OCTOBER DREAMS II

OCTOBER DREAMS II

EDITED BY
RICHARD CHIZMAR AND ROBERT MORRISH

CEMETERY DANCE PUBLICATIONS

Baltimore

❖ 2025 ❖

PAPERBACK EDITION
ISBN: 978-1-964780-42-9
Cemetery Dance Publications Paperback Edition 2025

October Dreams II
Collection copyright © 2014, 2016, 2025 by Richard Chizmar and Robert Morrish
Cover art by Glenn Chadbourne
Halloween Memory illustration by Keith Minnion
All other interior illustrations by Allen Koszowski
Dust jacket design by Gail Cross
Typesetting and book design by Robert Morrish
All rights reserved. Manufactured in the United States of America

Cemetery Dance Publications
132-B Industry Lane, Unit 7
Forest Hill, MD 21050
Email: info@cemeterydance.com
www.cemeterydance.com

Contents

MR. DARK'S CARNIVAL

Glen Hirshberg

"The Montanan is both humbled and exalted by this blazing glory filling his world, yet so quickly dead."

—Joseph Kinsey Howard

"So the first question, really," I said, leaning on my lectern and looking over the heads of my students at the twilight creeping off the plains into campus, "is, does anyone know anyone who has actually been there?"

Hands went up instantly, as they always do. For a few moments, I let the hands hang in the air, start to wilt under the florescent light, while I watched the seniors on the roof of Powell House dorm across the quad drape the traditional black bunting down the side of the building, covering all the windows. By the time I got outside, I knew, there would be straw corpses strewn all over campus and papier-mâché skeletons swinging in the trees. Few, if any, of the students who hung them there would have any cognizance of the decidedly sinister historical resonance of their actions.

"Right," I said, and returned my attention to my Freshman Seminar on Eastern Montana History. It was the one undergraduate class I still taught each year. It was the one class I would never give up. "Primary source accounts only, please."

"Meaning stuff written at the time?" said the perpetually confused Robert Hayright from the front row.

"That is indeed one correct definition of a primary source, Mr. Hayright. But in this case, I mean only interviews you have conducted or overheard yourself. No stories about third parties."

Two-thirds of the hands drooped to their respective desktops.

"Right. Let's eliminate parents and grandparents, now, who, over the centuries, have summoned and employed all sorts of bogeymen to keep their children careful as they exit the safeties of home."

Most of the rest of the hands went down.

"High school chums, of course, because the whole game in high school, especially Eastern Montana high school, is to have been somewhere your classmates haven't, isn't it? To have seen and known the world?"

"I have a question, Professor R." said Tricia Corwyn from the front row, crossing her stockinged legs under her silky skirt and pursing her too-red mouth. Around her, helpless freshman boys squirmed in their seats. The note of flirtation in her tone wasn't for me, I knew. It was a habit, quite possibly permanent, and it made me sad. It has taken most of a century to excise most of the rote machismo from Montana's sons. Maybe next century, we can go to work on the scars that machismo has left on its daughters.

"If we eliminate secondhand accounts, parents, and high school friends, who's left who could tell us about it?"

"My dear," I said, "you have the makings of a historian. That's a terrific question."

I watched Tricia trot out that string of studiously whitened teeth like a row of groomed show-horses, and abruptly I stood up straight, allowing myself a single internal head-shake. *My dear*. The most paternalistic and subtle weapon of diminishment in the Montana teacher's arsenal.

Pushing off the lectern and standing up straight, I said, "In fact, that's so good a question that I'm going to dodge it for the time being." A few members of the class were still alert or polite enough to smile. I saw the astonishing white hair of Robin Mills, the Humanities Department secretary, form in the doorway of my classroom like a cumulus cloud, but I ignored her for the time being. "Let me ask this. How many of you know anyone—once again, primary sources only, please—who claims to have worked there?"

This time, a single hand went up. That's one more than I'd ever had go up before.

"Mr. Hayright?" I said.

"My dog," he said, and the class exploded into laughter. But Robert Hayright continued. "It's true."

"Your dog told you this?"

"My dog Droopy disappeared on Halloween night three years ago. The next morning, a neighbor brought him home and told my dad a man in a clown suit had brought her to their door at six in the morning and said, 'Thank you for the dog, he's been at Mr. Dark's.'"

Mr. Hayright's classmates erupted again, but I didn't join them. The clown suit was interesting, I thought. A completely new addition to the myth.

"So let's see," I said gently. "Counting your father, your neighbor, and the clown—" this brought on more laughter, though I was not mocking—"your story is, at best, third-hand."

"Not counting the dog," said Robert Hayright, and he grinned, too. At least this time, I noted, everyone seemed to be laughing with him.

In the doorway, Robin Mills cleared her throat, and her mass of white hair rippled. "Professor Roemer?"

"Surely this can wait, Ms. Mills," I said.

"Professor, it's Brian Tidrow."

I scowled. I couldn't help it. "Whatever he's got can definitely wait."

Instead of speaking, Robin Mills mouthed the rest. She did it three times, although I understood her the second time.

"That fucker," I muttered, but not quietly enough, and my students stopped laughing and stared. I ignored them. "Does Kate know?" I asked Robin.

"No one's seen her yet."

"Find her. Find her now. Tell her I'll be there soon."

For a second, Robin lingered in the doorway. I don't know if she expected comfort or company or just more reaction, but I wasn't planning on giving her any. Brian Tidrow was a descendent of a Crow who'd married a white woman, scouted for Custer and eventually died with him. He was also a third-generation alcoholic, arguably the brightest graduate student I'd ever taught, and almost certainly the one I had enjoyed least. Now, he had finally committed the supreme act of havoc-wreaking he'd been threatening for years. He would get no more reaction from me, ever. I glared at Robin until she ducked her head and turned from the door.

"What was that about, Professor R.?" Tricia asked.

I avoided thinking about Kate. About Kate and Brian. What was there to think about? It had been years ago. By the time Robin located her for me, class would be over, and I'd be on my way. "You will notice, my young scholars, that I didn't even ask if any of you have been there. I have lived in Clarkston all my life, except for my eight years of university and graduate work. My parents lived here all their lives. My grandparents came from Germany right before the First World War"—'*at least several hundred years after my father, and half a century after my mother,*' as Brian Tidrow loved to remind me—"and never left until their deaths. In all that time, not a single member of my family has ever encountered anyone who has actually, personally, been. Ever. And that leads us to the most alarming, the most discomfiting question of all. Is it possible that Mr. Dark's Carnival—the inspiration for all our Halloween festivities, the most celebrated attraction or event in the history of Clarkston, Montana—never really existed?"

As always, that question took just a moment to land. It floated through the room for a few seconds like an Alka-Seltzer tablet dropped into a glass. And then it began to fizz.

"Wait," said one of the boys near Tricia.

"Oh my God, no way," said Tricia, her blue eyes bright as they blazed through boy after boy.

Robert Hayright shook his head. "That's wrong. You're wrong, Professor. I know it."

I put my hand up, but the fizzing continued a while longer. When it quieted at last, I started to smile, thought of Brian Tidrow with his great grandfather's Winchester rifle gripped in his teeth, and shuddered. *Goddamn him*, I thought. I refused to offer him any additional respect simply because he'd finally had the stupidity—he'd probably have called it guts—to go and do it.

"What do you know, Mr. Hayright?"

"I know there was a Carnival in 1926. It was out in the fallow fields by where the Gulf Station at the edge of town is now."

"How do you know that?"

"We studied it in high school. There were newspaper reports. Primary sources." He glanced up at me to see if I'd stop him, then went on. "Livestock that vanished. Some guy in a black robe seen drifting around on the prairie and lurking in the bushes. Three people died of fright, including a policemen sent to investigate all the screaming."

"There was another in 1943," I said quietly, to the suddenly silent room, as the icy twilight permeated the windows and seeped into the corners like floodwater. "That one was in particularly poor taste. Reportedly, it was haunted by dozens of people outfitted as dead soldiers. Upset a lot of parents whose sons were currently overseas.

"In 1978, there were no less than three so-called Mr. Dark's Carnivals rumored around town, though two of them were meant for small children and the third turned out to be a dance. I'm not saying no one has ever called their haunted house 'Mr. Dark's Carnival.' But as to the existence of the legendary, mystery-shrouded Carnival-to-end-all-Carnivals..." I waved my hand, started to smile, sighed instead. "The fact is that every year, we build our haunted houses and collect our children and head out to cover as much of our fair miniature city as we can, hoping for that supreme horrifying experience. That haunted house that will detonate our bowels, grind our chattering teeth to rubble, and blast us out the other side shaken and giggling and alive. That Mr. Dark's Carnival that we've been told, all our lives, might just be out there, on some un-named street, in some unexpected and unexplored corner."

For the next fifteen minutes, students hurled questions about the most persistent and ubiquitous elements of the myth: the tickets that had to be given to you or found somewhere; the ever-changing locations; the reputed deaths by terror. Most years, I let this part of the discussion go as long as it would, because I enjoyed hearing the variations on the legend, and the students enjoyed having the legend exploded. But this year, feeling increasingly disturbed that Robin had not floated back into the door to say she'd found Kate, and unable to shake the picture I'd formed of Brian Tidrow's last moments on Earth, I ticked off my myth-destroying points in mere minutes.

How many unexplored corners were there, exactly, in a town barely eleven miles square and 145 years old? How many new locations could there be? If tickets had to be found or given, who did the hiding and giv-ing? Given the elaborate nature of the illusions attributed to Mr. Dark's, where were all the workers necessary to perpetuate them?

Finally, Tricia once again asked the most significant remaining ques-tion. "Was there even a Mr. Dark?" she said.

"Oh yes," I answered, even more quietly, and the class hushed once more. "Although as to why this story has attached itself to him, well…"

It was at that moment, of course, that Robin Mills finally returned. How not surprising, I thought, indulging just a little selfish fury, that Brian Tidrow's farewell gesture should destroy my favorite moment of the teaching year. The only thing that even came close was the day I marched into my Graduate Seminar, laid a map detailing the progress of cattle introduction onto the Open Range over another showing the path of buffalo depletion, and proved, or at least suggested, that despite all our best efforts and a hundred years of imprecise historical accounting, it was anthrax, not white men—not directly, anyway—that killed the buffalo.

Outside, gray lines of snow began to drag themselves over the ground like the fringe on a giant, smothering carpet. The clouds hung heavy and low, and the first unmistakable winter wind gnawed and whined at the windows. I thought of Kate and forgot about anger, forgot about my teaching and my love for Halloween. I started to ache.

"Scholars, I apologize," I said. "There has been a personal crisis in the Humanities Department, and I need to tend to it immediately. So we will have to continue this discussion on Monday."

"What about Mr. Dark?" Robert Hayright whined, sounding almost angry. I didn't blame him. My class had been the most popular freshman elective for most of a decade, primarily because of the lecture I gave each year on this date.

I began to slide the notes I never used into my backpack, watched Robert Hayright slouch in his seat while Tricia rose in front of him. "Who knows?" I said, catching Robin Mills' agitated tapping against the doorframe of my room with a pen. "Perhaps one of you will find a strip of paper tacked to a tree-trunk tonight, and stare at it in disbelief. And you'll find the real Mr. Dark. And on Monday, you'll be able to tell me just how wrong I've been all these years. All right, I see you, Ms. Mills."

"Sorry, Professor," I heard her say. "Didn't even know what I was doing."

"Have a recommendation?" Tricia asked as the class began to file out. She was leaning forward over my desk, too close to me. Habit, again.

"About what, Ms. Corwyn?" I continued putting away papers but avoided brushing her sweater with my arm.

"Haunted houses we shouldn't miss? Particularly good streets? I hear they're going to have monsters in the river."

Startled, I looked up and found myself submerged in those too-blue eyes. "No one's done that for years," I said, and the last of my anger sank into sadness, though none of it was for Brian Tidrow. Other people have Christmases or High Holidays, and families to share them with. I have Halloween and these kids. This year I would have neither. "You'll have to tell me about it."

"I will," she said. "Thanks for the great class."

Seconds later, they were gone, and all the energy in the room went with them, and I was just another academia ghost, my skin sporting that translucent, sickly florescent tan, my hair succumbing to the color-leaching chalk dust and dead air. I wanted to see Kate. I wanted to help her fight through this. For the first time in my life, I wanted Halloween to be over.

"Where is she?" I asked Robin Mills.

"Your place," she said, with no trace of the contempt she might otherwise have attached to that statement. "She called from there. She was apparently the one who found him, Professor."

"Goddamn Brian," I said, starting past Robin. "Goddamn him to hell." I saw her start to register shock, because that's the emotion recommended, I guess, in the Judgmental and Officious Department Secretary Handbook for such comments and situations.

But then she said, "Tell Kate we're all thinking of her. Tell her to come see me Monday, or whenever she wants."

I turned, smiled, and realized that I'd worked near, if not exactly with, this person for fourteen years, and that it was time I got over myself. "I will," I said. "Thanks."

Seconds later, I was strolling through the deepening dark across campus. In the trees, paper men danced and spun on the frigid wind. I heard whooping sounds from the row of fraternity houses at the campus' south end, and scurrying feet as students raced excitedly for their assigned posts in haunted houses or collected dates for the evening tour through town. Underneath it all, I heard the ceaseless, sucking emptiness of the prairie, slowly pulling this town piece by piece and person by person back into the sea of cheatgrass and oblivion.

By the time I turned onto Winslow Street and left campus, the cold had crawled inside my insufficient fall windbreaker, and I could feel it creeping down my bones toward the dead center of me. The little kids were out already, racing down sidewalks lined with lit pumpkins in paper bags that glowed a glorious, leering orange. I saw a green-skinned zombie shiver up from a pile of dead leaves in the corner of a lawn and grab for two be-winged little girls who giggled and fled. The zombie watched them and smiled and shivered backwards and drew the leaves over himself again. He would be there all evening, I knew. He would keep his smile to himself for longer when the older kids came, grab a little more forcefully. He'd be frozen half through when he got home, and full of civic pride. In some towns, the neighbors force you to keep your yard tidy. In others, you're expected to show up in church or help out at the foodbank or on Clean the River Beaches Day. In Clarkston, you participate in Halloween.

A half-mile from campus, the houses spread out onto their lots, and the paths marked by the paper-bag pumpkins disappeared. But the festivities continued. Even the Country Club haunted its golf course every year and opened it to the entire town, though they taped tarpaulins down on the putting greens. At this hour, though, with full dark not yet fallen, these streets were relatively silent. The scares out here, it was understood, were for older kids. The zombies in the leaf piles sometimes held onto you if they caught you. I stopped just a moment outside Dean Harry Piltner's house and stood in the strings of snow. As usual, Harry had constructed a long, knee-high crawl-through maze of straw that zigzagged back and forth across his yard. I'd once asked him where he got the wolf spiders and finger-sized roaches he occasionally set free in there to scurry and hunt and, usually, die by squishing at the hands of some screaming teen. He just smiled in response and kept his Halloween secret to himself, like any good Clarkstonian. The homemade brownies his wife left at the exit of the maze were the best anyone I knew had ever tasted.

The Blackroot River bisects Clarkston five different times as it bends back and forth through town, creating miniature peninsulas. My house, a turn of the century A-frame built by one of the railroad masterminds of the Land Grab that brought homesteaders to the Open Range and, very nearly, civil war to the plains, rides the point of Purviston, the town's Easternmost peninsula, like the smokestack on a steam train. As I crossed the footbridge that leads directly to my door, I scanned my house for lights but saw none. Either Kate had left, or she was sitting in the dark. I suspected the latter. In moments of personal and professional crisis, Kate clung to the shadows. Otherwise, she'd never have let Brian lure her to Montana for her graduate work, leaving offers from four Ivies in her wake.

For just a moment, in the center of the bridge, I stopped to listen to the river. Already, its gurgle had an ugly rasp. By Thanksgiving, it would be frozen, and the streets would tuck themselves into their winter hibernation under a thick blanket of snow. I glanced back toward town, saw orange lights winking through the dark and heard a small child's scream erupt in the air like the call of a hunting osprey.

"You missed all the good stuff, Brian," I mumbled, surprising myself. I hadn't known I was thinking of him.

Even after I unlocked the door, it took me a few seconds to realize Kate was there, hunched on the couch by the bay window overlooking the river. She had the blue blanket my mother had knitted me, years and years ago, wrapped around her waist, and her long brown hair draped on her shoulders like a shawl. In sunlight, Kate's oddly sunken brown eyes made her look as though she never quite got enough sleep. In the half-light, the shadows lent color to her wan skin, and her eyes seemed to creep forward, and she became an astonishingly beautiful woman. At least, she became one to me.

"Hey," I said, started toward her, and felt just a flicker of the old uncertainty. I've long since gotten over my guilt about dating Kate; though she is a former graduate student of mine, she's 35, all of six years younger, with more of an academic pedigree than I ever had and no reason whatsoever to let me exploit her, or to exploit me. But I was eleven years without a significant relationship before Kate—Clarkston is a tiny, tiny place, the University tinier still, and I was born reticent, anyway—and even after two years, I've yet to regain my confidence completely.

This night, Kate did nothing to make it easy for me. She stared out the window. The window was closed, but the snow seemed to have seeped into the room somehow. I imagined I could see it winking near her ears like a cloud of will-o'-the-wisps, about to spirit her away. Stepping to the couch, I dropped down beside her. She started to cry quietly. I sat and held her hand and let her.

"He wasn't even a good friend," Kate murmured, after a long, long while. "He wasn't ever."

I touched her hair. "No, he wasn't."

"Too unreliable. Too wrapped up in his own pathetic problems."

"He was sick, Kate. He didn't have a choice."

For the first time that night, she turned and looked at me. The depth of her eye cavities made it seem as if I were peering into a cave. The effect always made me want to crawl in there with her. She smiled, and I felt like laughing but didn't.

"This is a reversal," she said.

"Don't get me wrong, Kate-O. I wish he'd never come back here—except for the bringing you with him part. I wish you'd never known him. You or anyone else in the damn department, because he had that mopey, haunted intensity that all you grad students flock to like bees to pollen, and then you spread it, and then everybody's mopey and haunted."

Kate laughed, and this time, the laugh inside me slipped out.

"He was a good historian," she said, returning the squeeze of my hand now.

"He was a promising historian. You're a good one. You do the research first, then have your insights."

Without warning, she was crying again, whether for Brian Tidrow or her mother, also dead by suicide more than twenty years before, or her vindictive father, or something else entirely, I didn't know.

This time, the crying spell lasted over an hour. I listened to her breath sputter and her voice murmur and choke, watched Halloween night settle over Clarkston. The snow thickened, gathering itself on the dead grass and in the cracks on the pavement. Even through the closed windows, shouts and screams and bursts of organ music reached us from across the river. "I stepped in some of his hair," Kate mumbled at one point, and I winced and squeezed her hand as she shook. I'd forgotten she'd found him.

It was at least eight and maybe later when Kate looked up at me. The shaking in her shoulders had stilled just a little. But what she said was, "This could go on all night, David. You should go."

I blinked, startled, not sure how to answer. "Go where? This is my home. And also where I want to be."

"It's Halloween. The best day of your life, remember?"

The sentimental response proved irresistible. I hadn't had many opportunities to try one, after all. "I've had other best days, lately," I said. Then I blushed, grinning like a six year-old, and Kate burst out laughing.

"Go haunted-housing. Come back with stories."

"Come with me."

Instantly, her smile vanished. "I've seen my dead person for the day, thanks. Oh, fuck, David." Her face crumpled again. I reached for her hand, but she shook it off. "Really," she snapped, and I jerked back. "I want you to go. I want to be alone."

"Kate, I want to be with you."

"You are with me." She was still snapping.

For a long moment, we stared at each other. Then I picked my coat off the chair where I'd draped it and stood. I started to ask if she was sure, but she was. And quite frankly, I was relieved, in all sorts of ways. I knew that I'd done what I could and that my actions had been noted. I knew that Kate loved me. And I knew that I wasn't going to miss Halloween after all.

"I'll bring you back a brownie," I said.

"God, you're not going to crawl through Piltner's maze, are you?"

I just stood there.

"You're an eight year-old, David."

"I'll check back in an hour. I won't be gone long."

"All right," Kate said, but she was already withdrawing into her crouch with her gaze aimed out the window.

I opened the front door, stepped outside, and the cold jumped me. It had teeth and claws, and the way it tore at my skin had me checking my coat front for rips. "Jesus," I said, started to turn back inside for gloves and scarf, and thought better of it. I didn't want to be gone long, anyway. And I didn't want to disturb Kate now. Shoving my hands in my pockets and blinking my watering eyes, I drove forward into the dark. Because I had my head down, I didn't see the thing on the footbridge until I was almost on top of it. Gasping, I jerked to a stop.

At first, all I saw was a newspaper blown open. Then the wind kicked up, and the edges lifted like wings but the paper itself stayed put, and I realized there was something underneath it holding it in place. A half step closer, and I thought I could see a head-shaped shadow lying in the larger, deeper shadow of the overhanging poplar trees like…well, like a head in a pool of blood.

Goddamn Brian Tidrow, I thought again, and started forward. The man lay straight across the bridge, in the dead center of it, with his head against one railing and his feet dangling over the river on the far side. I've often wondered where all the homeless people in Clarkston come from, and why they stay. I never recognize any of them—they're no one I ever knew—despite my years of living here. And the climate can't be conducive to life on the street. Maybe the citizenry are generous, or the food at the shelters is good, or else the plains loom like the roiling oceans of nothing they are and obliterate hopes of safe passage.

This man, I decided, was sleeping or stone drunk. You'd have to be drunk to sleep in this spot with the wind crawling over you. The only movement as I approached was the fluttering of the newspaper. The only sounds came from the river below and the town beyond.

"Hey, man," I said softly. "You all right?"

The newspaper fluttered. The river hissed. The man lay still. I thought about going home to call the police. I had nothing against the poor guy sleeping on my bridge, but jail would be warmer. Kate wanted me gone, though. And sometimes, I thought, with the fatuous logic of the comfortable, there are better things to be than warm. I planted one foot, lifted the other so that I was straddling the man, and he sat up.

It was the hand he snarled in the belt of my coat, I think, that kept me from leaping straight over the railing. Clumps of curly black hair flew from his scalp like strips of shredded steel wool. His lips were white-blue with cold, his eyes so bloodshot that the red seemed to have overrun the irises and pooled in the pupils.

For a few seconds, he held me there, and I held my breath, and nothing moved. He wasn't looking at me but beyond me, past my hip at the trees and the riverbank. The intensity of his stare made me want to whirl around, but I couldn't rip my gaze from his face.

Finally, I managed to gulp some air into my lungs, and the cold shocked them out of paralysis. I coughed. The man gripped my coat, stared behind me, and said nothing.

"What?" I finally said.

The hand at my waist did not relax. The direction of the gaze didn't change.

"Are you cold? Can I—" I looked down and saw the crumple of black paper pressed between the man's palm and my stomach. A whole new shudder rippled through me, drawn from a long forgotten childhood reservoir. Blind Pugh, and the Black Spot, and the Admiral Benbow Inn. *Until dark*, Pugh told Billy Bones, on the day of Billy Bones' death. *They'll come at dark.*

I put my hand on the paper, which turned out to be surprisingly heavy. Construction paper. Instantly, the homeless man's hand ricocheted back to his side as though I'd triggered a catapult. The whole body beneath me jerked backward into a prone position, and the newspaper snapped into place around him. Uncrumpling the construction paper, still shuddering, I stepped back and looked at what I'd been given.

"Oh," I said. Then I said it again. Then I turned and raced for home.

Kate was still crouched by the window when I burst in. She didn't look up to ask what I'd forgotten. She looked only a little more conscious than the man on the bridge had. I marched straight to her anyway.

"Look," I said, and held the construction paper toward her. "Kate, I'm serious, look."

Her sigh came from way down inside her. Slowly, she took the paper from me, tilted it toward the light coming in the window. She read it twice. Then she stood up. The blanket stayed wrapped around her waist.

"God, David, we have to go," she said. "I'll get my coat."

"I'm going to marry this woman," I said aloud to the window as Kate stepped toward the closet. By the time she returned to me, buttoning her heaviest black overcoat around her, her movements had regained most of their usual speed and grace.

"You have to understand," I told her, touching her hair with the back of my hand. Her face still looked wan, but her eyes were bright. "This won't be my first Mr. Dark's Carnival."

"What do you mean? You don't even believe it's real."

"I've been given tickets on three previous occasions. Twice, I followed the directions on them and wound up at a frat party. Little Halloween prank from my students. The third time, I wound up at a very fine haunted house indeed, right here in Purviston, not five hundred feet from this door. Unfortunately, I happened to recognize Harry Piltner's stoop under his black cowl at the doorway, and because I'm a jerk, I said, 'Do I get a brownie, Har?' And Harry kicked me."

"So why are we going?" Kate said, shepherding me toward the door.

"Get gloves. Hat, too. It's unbelievably cold."

We were outside now, and Kate threw her head back and stood a moment in the chill. She didn't even have her coat all the way buttoned.

"You're insane," I said, jamming my gloved hands into my pockets and hunching against the snap of the wind. "We're going, first of all, because someone went to a lot of trouble to get me these. Get somebody these, anyway. And they did it with high Clarkston Halloween style, so I can't ignore it. Secondly, even if it's a frat party, the beer'll be good."

"Oh, right. You don't even drink."

I held the door of my rusty red 1986 Volvo open for her and kissed the top of her head as she bent to climb in. "You're freezing," I said, "put on your damn hat."

"Thirdly?" she said, and smiled up at me. At that moment, she seemed even more excited than I had to admit I was.

"Thirdly, I had a feeling you'd come, in spite of everything."

Her smile widened.

"And fourthly, Kate dear," I said, glancing toward the bridge, which was empty. Purviston tickets distributed, I thought. I wondered where the homeless man would lay himself and his newspaper next. "Fourthly, one just never knows, does one? I don't, anyway." I shut her door and got in on my side.

The car took four cranks of the ignition key, but it did start. It always starts. "Where to?" I said, gesturing toward the black construction paper in Kate's lap. On it, in gray-white chalk, was a map of Clarkston with a white dotted line snaking through it and the words *Mr. Dark's Carnival Welcomes You* underneath. No skull and crossbones this time, and no come-if-you-dare warning. A classier prank, at the very least.

"Get to Winslow," Kate said, without looking down at the paper. "Take it south all the way out of town."

To my relief, she sounded excited. Exhausted, wrecked, but excited. I threw the car's heater on, blasting us both with frigid air, and grunted. Kate stared out the window at the dark.

By now, even the streets of Purviston were alive with costumed revelers. A group of rubber-masked teens came hurtling down the sidewalk from the direction of Harry Piltner's, their wigs and winter coats caked with straw, hands flashing all over themselves in search of bugs that had probably long since dropped off. I smiled.

In town, the activity level seemed just slightly lower than usual because of the cold. By 9:30, most Halloweens, the college kids who worked the little-kid haunted houses had been released from scare duty, and they clustered around parked cars or outside the Rangehand pub downtown and blasted hip-hop and waited for midnight, when the frat parties began in earnest and continued until the police shut them down. But this night, the trick-or-treaters had long since retreated indoors, and the partiers had stayed in their dorms, and the only people out were the heartiest Clarkstonians, tracing their habitual routes from one fright sight to the next.

In a matter of minutes, we were out of town. At the two-mile mark, the last streetlamp stuck out of the prairie like a flag left by a lunar expedition, and then we were in darkness.

"Still know where we're going?" I said.

"Says seven miles."

"Air's getting warm."

Kate didn't answer. Snow glittered on the asphalt and the endless stunted grass all around us, as though the sky itself had shattered on the ground. The Eastern Montana plains on a snowlit night are limitless as deep space and just as empty.

After a minute or so, Kate shifted in her seat. She spoke slowly, softly. She sounded barely awake, and most likely she was after the day she'd had, and now the warming car, the chattering road, the silence. "Tell me again what you think you know, David Roemer, about Albert Alouisius Dark?"

Instantly, the last of my classroom lecture leapt to my lips. "Delighted you asked. Thought I wasn't going to get to tell anyone this year."

Kate smiled.

"Judge Albert Alouisius Dark. Born God knows where, educated God knows where, because that's the first intriguing thing about him, isn't it? There's no record of him in this state—it was a territory then, of course—before his appointment to the Bench in September, 1877. In fact, there's no record of him anywhere."

"You mean you haven't found records of him yet."

"You're not the only competent researcher in this Volvo, O Barely Speaking Woman. And I'll thank you to remember the Civil War, and its prodigious though little noted effects on the record keeping of our fair cities and towns."

Kate nodded. "Go on."

"For eight years after his appointment as ranking barrister in this desolate region, Judge Dark maintained a consistently moderate record. Right up until Christmas Eve, 1885. That ni—"

"Turn here," Kate said, and I jammed on the brakes, dragged the car to a stop, and stared.

"Turn where?"

"Back up."

I looked over my shoulder into the black, snow-streaked nothing. "Maybe the map's upside down."

Kate grinned. "Just back up, idiot."

I tapped the brake pedal, held it down so that my taillights illuminated the blackness. There, fifteen feet or so behind the car, limned in red paint of some sort, were two tire ruts snaking between two bedraggled plains shrubs and away into the grass. Way down in my stomach, something twitched. Nervousness. Uneasiness, maybe. Disbelief. Hope. If this was a prank, or an imitation, it was the best yet. And if it wasn't a prank...

"How the hell did you know that was there?"

"The map."

"But how did you see it?"

"I was looking for it. David, let's go." Kate looked at me. Her face was still red, but whether from crying or excitement, I couldn't tell.

Backing us up, I paused just a moment at the lip of the path. I cracked my window, and the whistling silence sucked at our little bubble of life inside the car.

"What are you thinking?" Kate said softly.

"Little Big Horn. The Donner Party. Fifteen or twenty other examples of overconfident white people overestimating their power over the West."

"This really could be it, David. Couldn't it?"

"It really could be something."

I pushed my foot on the gas, and we were off the highway, jiggling over the dirt.

"How far?" I mumbled.

Kate glanced down at the map. "Three miles, maybe." I groaned. Kate said, "Christmas Eve, 1885."

I watched the grass disappear under our tires, the snow that seemed to float on ground so flat and featureless that it didn't even really seem to be there. "On Christmas Eve, 1885, at approximately 8:45 p.m., a group of local ranchers calling themselves the Guardians of Right appeared at the door of Judge Dark's rather lavish creekside home—it was destroyed by fire, incidentally, in 1956, and is now buried under the high school football stadium—and demanded entrance. With them, the Guardians had brought a Chinese homesteader who'd been hitched to a wagon with his feet bound and made to hop all the way from his claim two miles outside of town."

"How do we know this?" Kate asked.

"Primary source, of course, of course. And no one can talk to a source, of course."

An old, habitual joke of mine. Kate ignored it. I went on.

"The judge himself kept an impressively detailed notebook. The Guardians demanded immediate entry, a trial right then and there, and a hanging verdict. And Judge Dark, inexplicably, showed the men into his living room, then called his wife down to act as court reporter and witness. The prosecution case lasted ten minutes, and involved somewhat circumstantial but undeniably incriminating evidence of the theft of foodstores and two horses. There was no defense, seeing as how the homesteader in question did not speak English and couldn't even stand because the bones in his feet and ankles had been smashed during his trip to the Judge's door. The guilty verdict and death sentence apparently came so fast that even the Guardians were startled to silence. The Judge makes specific and rather self-satisfied note of this effect.

"What the Judge actually said next, I cannot tell you. But I can tell you what he wrote. And I can tell you that word for word: '*I attached a single condition: that the prisoner be hanged by no hand but my own, and that he stay this night, his last on this Earth, in my home, under my care.*' This was assented to, and the stunned Guardians left. And on Christmas morning, in front of over a hundred witnesses in what was then the town square, Judge Albert Dark wheeled the homesteader to a poplar tree, strung a rope around his neck, positioned him in a sort of crouch in the back of a wagon, and executed him, cleanly and quickly. No one yelled '3-7-77.'"

"What does that mean, by the way?"

"No one knows, really," I said. "None of the original Virginia City vigilantes ever said. They just left those numbers pinned to their victims. Anyway, the homesteader, by every account, said not a word, and made no sound. But he did look up, right as the wagon fled him and the rope bit into his neck. Two of the four published accounts claim he was smiling. Kate, what the hell is that?" But I could tell what it was. It was a kid. In pajamas.

He was barefoot in the grass, straddling the tire ruts with one arm stretched perfectly perpendicular to his shoulders, pointing off into the blackness. His skin glowed white in the headlight beams, as though the snow had somehow sunk inside it. He had short blond hair that stuck straight up. His pajamas had zebras on them.

I hit the brakes, started to slow.

"God," Kate said as we rolled to a stop fifteen feet from the kid. "How old do you think he is?"

"How *cold* do you think he is?" I muttered, staring at the kid's feet.

He was about as tall as the top of my windshield. I rolled down my window and leaned out, but the child made no move toward the car, and he didn't lower his arm. It occurred to me that maybe he was an astoundingly realistic scarecrow. But he wasn't. I could see his lips, blue with cold, twitching when the prairie wind whipped across them.

"Are you all right?" I called. The child didn't move.

Then, abruptly, I smiled. I hadn't even gotten to this latest Mr. Dark's Carnival, and already, it had me pleading with the ghouls, trying to get them to break and speak to me. The bubble of nervous excitement inside me swelled.

"Follow the yellow brick road," I said, and turned in the direction the child had pointed.

There were other tire tracks, I noted, all around us. I took an absurd amount of comfort in the fact that we weren't the first ones out here. I drove slowly, letting the prairie drum against the underside of the car like a choppy sea against the hull of a sailboat. Except for the dirt we stirred, nothing moved.

"How many did Judge Dark hang?" Kate asked, though her eyes, too, were straining forward into the void.

"Four that we know of between 1885 and statehood, when he drops from the official record as abruptly as he appeared. In each case, he allowed a local vigilante group to bring suspects to a lightning trial, convicted the suspects, then kept them all night in his home, where one assumes he served as confessor and last meal chef or possibly something completely different, and then performed the killing the next morning. He apparently was a master executioner, because, according to the *Plains-Ledger, 'not a single one of his charges so much as danced. And none of them said a word before they went to their makers.'*

"Look," said Kate, but I'd already seen.

Drawing the car forward, I pulled into a space between two pick-up trucks and switched off the ignition. There were six other vehicles arrayed around us in a makeshift parking lot. Of the drivers and passengers, I saw no trace.

I looked at Kate. We listened to the snow tap the roof of the Volvo. Beyond the impromptu circle of cars, the prairie grass rolled in the raging wind.

"So remind me," Kate murmured. "How did this murderous judge, whoever he was, become part of the Carnival myth?"

"Can't remind you," I said. "'Cause I never told you. 'Cause I don't know."

"And why 'Carnival?' Why not 'Scary House?'"

"Got me yet again."

Suddenly, Kate was smiling once more, and the red in her lips spread up her cheeks, and I felt so grateful, so lucky that I wasn't even sure I could move. "Thank you for coming to get me," she said.

"Thank you for coming along, my love."

Kate blew me a kiss. She jerked the door handle down, still smiling, and—gently, as though easing into water—climbed into the night. I opened my own door and joined her. We stood at the hood of the car and stared around us.

There was no sound except the wind in the grass. No child in pajamas appeared to point us the right way. I jammed my hands into my pockets as the cold gnawed at my wrists.

"There," I said.

"I see it," said Kate.

It was just a glow, barely brighter than the moonlight on the snow. Distances are hard enough to gauge on the plains in broad daylight. But given the limited visibility, I decided the glow couldn't be more than a half-mile away, straight out from the highway into the grass. We started walking.

It was an illusion, of course, that the dark got darker as soon as we left the circle of cars. Nevertheless, I could feel the Eastern Montana night sweep over our heads on its enormous wings. I could feel its weight up there, and its talons. I kept my head down and walked. Kate walked beside me, the sleeve of her coat brushing rhythmically, repeatedly, against my own. We'd gone maybe 300 yards when both of us looked up together and saw the house.

It loomed out of the prairie shadows, black in the moonlight, inexplicable as the monolith in *2001*. The glow we saw came from a lone floodlight buried in the grass and aimed at the white fence surrounding the structure. As we got closer, I saw that the building wasn't black but barn-red, single storied and rectangular and long. In the yard demarcated by the fence, people-shaped figures glided back and forth.

"If it was nothing else but this," I said, staring at the tableau before me, "I think I'd be satisfied."

"It's like something out of a painting," Kate said, and that stopped me. The chill that flooded my mouth seemed to have come from inside rather than out.

For a second, I couldn't place the source of my discomfort. I looked at the structure. I looked at the floating figures, just beginning to acquire distinct faces from this distance. I looked at the fence, and then I had it.

Because it wasn't a fence. And the scene didn't remind me of a painting, but of a photograph. The one on page 212 of the Montana History Primer I'd penned, to be exact, that showed the stacks of jumbled buffalo skeletons piled on the plains during the years the Federal Government paid the most desperate or ghastly Montanans to shoot every bison they could find and export the bones downriver.

I started to speak, had to wet my lips, tried again. "There, um, been any recently reported mass murders of oxen in the vicinity?"

Kate turned, her brow furrowed. "What?"

"Take a good gander at that fence, Kate."

She did. Then she said, "Ooh. That can't be real."

"One hopes not. One hopes there is a large placard pasted over the entry reassuring us that No Animals Were Harmed or Mistreated During Creation of This Carnival. But one is disturbed."

"Come on," Kate said, and on we went.

Up close, the bones looked a little less real, if only because they were reassuringly clean. Somehow, I'd been expecting bits of gristle to be hanging from them like party streamers. The four figures gliding back and forth in the house's mock garden were all young women, and they all wore long, white nightgowns that flowed down their forms like liquid moonlight. They were bare-armed, black-haired, and they might have been sisters. Certainly, they all had the same porcelain skin pallor, the same slightly upturned noses, the same half-smiles on their red-black lips. I found the sight of them slightly disappointing. After everything that had come so far, this seemed too familiar a horror movie image, and something of a failure of imagination.

The mound of bones—up close, it was more hedge than fence—had one opening off to the right side of the house. Crouching beside the opening, staring straight past us at the eternity of nothing beyond, was another child. This one wore a green overcoat belted at the waist. He had jet-black hair that made his skin look bleached of features, like a face in a photographic negative. He, too, was barefoot.

When Kate and I moved toward the opening in the bones, the child stood up and stepped in front of us. We waited for him to speak, but of course he didn't. He didn't move, either.

"Now what?" I finally said.

The nightgown wraiths weren't the only people in the yard, I could see now. There were other people with plain old Montana-pale skin and good winter jackets and gloves and scarves. Hauntees. Maybe eight of them, milling about.

Slowly, still looking beyond us—just like the man on the bridge, I realized, and wondered if this particular Mr. Dark ran an extended and brilliantly effective training program for his employees—the gatekeeper child raised his arm, palm upward, and held it toward us.

"Blood?" I muttered to Kate. "Cheez-its? What does he want?"

After a long moment, Kate dipped her hand into her coat pocket and withdrew the black construction paper. "Ticket," she said happily.

"Oh yeah. Wouldn't want any party crashers," I said, but I moved forward with Kate as she placed the folded paper in the child's hand.

"Brrr," she said as she touched him. "Honey, you're freezing."

"It's not so bad," said the child, and my mouth flew open and my knees locked. I'd gotten used to the lack of response.

Kate maintained her poise better than I did. She glanced at me, then back at the child. Then she nodded. "You're right. It isn't." Taking my glove in her hand, she drew me forward through the bone hedge into the yard.

We'd taken all of three steps when one of the winter coat-wrapped figures threw back the flaps of its red wool cap and squeaked, "Professor R!" at me.

I blinked, glanced at Kate, then back at the person flouncing toward us. "Um," I said. I run into students every time I leave my house in Clarkston. But somehow, for no good reason, I'd forgotten it was possible tonight. I blushed. "Hello, Ms. Corwyn."

"And who's this?" said Tricia, completely unaffected.

My blush deepened, and I felt a flicker of annoyance. Surely, at age 41, after seventeen years in the classroom, I'd stopped being embarrassed about the gaps that existed between my teaching self and my home self. But that didn't mean I'd found a way to bridge or even explain them. I don't know anyone who has. "This is Kate," I finally answered.

I turned to Kate for a smile, a gently mocking putdown, something. But the expression on her face had sagged. She looked at me, and she seemed so tired, all of a sudden, and I knew Brian Tidrow had floated up over her shoulder. He'd done that periodically, even when he was alive. It wouldn't be the last time, I knew.

"Okay," she said, and wandered away into the garden. I had no idea what she meant.

"Hmmm," said Tricia.

Instantly, with Kate out of earshot, I was Professor David once more. "You just keep those fast-developing observational skills to yourself," I said, and smiled with my mouth closed. A teacherly smile.

"Is this unbelievable or what? This corpse crawled up out of the river and gave me a map."

"A corpse."

"All white. I don't even know how long he was down there, because I sure didn't see him. Robert and I were walking along the bank in Poplar Park and suddenly this *thing* wriggled up out of the water at our feet. He was stark naked except for a Speedo. Robert almost flew up the nearest tree."

I went right past the corpse. A Speedo-wearing corpse in a half-frozen river did not seem so very strange on a Clarkston Halloween night. At least, not this Clarkston Halloween night. "Robert," I said. "Robert Hayright?"

"Yeah," said Tricia. "Why?"

I felt my jaw start to drop, clamped it shut. Annoyance flared in me, though I had no idea why. I needed to go to Kate. And I wanted to get lost in the marvelous atmosphere of this haunted house. But I couldn't quite wade out of Tricia's blue eyes yet. And I couldn't get comfortable with the way she floated through the world. I'd met people like her before, of course. A few. The ones born with smarts, beauty, self-confidence, everything, gliding on their own private seas, remote and mesmerizing as lighted yachts as they drift among the teeming rest of us, struggling in our leaky johnboats from one shore we can't remember toward another we'll never know.

"How did that happen?" I said.

Tricia shrugged. "Robert? He asked."

Good for both of you, I almost said, then decided that was beyond condescending. "I have to go find Kate."

"Don't miss the booth. It's weird as hell. Professor R., do you think this is it? The real Mr. Dark's?"

I studied her cold-flushed, happy, markless face. And my annoyance transformed into sadness, still and deep. "I think it may be our Mr. Dark's, Tricia. I think this may be as close as we'll ever get." Not until I was several steps away did it occur to me to wonder where Robert Hayright was.

In the back left corner of the house's backyard sat a game booth draped in red and yellow carnival bunting. Kate stood to the left of it, but she wasn't playing whatever game the booth offered. She was looking at the prairie outside the bone hedge.

I was fifteen feet away, closing fast, when two of the nightgown girls appeared on either side of Kate, took her arms, and spun her, gently, toward the house. I hurried forward.

"Wait," I called.

"Move it, come on," Kate answered, turning her head toward me but letting the nightgown girls lead her. The spirit of the evening seemed to have seized her once more. "I think it's our turn, David."

They were guiding her around the side of the structure toward the front door. Like all haunted houses, I surmised, Mr. Dark's could only accommodate a few guests at a time. Then the illusions had to be reset, the trap doors and lunging scarecrow monsters propped back on their springs, the fog machines reloaded. I had just about caught up when a third nightgown girl drifted directly into my path, held up a warning hand like a school crossing guard, and stopped me.

"No, no," I said. "I'm with her. I came with her." I stepped to the side, and the nightgown girl stepped with me. Her bare feet made cracking sounds in the snow-caked grass and left half formed impressions. Her hand remained extended, blocking me. For several seconds, we stared at each other.

"They've been doing that since I got here," said Tricia, walking up next to me. "No one gets to go inside with the person they came with."

"Forget that," I said, ignoring Tricia, watching Kate. The nightgown guides on either side of her still held loosely to her arms, but they'd stopped walking, allowed her to turn around.

Kate's eyes were hooded in shadow. I couldn't tell if she was steeling herself or enjoying the whole thing or resigned or what. All she said was, "It's okay. It'll be fun."

"I came here with you," I said. "I want to go through it with you."

"Guess there are still at least a few things we don't get to go through together," said Kate. Then she smiled another of those wide, blooming smiles, but she aimed it at Tricia. "Take care of the poor professor. See you out the other side, David."

She stepped forward, surprising even the guides, I think. The one on the left lost her hold on Kate's arm. The house had a white front door with a giant, ear-shaped brass door handle that flashed in the icy moonlight. Kate closed her hand over it and glanced back one more time.

She was still smiling. Then the door was open, and the blackness inside seemed to spill, for just a second, into the lawn. The door closed, and Kate was gone.

"It's not even fair," Tricia said. "I've been here longer than you guys."

"How long *have* you been here, anyway?" I muttered, unable to pry my eyes from the door. The dark in there had seemed almost solid.

"Half an hour, maybe? There doesn't seem to be an order, though. They just come and get you. They got Robert maybe fifteen minutes ago."

"They make you go alone?"

"Some people. Some get to go in groups of two or three. Just not anyone you came here with. Think that's part of the plan? A way of making you uncomfortable or something?"

If it was, I thought, it was working. "Show me the game booth," I said, mostly because I didn't like standing staring at the door. And somehow, I suspected I wouldn't be summoned as long as I did so.

I had my hands in my pockets, my arms tucked in tight at my sides because I thought Tricia might take my elbow or something, and I didn't want her to. But she just flicked her head in the direction of the backyard, smiled at me, and walked off. I followed, watching the house, listening for screaming, but there was none. There was no sound at all. Other people, I thought, must have gone in before Kate and joined her to form a group, because there were only four or five hauntees left in the yard now.

A long, folding table lined the back of the first game booth, and on the table sat a row of foot-high stuffed elephants, all crouched back on their haunches with their trunks in the air. The elephants seemed disconcerting only in their ordinariness. Once again, I was confronted with the contradictions of this place, the completely unique and elaborately controlled atmosphere and the utterly prosaic imagery. Surely, finding and playing this particular game deserved more significant reward.

Leaning against the table, smoking a cigarette, stood a gray-haired, stooped old man in a cloak. He had his chin tilted back, his eyes aimed at the roof of the booth. For a second, I thought he might be impersonating the stuffed elephants, and I started to smile. The old man lowered rheumy, red-streaked gray eyes and looked at me, then Tricia. "Only one play per traveler," he said, his voice more smoke than sound.

"I'm not playing," said Tricia, cheerful as ever. "He is."

The old man dropped his cigarette to his feet, where it hissed in the grass. "Spin the wheel," he said to me. "Test your fate."

The wheel sat on another folding table that ran along the front of the booth, looking as though it had been ripped from a *Life* game board and enlarged. It was made of white plastic roughly three feet in diameter. Positioned underneath the indicator was a circular piece of black construction paper. There was a single wedge of red paper taped over the black at roughly high noon, with white lettering on it. The lettering read, SPINNER WINS ELEPHANT. There was lettering on the much larger black section of the circle, too. It said, DEALER LOSES HAND.

"I won Robert an elephant," Tricia told me.

I put my fingers on the wheel, then jerked them back. The spinner wasn't plastic; it was bone. And freezing.

"Jesus Christ," I said.

"Oops," said Tricia, laughing happily to herself. "Forgot to mention that, didn't I?"

The gray man was no longer looking at us. He was looking beyond us. Remembering his training, I supposed. I put my hand back on the spinner, glanced at Tricia, thought of Kate, and spun the wheel.

Around and around it whirred. It made no sound. The indicator circled the grid, and eventually glided to a stop deep in the black.

"No elephant for me," I said.

Sighing, the old man dropped his arm on the table in front of me. With his other hand, he withdrew a hacksaw from inside his coat, sighed again, shrugged. Then he drove the hacksaw straight down into his wrist, straight through to the table, where it vibrated a few seconds in the frozen wood.

"Holy *fuck*," said Tricia, and flew backwards.

I stared at the hand on the table, severed now, a single, long tendon dangling from it like a tongue. The old man was staring at the hand, too. Mouth working, I took a step back. It had happened so fast that I couldn't quite grasp it yet. But there was no blood. No blood. Exquisitely realistic tendon, but no blood.

"You're awfully good," I said to the man.

He nodded, lifted a garbage bag from under the table, and swept the severed hand into it with his stump. Then he retreated to the back of the booth, placed a fresh cigarette between his lips, wiggled the stump into a pocket in his cloak, and reassumed his position.

"Oh my God," Tricia said, and now she did grab my arm and held onto it as she went on laughing. Her laughter was irresistible, infectious, like a tickle. I felt myself burst into a smile.

We stayed arm in arm, watching the carnival booth, waiting to see what happened when the next *traveler*, as the man had called us, came to play. I at least wanted to see if the gray man had new fake hands in his cloak and could attach them without turning away and blocking our vision. But a scant minute later, the nightgown ghosts appeared, one on either side of us.

"Finally," Tricia breathed.

"You're sure you're up for this?" I asked, feeling almost giddy now. I couldn't wait to tell Kate about the booth. I couldn't wait to find her again. Besides, teasing Tricia was as irresistible as laughing with her.

Of course, she was better at teasing. "I've got my big, bad Prof," she said, squeezing my arm. I blushed, and she looked at me, and we let the nightgown ghosts lead us back around the long, red house toward the white door, the waiting dark.

I had two wild, ridiculous thoughts as I was led up the stoop. The first was that I'd just met Judge Albert Alouisius Dark, that he'd found the fountain of youth somewhere and decided to spend his eternity huddled away on the plains, plotting yearly appearances with selected friends. The faintly perverse, perpetually bored Santa Claus of Halloween. The second thought I said aloud.

"Where's the exit?" I said.

"What?" said Tricia.

"You said Robert went in, what, twenty minutes ago now? Where did he come out?"

"I thought of that."

"Did you think of an answer?"

Tricia grinned. "After you, Professor R."

One last time, I considered the possibility that this was all a hoax, the best ever perpetrated, at least on me. God, even Brian Tidrow could be a hoax, I thought, then dismissed the thought. I glanced at Tricia's face. Her red mouth hung open just a little, and her blue eyes were bright. This was no joke. None she was in on, anyway.

I took the handle, which, to my relief, felt like a door handle, and shoved. The door didn't creak but swung smoothly back. I glanced over my shoulder and gasped and stumbled forward, dragging Tricia behind me. The nightgown ghosts had been right on top of us, brushing against our backs. One of them smiled blankly at me, put her hand on the handle, and pulled the door closed.

For a minute, maybe more, we just stood in the dark. I kept waiting for my eyes to adjust, but there was nothing to adjust to. This was blackness and silence, plain and simple. My ears almost stretched off my head, searching out sounds of people scrambling into place, spring triggers being set. Then they searched for just plain breathing, the tap of snow against outside shingles, anything at all. But there was nothing. Stepping into that foyer was like stepping into a coffin. Worse, actually. It was like walking completely out of the world.

"Professor R.?" I heard Tricia whisper. Somehow, I'd lost her elbow, but I felt her hand crawl up my sleeve now, take hold of me.

"Right here," I said, though I was at least as happy to hear and feel her as she must have been me. I found myself hoping, desperately, that Kate had been allowed some sort of group to go through this with. The idea of her standing here this long, with Brian Tidrow's blown-apart head leering under her eyelids, was more than I could bear.

The house's first overture was a touch. It was so subtle that I mistook it, for a moment, for Tricia's breath near my cheek. But then I realized I could feel it on my hands, too, a gentle, intermittent rushing of air. The first warm anything I'd encountered since the car heater.

It did feel like breath, though. As if there were dozens of people crouched right up against us, just breathing.

"Hey," I said, because even as I'd had that thought, I knew it wasn't true. Because I realized I could see, a little. Something, somewhere, was casting a faint, green glow. I glanced toward Tricia, saw her outline.

Tricia glanced back at me. "I can see you," she said.

"Feel better?"

"Nope." Even in that dim light, I could see her teeth.

"Smart girl."

We were in a sort of hangar-style chamber, long and wide and empty. There was a doorway, however, fifteen feet away on the left. The glow came from there. The little puffs of air came from everywhere, but the glow was on the left.

I tugged Tricia's arm, and we started that way. Nothing dropped out of the ceiling. Nothing moved at all. As we approached the opening, I noted the crawling pace we adopted. Walking a haunted house properly is a lot like making love, I'd decided years ago. Maximum enjoyment requires concentration, the patience to allow for moments of electric, teasing agony, a suspension of disbelief in your own boundaries, and most of all, a willingness to pay attention. Despite my yearly visits to every spook joint in Clarkston, I hadn't paid so much attention since high school. In spite and because of everything, I smiled.

We stepped into a hallway that ran ahead for fifty feet or so and then jogged to the right.

"See, they understand, these people," I said. "You don't need fog. You don't need rubber hatchets in your head and things lunging out and grabbing your hair. You just need the dark and the silence and some imagination and—"

"No lectures, Professor," said Tricia.

My smile widened unconsciously. "But lecturing makes me feel better."

"Exactly," said Tricia, and I could see her eyes flashing. Her concentration on this moment was total. She led me forward, and I let her.

We'd gone perhaps fifteen feet when my foot hit the floor and sank, and I jerked it back. I hadn't sunk far, but I didn't like the squishiness where wood or cement should have been. I'd seen and felt and imagined too many bones tonight. I thought of the soft spot on a baby's skull and shuddered. I lifted my foot again, put it down to the left of where I'd put it before. It sank again.

"Is this carpet?" Tricia asked.

"No idea."

"Feels gross."

"And you didn't even know Brian Tidrow."

"What?"

"Just walk, Tricia. Let's walk."

It was like I'd imagined stepping onto the moors would be as a child, after I'd been read my first story with quicksand in it. For weeks afterward I'd been terrified of walking in the grass. I'd had such total, unwavering faith until then in the ground.

Sometimes, our feet hit solid surface. Sometimes, the surface gave, depressing downward a little. This might not even be an intended effect, I decided. This could just be old, rotting wood. I didn't believe it, though.

As soon as we reached the spot where the passageway veered, the glow became a full-fledged spill of light from another doorway ten yards ahead. Without a word, we turned that way and crept forward. The floor beneath us became solid again. The rushes of air diminished, then disappeared altogether. But there were other sounds, now. Rustlings from down the hall, and a sort of drip and slosh from nowhere in particular. If the night had been warmer, I'd have assumed that ice was melting off the roof outside.

No sound came from the room with the doorway, though. We reached it side by side, turned toward it together, and Tricia said, "Oh" and started to giggle and stopped. The effect was delayed on me, too, because the whole thing had been so studiously constructed to look real rather than ghoulish.

On the ceiling in the center of the room, right where a light fixture should have been, a shining metal hook glinted in the seemingly sourceless green light. From the hook, not swinging, hung a slightly pudgy, pale boy, maybe eight years old. The noose around his neck, right above the collar of his Minnesota Twins baseball jersey, appeared to have bitten straight through his skin into his muscles and veins, which you could just see, little red tangles in yellow twists of twine. His tongue didn't bulge and it wasn't blue. It just drooped out the side of his lips in a peculiarly childlike way, like the untucked tail of a shirt. The boy's bare feet were at least half a yard off the floor.

A red velvet rope barred Tricia and me from entering the room. But we stood a while, waiting for the kid to blink, yell "Boo," jerk forward, do any of those comforting haunted house things. But he didn't. He just hung.

Back down the hall, I heard the thud of boot on floor. I looked that way, saw a person-shaped bulk detach itself from the massing shadows and step toward us.

"Time to go, I think," I said.

"Professor R.?" Tricia said. For the first time in my experience of her, she sounded like a teenage girl.

"Let's just keep walking." I'm not sure which of us took the other's hand. "Just imagine the stories we're going to be telling on Monday."

"Monday?" said Tricia. "Shit, I'm calling everyone I've ever met as soon as I get home."

Twenty steps ahead, the passageway ended in a T. To the right, we could see one more strip of light, flickering and yellow, down near the floor this time, so we went that way. Soon, we realized we were approaching a plain wooden door pulled most of the way shut. My least favorite door position. At least when a door is completely closed, you assume that nothing will come out *to* you. I heard footfall again, glanced back, saw the person-shaped shadow reach the T in the hallway and turn in our direction. Whoever he was moved just slightly more slowly than we did. But he kept coming.

We were a few feet from the door when the grunting began. For a single second, simply because we'd heard virtually nothing since we entered, it startled me. Then I started to smile. The grunt was distinctly human. Human-playing-ape.

"Oooh," it went. "Oooh-oooh."

I started to say something to Tricia and finally noticed the pajama child cloaked in the black shadows near the door. As soon as I saw him, he took a step forward. He was a bit older than the hanging boy, with long hair that lay in a black, wriggling mass on his shoulders and made his head look like it was encased in snakes. It could have been a wig. His pajamas were yellow and baggy.

"Watch the gorilla," he said flatly, pushed the door open just a bit more, and stepped back into the shadows, his movements precise and mechanical as those of the robot pirates at Disneyland.

"Gorillas scare me," said Tricia.

"Now, have you ever taken the time to sit down and talk to one?" I said, and she elbowed me in the ribs. The pressure of my coat against me reminded me that I wasn't warm. The house had not been heated, apparently.

Right as we reached the door, I saw the cage on the other side of it, and for the third time experienced a flicker of disappointment. The cage had been dug into the wall, lit by torches that guttered in sconces. In the cage, '*ooh-oohing*,' was a tallish person in an old and painfully obvious gorilla-suit.

"Okay," I said, and started forward, pushing the door all the way back. The gorilla guy lunged at his bars, jammed one rubber arm through at us, grunted. My pride was up. I stared right into his eyes, tugged Tricia beside me, strolled past. When the second gorilla dropped on us from behind, I flew fifteen feet down the hall and shouted. Tricia screamed. Then both of us whirled, stunned, laughing.

The second gorilla stood in the passageway, hunched, huge, panting. He did not say '*ooh*.' His skin still didn't look quite real, but it didn't look rubber, either. Mostly, it looked unhealthy, clinging in strips to whoever was underneath there like black, desiccated mummy wrapping.

"Classic misdirection," I panted. "That guy was just sitting there on the wall if we'd looked, see? But they got us focused on the one in the cage."

"You're doing it again, Professor."

"That's because that scared me shitless, Tricia."

"I noticed that."

The door behind the gorillas creaked. Something else was pushing through. The shadow that had been herding us along, I suspected.

"On we go," said Tricia, pulling me forward, and we continued down the hall.

We walked twenty paces, then twenty more. I began to wonder just how big this house was. It hadn't looked forty paces long in any direction from the outside. Nevertheless, we'd gone nearly a hundred before we hit the stairwell.

The architects of this funhouse had thoughtfully provided a single torch, licking the wall at eye level, to alert passersby that they could plunge to their deaths here. Maybe this house had been built on the prairie because it was outside the jurisdiction of Clarkston's increasingly specific and stringent haunted house safety code.

"We in the right place?" Tricia said.

I thought about that. "The only way to know for sure is to wait and make sure the big thing behind us catches up."

"Or we could keep going."

The stairs were cement, but ten steps down, the walls lost their comforting wooden skin, became dirt. Ahead was a floor, or at least a landing, and the stairwell banked to the left into total darkness.

I stopped, listened, hissed for Tricia to stop too. For the second time, and much more loudly now, I heard the dripping, sloshing sound. It came from ahead of us.

"Maybe we *are* going the wrong way," I said.

"I don't think so," Tricia murmured, her eyes raised above my head, and I turned and saw the shadow-shape fill the doorway. Whatever it was wore a black cowl, complete with hood, and it was big. Six and a half feet tall, at least. I couldn't see its face. But it was carrying a gavel.

"Okay," I said. "Down, Tricia."

Down we went. The shape stayed where it was until we reached the landing, then took a single step after us. Tricia reached the landing first.

"What's below us?" I called, catching up.

"More stairs," said Tricia, and the torch behind us went out. "Fuck."

"Let's go. Forward is homeward."

"Arm, please, Professor R."

I gave her my arm. We continued down. Five steps. Ten. Down. Down. Every few seconds, we heard a single creak as the Judge-thing in the cowl pursued at its leisurely pace.

From deep inside me, a laugh swelled. I felt it crest in the back of my throat, then break into the open air.

"Oh my God, shut up," said Tricia.

But I kept on laughing. Truly, I thought, this was the best I'd ever seen. Then my foot plunged ankle deep into water, and I shouted and teetered backward.

"GROSS!" Tricia yelled. She fell back beside me, shaking her leg, and we lay together on the steps.

Somewhere above us, a stair creaked.

"Kate hates puddles," I said, trying to imagine her coming through this. Abruptly, I had no laughter left. I was just overwhelmingly tired. And Brian Tidrow was dead. I hadn't liked him. I liked his being dead even less.

"What if they just lead everyone down here and drown them?" Tricia murmured.

"That would lower my overall rating of the experience," I answered, trying to rouse myself to push ahead. How much longer, really, could all this be?

"We could be walking in a sewer."

"There aren't many people out here, though. So the amount of actual sewage—"

"Shut up, Professor R.," said Tricia. But she laughed, or at least expelled the air she'd been clutching in her teeth.

I got up. Tricia got up, too, and the stairs above us creaked again. But there was no light to see by. Gritting my teeth, I stepped straight down into the wet, tugging Tricia behind me. The floor underneath was solid, anyway. Tricia moaned as her ankles sank, but she didn't say anything. We went forward.

Mostly, for the first few feet, I was listening. I wanted to hear where the water we disturbed rolled into a wall, thinking maybe I could judge the size of this tunnel, space, whatever it was. But I couldn't.

"Tell me this is water," Tricia whispered.

"Hadn't even thought of that. Thanks, Tricia." I shuddered. I was whispering, too.

We'd gone another fifteen steps when overhead lights burst to life, blinding us, and shut off just as quickly, igniting fireworks on my retina. I stopped hard, the water sloshed, and the disturbed dark flapped and fluttered around us.

"Now what?" Tricia said.

"Let's see if that happens again. Maybe we can figure out where we are."

We waited maybe a minute, which felt like twenty. Nothing happened. Shrugging, I tugged Tricia's arm, took a step, and the lights bloomed, held a split second longer this time, and died.

"Hmmm," I said, and started forward again.

Five steps later, the water got deeper. It happened in a quick, slipping slope, and we were up to our knees, then nearly our waists. I continued to insist to myself that it was water. At least it wasn't cold. If anything, it was a little too warm.

This time when the lights flashed, they stayed on a good five seconds. My pupils telescoped, my brain locked, and I got just a glimpse of wooden walls to the sides and another staircase less than fifty feet ahead, leading up. Then the dark slammed down.

"Okay. Exit ho," I said, and felt the first bump against my leg. "Uh-oh."

"What?" said Tricia.

"Just walk."

"Hey," Tricia said, and then, "*Jesus.* There's something—"

"Walk, Tricia. Wait for the lights."

"I don't want to see."

The lights exploded. I was watching the water. I very nearly fainted into it.

Drifting on the black, rippling surface were fingers. Thumbs. Dozens of them. Hundreds, floating like dead fish in a dynamited pond. I saw part of an ear. The lights went out.

"Professor," Tricia said, her voice very small. "Did you see—"

"Walk, Tricia. Fast."

Mercifully, the water got shallower just a few steps farther on, but the things in the water swirled more thickly around us. I kept my hands locked against my chest and burrowed straight ahead. Tricia was even faster, very nearly running as we scrambled up another slope. The water level fell toward our knees. Both of us heard slower, steadier sloshing behind us. But when the lights came on again, neither of us glanced back.

Seconds later, we were on the stairs, breathing hard. I might have bent over and kissed the firm, dry wood beneath me except that my pants were soaked and felt awful when my skin pressed against them. Walking sopping wet across the frozen prairie to the car would be fun, I thought.

But worth it. The whole damn thing had been more than worth it. I couldn't wait to grab Kate, hold her, laugh with her. I couldn't wait to start digging around town for wood-purchasing and electricity records in the hopes of tracking down the creators of all this. I couldn't wait to interview Robert Hayright and everyone else who'd been here about exactly what they'd seen. For the first time in years, I felt like writing.

More than anything else, though, I felt grateful. All my life, I'd considered myself a sort of library phantom, haunting the graveyards and record morgues of my own history without ever, somehow, materializing inside it. But I was soaking in it, now, shivering in the relentless, terrifying rush of it.

I looked up and saw the exit sign glowing plainly, redly, twenty steps above me.

"That's it?" Tricia said, clutching her arms against herself and holding her sopping pantlegs very still.

"Are you joking?" I answered, but I knew what she meant. I didn't want to leave. I wanted to go on being this kind of scared forever.

Except that I didn't really want the Judge-thing to catch us. So when I heard him sloshing closer, I started up the steps. I had reached the landing, halfway to the top, when the strobe light strafed us, and the pajama people stepped out of the wall on either side of the staircase. There were two on every stair.

"Bummer," I said, because I knew this trick. I'd seen it in half the haunted houses I'd ever visited. True, I was impressed by the doors cleverly carved into the walls to hide all these people until we were right on top of them. But now, I was going to start up the stairs, and the pajama-people would produce hatchets and clubs and raise them, slowly, looking all lurchy in the twitches of light, and then they'd lean in and menace us as we made for the door.

"Ohhh," I heard Tricia moan. I also heard a slosh and then drip from below, and I knew that the Judge-thing had reached the foot of the stairs.

"No worries," I muttered, and, ignoring the wetness in my legs, started upward again.

"I hate strobes," said Tricia. But I heard her stepping behind me.

I had my hands in my pockets. As I passed the pajama people, I glared straight into their eyes. The only thing that surprised me was that none of them made any sort of mock-threatening motion. In fact, they didn't move at all. They just stood, silent as heralds in a painting of a medieval procession, and watched me go.

"Unnh," I heard Tricia say, and looked back, and everything went to hell.

Full-blown, blazing, ordinary light flooded the space down there, more than enough for me to see the Judge-thing. He had not actually stepped onto the staircase and was instead standing knee-deep in the black pool of wetness we'd traversed. I couldn't see his face because of his cowl. But I could see the fingers and thumbs floating around him.

They were moving.

Dozens of them clung to the fringe of his cloak or crawled blindly up his hanging arms, wriggling. Like bees over a beekeeper, I thought wildly, and my breath flew from me, and Tricia screamed and shoved me out of the way and hurtled out the exit door.

Staggering, I tore my eyes from the Judge-thing and stumbled up the last few stairs. Still the pajama people made no move to hold me. Tricia had left the door half open in her flight, and I scrambled for it, very nearly tumbling to my knees. Three steps more. Two.

Then I was out, in a sort of clearing on the prairie, several hundred feet from the red house, and the door was starting to shut, and a crushing burst of desperate longing exploded through me. For a split second, I thought it was for the house. The knowledge that I would never experience another like it. That the eternal Halloween search of the lifelong Clarkstonian was over for me.

Then I realized what had been so strange about Tricia's flight from the house. Or rather, the moment just before it. When she'd screamed, she hadn't been looking at the Judge-thing. She'd been looking into the shadows right beside her. And the look on her face wasn't terror, or not only terror. It was also recognition.

I knew, then. I knew even before I turned around. And I thought I understood, at least a little. The wriggling fingers. The Judge-thing, and the nature of its power. The barefoot pajama boys and the decrepit gorilla. Not why. Not how. But something. And I knew the plains weren't empty after all, not the way we'd thought all these years. In fact, they are overflowing, overrun with Native Americans, homesteaders, dancing girls, ranchers, Chinese, buffalo. All the murdered, restless dead.

I watched Kate watch me from the top of the stairs. She hadn't been issued her pajamas yet, I guessed. Her coat was open, at last, and there was no blanket around her, and I could finally see the hole Brian Tidrow must have blown in her stomach, just as she walked in his door, in the seconds before he'd shot his own head off.

"No," I said.

"Goodbye, David," Kate said softly, and the door swung closed as she blew me a kiss.

Universal Horror

Stephen Graham Jones

The game was the same as every year. Rachel could have called it in July, if she'd wanted. For every age-inappropriate costume that knocked on the door of their no-kids party—six-year-old sexy nurses, second grade saloon girls—Bill had to do a shot. For every comic book or television character, Nalene had to do a shot. Usually David got drunk off ethnic-insults-on-parade—kids in headdresses, kids-as-pimps—but three months ago his girlfriend 'Carrie' had given birth to a bouncing baby boy, so he wasn't even at the party this year. David's ex Jen always called animal-costumes, but, like David, she was starting over somewhere else.

Last Halloween, Rachel had had pirates and soldiers, a category she'd come up with herself, that had got her thoroughly sloshed by eight o'clock, in need of a restorative bump from Bill's famous stash. This year she'd gone Russian roulette, just pulled a strip of paper from the salad bowl in the kitchen.

Universal Horror.

"But that's everything?" she'd said, holding it up like she wasn't going to fall for this.

Bill, their expert, groaned.

"Think thirties, forties," he said, gesturing with his tumbler. "Frankenstein, Dracula, Mummy, Wolf Man. Phantom of the Opera." He sung the last part, and gestured his arm wide and grand, to encompass the whole neighborhood.

"Kids don't listen to opera anymore," Nalene said.

"Anymore?" Rachel said.

"Black Lagoon, Invisible Man, Bride of Frankenstein…" Bill was still reeling off.

And so the night began.

The No-Kids Pre-November Drunkfest had started right out of college. Now Bill and Nalene and Rachel were the last hold-outs, the 'loyalists' as David had called them when he was one: the diehards still sticking to their ideals of ten years ago, when they were never going to sell out, never going to buy in.

There'd been eight of them, then. Four couples against the world.

The only couple left standing now was Bill and Nalene.

"Our ranks are thinning," Bill had been noting out loud since Rachel had walked over at five, and then he'd lift his tumbler to who they used to be.

Aside from David stepping out on Jen with Carrie the house-sitter, a development so ripped-from-the-sitcoms that Rachel could hardly even muster an ironic smile, Ali and Bethany had packed up and moved way (the farewell party had been epic, a throwback), were rumored to be pregnant-at-a-distance as well, having their progeny in shame. In a not-so-generic move, Ted had left Rachel in August for a willowy bag boy he'd found at the neighborhood grocery store.

Ted claimed not to be gay, to just be in love, but Rachel wasn't stupid. He was being Ted: polite to a fault, careful of her feelings, trying to pull all the blame onto himself.

Instead of having the balls to just tell her it was over, that he'd never expected it to last this long, he was feigning infatuation, trying to make himself out to be a victim of love, caught in sudden headlights out on the highway of life.

It was pretty cliché, Rachel guessed. Except for the groping in the dark with a younger version of himself part. Really, it was pathetic—though Rachel did get a rush from trying to imagine how he had to hold his eyes when pointing his fingers to shove his left hand down into the hip-hugging pants of his bag boy. And it was delicious, too, how they probably had to be fast—breaks are fifteen minutes—and quiet, because the coke machine they were pressed up against was high traffic, and the assistant manager of produce had already warned them once, about love.

So, for the first time in better than a decade, she was alone for Halloween.

And now the doorbell was ringing with the first trick-'r-treater of the night.

Bill popped his plastic fangs in, said to Nalene and Rachel, "Bottoms up, ladies?"

Some things you don't even dignify.

It was a little mummy, all alone.

Rachel, at the door, looked back to Bill like he'd set all this up, hadn't he?

"Like you came here to be sober?" Nalene said, nudging into the doorway with Rachel.

The rule was you take your shot after you shut the door. Because there were always parents watchdogging it at the curb, their flashlights forming yellow puddles of fear at their feet.

"A scary mummy," Rachel said, holding the plastic bowl of candy out between.

"That's real gauze," Nalene said, rubbing a trailing piece between the pads of her fingers. "Hospital grade."

"Trick 'r treat," the kid said, or something with that singsong lilt. There was no mouth hole, just too many layers of grimy white.

"Oh, yeah," Rachel said. "Um, trick?"

She couldn't remember the exact protocol. Did this mean she was asking for a trick, or promising one?

"Hey now…" Nalene was saying now.

Rachel refocused.

The little mummy had produced a foil-wrapped square skewered on a toothpick.

"Did you make this?" Rachel said, playing impressed (she had nieces and nephews), and took it, rattled the candy bowl like shaking up the secret candy from the bottom.

The little mummy's gauze fingers went in, shoved around, came out with a single piece, and then he coughed under all that gauze, his mouth-fabric staining red.

"There's your trick," Nalene said, impressed. She called back to Bill, "Have you still got some of those?"

Bill looked around, said, "Blood capsules?"

The ritual over, the little mummy stepped off the porch.

Rachel looked around for the mummy's mom, saw the dad instead in a una-bomber hoodie—costume? no? He stabbed a cigarette into the deep shadow of his face, was already casing the next house, holding his smoke in for longer than Rachel could have, like savoring every last grey swirl.

Not a neighborhood dad, Rachel figured. A weekend dad, bringing his kid to where the good candy was.

"Next?" Nalene said, leaning out.

It was early yet, hardly even dusk.

"Think he made it himself?" Rachel said, peeling the foil from the bite of brownie, letting it bloom at the top of the toothpick like a husk just opened.

"Special brownie…" Bill said, balancing Rachel's first shot over.

"It's us who poisons them, right?" Rachel said, popping the brownie in, "not the other way around."

"There's probably Crayola in it," Nalene said. "And cooties."

Rachel chased the brownie with the shot.

It made her eyes water.

Twenty minutes later—an astronaut they'd all had to drink for, as he filled no category, and a band of miniature pirates Nalene graciously claimed—Bill came back from the kitchen with the videocamera.

"Liver Chronicles time…" he announced, as if there were more of them than there were.

"We still doing that?" Nalene said.

She was digging through the candy bowl for butterscotch. This was the one night of the year she allowed herself to indulge.

"Do you ever watch them?" Rachel called to Bill over the back of the couch.

"Every day," he said, and plopped down. "I call them the Blackmail Tapes, actually."

"There's not enough of us to make it fun," Rachel said.

"What the—?" Nalene said.

Rachel and Bill looked over.

She was extracting something from the candy bowl.

A bloody fingernail.

"Trick," Bill said, and spit his fangs out into his palm, delivered them to a coaster on the coffee table.

"It's fake, isn't it?" Rachel said about the scabby fingernail.

Nalene was holding it up, inspecting it against the lamp.

"I don't think I'm hungry anymore," she said, and deposited the fingernail in the trashcan they used for umbrellas.

The doorbell rang again. Witches.

"That'd be David's shot, for ethnic insult," Bill said, getting the camera cued past last year's confessions. "Witches have gypsy noses. Like in Oz. Tell me I'm wrong."

"Magical creatures," Rachel corrected. "That's Ted."

She took the shot, had to close her eyes to swallow it down.

"You all right?" Nalene said.

"Good," Rachel coughed out.

"Who's first?" Bill asked.

The Liver Chronicles were campfire stories, minus the campfire. Secrets you tell when you're drunk.

"I don't have any left," Nalene said. "I didn't last year either, remember? I just told that one about pouring nail polish remover on that cop car."

"That wasn't even you," Rachel said.

"I was there," Nalene said.

The rule was it had to be something punishable by law.

Bill turned the camera on himself.

"When I was sixteen," he said, taking a long drink to let the tension build, "we used a sandwich bag for a rubber once."

"Mixed company?" Nalene said, playing offended. "As in, there's wives here?"

"Wife singular," Rachel corrected, swirling her finger around to point it back at herself.

This time when the doorbell rang, they looked in that direction like it was already becoming a chore.

"Okay, okay," Rachel finally said, and poured herself off the couch, collected the candy, swung the door back.

"Another mummy," she said loud enough for Bill and Nalene.

That wasn't exactly right, though.

"Have I seen you before?" she said down to the little mummy.

"Ask if he has another brownie!" Bill called.

"Here," Rachel said, and offered the bowl.

The mummy hauled his arm up, sifted through. Rachel didn't watch his fingers, but his one eye. He either had a filmy contact in—you can buy something like that for a kid?—or this was a real live mummy.

"Good gauze," she said, just for herself, letting the back of her index finger brush the little mummy's mummied cheek.

"Dirty gauze," Nalene said, suddenly there again, rubbing a trailing strip between her fingers, careful to avoid the stained parts that were supposed to be old blood. Or embalming fluid? She leaned down to look into the mummy's face. "You're not going to leave us any surprises in with the candy again, are you?"

"Leave him be," Rachel said, and pulled the bowl away, her eyes trying to see the whole sidewalk at once. Trying to see the hoodie-dad, so she could tell from his stance whether he knew this was the same house or not. So she could tell if he was in on this or not.

"Good trick…" Nalene was saying to the little mummy.

Rachel backtracked, saw: the little mummy had three pieces of candy in his wrapped fingers, but his trailing gauze was still sticky on the back, it seemed. It had collected a butterscotch.

"That was mine," Nalene said, reaching for it.

The little mummy twitched the candy away.

"Where's your dad?" Rachel said to the little mummy, looking past him again.

"Why?" Nalene said, tiptoeing to look. "Is he a candidate?"

Rachel shut the door.

Because the little mummy's costume had been so good, Rachel did the one shot she had to, since he was a monster from the thirties, but then she poured another, carried it with her the way Bill always had his cut-glass tumbler.

He lifted it to her and she nodded, drank a sip, and raised the camera to her.

"Do we have to?" she said.

"Tradition," Bill said, squatting to track her face.

Rachel crossed to the couch, sat all the way back into it and shook her head like she wasn't going to do this.

But she already was.

"There was one I never told," she said. "Because, you know. Ted."

"Is he in it?" Nalene asked, thrilled, her bare feet tucked under her on the couch beside Rachel.

"I couldn't tell it because it wasn't him," Rachel said.

"Now we're getting somewhere…" Bill said, putting his fangs back in in a way that Rachel could see him at seventy, with dentures.

"Don't record this one, though," Rachel said.

"Just with this," Bill said, tapping his temple with his middle finger.

"That means turn the camera off," Nalene prompted.

Bill hissed a vampire hiss at her and clapped the camera in his lap shut.

"Thanks," Rachel said to Nalene, then looked at the door like it was the only thing that could save her now. When it didn't, she came back, chewed her cheeks in like she hated, and said, "Remember Craig D?"

"Which one was he?" Bill asked.

"Davidson," Nalene filled in. "The other was Morrison."

"Morissey," Rachel corrected. "We never dated, really. We just went out twice, I guess."

"And you couldn't tell Ted about this?" Bill asked.

"I could now," Rachel said. "Let's just say we were driving. And only one of us was watching the road."

"Oh," Nalene said, her lower lip sucked in, eyes hot.

"Second date?" Bill said. "What, were you a prude back then?"

Rachel flipped him off, kept going. "We were out in that industrial park place, just kind of taking random rights."

"The road to heaven is paved with—" Bill started, but Nalene saw his hand-mouth motion coming, was already tossing a pillow at him.

"Go on," she said.

"That's it, really," Rachel said. "Remember how there were all those rabbits out there, though?"

"You killed Thumper?" Bill said, impressed.

Rachel drank a sip, then just shot the rest.

She wasn't going to make eight o'clock this year either, she knew. Not without help.

"We hit something. I felt it, like, in the floor. When we got back to my apartment, there was blood and hair on the front of that Camaro he had? The red one?"

"He had a name for it," Bill said, looking past Rachel, at the door.

"I'm sure he did," Rachel said. "Like I said, it was just that once. But then—do you remember that week? Right before finals, junior year?"

Nalene let her eyes scan all the internal headlines she always had on instant. "No," she said, when she got to that week.

"I—I don't know," Rachel said.

"What?" Bill said, leaning forward, picking up on the seriousness in Nalene's tone.

"That kid, the hit and run," Nalene said, staring at Rachel, waiting for Rachel to smile, waiting for this all to be a joke. "We went to the vigil, remember?"

Bill looked up to the right corner of the room, nodded, came back with, "That thing at the flagpoles, where we all had candles but nobody lit them, yeah."

"Because he was burned by the time they found him," Rachel said, shrugging like it didn't matter. "Whoever hit him, they went back. To hide the evidence. Right there in the road."

"You can't burn a whole body with gasoline," Nalene said.

"You can burn paint off that body, though," Rachel said.

"Returning to the scene of the crime," Bill said, shaking his head at the stupidity. "Neither of the Craigs were in any danger of going genius, I don't guess."

"And so—" Nalene said, getting her words right, "and so you've, ever since then, you've been thinking it was you? That it was because of you?"

Rachel shrugged again.

"Even if it was Craig, then it was Craig," Nalene said. "You were just an innocent bystander. You wouldn't even count as a witness."

"I'd probably count as something," Rachel said, watching Bill's fangs on the coffee table again.

"I don't think he's ratting you out, anyway," Bill said.

They both turned to him.

"Craig Davidson," he said, and when they both still just stared, waiting, he said, "Do y'all, like, live in this city?"

"What?" Nalene said.

Bill cocked a hanging hand around an invisible noose and kicked his head over sideways, tongue lolling. "Last Halloween..." he croaked, trying to roll his eyes back. "Best trick ever..."

And then the doorbell rang again.

Rachel flinched hard enough that her drink would have spilled, if it wasn't already gone.

"Your turn," she said, and climbed up from the suddenly-deep couch.

She was talking to Nalene, but it was Bill who rose, leading with his glass.

"Oh shit," he said.

It was a squad of zombie cheerleaders. Sexy zombie cheerleaders, none of them past fourth grade yet.

On her way past, for the guest bathroom, Rachel picked the cheer-leaders' den mom out at the curb, the side of her face lit with a cellphone, her skirt just as short as the cheerleaders'.

In the bathroom, Rachel just had to get her face close to the toilet to start vomiting. She splashed all her shots into the toilet, along with the crumbled, soggy bite of brownie.

And—what the hell?

Squirming blind in the puke water, trying to live, were four or five blind maggots.

Rachel threw up again, from deeper, and flushed before opening her eyes this time.

"It's for you!" Nalene was calling through the door. "You all right in there?"

Rachel wiped her face, pulled herself up with the brass doorknob.

No doorbell, but when there was a line off the porch like rush hour, you just stood there, waited for the next little monster.

"C'mon already…" Nalene said, hooking her arm through Rachel's, dragging her to the front door.

The little mummy.

"Told you," Bill said, and clapped his sixth consecutive shot down onto the coffee table. Because there'd been six zombie cheerleaders.

"How long was I in there?" Rachel said, looking back to the bath-room.

"Here," Nalene said, thrusting the candy bowl into Rachel's gut, pushing her at the little mummy.

"We know what you're doing," Rachel said to the little mummy. "It's called cheating."

The little mummy guided its trembly hand into the candy.

"And stickies don't count," Nalene said over Rachel's shoulder.

The little mummy creaked something and Rachel nodded like she understood, was already dreading the next shot, then, as the door was closing, she keyed on the hoodie-dad out at the curb. A line of smoke seeped up from the shadow his face was, then dissipated up into the night.

"Wait—" she said, trying to catch the door.

It opened again, onto three teenage Wonder Women, their star-spangled bustiers dangerously loose.

"A twofer," Rachel said, or, heard herself saying.

Because of the comic book origins, Nalene had to drink. Because of the skin-on-display, Bill had two more shots coming.

"And one for me," Rachel said.

Because of the mummy.

For the first time Rachel knew about since college, Bill passed out before the party was over. Before it really even started.

"He started at lunch," Nalene said, positioning a couch pillow under his head. "Guess we're getting old, right?"

Rachel didn't answer.

"Not that you look it," Nalene said, lifting Rachel's hair on one side. "That brownie was good for you, girl. Ted doesn't know what he's missing."

"I don't have the right parts for Ted anymore," Rachel said.

"World's full of Teds," Nalene said, and opened the liquor cabinet like the door to another world.

"Think I need a little boost," Rachel said, touching the side of her nose Santa-style so Nalene would hear the snow in her words.

"You and me both," Nalene said. "But sleepyhead over there—you know how paranoid he can get? He keeps his stash somewhere in the garage. Says it's better if I don't know."

Rachel was too out of it to even be amused.

"We are getting old," she said.

"You ever think about it?" Nalene said, pouring herself something opaque. "The biological clock, I mean? Tick-tick-tick?"

"I'm not a bomb," Rachel said, and took Nalene's drink from her, took a deep swig. "I'd be a terrible mom, though."

"You seen some of the costumes out there?" Nalene said. "I don't think there's exactly a lot of adult supervision going on."

Rachel took another bitter drink.

"I should buy some water," she said.

Nalene studied her, didn't follow. Rachel didn't explain. Her garage had some thirty five-gallon jugs of water stacked all across it. It was because she liked to watch Ted's bag boy carry them out, try to fit them in the trunk.

Initially, her thought had been to tip him, not have enough money, then invite him back to her place for some real gratuity.

He was so pretty, though. So young. So unaware.

Let Ted keep him, she told herself. Ted deserves someone nice, someone good.

This time when the doorbell rang, she didn't even flinch.

"I already know," she said to Nalene, and killed whatever her vile drink was.

Instead of the mummy, it was a werewolf. Or, an adult werewolf mask on a kid who could maybe spell his name, if given three tries and a running start.

"I like you," Rachel said, and squatted down, shifted through the candy bowl, finally came up with the swirly lollipop that somehow hadn't been grabbed yet.

"You just want him to mess up his costume," Nalene said, the two of them watching the werewolf cub waddle away.

"I don't want one, no," Rachel said. "I don't deserve it."

Nalene looked over to her, her eyes holding Rachel's.

"Nobody deserves that," Nalene said.

Rachel closed her eyes, the house spinning around her.

Next up was the Legion of Doom, or some superhero team.

Nalene curled her shoulders forward like she'd just been punched in the gut.

Rachel opened another bottle, started pouring.

I t was a ghost who found what was hiding in the candy bowl.

The reason it was a ghost was that he didn't have gloves, just had little-kid fingers to reach out from under his sheet.

It wasn't quite a maggot, but it wasn't quite a fly yet either.

Worse, it seemed to be looking up at Rachel and Nalene. Like it was well aware what a vulnerable state it was in. Like it expected whatever they had to do, here.

Nalene opened her hands, the bowl falling for minutes, it felt like.

The next group of kids—soldiers, which would have been deadly last year—fell to their knees, stuffing their cargo pockets and cartridge belts with candy.

"What's happening?" Rachel said to Nalene, clutching her forearm hard.

Nalene shut the door, spun the deadbolt in and smeared her hand across the bank of switches, turning the porch light off the same way people in movies close the eyes of dead people.

"We need that bump..." she said, which is how her and Rachel ended up in the garage, neck-deep in Bill-land.

Thirty minutes later, Nalene caught the back of her ankle on some hidden blade in what felt like the lawn maintenance corner, and it bled and bled, and then bled some more.

In the bathroom, on the sink, she collapsed in laughter.

Rachel had jammed cottonballs between Nalene's toes like this was a pedicure.

Rachel caught the laugh, couldn't stop.

At the end, she was crying.

"I think I miss him," she said, looking up to Nalene. "How stupid is that?"

Nalene, never mind her ankle, stood, hugged Rachel close and patted the back of her head.

"We'll kill him," she said. "You didn't deserve this, girl."

Rachel's breath hitched and then she was really crying, Nalene stroking the back of her hair flat.

"There, there," she was saying.

In the mirror, Rachel caught her face. She pushed away, looked harder at her reflection.

"I'm breaking out," she said, turning her face sideways for the cloud of red at the corner of her mouth.

"Stress," Nalene said.

"There was something in that brownie," Rachel said.

"Like a reaction?"

"Like I don't know. They're not from this block."

"Damn foreigners," Nalene said, sure to use her family's accent.

Rachel closed her eyes, tried to think.

Somewhere in the swirly center of that moment, the doorbell rang.

"But it's him!" Rachel said, Nalene holding her by the wrist, keeping her from the door.

"We don't have any more candy," Nalene said.

"I don't think he wants candy," Rachel said, and jerked away, cracked the complicated mechanics of the deadbolt—it was the kind with a key to turn it—and swung the door back fast enough that her hair sucked forward.

She was looking down at denim knees. At jeans.

She tracked up, up.

"David," Nalene said.

"And David, Jr.," Rachel added, already looking past them, to the sidewalk.

"Is he—is he—?" Nalene was trying to get out.

David finished it for her: "Spider-Man."

Rachel felt Nalene deflate beside her.

"You knew, didn't you?" Nalene said. "Did Bill call, tell you?"

"Bill?" David said, craning around then saying it: "Oh, man. Party foul. Early ejection."

It was what they'd all used to say.

David was holding a baby now, though. One he'd made. One he'd dressed up as a superhero. One too young to even gum any of this candy.

Rachel pushed past him, onto the lawn.

"Have you seen a mummy?" she asked.

"You mean Carrie?" David said.

"She thinks this cute little mummy has it in her for," Nalene said, out on the porch with David now. "He stole all our candy."

"Seriously?" David was saying behind Rachel. Like in another world.

Rachel was to the sidewalk now. Looking one way then the other.

There were enough shots out here to drown a whale.

Walk far enough one way, and the parking lot of the grocery store would open up. Back the other way there were just houses forever, cul-de-sacs and dead-ends and streets named after trees and presidents.

"Here, mummy mummy mummy," Rachel said.

As if in answer, a pale piece of trash in the street flopped over in the breeze.

A strip of gauze.

Rachel stepped out, was squatted down to peel it up from the hot asphalt when her world went white and loud.

The car had stopped six inches from her face.

She stood holding the fluttering gauze, like that would explain it, and then Nalene was there, limping to the rescue, making things worse by yelling at the driver, who'd spilled his beer into his lap and was yelling, too.

Finally David, his baby on his hip, was able to calm the driver, get him to move on past.

"Nothing to see here," Rachel said to herself.

When Nalene guided her back to the porch, Rachel having to help Nalene stand, David didn't follow.

This is how goodbyes work, she knew.

"How did you not know about Craig D?" Rachel said.

They were on the couch again.

"I don't, like, stalk everyone I used to know," Nalene said, holding her hair away from the coffee table so she could inhale a generous second line.

She offered the ceremonial straw to Rachel but the back of Rachel's throat was already that hot kind of drippy, her thoughts already that grainy kind of cold.

"But you've got that memory," Rachel said, using her fingers to indicate Nalene's big brain.

Nalene sighed back into the couch, either had no answer or no interest in answering.

The way they'd found the stash was by waking Bill. With the old trick of ice cubes on his closed eyes. He'd staggered up, fell halfway down, and for his few moments of groggy awareness Nalene asked him where the stash was, the stash the stash the stash.

Bill mumbled something about fishing, and tried to do his hands around an imaginary rod and reel but couldn't seem to remember if he was right- or left-handed. It was enough.

Now they were here, deeper into the night.

"Think that's the one?" Nalene said, pointing her finger in the general direction of the sandwich bag the stash had been sleeping in.

"He had to be lying," Rachel said. "No girl would ever let—" but lost the tail of the thought, once the words turned into an image.

"Girls he knew in high school—" Nalene said, and wowed her eyes out like not much would surprise her, here.

"Girls he knew in college…" Rachel said back, meaning the two of them.

Nalene threw a balled-up napkin at her.

This time when the doorbell rang, neither of them looked back to the door.

"Ali and Bethygirl," Nalene finally said, her voice slurring. "Big re-union tour."

Rachel did her hands around the idea of a pregnant belly.

They collapsed into spasms of laughter.

Nalene rose, did Rachel's line, then wiped her nose on the back of her hand and looked at it, held it back to her right nostril.

"I'm not letting you walk home like that," she said to Rachel.

"You're the one with the ankle," Rachel said.

"I mean," Nalene said, doing her fingers by her head to show, "your state of mind."

Rachel shrugged, looked back to the door just when the bell rang again.

"This is it," she said, and vaulted over the back of the couch with more Mary Lou Retton than she'd have thought she had.

"No, don't—" Nalene said, reaching across Bill, but it was too late.

Rachel opened the door hard, let its knob clap into the wall, shake all the pictures.

"Oh," she said.

A fourth-grader in a white t-shirt, something clever written on the front in marker. Something saying what this lo-fi costume was.

Instead of staring until her eyes could rearrange the letters, she reached back for the candy bowl that wasn't there.

"Oh, shit," she said, and the fourth-grader snapped his eyes up to her about her slip then out to the huddle of parents at the sidewalk, watching. Lip-reading.

"No, no, here," Rachel said, dropping to her knees.

Wedged against the sun-bleached stone frog guarding the top of the stairs was some chocolate doodad in wax paper.

Rachel held it up to the fourth-grader.

When he didn't understand, she grabbed his hand, forced the candy into it, and folded his fingers back.

Now one of the dads was walking across the grass, to stop this.

Rachel straightened her left arm to lean against it better—what she'd always considered a Scarlet O'Hara pose for some reason—and waited for whatever was next.

When Nalene couldn't find the shot glass for the shot she owed the world—the marker on the fourth-grader's chest has been T-SHIRT MAN—she just curled up around the bottle.

"This isn't a good sign," Rachel said, afraid to sit down now. Because she might not be able to haul herself back up.

"We're getting old, girl," Nalene said, and took a swig.

"Speak for yourself," Rachel said, pushing away from the back of the couch. "I'm going to bed."

When the deadbolt didn't work anymore, she looked back to Nalene for help.

Nalene held up the deadbolt key, then slid it neatly down the front of Bill's pants.

"You don't think I'll do it?" Rachel said.

"Let me," Nalene said, and rolled over on top of Bill, her hand back down the front of his pants, her body trying hard to writhe him awake.

Rachel watched until she didn't want to see anymore, then zeroed in on the banister, let it deliver her upstairs, to the guest room.

Piled on the bed and avalanching off it were the bags of yarn Nalene always had.

They were in plastic shopping bags.

Rachel lifted one, smelled the handle-part for bag-boy scent. For Ted. And then she had to balance her face up to keep her eyes from spilling.

She turned around, fell backwards into the pile like a tea commercial.

The yarn was soft, the plastic crinkly and loud.

She blinked once, blinked again, and there was already crust in the corners of her eyes.

It wasn't morning yet, she professionally surmised. The window was still black.

Her mouth was tacky, tasted bad.

She'd left the hall light on, too. Now that she could see it, it was too bright.

"Stupid, stupid," she said, and rolled out of the pile of bags, her hair and fingers trailing yarn. One red strand even hooked to the back of her earring.

When the light switch sucked the brightness back into itself, it brought a different kind of quiet with it.

Something was dripping downstairs.

Rachel reeled back through the evening, settled on Nalene dry-humping Bill, the bottle a casualty of love behind her.

But this was thicker. The sound. Slower, more deliberate.

Rachel cocked her head over, swallowed, and for a bad instant flashed on Nalene and Bill tangled on the couch, each of their throats smiling, those bright red smiles arranged against each other for a last kiss.

She threw up, right onto the brand new carpet.

"Sorry, sorry," she said, trying to wipe it away with her hands, and then a car honked once out in the street, like a date.

When it honked again, Rachel slung her face up, crossed fast to the window of the guest bedroom, pulled the mini-blinds open hard enough that they stayed.

Stopped in the street, its parking lights orangey-yellow at all four corners, its headlights glowed down, was a cherry red Camaro.

The driver door was open, the driver leaned back against the hood, his legs crossed at the ankle.

A breath of smoke seeped up from his hoodie and he lifted his cigarette hand to Rachel, saluted her seeing him.

Rachel fell back, into the bags and the yarn.

"Nalene!" she said, her voice rising to a scream. "Nalene!"

Nalene was dead, though. She knew that now.

Rachel grabbed back for a shopping bag, poured its yarn out, breathed into the bag four times, five.

And then she realized her hands were on the handles of the bag. That she could put it on like a hat, snug it down tight at the neck. That it would be so easy. Just like it had been for Craig D.

"No, no," she said, standing, shaking the bag away.

There was something else sticking to her hand, though.

The gauze.

When she pulled it away, it took a patch of skin with it.

Rachel fell to her knees, her mouth open in shock and pain, her left hand clapped over the torn spot on her right wrist, and then became sure something was about to stand from the pile of bags. Something draped in yarn. Something rotten under all that color.

She kicked back, away from the bed. Pressed her back against the wall.

"Nalene," she said, quieter now, because Nalene couldn't hear.

Would Nalene even know that was Craig D. out there in the street? That he'd stepped over, become something else?

He was asking Rachel to come with.

Just for a quick ride.

That had been his name for the Camaro: Quick Ride.

Rachel felt a laugh burble from her lips and held her hand over it, and in that moment there was a distinct knock, one-two-three.

From the door beside her. The closet.

When Rachel didn't answer, it knocked again, harder. More insistent.

Shaking her head no about it the whole time, she stood, faced the door, and twisted the knob.

Because it was a dream, she was telling herself. Because at the instant in her dreams that a scary thing showed itself, she always shook herself awake.

It was time to wake up.

She pulled the door back, ready to fall into the next day's morning—into November—but, instead of waking, she saw the scary thing.

The little mummy.

"Trick 'r treat," he said, through the gauze.

Because that's what they do for burn victims. That's what they do for kids who weren't really dead when they were burned alive.

The little mummy held his hand up to Rachel.

"I'm—I'm so sorry," Rachel said.

The little mummy nodded, knew, its one eye even holding a teaspoon of pity for her, it seemed.

His hand was sticky. From the gauze.

"Oh," Rachel said, when he turned, led her back into the vast blackness of the closet.

Rachel's breath when she breathed, it was delicate and white, but just for a moment.

Then it was gone altogether.

PERSPECTIVE

Michael McBride

In Colorado, the first snow of the year falls on Halloween with such regularity that you can pencil it in on your calendar when you buy it. Not this particular year, though. October 31, 1987 was unseasonably warm and—thanks to the most rare and cherished of anomalies—landed on a Saturday. As fourteen-year-old boys, it was our duty to seize the opportunity and write our own coming-of-age story, the kind that promised we would stare death in the eye before the day was through. It was with such lofty aspirations that we embarked upon a journey into the sordid history of our little part of the world.

The buffer between Colorado Springs proper and the Air Force Academy to the north is a heavily wooded dale called Woodmen Valley, hidden inside of which is a semi-rural community where a quarter-century ago the horse properties were only beginning to make way for matchbook housing developments. My friend Jeff lived in one of the first houses to be built in the middle of the dirt grid of unpaved roads and the forest of stakes delineating the individual lots. It was in one of these lots—as far as we could get from his parents, while technically remaining within sight of his house—that we pitched our tent and prepared for the greatest Halloween of our lives.

Initially, our plan had been merely to close down the town trick-or-treating and gorge ourselves on candy until our stomachs ruptured. Our thoughts were solely on filling our pillowcases with chocolate, until we ran into Clint.

Growing up, everyone knew someone like Clint. He was a friend of convenience—the most convenient thing about him being his hot sister and her even hotter friends—the kind of guy you hung out with when no one else was available, and even then you did so with reservations because you knew there was no shaking him after that. It was Clint's idea to launch our paranormal investigation.

We'd all heard the stories. You know the kind, the ones passed down by the *older kids*, whose knowledge and integrity were so unassailable that their words might as well have been carved in stone, because everyone knew that with age came the perspective and wisdom to see the world as it truly was. So when Clint claimed the *older kids* had told him that there was a tunnel that ran from Woodmen Valley to that notorious den of satanic activity, Manitou Springs—the small town just on the other side of the Garden of the Gods from where we lived—we knew better than to dispute the assertion. After all, it was common knowledge that Anton Szandor LaVey wrote the *Satanic Bible* in Manitou and everyone had heard the rumors about the secret tunnels running beneath our feet, the most notable of which included the warrens beneath the old sanatorium, where the ghosts of the tuberculosis-afflicted still shuffled through the darkness, coughing up their black lungs.

Even better, Clint claimed the older kids told him where the entrance to the tunnel was.

Thus, we set out under the warmth of the mid-afternoon sun (we weren't stupid enough to go there after dark), Clint on his dirt bike and Jeff and me on our ten-speeds (before it became mandatory to wear spandex while riding them, kids), bound for the old convent. It was a bastille-like fortification set high up in the evergreens at the end of a winding single-lane road no one dared travel, to either side of which various outbuildings resided in the perpetual shade of the pines and skeletal aspens. (That the convent was a place where nuns lived meant nothing to any of us. It was *The Convent*—duh-duh-dahh—a dark place where even darker deeds were committed by the darkest of people, whom no one ever saw, except as fleeting glimpses of long black cloaks through the trees.)

We rode for hours until we finally found a small white house, or at least what was left of one. The gray wood showed through the peeling paint and dead junipers framed a concrete porch with stairs that had deteriorated to a gravel and cement-dust slope.

I vaguely remember hiking around the side of the house through the tall weeds and plucking spear grass from my socks while Clint opened the back door wide enough for us to squirm through. We entered a kitchen stripped of all of the counters and appliances. Clipped plumbing and wiring protruded from walls covered with graffiti with no artistic value, only various combinations of four-letter words, declarations of teenage love, and pentagrams. We stood on the warped wooden flooring, where once there had been linoleum, and knew we'd found the right place. I mean, the pentagrams were a dead giveaway, right? So, having found what we'd set out to find, Jeff and I decided we were more than ready to go.

Not Clint, though.

A crash of shattering glass and we ran into the main room to find Clint hurling a metal-framed chair against the windows, which were boarded over from the outside. Broken glass sparkled on the ground all around him. The carpet had been pulled up and rolled into a moldering burrito against the far wall. There were broken bottles everywhere and faded Coors cans in the corners. And graffiti, although not nearly as much as there had been in the kitchen, all of it black.

Apparently I was all for a little B&E when it came to an abandoned house, but vandalizing it was a line I wasn't prepared to cross. However, every time I told Clint to knock it off, he broke another window, so I learned my lesson and tried to distance myself from the destruction by walking down a short hallway toward what must have once been a bedroom, the inside of which will always remain fresh in my memory.

Every. Little. Detail.

I stood in a doorway from which the door had been removed and stared into a room carpeted with dead bees. Every inch of the floor was covered by a single layer of carcasses, one right next to the other, all the way from the far wall to the perfectly straight line that defined the threshold in front of my toes. A chair like the one I could still hear crashing through the windows was positioned in the dead center of the room. There was no hive. No buzzing. There wasn't a living insect in the room that I could see or hear. I recall thinking just how long it must have taken to arrange all of the dead bees so meticulously and the kind of patience required to essentially assemble a hundred thousand-piece jigsaw puzzle bristling with stingers. And then I saw the blood. Or at least what I thought was blood.

The closet doors were long gone and their absence revealed the lone shelf inside. It was a plain white board on top of which sat three glass bottles that reminded me of moonshine jugs. The fluid inside of them was a deep red bordering on brown. Someone had written on them with black ink, but I couldn't read the words (not that I tried especially hard).

The creaking of footsteps behind me announced the arrival of my friends. None of us said a word, nor did we cross the threshold and tread upon the carpet of dead bees. I don't know how long we stood there in silence or who finally broke it, only that when we finally turned our backs upon that dreadful room and walked away, we scoured the floor in the main room and the kitchen on our way to the back door and didn't see another dead bee. Not one.

I distinctly remember standing at the back door while my friends squeezed through the jimmied opening and looking at the narrow entryway to my right and the even narrower staircase leading down into the basement. I don't know what made me decide to go down there (believe me, it's out-of-character), but that's exactly what I did. We'd come to find a tunnel and after seeing the bee room, I had a hunch there just might be one, which, until that moment, I'd thought of in abstract terms.

I was standing on an earthen floor in the cool darkness when I heard the wooden stairs behind me groan. When I turned, Clint shined his flashlight into my eyes and then walked past me into a cellar with concrete walls. The rafters were draped with cobwebs and the aged timber that supported them divided the space into non-rooms. The only thing down there was an old hot water heater and it wasn't even connected. It was just leaning against the wall beneath an overhead bulb on a pull-string, but behind it was a hole in the wall, through which I saw excavated dirt and what looked like a tunnel. Or merely a root cellar that extended beyond the limited reach of the light. There was only darkness and the sensation of depth, yet the hackles rose on the back of my arms and I felt an uncomfortable coldness that even today I can't clearly define.

Clint never noticed that hole, and I didn't share my discovery with him or Jeff—although I thought about it the whole ride back, through an evening of trick-or-treating (in a glow-in-the-dark hockey mask), and a night shivering inside of a sleeping bag with a belly roiling with candy—and still couldn't understand why I'd decided to keep it a secret.

I think maybe I just liked the idea that the tunnel existed, that shining a light into what turned out to be a root cellar would ruin the mystery every bit as much as exploring a tunnel that might have actually led somewhere, although I doubt it could have traveled a dozen miles through the rocky earth. Who knows, though? Between the documented tunnels beneath the sanatorium and the countless coal mines into which the occasional driveway collapsed, it could have been possible.

I didn't go back to that spot, not until more than fifteen years later, but by then the house was long gone. Cloned tri-levels had replaced the pines and aspens and the convent had become a nursing home. I slowed as I passed the houses built upon the ground where once that bungalow with its carpet of dead bees had squatted and realized that if there had been a tunnel, they undoubtedly would have found it when they dug the foundations. Maybe the entrance to it had collapsed when they razed the old place and the remainder of the tunnel, dark and strung with cobwebs, still cuts through the earth beneath all of those houses, leading to a destination known only to those who originally excavated it.

Age might have brought the perspective and wisdom to see the world as it truly was, but I think the mere idea of the existence of a house carpeted with dead bees and its mysterious underground tunnel is worth more than any amount of three-hundred-thousand-dollar houses, one of which, I can only hope, has a basement wall that will one day crumble and reveal a hole that might—just might—lead into the great unknown.

THE SCARIEST THING I KNOW

Dean R. Koontz

When I was twelve years old, in seventh grade, I was a disaster waiting to happen. I wasn't the equivalent of a simple flood or a mere train wreck. I was an earthquake in ragged sneakers, a tornado in patched jeans, ready to bring tremendous ruin down on myself and on everyone around me.

I didn't realize I was a loser. I thought I was smart and tough.

I was so smart, I *knew* school was a concentration camp where they brainwashed kids to be good citizens and spiked the lousy cafeteria food with be-nice pills. To me, being an upstanding citizen meant working your whole life for nickels and dimes and having no fun. I preferred to be bad.

And tough? Other kids called me *Stony,* because I was hard. You didn't want to mess with me. I had my secret smokes—Lucky Strikes, the smokes of tough men—and recently I'd started carrying a knife. Five-inch blade, gravity release. I hadn't used it in a fight—not yet—because so far I'd never been in danger of losing with my fists alone.

Looking back, I can remember the anger that was in me, the storm of violence waiting to break, but I can't *feel* it anymore, not the way I felt it then. The twelve-year-old me is more unknowable than a stranger. He's an alien from another world.

I'm grateful I didn't grow up to be him.

My name is Nicholas Loffman. My friends call me Nick or Nicky. No one has called me Stony since I was twelve, thirty-eight years ago.

Halloween 1963 was the night my life changed forever. I didn't believe in spooks and such. The world held no mystery for me in those days. I saw everything simply, clearly: There were people who always got what they wanted—and people who never did. I was determined to be one of the always-gots, not one of the never-dids. I intended to take what I wanted, no matter what the risks.

That Halloween, most other twelve-year-olds were still doing the witch-vampire-skeleton thing, toting huge shopping bags door-to-door, hoping to fill them with enough candy to rot their teeth before Thanksgiving.

I was looking for bigger loot. My English teacher, Mrs. Carson, was going to be away from home for the evening. She and her husband, who taught twelfth-grade English, were chaperoning a corny "Goblin Hop" at the high school. I figured I could jimmy a window at their place, without much chance of getting caught, and see if I could find some loose money or anything else I wanted.

I didn't have anything against Mrs. Carson. She never sent me to detention. She tried her best to teach me. And I didn't even know her husband, though I did know he was a coin collector, and I figured maybe there would be some significant change lying around.

The word *burglary* never entered my head. As I saw it, if I had the nerve to take something I wanted, then it was rightfully mine. In school, we'd learned about evolution, the survival of the fittest, predators and prey. I was fit, strong for my age, bold—so, hey, I was just fulfilling nature's plan.

Late in the afternoon that Halloween, nature's plan had to be put on hold when my mother informed me that I had to accompany my little brother, Dink, when he went trick-or-treating.

By twelve, I was a thief and a bully, but I couldn't say no to my mother when she asked for my help. I was perpetually angry with her. I'm ashamed to say that she embarrassed me, that I had no respect for her, that I shrank from her touch and was often rude to her. But when she asked me to do a chore, I did it. Never with a smile, always with a display of contempt, but I did the chore. This curious obedient streak frustrated and puzzled me. I didn't understand why she had this power over me—because back then, I didn't realize that I loved her.

This is very hard to tell you, very hard, but if you're to believe what follows, I need to be painfully honest and admit that she embarrassed me because she was constantly tired, endlessly worried about one thing or another, every day counting pennies and cutting corners and planning for crises that might never come. We were poor, and I blamed her for our poverty, because it seemed to me that she had just *accepted* it.

In reality, she was tired all the time because she worked six and sometimes seven days a week as a waitress at the Good Plate Diner out on the state highway. She sewed her own clothes and some of ours, and she could stretch a grocery dollar until it would kill you if it snapped. She was only thirty then, but worn thin and pale with care.

My father walked out on us the year that Dink was born, when I was three, and we never saw him again. I blamed her for that, too, because my father wasn't there to take the brunt of my anger. And even Stony Loffman, young thug in the making, wasn't heartless enough to blame his brother Dink.

His name wasn't really Dink. Walter John Loffman. He waited to be called Wally but I called him Dink because the name peeved him.

The world over, little brothers—he was nine that October—are an irritant to boys on the cusp of adolescence. Often, however, I was prickly with Dink because he so strongly resembled our mother, while I was the image of my father, whom I knew from photographs.

I hated my father and loathed my resemblance to him. Mother tried to counsel me out of my hatred. She said my old man wasn't evil, not even bad, really, just weak. She forgave him, but I would not.

The creep had abandoned us for many reasons, but the deciding event had been Dink. My brother's left side was unfinished when he was born. His left arm measured two inches shorter than his right, and had three fingers. His left leg—withered, seated in a distorted hip socket—required a brace to support him.

One thing I can be proud of: I never made fun of Dink's disabilities or expected less of him because of them. Anyone who dared to tease him carried my signature bruises for a week.

Yet I remained prickly with Dink, impatient, uncommunicative.

An hour after sundown, we set out. Using Mother's black cardigan as a tunic and a pillow as a hump, wearing a dime-store mask, Dink had dressed for trick-or-treating as the Hunchback of Notre Dame. He was never self-conscious about his arm and leg; now it tickled him to emphasize his deformities. I wore no costume, none of that kid stuff. I was strictly Dink's chaperone, bent on hustling him along, getting his treat bag filled, so I would be free to search Mrs. Carson's house while the Halloween hop was still hopping.

In those days, in our quiet town, kids could safely go roaming on Halloween without clench-jawed adults accompanying them. The candy collected didn't have to be fluoroscoped for hidden razor blades or chemically analyzed for poisons. But, of course, that was in another century.

Trick-or-treaters banded together in groups, to goof with one another and to play at being spooky. We walked four blocks from the trailer park where we lived before we encountered others in costume, but by the time we'd traveled two blocks farther, there were twelve of us, some kids as young as six, a couple as old as me.

Witches, vampires, skeletons: They were the usual suspects, less convincingly monstrous than they thought they were.

A little girl, about Dink's age, missed the point altogether; she ventured into the haunted night as an angel, dressed in white, with white feathered wings. When the others ragged her mercilessly, she said, "I *like* being an angel, and so would you if you were good enough to be one." This earned her even more jeers and taunts, in response to which she merely smiled and curtsied—eliciting additional mockery.

One kid, masquerading as Death, had a genuinely creepy costume. He was shorter than me, maybe ten years old. He wore a black robe that dragged on the ground, a deep hood over his head. He'd painted his face black, so it vanished in the hood.

The long sleeves of his robe hid his hands. But from time to time, he raised an arm and pointed at one of the other kids, and from the sleeve came the bony fingers of a skeleton, no doubt a plastic, novelty-shop gag that he was holding in his real hand.

Three things about his performance were genius. First, he never spoke. No amount of taunting or wheedling could pry a sound from him. Second, he stank like death. Perhaps with a chemistry-hobby set, this weirdo had concocted a putrescent stench and sprinkled it on his robe.

We recognized some of the kids. Some we didn't. Kid Death, as I came to think of him, surely seemed to be a stranger, because neither Dink nor I knew anyone who had this cool an imagination.

From house to house, we proceeded, and the trick-or-treaters grew increasingly terrified of Kid Death. They were convinced the stinky one was real, not one of them, but the Grim Reaper in miniature.

I could have grabbed the little geek, wrestled him to the ground, and yanked his hood back, but he was smaller than me. And as bad as I was, I never fought anyone unless he was my size or bigger. Picking on someone smaller was a sign of weakness, and I was not my father.

Besides, I just wanted to move this show along and get to Mrs. Carson's place.

The third bit of genius in Kid Death's performance: He wasn't carrying a shopping bag, and he showed no interest in candy. He held back, at the periphery of the group, watching, pointing. If he didn't want candy, then the logical conclusion, among the small fry in our group, was that HE WAS REALLY DEATH, AND HE WANTED THEIR SOULS!

Before long, Dink was staying particularly close to me. In fact, all the kids were huddling around me.

"He's no kid," said Dink. "He's real."

"Get real," I told him. "He's no bogeyman."

Just then, when Kid Death turned to us, moonlight flared in the whites of his eyes. The moon was full, pocked and yellow, with rags of clouds trailing from it, like the face of a mummy revealed between unraveling bandages. His eyes, therefore, were yellow and unearthly.

Pent-up terror exploded through the group. When yellow-eyed Kid Death pointed at them with his bony hand, the munchkins screamed and ran, having worked themselves into a state of high anxiety.

I lost Dink. Then I saw his small form with the fake hump and the real limp, stumbling into the street. I saw, too, the onrushing truck.

Strong as I was, tough as I was, I couldn't reach him fast enough to sweep him out of danger. I ran toward him, knowing it was hopeless.

That's when time stopped. Not for me. But it stopped for Kid Death and all the trick-or-treaters. They were frozen in midstep, in midbreath, like statues. The clouds ceased unraveling across the face of the moon. The breeze died in an instant, and not one leaf stirred on the trees. The world was suddenly without sound: not a tick, not a click, not a whisper. I thought I'd gone deaf.

Time stopped for Dink, too, and for the speeding truck. At first I alone was moving in a petrified world—but then I saw the little girl dressed as an angel. She moved faster than I could, straight for Dink: She was *flying*, she swept Dink off the street, carried him past the truck, and time started moving again. The truck roared by in a blast of wind, and all the munchkins were screaming, and Dink was safe with the white-winged girl on the other side of the street.

By the time I reached my brother, the girl was gone. I never saw her vanish. I hugged Dink so hard.

When the other trick-or-treaters gathered around, I plucked off Kid Death's hood. He was a boy we knew, a geeky sixth-grader.

Dink didn't remember the angel girl. He thought I was the one who pulled him out of the path of the truck. That's what he still believes, all these years after that night.

Indeed, no one remembered her but me. She had been sent to save Dink, but even back then, hardcase Stony Loffman realized she had been sent to save him, too. Which is why time didn't stop for me, why I was allowed to see her fly.

I never went to Mrs. Carson's house that night. I never stole again. I threw away the knife.

Dink grew up to be a doctor of biology and a medical researcher whose discoveries have saved uncountable lives.

Me? I've become a popular writer of suspense novels, scary stuff. Married, with two kids of my own. I was successful enough, early enough, to give my mom ten years of easy living before she died.

Because of what I write, people often ask me what is the scariest thing that's ever happened to me. I tell them, instead, the scariest thing I know: that there is a purpose to life, and meaning, and that everything we do counts in the end. This is the scariest thing I know—but also the most wonderful.

GUISING

Gemma Files

When I was a kid, out in the woods on the Dourvale Shore, I saw faces in the bushes, sometimes: wizened like nuts, smooth like peeled birch, smiling, snarling, but always with holes—small or large, dark or empty—where you'd expect their eyes to be. Sometimes, at night, I saw wavery little versions of those faces looking out of my bedroom walls, from the spaces in the pattern of the wallpaper.

You probably think I'm speaking metaphorically. Everyone else did, for years—said it was just hypnagogic imagery, a kind of waking dream, a manifestation of the trauma going on around me. And after getting tired of attempting to persuade them otherwise, I eventually managed to kind of convince myself they were right.

But I really wasn't speaking metaphorically then, and I'm sure not doing it now.

I remember trying to draw the face I saw most, then having that drawing taken away from me by my grandmother, who burnt it in her iron-bellied kitchen stove. I remember she and my Dad arguing about it, later on, when they thought I couldn't hear.

This was just after my parents broke up, when Dad took us home to Overdeere, to stay with his mother until he got a job that'd support us. He'd been a late baby, and as a result, my grandmother was the single oldest person I'd ever seen. Her heavy braid of hair was the dull brownish-yellow of nicotine stains, matching the DuMaurier cigarettes she was always chain-smoking, her hands wrinkly-soft and peppered with age-spots. She kept her teeth in a jar and her own "eyes" in a case—they were contact lenses, really, but that didn't stop my Dad from telling me, when I asked once where Grandma was: "Oh, she's upstairs, sweetie, taking her eyes out."

"I'll be out of here by Christmas," Dad told her, to which she simply sniffed. "You'd better be," she replied.

Dad and Mom just didn't get along anymore, was how he'd eventually explained it, and I'd nodded as though I agreed—though, looking back, I found I couldn't really remember when they *had*. They were different people, to say the least; she came "from town," which in this case was Barrie, and had hoity ideas about what constituted decent living standards. Dad, on the other hand, was a Lake of the North boy, born and bred—managed to bull his way through a Forestry degree, but not quite to find a place in his preferred area. She'd stood there with a disapproving look on her face, watching him slip down into a Rona Gardening job ("You'd be a glorified florist, Kieran!") which eventually became unbearable, after which he got his trucker's license and began to do long-haul, gone three weeks out of every four. Her own stuff she could do from home, at night—she'd majored in Computer Tech, with a Design minor, which kept her busy building other people's websites. But it wasn't enough.

I don't blame her, I guess—not now, anyways. But I did then.

Most days, in fact, I can barely remember her face, aside from that one photo the papers found, reduced to newsprint or LCD pixels. All I have left of her is her scent, a celebrity perfume they don't make anymore, and the memory that the day she finally took off, she was wearing her favorite set of green ribbons trimmed with silver foil in her long, dark hair. Just gone, out the door and down the road in a cab to meet the boyfriend we'd never known she had. And the next day, Dad's car pulled out of our former driveway in the exact opposite direction, with me riding shotgun and everything we had in the back.

A week later, we were setting up in my grandmother's spare room, where the air stung with dust and the furniture hadn't been updated since 1973. Its single window looked straight out into the top sections of a British-style boundary-setting hedgerow whose roots her own grandfather supposedly laid, but which had been left to grow wild since the Korean War. Before that, however, the old man had done his work well—the fruit of his labors grew ten feet high and three feet deep, forming a close-knit lattice of stick-bone bars in winter, a mulch-fed mini-forest every other time of year. What light seeped through was green, and when you stood right next to it, your hands and face turned pallid, bruisy, veins gone suddenly delicate under leaf-thin skin. The shadows it cast made you look as though your blood had turned to chlorophyll.

"Best to stay out of the woods, kiddo," Dad told me, that first day. "It's an obstacle course, back there—deadfalls everywhere. A kid I knew growing up fell down a crevasse once, broke his leg, didn't get found for almost a week. Never was right in the head, after that."

"Don't forget the Hell Holes," my grandmother called, from the kitchen.

"Yeah, that's right." To me: "There's Hell Holes, too—sudden falls, straight down, nobody even knows how deep. The limestone forms bubbles, just gives way underfoot."

"It's because of the swamps. That's where the sulphur gas comes from, too."

"Methane, Mom. It just smells like sulphur."

"Same difference! That stuff'll knock you out, and it catches on fire, if you aren't careful. So no mucking 'round with matches!"

"She's not gonna do that, Mom. You're not gonna do that, honey, are you?"

"No, Dad," I lied.

It was hard to find a way under the hedge, but I finally managed it. I had to dig around at the bottom, where the stakes holding the ethers in place had started to break down, 'til I found a place so damaged by underground digging, frost, and blight that a pathway large enough to crawl through had opened up. It was narrower than me, but I wriggled through, like a worm—emerged on the other side covered in juice-stains and dirt, with cobwebs in my hair and bugs down the neck of my sweater. When I slid it off to scrub my face, a grasshopper fell out, still kicking.

Beyond, the woods began in progress, with no clear line of demarcation. You just looked up, and there they were; there *you* were, more to the point. Where the trees came in so close they shut out the sky, ferns grew so deep you couldn't see where to step, and every weed you brushed past left part of itself behind—clinging, scratching, stinging. The only way out was up, through the underbrush, the terrain getting steeper until weeds gave way to moss and the hill beneath emerged: a massive, pinky-grey blister of granite scored with hand-deep gouges where fresh acorns collected, cushioned on a rotten mush of old ones.

When I got up high enough, the rock flattened out, forming a little shelf, maybe three feet by six. And on that shelf I found an equally tiny camp-table center-set, haphazardly nailed together from wood, stripped grey by weather. The hill went up behind it, so slanted it formed a sort of seat, so I plumped myself down and looked at the table-top, where a word had been carved, in strangely beautiful script: *SARACEN*.

"That's my cousin's name," a voice said, from behind me.

Another little girl had come up, so silently I'd never heard her. She was literally leaning out of the brush above, hanging in over my shoulder, so close I couldn't even jump; denied room to react, my heart just gave a little knock, and I looked at her, swallowing.

"Oh?" I managed, finally. "Uh…that's cool. I never heard of a guy named Sara…"

She corrected me: "Sara*cen*, his name is. They're folk from away, unbelievers in Turkish climes, on the other side of the world. My mother says his mother liked the sound of it, when she was carrying." She peered down at the carving with interest. "Must be he played here too, once, though I can barely credit it."

"They live nearby, your family?"

"All around. We're many, hereabouts."

"We just moved here. Well, Dad and me."

"Aye, I ken. You're Jess Nuttall's boy's girl."

"My name's Nuala. What's yours?"

"They call me Leaf."

She had a high, hoarse voice, not much wind to it, and rough, though that might have been the rhythm of her speech. I was too young to know her accent—it all just seemed strange to me, foreign somehow, with no clear idea beyond that. Years later, it occurred to me that she sounded as though she'd learned English from someone with a thick Scots burr, but spoke it with most of a North Ontarian honk, aside from certain differences of pronunciation.

"How old are you?" I asked. "I'm nine."

She struck a theatrical pose and told me, deadpan: "Oh, I am old, old. I have seen five forests come and go, but never before have I seen beer brewed in an eggshell."

I goggled at her. "You're kidding, right?" And she laughed, high and sweet, a child's laugh like any other, save how I immediately wanted to hear it again.

"Cert," she said. "I'm…kidding, only. I have nine years as well, myself."

Looking back, I can see that she said the word—"kidding"—as though she'd never heard it before, but liked it. It made her grin, wide, which in turn showed how charmingly gappy her teeth all were, not to mention larger than you'd expect given her size. So much so that when she put her jaws back together, I swear I saw her bottom canines slightly dent her upper lip.

"Do you guise?" she asked me, a moment later. Then explained, spurred by my obvious bafflement: "Put on a face, I mean—make masks, pretend."

"Like…play dress-up, is that it? Or like for Hallowe'en?"

"Aye, that: All Hallows. Samhain Night."

"Well, sure, I guess. Don't you?"

"Aye, ever. We call it the glamour."

"*The* glamour?"

"So I said."

Leaf and I played for what didn't seem like hours, but when I realized the sun was going down, I started back. "You could come for dinner," I offered, not actually knowing if that would be okay with my grandmother or not. But she just shook her shaggy head, solemnly.

"I'm wanted home," she said. "And besides…no, better not."

"You can come anytime," I said. "Tomorrow, maybe."

"Or you, up here."

"I'm starting school soon. Will I see you there?"

"Not too like."

"…tomorrow, then. Here."

She laughed again. "Aye," she said. "If I don't see you, first."

You're wondering why I'm telling you all this, no doubt. Like *what's the damn point, Nuala?* And then you maybe remember what I let slip about my mother, back there—what I grazed over, more like, without explanation—and think, annoyed: *More about* that, *that's what I'd like to know. Not all this backwoods* Stand By Me *crap—"it was the best of summers, it was the worst of summers…"* I mean, Jesus.

Well, at the time, for me, my mother had *already* disappeared. None of us would know anything more until six months later, when two nice officers from the Ontario Provincial Police came asking whether or not we'd had contact with her since a month previously. We were as surprised as anybody else to discover she'd apparently left that boyfriend of hers the same way she'd left us, except far more precipitately: without warning, in the middle of the night, leaving all of her stuff behind. None of which kept the OPP from making him their primary suspect; he had a record, after all, though most of it was for minor drug charges and public intoxication.

A year after that, some hikers exploring the fens around Chaste found her purse nestled high in a tree. Inside was her wallet, most of her hair and a few of her teeth, fresh enough to get DNA from the pulp and roots. My mother's boyfriend was arrested, protesting vociferously. The Crown argued that he probably threw her down a Hell Hole, of which there are several in Chaste's vicinity, though why he didn't do the same with her purse was never explored. That they found a thriving grow-op inside his garage probably didn't help.

He's been in jail for over ten years now, up at the Kingston Pen. I was asked to make a victim's statement at his first parole hearing, but I told them it would upset me too much, which they accepted. I was later informed that he did not, in fact, make parole, because he'd been caught multiple times holding drugs for other inmates.

These are the facts. The truth, so far as I've since been able to figure it, is rather more slippery, and difficult to prove—as it often is. But here, in particular...

Much like beer brewed in eggshells, what came next is definitely odd enough to merit comment, no matter *how* old you might be.

At school I soon fell in with a little group of kids my age. Still, I always found a reason to sneak off and meet up with Leaf, at least a couple days a week. She showed me paths I could never find again on my own, taking us all around the area: to the Lake, the dumps out back of the Sidderstane cannery, even that overgrown ghost-village by the Dourvale Shore my new friends talked about in whispers. One afternoon in October, we sat together inside a salt-box house whose interior had fallen to ruin, leaving only the outermost portions: four windowless walls, crooked and rickety, held together mainly with vines. Two trees grew up through the middle, where the floor used to be, and their branches made a sort of roof.

"And where's she now?" Leaf asked.

"Don't know," I replied. Then added, quickly, as though to convince myself: "Don't much care, either. She never bothered to call since we got here, never even bothered to write...I mean, not like she doesn't know where we *are*. She just doesn't give a heck, so screw her."

Leaf nodded. "Mothers shouldn't leave," she said. "It's not right."

I laughed, bitter. "I'm okay without one, I guess," I said. "So, what about *your* Mom? She nice?"

"Oh, I love her dearly. Her, my brothers and sisters, our cousins..."

"No Dad?"

"Somewhere," she said. "We don't make ourselves, aye? But he's no part of us, really." Since I didn't know what to say to that, we sat a few more minutes in silence, watching the trees move overhead—comfortable, somehow, even in our discomfort. I could hear her breathing, a faint, sighing song, same as the wind that scattered dead leaves at our feet.

"I'd help with your sorrows, Nuala, if I could," Leaf told me, eventually, putting her cold little hand on mine, with an odd gentleness; I remember how overlong her nails were, black at the broken tips, and that they scratched just a bit, for all her restraint. Looking up at me under the shaggy fringe of her hair, her eyes ever-so-slightly agleam, and asking: "You know so, don't you? For you're my friend, my only."

"I know, Leaf."

"Though you have friends elsewhere, now, I hear."

"What, Grace and Milton, Heather? They're just kids in my class, like—somebody to eat lunch with, or hang at recess. *You're* my *best* friend."

"And you, for me, always." She nodded at the sky, like she saw something floating up there, coming closer. "Will be All Hallows' soon. Do you think to guise that night, and walk out begging?"

"Um, not so much. I mean, there's that thing at school, the costume party. But we're all a little old for trick or treat, right?"

Her face fell. "I'd hoped you would," she said, at last. "For my family celebrates that night, and I'd have you meet them, if I may. 'Tis a great rout, always."

"Well…" And now I felt bad. "Where do they have it, usually?"

"Oh, hereabouts. The Shore's ours, to do with as we please." She gave me a shy glance. "I could come meet you, the night of, at your school. Bring you here."

I hesitated. "You do that, the guys'll want to come along too."

"Then let them. All will have safe passage, so long as I'm near."

In the trees, a bird sang; the sun was sinking, colors changing. The wind blew a little colder, and I shivered, even in my jacket.

"Sure," I said, finally. "That'd be good."

Dad was out on a run, Hallowe'en week; he'd gotten his passport updated the month before, so it probably involved crossing the border. Which left my grandmother and me rattling around together, me working on my costume, her doing the stuff she usually did.

"What do you know about fairies, Nuala?" she asked me, the night before: Devil's Night, Mischief Night, when all the older kids were supposedly out egging houses and TP-ing trees. Then continued, not waiting for an answer: "In the old days, my folks used to say Hallowe'en was when they let the ghosts of the damned out of Hell, and that's why we dressed up—so they wouldn't know who we were, if they met us out after dark. You go back further still, though, it wasn't ghosts they meant at all, but the *Daoine Sidhe*, the good folk. Them under the hill."

"What hill, Grandma?"

"Any hill, I guess. But 'round here, they mostly meant Druir Hill, on the Dourvale Shore; don't suppose you go anyplace near there, do you, when you crawl out under the hedge?" At that I looked up, shocked, which made her give a grim little smile. "Oh yes, my girl, I know all about that—think you were the first ever got that same notion? Think again."

"*You* did?"

"Many a time. Up the hill, past that table…there was a boy I'd meet there, sometimes, came right out of the woods. Mrs. Sidderstane's son, from up at the big house, who wrote his name on the table-top with his knife."

Saracen, I thought. *Unbeliever, from away.*

"Oh, and he was handsome, too, with his blue eyes, though there was something about the way he looked at you…" She shook her head. "Any rate: the Shore's not a good place, 'specially at night, though I know you kids think it's some sort of amusement park. All the things your Dad and me warned you about, they go double, up there. And Hallowe'en's the worst time to go, bar none."

"Because of fairies?"

"Because I say so, miss. Now promise: you go out in *that*—" She nodded at my princess dress, my tinsel crowd, the little mask of tissue-paper veiling I was pinning to it. "—you stay away from there, far as you can get. Or you don't go at all."

"I promise," I said.

"I wish I believed you."

"I *promise*, Grandma."

"Well, it's on you, now. I've said what I could."

And she shrugged, turning back to the stove, where she had biscuits baking. But I could see her eyes were wet.

Why wouldn't you want them to know it was you, though? The fairies? That was what I should have asked—so she could tell me about change-lings, or girls caught in rings, boys caught under hills. How time bends in the tunnels, so you might come in one end a child and leave the other an old, old man. How no matter what they serve you, you shouldn't eat, because then it gives them power over you…and besides, it's all nothing but dead leaves, really: leaves, and mulch, and bones. Nothing but glamour.

God knows I *would* have asked, had I only known to; just like I wouldn't have done what I did the next night, I'd only known it was a bad idea. But I guess you can say the same about a lot of things.

Heather was a princess for Hallowe'en, too, it turned out—a *space princess*, like from *Star Wars*. Grace was a kitty-cat. And Milton was doubling his fun by wearing a werewolf mask on top of his hockey sweater, so he wouldn't have to choose between the two things he liked best, monsters and sports. "I can play goal for Frankenstein against Dracula, now," he told us, muffled. "Beat *that*, Barbies!"

He danced with all of us in turn, though, once the music started—and later we all danced with each other, bopping around in tandem to Men Without Hats while the big kids passed tissue paper in front of the disco lights to make them strobe. Then grabbed a few Cokes and went outside to cool down, chatting our way past the smokers, the neckers and the scrappers, right to the forest's edge. Which is where Leaf met us.

Not much of a costume, per se—just her usual clothes, threadbare and dusty, so out of fashion they almost looked cool. But she was wearing the best mask I've ever seen bar none, before or since: close-fitted enough you couldn't see any seams, moving with her breath. It had lumpy skin, pale like a potato, a pig's nose and dim little red eyes, and the mouth stretched so far in either direction that if the corners hadn't hit its ears—those lobeless curlicue holes, with their flared and pointed upper ridges of cartilage—it almost looked like they might have just kept on going 'til they met, and the whole top of her head popped off.

"Nuala," she greeted me, her voice hardly even muffled. "And these your friends, of course: Heather...Grace. Milton."

Milton didn't quite recoil. "Uh...yeah, hi. Nuala, who's this?"

"Leaf," I said. "*You* remember. She's taking us to a party, at her place."

"Leaf who, though?"

I shook my head, only then realizing I'd never actually asked. But: "Redcappie," Leaf replied, without hesitation. "Leaf Redcappie, they call me."

Grace made a little noise. "I have to go home," she said. "Heather— you should come, too."

Heather snorted. "What for?"

"*Redcappie,*" Grace hissed back, and Heather swallowed, starting as though she'd suddenly remembered something, while Milton and I just watched, confounded.

"Oh yeah," Heather said, at last. "Yeah, we—have fun, you guys."

"Heather?"

She and Grace had already grabbed hands, however, eyes darting, poised to turn. "Have fun," Grace threw back, over her shoulder. "And, um, nice to meet you, Leaf. Tell your folks...uh, anyhow."

"*Grace,* what the *spit,* man!"

But they were out of range now, almost out of sight. They didn't look back. Milton and I swapped glances, then looked to Leaf, who didn't seem surprised.

"Wish them good even," she said, "and you two as well, if you'd rather not come with, also. For 'twas good enough to see you the once this night, Nuala, in your guise."

I looked back at Milton, who shrugged. "Let 'em go," he said. "I'm always up for a party, 'specially someplace new. This one's been pretty lame, so far."

Then he smiled at me, so I smiled too—and from the very corner of my eye, I almost thought I saw Leaf smile, even through the skin of her amazing mask. She reached out one hand, and I took it.

Into the woods we went, all three—but when November finally dawned, on the cold hill's side, only one of us came back.

I remember waking up, on my back, covered with dew. I was cold, and my eyes hurt. I think I'd been crying.

I remember stumbling home, through the woods. Crawling back through the hedge, so clumsy I tore myself on its twigs.

I remember what Dad's face looked like, when he opened the door and found me wavering there. My grandmother sitting at the kitchen table, face in her hands, her shoulders shaking.

Heather and Grace came to visit me in the hospital, two days later, and stood looking at me for a long minute, still hand in hand, like they'd never broken apart in the last seventy-two hours.

"We thought you'd be okay, is all," Heather said, finally. "You guys. Because you *knew* her."

"Uh-huh," I replied, voice slow and grating, through my swollen throat. "I...*thought* I did, yeah."

"So what happened?" Grace asked. "To Milton?"

"...don't know."

And after we'd all taken a few minutes to digest that: "Well," she couldn't quite stop herself from saying. "You know that's your *fault*, right?"

(Right.)

Once I was well enough to travel, my Dad finally left Overdeere again, taking me with him. We moved first to God's Lips, then Barrie (ironically enough), then Mississauga, then Toronto proper. I graduated high school there, made Ontario Scholar, got into U of T. My grandmother was dead by that time, of course; she left everything to Dad, who left it in turn to me, as I only discovered after he had a fatal heart attack earlier this year.

I majored in History, with a minor in Library Sciences that I parlayed into my own personal line of research. Eventually, I stumbled upon the Connaught Trust, where the records that had eluded me thus far are kept. Which is how, years on, I learned the truth behind the Dourvale Shore's legendary reputation—about those three bloodlines of Overdeere that supposedly trace themselves back to Scotland, to the fairies, each family's lineage weaving back and forth and in and out of the others' like worms through a dead dog's heart: the Druirs of Stane Hill, lofty and secret, plus their descendants the Sidderstanes, who lend their name to the Cannery, and own most of Overdeere proper. Not to mention the poorest of all their many poor relations, the Redcappies.

Though few of this latter clan have ever been seen in town, they did once own a set of houses in Dourvale in 1935, before the development collapsed, leaving the village untenanted and derelict. And this also happens to be when the youngest Redcappie family member was a nine-year-old girl named Duille, which—in Scots Gaelic—means "Leaf."

Old, old, her voice sighs through my head sometimes, at night, when I'm alone. *Old, I am, and so strange. Like beer brewed in an eggshell.*

But that's not the whole of it, not yet.

Roughly a year after that Hallowe'en, two hunters tracking a downed duck found the hairy tip of a werewolf mask's ear poking up out of the sod on Stane Hill. Their dog began to whine and dig at it, and as they struggled to pull him away, one hunter felt rather than heard a faint, erratic knocking from beneath their feet. Ten minutes of frenzied excavation later, they broke through a blister in the earth and uncovered a thin, dirty boy in a hockey sweater, his mask's orifices clogged with dirt. When he finally stopped crying and screaming, he told them his name was Milton Recamier, and that he thought he'd been trapped down there for a few days. Maybe a week.

The authorities said he must have fallen into a Hell Hole and been trapped underground, but Milton claimed he'd been stuck inside the Hill itself, breathing its rock like air. Unsurprisingly, he quickly ended up in a mental institution, where he stayed until he changed his tune.

When we were both sixteen, I was visiting friends in God's Lips when he suddenly walked up to me on the street. He looked ragged, literally and figuratively, with a weird sort of eczema at his temples that I later realized might have been the result of electroshock therapy.

"She told me to give this to you, if I saw you again," he said, handing me a package.

"Who?"

"Leaf."

It was an old paper bag, the opening folded and scotch-taped to create a seal, and by the time I'd unwrapped it, he was already too far away to call after him, even if I'd been capable. Instead, I just looked down, frozen, my chest hot and hollow. Because what it held was—a knot of ribbon.

Green.

Trimmed in silver foil.

The kind my mother was wearing, the day she left.

I'd help you if I could, Nuala. For that you're my friend. My one. My only.

So little of that night I recall, still, at all. Shreds and patches.

Inside Leaf's relatives' house—the Hill?—it was bright (dark), and hot (cold), full of figures (yes) in costume (no), adults and children (maybe), men and women (likewise); I remember shouldering my way through a crowd of whirling, laughing, dancing creatures, humming along and toe-tapping to music I thought I recognized somehow, even though I was equally sure I'd never heard it before. Milton was spun off, whirling away through the darkness, borne on the riotous tide; Leaf clutched me close and let him go, pulling me past reams of food spread out on tables, glistening and delicious-smelling, a feast for the ages. (But: *Don't eat any, Nuala, not one bite,* I felt her say, right into my ear's hiddenmost whorls, so they vibrated secretly. *It will do you no good, if you ever wish to leave here.*)

Milton, in the distance, was cramming his face, with both hands. He looked like he enjoyed it, at the time, and whenever I think about it now, I really hope he did.

"Have to sit down," I told her, indistinctly, to which she shook her head: "Nay, but keep on, I pray—slack not, 'tis only a little way further. We're almost through."

Pulling me on, on, ever on, past men with horns and girls with tails, faces with two mouths, faces with none. Eyes and teeth and glittering scales, leaves and vines and fruit blooming straight from skin, crowns of candles lit like marsh-flame, guttering in the darkness. Past the flap of wings and the brachiating leap of things high above, hurling themselves back and forth as though from branch to branch in some massive, invisible copse of trees.

And then, suddenly, in the very midst of it all—a dark young man, blue-eyed and handsome, emerged full-blown, coming towards us through the crowd. Leaf tried her best to avoid him, but he eddied forward, blooming up between us with his arms crossed, frowning down. And I saw (*thought* I saw) that when he blinked, his lids—long-lashed, luxuriant, shadow-touched at their rims, as though lined with kohl—shut the wrong way 'round entirely: not from the top, down, but from the bottom, up.

"Cousin Saracen," Leaf murmured, masked head suddenly hunched, as if she feared to be hit. And: "Leaf," he said, his voice strongly Scots-burred, original template to her merest imitation, "what is't ye've done, my poor, small fool? Tae bring *this* one here, tonight..."

"I thought to show her, only. Only that."

"Ye should not have, as well ye know."

"Yet she's blood, kin—Jess Nuttall's girl's boy. You remember, aye? And...my friend, also."

"That's no account of mine, girl. Ye know my mother's views."

"But—"

He waved her protest away. "Show her the whole truth, Leaf, then loose her tae go, while she still can. Bid her see straight what she half-glimpses already, and let that be an end on't."

"And what of her company?"

"Him? Oh, he's e'en now caught, mazed fast—our families must have their will of him, to work away his debt. No concern of either of ours, therefore—not like her."

Leaf sighed. "I know it," she said, softer still, almost into her neck.

And...first we were standing there, then we weren't, swerved sidelong into some smaller chamber all filled with moss and apples, sticky-sweet and vaguely rot-stinking. By my foot, the pale flower of some woman's hand reached up from further down, submerged below the wrist in the rocky floor, splayed fingers discolored by decay.

"Don't look there," Leaf told me, raising my head by the chin, as my vision swam. "Here, Nuala, best of all friends. Look to me, only. Look to me."

And her mouth opened, the mask's mouth, wide and wider, wider still. Till it seemed the entire top of her potato-pale skull might tip back, drop free and roll away, leaving her nothing but teeth and tongue, gaped open wetly to the world. Except…

…it wasn't a mask, of course. At all. Just her, the real her, finally visible, without the lies. Without—

—"the glamour."

I don't know what I said. What noises I might have been making. Which is odd, because I know for sure that I could hear *her*—Leaf, bending in above me herself as her cousin watched, lowering herself so we were eye to eye once more, where I crouched gibbering on that half-rotten, hand-flowered floor. And saying, sadly, as she did:

"Tonight we guise no more, for 'tis the time of it—this one night of all the year, when we may walk abroad unremarked-on, wearing our own faces in jest as we cannot, any other time, or risk a broken covenant. And I did so want you to see me true, if only for the once."

I gaped, and she sighed, and her cousin reached out a six-fingered hand to my shoulder, pushing me out through the Hill's wall. I saw the roots and stones rush by me, *through* me, sifting my very atoms, unresisting like rain. And then it was dawn, the cold light of day, and I was lying staring up into the sky, my spine hurting, every bone in my body lit up with what seemed like one single, awful ache.

They still ache like that, sometimes, even now. That's when I know I'm seeing something I should probably pay attention to.

Here are some things I believe, now, though I have little or no proof for them:

My mother is probably the tree they found her purse in, hands up-flung into pleading branches like Daphne, with bark growing over every part of her. Or maybe she's a stone instead, standing frozen somewhere on Dourvale's streets, with only the sun crawling across her skin to tell her time is passing. Maybe she's buried in Stane Hill, same as Milton once was, except further down. One way or the other, I don't expect to find her alive. I don't expect to *find* her, not even if I were to finally start looking.

At Stane Hill, the Druirs' seat, Leaf touched me to get me in, not that she probably needed to, and I touched Milton to get him in, not knowing he wouldn't be able to leave without me till he'd worked off the food he took. Blood opens the door, you see—both ways, probably.

The older I get, the more I watch Leaf's cousin surface in me—handsome Saracen with his poison-blue eyes, eternally young and unspeakably old, who once carved his name on a table to impress my grandmother, back when she was still sweet young Jess Nuttall. I sit in my apartment with my part-fairy bones aching, off and on, longing for my great-grandfather's hedgerow, the hole beneath and the woods beyond. It's my inheritance, after all.

We have the stink of human on us, we quarterlings, too much so for the eldest of our blood to ever find us sweet, Leaf's voice whispers to me sometimes, late at night, whether I'm dreaming or awake. *The hills will not open for us; the rings are closed forever. Who can we turn to, therefore, except each other? Which is why no one will ever be coming for you but me, Nuala, just as no one will ever be coming for me, in the end, but...probably, possibly, if I only wait long enough...*

(Oh, how I hope, my dearest, my only friend. Oh, how I pray.)

...you.

I know myself, you see, at last. I'm no monster; not that Leaf was one either, not entirely. But in one particular, I agree with her, completely: this Iron World hurts me, and I'm tired of guising. I want to take off my false face and see the one beneath, maybe the same one I used to draw, over and over: wrinkled like a nut, peeled like birch. And one day soon...

...*very* soon, most likely, given it's October again, and Hallowe'en draws near...

...I will.

GORT KLAATU BARADA TRICK OR TREAT

Nancy Holder

I was nine.

He worked for weeks on my robot costume, my dad did. In the garage, drinking beer, listening to the radio, he constructed the torso out of two-by-fours and covered them with pieces of Styrofoam covered with aluminum foil. This structure went over my head and two thick straps (belts from his khaki uniforms; he was a psychiatrist in the navy) crisscrossed my shoulders to bear the weight. Thus I was encased in a rectangular prison. He added a tube made out of paper towel rolls that was pointed at my mouth. When I demanded "Trick or treat!" I sounded like Darth Vader. I could snake my right hand up just enough to yank on a pulley, which would cause a fake arm wrapped in silver spray-painted cardboard to jerk upward. At the end of the arm was a hook from which dangled my trick-or-treat sack. Images of Houdini's "Chinese Water Torture" tank and The Mechanical Turk chess player spring to mind now, but at the time all I could think of was how cool my robot body was, and how very, very much it weighed.

Next came the head, a fencing mask attached to the top of my rectangle. Thus I was about seven feet tall. Both my parents owned fencing masks, but I had never seen them fence, and they had no photos of themselves in action, but I imagined they were like John Steed and Emma Peel. Or Arnold Schwarzenegger and Jamie Lee Curtis in *True Lies.* And a mask that awesome was perched on the top of my costume!

Sensing a practical problem, my father cut a very small slit in my Styrofoam torso so that I could look out at the world. He covered it with mesh. No one noticed the slit. They all talked to the mask. Psych!

He added silver spray-painted sections of cardboard to cover my jeans and tennis shoes. I do not know why he didn't make the brace sections of my torso out of spray-painted wrapping paper tubes, say, instead of the carefully chosen, very heavy wood from the lumberyard. All I know is that he didn't.

Once I was assembled, my back bowed a little (from the weight) and my shoulders began to spasm (from the weight) but I didn't say a word. With his help, I shuffled across the street to Evie's house in gut-wrenching pain, and I could barely contain my excitement.

Evie (last name redacted) had dressed like a sort of Colonial girl, or maybe she was a doll. I wasn't sure but I told her she looked radical. Her costume consisted of a high-necked Victorian blouse, a large blue skirt, her black hair pulled back into a bun, and rosy circles applied to her cheeks with lipstick. My father made sure we had our flashlight (we were sharing), left us to our independence, and off she and I scurried. Or rather, she scurried, and I truly shambled, in the best Stephen King sense of the word.

We rang the first bell. The door opened, and I said "Trick or treat!" into my tube. The woman who stood on the threshold did a double-take and shouted "Wow!" She ran off to get her husband to take a picture.

Of *me.*

People who were in the house watching TV came to take a look.

At *me.*

Evie lasted about five houses. Then she stomped home in wounded, jealous tears…taking our single flashlight with her in her ire. I couldn't see anything through my tiny little slit, and my father found me clanking around in a cul-de-sac, crying and whispering, "Help!" through my paper towel tube.

He walked me home and in the privacy of our garage, he lifted the weight of the world off my compacted spine, blanched at the blisters on my shoulders, saw the paltry clutch of candy at the bottom of my space-age Halloween trick-or-treat bag, and told me how very, very sorry he was that he had ruined my Halloween.

I think then and there I became a writer, as a funhouse maze of emotions wobbled their reflections in my aching brain: Part of me was so disappointed, for yes, Halloween had been ruined. Another part was enchanted by my mad scientist father, who had so earnestly concocted this amazing costume out of the detritus in our garage. And another part felt this need to protect the feelings of this dolt above all else, a prime directive tinged with shame and embarrassment on his behalf, because really, all you had to do was hold that costume for a minute and you would realize how impossible it would be for a dinky nine-year-old to wear it.

Of course this is *the* Halloween of all my kid Halloweens. It was the best of, it was the worst of. But it makes a fantastic story. And that makes up for the candy.

But not the blisters.

Or the fact that Evie took a contract out on my life and I had to commit unspeakable crimes in order to survive.

But it almost does.

Under The Autumn Stars

Tim Waggoner

I once read that every moment of our lives is recorded somewhere in our brains in perfect detail, and that if we knew how, we could recall those moments with such vividness, it would be like we're living them all over again. I'm not sure this is true, and if it is, there are plenty of memories rattling around in my skull that I'd just as soon fade and never return. But I do have a couple fragmentary memories from the first year of my life that make me wonder if we really *do* keep every experience stored away deep inside our minds, just as if we were computers. And one of those early memories is about my first Halloween.

Now some of you might be skeptical, and if so, I don't blame you. I'm a fiction writer, and I make things up for a living. Who remembers stuff from when they were a baby? *Hell, I don't remember what I had for breakfast this morning,* you might be thinking, and I'm right there with you on that one. An eidetic memory I definitely don't have. Plus, I read something else about human memory—which just so happens to contradict what I wrote earlier. Each time we recall a memory we have to store it again, and when we do so, the memory changes. Just a little, perhaps, but it's no longer one hundred percent accurate. And the more often we remember things, the more those memories change when we store them. It's like an ongoing process of imperfect fossilization, with more and more errors appearing as the years pass. So by the time you're older—I'm forty-nine as I write this—you have to wonder, how much of our memories are true? What the hell *is* true, anyhow?

All I can tell you is that I checked the memory of my first Halloween with my mother, and after I related it to her, she said, "How can you remember that? You were just a baby!" So whatever this is that I'm about to tell you—a true memory or an altered one—at least my mommy vouches for me. So there.

I was born in March of 1964, so the Halloween I'm talking about occurred in that same year, when I was just shy of eight months old. I was my parents' first child, and my mom was excited when Halloween came around. She dressed me in a pink bunny costume—a fuzzy one-piece with footies that zipped up in the front and had an attached hood with floppy bunny ears. I had no idea why she put me into this outfit. I'd never worn it before, and it was nothing like my usual clothes. I'm fairly certain I recognized it as a bunny costume, but I'm not sure how I knew this. Maybe I'd seen bunnies in picture books or on TV. Soon after I was dressed, Mom put on a light jacket, picked me up, and headed out of the house. Dad didn't come with us. I'm not sure why. Maybe he stayed home to pass out candy to trick-or-treaters. Or maybe he wasn't that into the baby thing. He was only twenty-five, and a man of his time. Back then, only women did baby stuff. Men just stood by, feeling out of place and useless—if they felt anything at all.

It was cool out, but not cold. No rain, either. It's not uncommon to get a cold drizzle on Halloween in southwest Ohio, but that night, the weather was near perfect. I hadn't been outside at night before, at least not for very long, and I was fascinated with how different the world looked. It seemed bigger somehow and quieter, although the sounds I did hear came clearer and sharper to my ears than sounds did during the day. And the shadows! The darkness smudged objects, softened them, concealed details that were all too visible in the light of day. I wasn't scared, though. I'm not sure I knew what fear was yet.

We lived on a very small cul-de-sac—there were only two houses—and as we started down the sidewalk, there was no one else around. But as we left the cul-de-sac, I saw people walking on the sidewalks, most of them small, but there were some mommies and daddies among them. I'd never seen so many people outside at once, and while I recognized there was some sort of order and a common purpose to their movements, I couldn't figure out what they were doing. As we drew closer to some of these others, I saw that the smaller ones all looked different. Their clothes—some dark, some colorful—were like nothing I'd ever seen before. And their *faces*... They were strange and distorted, features frozen in unchanging expressions. Some smiled, some snarled. Some had straight white human teeth, some had sharp animal teeth. At first I wasn't sure what these creatures were, but after a time I came to realize they were smaller humans—I'm not sure I understood the concept of children yet—and that their bizarre faces were like my bunny outfit. I don't know how I figured out this detail. Maybe I noticed some of the kids had outfits that didn't require masks. Or maybe I saw a few kids slip off their masks, probably because the damned things were so uncomfortable, or maybe so they could eat some of the candy they'd collected. Or maybe this is a revision I made to the memory when I was older and understood what a mask was.

I watched kids go up to houses, knock or ring the bell (although a lot of folks had their doors open, so there was no need to do either), chant some words I didn't recognize, and hold out bags or plastic buckets. The grown-up who lived at the house would compliment the kids on how scary they looked, and then toss a few small somethings into their bags. The kids would say thank you more or less in unison, and head off to the next house, running across lawns, laughing and shouting.

Mom took me from door to door to show me off to the neighbors, and whoever answered her knock—usually a woman—made a fuss over how adorable I was. I understood Mom was presenting me to the neighbors, but I had no idea why, nor did I understand why they made such a big deal over me simply because of the clothes I was wearing.

And that's where my memory of that night ends.

So what does this all mean to me now, almost half a century later?

For one thing, I'm amazed at how aware I was as a baby, and how despite the fact that my brain was still developing, I seemed to be able to process information in a cognitive fashion. I also was self aware, and had a sense of identity. Not as a person named Tim, though. What I'm talking about runs deeper than that. It's something primal, and I can still feel this same "me-ness" inside to this day. Does all this mean that we're able to think in more sophisticated ways much earlier than most of us imagine? That we are born with a Self that in many ways remains the core of our identity throughout our lives? I have no idea, but I'll tell you one thing. I always do my best to treat people as fully formed individuals deserving of respect, regardless of their age.

As profound as all that may (or may not) be, this memory makes me wonder if that experience was the birth of my love for all things dark and wonderful. Horror movies, toys, comics, magazines, novels—all eventually leading to my own work in the field. And I can see the seeds of my own writing style in my memory of that long ago night. The surreal nature of the experience, a "character" trying to understand the strange transformation of the world around him... Even my fondness for writing with an immersive point of view. So much of who and what I am, and what I've given the world, can be traced to that one Halloween, and to a young mother who thought it would be fun to dress her baby in a silly costume and carry him around the neighborhood.

Thanks, Mom.

MONSTERS

Stewart O'Nan

They were going to be monsters, for the church—Creatures from the Black Lagoon. Mark wanted to be Dracula, but Father Don said only one person could, and Derek convinced him it would be more fun. You got to wear a suit with a zipper up the back and a head that fit like a diving helmet. They could scare the little kids and gross out the girls. No one would know who they were.

"Plus it's boring by yourself," Derek said. "You just sit there."

"Yeah," Mark said, partly because he was secretly afraid of being in there by himself in the dark. "Do we get fangs?"

"You don't need fangs," Derek said. "There's already teeth in the head."

It was Mark's only argument. It was like that with Derek, he was always in charge, which was all right, because Mark was shy and terribly aware and ashamed of it. Plus Derek never ditched him like Peter did. Peter was his brother; he was only two years older than Mark. They'd always played together, ever since they were little, but since Peter started at the high school this fall, he was never home after school. At dinner when Mark brought it up, his father just sighed. "Why don't you go next door?" he said. "You and Derek should be able to find *something* to do."

That's what they were doing, just messing around. It was a Thursday after school and there was nothing to do, so Derek brought out his Daisy and they took turns plinking the same six pop bottles off some old railroad ties Derek's stepfather had piled in the back lot. The gun was so weak they didn't even fall over sometimes, just tinked and wobbled.

It was Derek's idea to play Shooting Gallery. One of them hid behind the ties and then popped up and you had to shoot him. You only pumped the gun once, and they had their jackets on; it only stung if it hit bare skin. You crawled around behind the ties and then popped up and the other person tried to shoot you.

They did that for ten minutes but it was boring. Then Mark came up with Moving Target. In this one, you jumped up and ran and then dove behind the ties. This was even more boring because no one got shot.

Then Derek made up Ambush. The guy with the gun hid somewhere behind the piles of woodchips and gravel, and the guy who popped up threw hand grenades—just round stones Derek's stepfather used to edge the little goldfish ponds he built.

Mark had the gun. He pumped it once and crouched behind a sharp pallet of bricks, waiting for Derek to lob one of the stones. They were a little smaller than baseballs, and he didn't want to get hit with one. He peeked around the corner and saw Derek start to pop up and toss the grenade like a soldier, like a hook shot—saw the stone leave his hand and arc towards him.

He'd have time to think about this later: how impossible it all was. He saw the stone was going to miss, so he ducked around the corner, firing without even bringing the gun up. From the hip, just like in the movies.

He expected Derek to run but he was watching the grenade like it might really explode.

It was just one shot, from the hip.

Derek grabbed his face and bent over, holding it.

Mark thought he was faking. He loved death scenes on TV, dropping to the carpet in their rec room, one hand clutching his heart as he gasped out his last words, the other reaching for Mark's sneaker. But then he was screaming—high and loud and over and over—and walking fast toward his backdoor, his hand still there, as if he were trying to keep the eye in.

Mark dropped the gun and ran over and walked along with him. "Are you okay?"

"No."

"Let me see."

"No." He was walking slower now, and Mark could have stopped him, but there was blood coming out between his fingers and Mark couldn't think. He went up the porch stairs in front of him and opened the storm door. He saw his own hands were empty, and thought: I shouldn't leave the gun out there.

"Sarah!" he called inside, because Derek's sister was the only one home. He went through the kitchen into the front hall and called her, and she came running down, asking what had happened. When she saw the blood she grabbed Derek and hauled him to the sink and started running water. Mark had a crush on her—her lip gloss, her purple scrunchy, the way she bowed down and then reared up and flung her hair over her head—and her taking charge made her seem heroic, older, even more unreachable.

"What happened?" she asked.

"It was my fault," Mark said. "We were playing with the gun—"

"God damn it," she said. "I can't believe it, you're so stupid, both of you."

Sarah ran some water on a dishcloth and got right up next to Derek. She told him it was okay, everything was okay. They needed to see how bad it was. Derek wasn't screaming anymore, it was more like crying, trying to breathe in too fast. She had her arm over his shoulders, her face so close they could have been kissing. "Yeah, I know," she said, "it's all right, we just need to see."

He nodded and Sarah took his hand away from his eye.

"Oh my God," she said, "Go get your mom," and Mark ran.

There was a path worn between their backdoors. He dodged the kitchen table, gave it the same move he did when Peter was chasing him in from something. "Mom!" he called, "Mom!"

She was upstairs sewing costumes for the haunted house, pins between her teeth. She was so used to him screaming she didn't even get up. She talked out of the side of her mouth. "What is it now?"

"I shot him," Mark said, and tried to explain, but suddenly he couldn't talk, and then he was crying just like Derek, trying to get enough air.

His mother spit the pins out and grabbed his arm, dragged him along behind her as she ran down the stairs. He couldn't believe she was so fast, banging out the storm door and flying across the yard and into the Rotas'.

Derek was sitting at the kitchen table with Sarah holding a baggie of ice on his eye. He still had his jacket on. He wasn't crying, just hunched over, rocking back and forth, saying, "Ow, ow, ow."

"Is he all right?" Mark's mom asked.

"No," Sarah said. "It's his eye. I called 911, they said they'd send an ambulance."

"Let me take a look at it." His mother plucked the bag away and put it back fast. "When did they say they'd get here?"

"Five minutes."

His mother sat down, then got up again and walked around the room, biting her thumbnail and looking out the windows.

"I'm sorry," Mark said, and again he began to cry, right in front of Sarah.

"It was an accident," his mom said.

"It's okay," Derek said, but this only made it worse, and Mark ran out into the yard and didn't stop until he reached the back lot.

There was the gun next to the pallet of bricks, and there on a yellow leaf was a dark spot of blood, and another.

"Mark," his mom called. "Mark, get in here now!"

He picked up the gun and the BBs shifted and clicked in the barrel. He loved the Daisy, the afternoons they spent winging cans and bottles and old archery targets Derek's stepfather kept in the shed, but now as he walked across the yard, he promised—honestly, to God—that this was the last time he'd ever touch a gun.

It wasn't even a real gun.

"Give me that," his mom said on the porch, and snatched it by the barrel, something you weren't supposed to do. He knew to just keep quiet.

The kitchen was empty. They'd moved Derek to the front porch to wait for the ambulance. He sat on the glider, still nodding and rocking, making it move. "It hurts," he said.

"I know," Mark's mom said. "It'll be here soon." To Mark, she said, "I'm not mad at you, no one's mad at you, just don't run off like that."

"I'm sorry," Mark said.

"We know you are," she said. "It was an accident, everyone knows that, now just calm down."

"Here it comes," Sarah said, pointing at the ambulance.

It didn't even have its lights on, or its siren. It pulled into the drive and the EMTs jumped out. One looked at Derek while the other talked with Mark's mom. The one with Derek knelt down by the glider and pulled out a mini-flashlight and waved it in front of his face.

"Can you see it now?"

"No," Derek said.

"How about over here?"

"Yeah."

The EMT stood up and told Mark's mom they were taking him to Butler Memorial and that she should contact his parents.

"I already have," his mom said.

They put him in the back, and the one got in with him.

"You can follow us if you want," the other one said.

The nurse at the emergency room said Mark's mom could go in with Derek but Mark and Sarah would have to wait outside. Sarah lost herself in *Cosmopolitan* and Mark got up and looked at everything in the vending machines. The hospital had taped up the same cardboard decorations his Sunday school class had—the same pickle-nosed witches and rearing black cats and ogling, wide-eyed pumpkins. Mark tried to read a *Sports Illustrated* but it was too old. The last time he'd been here was when he broke his wrist trying a grind on a concrete bench in the back lot, and now he wondered if he was bad luck, if the rest of his life would be like this. It would be okay, he thought.

Derek's stepfather showed up first, his work gloves stuffed in his back pockets. He was small but he had a huge mustache; he wore his Steeler cap everywhere except church, where he played guitar up front with Mark's dad.

Mark stood up but he went straight to Sarah.

"They were messing around with the BB gun," she said, pointing to Mark.

"Is that right?"

"Yes sir."

"I thought I showed you two how to handle that thing."

Mark just nodded.

"Well, accidents will happen, I guess. Are you all right?"

"Yeah," Mark said.

"Okay," he said, and put his hand on Mark's shoulder and gave it a squeeze before he went off to find the nurse.

Ten minutes later, Derek's mom ran through the electric doors. She was dressed for the mill, still wearing her clip-on nametag, and she smelled like pencil lead. She had steeltoed boots like Mark's father and a line of grease across the front of her uniform. It looked like a costume on her.

"How is he?" she asked Sarah, and when she didn't like her answer, stalked right past Mark to the nurse.

Mark's mom came out after a while and said the doctors weren't sure. He might lose the eye or it might get better, only time would tell. He'd probably have to stay in the hospital for a day or two, they'd see. While she was explaining everything to them, Mark's dad walked in.

The first thing he did was sit down. It was a thing he had; anytime they had to discuss something serious, he made everyone sit down. His other rule was no shouting, no matter how angry you were. His mom told him the whole thing, and then he stood up and took Mark's hand and then his mom's and then Sarah joined the circle and they all bowed their heads and they prayed.

"Amen," his father said, and gave a little squeeze which Mark returned out of habit.

Sarah suddenly broke into tears, and his mom held her for a while, and then Derek's stepfather came back out and gave his father a hug.

Derek was resting, they'd given him something; Derek's mom would stay with him tonight. Meanwhile it was probably best if they all went home.

"Can we visit him later?" Mark asked.

"Tomorrow," his mom said.

It was night out now, the moon almost full. In the parking lot they split up. "Why don't you go with dad?" his mom said, so Mark climbed into the pick-up and buckled himself in.

His dad would tell him a story, Mark knew that. It would be something from the Bible, a parable Mark could learn from, and he waited for it as they got on the highway and headed out of town. It wasn't until they passed the salvage yard by the firehouse that his dad cleared his throat and said, "You know something?"

"What?" Mark said.

"It could have just as easily been you. You know that."

"Yeah."

"Do you remember what it says in John about the two farmers?"

"No," Mark said, because he never knew what the Bible said. In Sunday school they read stories together that everyone had heard before, but his father knew all of it, pulled it out like a favorite wrench.

"There were two farmers who lived next to each other, and one day a plague of locusts came along, so thick they could hardly see. When the locusts flew off, the one farmer's crop was all gone, bitten down to the roots. But the other farmer's crop wasn't touched at all. It was like a sign, people said."

His dad looked to him, and Mark said, "Uh-huh."

"The farmer who lost his crop thought it was the work of sorcery. The farmer whose crop wasn't touched thought it was the hand of God. The two of them accused each other of being in league with the devil. Each of them set about to prove it in the courts. In the meantime no one was tending the fields and it was high summer. And you know what happened?"

"What?" Mark said.

"The whole crop burned up and was lost."

His dad looked to him again as if to make sure he understood, and then they drove along, nothing but the truck's engine and the tires whining over the road.

It was past supper so Mark's mom heated up some lasagna from yesterday. Peter was home, and they had to tell him what happened.

"Your brother and Derek were playing around out back," his mom said. "And somehow…"

Every time Mark heard someone tell it, he could feel them blaming him. That was fine, it was his fault; he just wondered if it would get better. He hoped so.

Peter washed while he dried and put the dishes away.

"You weren't *trying* to hit him," Peter asked.

"No," Mark said, angry at him. But was that really true?

It was just a game. Now the crop was gone, the fields burnt.

"He'll be okay," Peter said. "Plus he's still got the other one, it's not like he's blind."

"Shut up."

"I'm just saying," he said.

It was a schoolnight, and they had homework to do, and then when they were done they were allowed an hour of TV. His dad went over to the Rotas' during *Seinfeld* and came back during *Suddenly Susan*. Nothing had changed; Derek's mom was still at the hospital. Maybe they'd know something in the morning.

In bed, Mark pictured the celebration they'd have when they found out Derek was okay. His dad would call for a prayer circle and they'd bow their heads and all of them—Mark, especially—would thank God.

But in the morning Derek's stepfather said the doctors still couldn't say one way or the other. Derek's mom was taking the day off to stay with him. Peter and Sarah walked together to the bus stop; the grass was frosted and they left footprints. Mark's bus came later. He scuffed through the drifted leaves, his backpack a load on his shoulder. It was the last stop on the route, which was good in the morning but bad after school. On a regular day, he and Derek would jag around, maybe play kill-the-man-with-the-ball until the bus came. Today it was just him, and he waited outside the shelter, kicking stones across the road and thinking how impossible the shot was, the terrible odds of it, and how unlucky it was that the person firing the rifle had been him. Sometimes he couldn't believe it was real, he could pretend it never happened. But it did.

In school he didn't mention it.

"Is Derek sick, do you know?" Mrs. Albright asked him, and he said yes.

After school he had haunted house practice, but his mom called Father Don, who said it was okay if he missed it to visit the hospital. The Creature from the Black Lagoon suits weren't in yet anyway, and they knew what to do, they didn't have to practice being monsters.

"Do you not want to go?" his mom said in the car.

"No, I do."

"He's not going to be mad at you, if that's what you're worried about."

"I know," Mark said, but he was thinking about the farmer who'd lost his crop. How could you not be angry?

Derek's room was on a floor just for children; the halls were crowded with parents, and the decorations were the same as downstairs. The shades were down and Derek was asleep. His stepfather and mom were both there. His roommate had just been released, so there was an empty bed next to his. Derek's mom took them out in the hall to talk to them.

"They say the eye itself isn't as bad as they thought, but the thing is lodged in there. They're going to try to get it out but they say there's a chance the retina might detach."

"Is there any way to reattach it?" Mark's mom asked.

"No, if it detaches you lose the eye."

The surgery was scheduled for tomorrow morning. That night they prayed for him, Mark's father talking about the mystery of God's purpose and their acceptance of His will. Mark thought it was wrong, that there must be something they could do to fix things. It felt like giving up to him.

And then after the surgery they still had to wait another day to see if it worked. The doctors said everything went well but with something like this there was no guarantee.

Sunday before church Derek's mom came over; she was in the same clothes as yesterday and said she hadn't slept. They weren't going to be there, so she wanted Mark to say Derek's name during the Prayers for the People. Everyone thought it was a good idea, and Mark did too. Maybe this would help a little. He'd already planned what he was going to say during the Confession. It would be like an offering. He didn't think it would change anything, but still, it was something.

His mom laid out his good white shirt and Mark buttoned it till it pinched his neck. His hair was still wet; it combed down dark in the mirror so you wouldn't know he was blond. He fixed his part and leaned close to his own reflection, looking at his eyes, one and then the other. The black part and the green around it and then the white was like a bullseye, three rings. He put his hand over his right eye and everything off to that side disappeared.

It wasn't that much different, was it?

But he could always take his hand away, he thought. Derek couldn't.

His mom drove and he and Peter sat in the back, his dad's guitar case across their laps. Even the new part of the parking lot was full; Mr. Jenner waved people in with a blaze orange vest and parked them on the grass. Mark waited for his dad to slide his guitar out, then followed him around the car to where Peter and his mom were waiting. He saw the Tates across the lot, all dressed up, and Mrs. Lerner in her white gloves, carrying a lily in purple foil. The bells were playing from the loudspeakers above the front doors, and everyone was headed for them. It wouldn't be hard, Mark thought. All he had to do was stand up and say Derek's name.

Inside, it was warm with voices. Since Derek's stepfather wasn't there, Charlie Wycoff was up front tuning up, and Mark's dad needed to go over some changes with him.

"Play well," his mom said, and gave him a kiss.

She let Mark into the pew first and sat down with Peter on the other side of her, on the aisle. They shared the pew with the Rotas, and Mark wasn't used to all the space. His slacks slid on the wood, and he pushed himself side to side like a goalie fixing his crease, his feet on the kneeler. "Stop," his mom said, a hand on his leg. "Now are you all set with what you're going to say?"

"Yes."

"Here." She had her prayer book open to where they said it. "Right after Father Don says this here."

She marked the place with a white ribbon and gave him the book.

His dad and Charlie Wycoff started playing and people stopped talking. Father Don came out in his robes with his old Bible and raised his arms to welcome everyone, and Mark wondered what Father Don would say to him. It wouldn't be like his dad and his farmer story, it would be different. If Derek's eye was all right, then it was a chance for Mark to learn something. In school, Mrs. Albright drew a minus sign on the board, then waited a second till they all saw it and made it into a plus. "Make a positive," she said, "out of a negative." Now Mark wondered how that fit with the two farmers. What could you make from a burnt up field?

Not much.

It was just a story, it wasn't something that actually happened.

They stood to sing and knelt to pray, and he read the whole program, seeing who donated the flowers for the altar this week, whose birthday was coming up. During the announcements before the sermon, Father Don reminded everyone that there would be a sneak preview of the haunted house this Wednesday for church members only, so it would be a good time to beat the lines. Last year they raised over five thousand dollars, so how about a big hand for all those folks who helped put it together?

"That's us," Mark's mom said as they clapped.

And then the sermon, which seemed long, and the offering, and another hymn, until finally Father Don raised his arms and said, "Let us pray," and lowered them for everyone to kneel down.

Mark had the book turned to the right page. They prayed for the president and they prayed for the bishop and for Father Don. They prayed for all those struggling against injustice and oppression and for the poor and the unfortunate. And then they prayed for the sick and infirm, and Father Don asked God to especially keep in mind those members of the congregation in special need of His healing.

It was quiet then, and Mark's mom touched his arm. He stood up.

The church was a field of heads bent down, and he was taller than all of them, except Father Don, who turned to look at him, as if he expected this.

"Derek Rota," Mark said, and Father Don nodded.

He wasn't loud enough, he thought, but it was too late and he knelt down again.

"Eileen Covington," someone else said, and then it was quiet.

"Gertrude Wheeler."

"Jan Tomczak."

It went on for eight names. Mark thought it was a lot, all of those people in the hospital, and all their families worried about them. Some of them were probably going to die. He'd barely noticed this part of the service before, and now it seemed terrible to him, proof of something gone wrong.

But none of the other people had shot anyone, had they?

They finished and everyone sat up with a rumble of kneelers. "You did very well," his mom said, and then his dad stepped to the center and played and they all stood up to watch the altar boys take the cross away.

In the receiving line, Father Don shook his hand in both of his. "Are you ready to be the Creature?" he said, because the suits had come in yesterday.

"Sure."

He'd have to come by and try it on tomorrow. Mark's mom said it wasn't a problem.

Outside, the little kids were running around on the new sod, one girl crying because she'd gotten grass stains on her white dress. They waited for Mark's dad, who had to pack up his stuff. When he came out he was still talking with Charlie Wycoff.

"He's pretty good," Mark's dad said in the car. "He's really been practicing a lot."

"I thought Mark did a nice job too," his mom said.

"I heard. Good projection."

In the back seat, Peter made a face, and Mark elbowed him, and Peter went to hit him but stopped short just to make him flinch.

Outside the fields went by, long harvested, the stubble white and bent down by the reaper. He could smell someone burning leaves; you weren't supposed to but people still did.

Nothing had changed, Mark thought. Nothing had happened. He'd just said his name, that was all.

But what if saying his name saved his eye? That was possible, wasn't it? That's what faith was. If the two farmers had had faith—was that the meaning of it? He wanted to ask his dad: What were the farmers supposed to do?

It was dumb thinking about it; it was just made-up.

At home they changed clothes and ate lunch and put on the Steeler game. It was dumb; they were beating up on Houston. Mark was thinking about going out and raking the yard when Derek's stepfather came over.

Mark answered the door. Usually he'd just let him in, but Derek's stepfather asked if his dad was around.

"I'll go get him," Mark said.

His dad was lying on the couch with the football in his lap. He looked surprised and got up and handed off to Peter, and Mark knew not to follow him.

His dad didn't come right back. He closed the door and went upstairs where his mom was working on the costumes, and then in a while the two of them came down together. Peter looked at Mark like this was about him.

His dad clicked the set off and had everyone sit down.

"Take hands," he said, and they did.

"Mrs. Rota just called. The doctors said Derek's eye was just too badly damaged."

He went on, but Mark had stopped listening, concentrating on the shot, that one stupid moment with the gun. It was Derek who made up the game, it was Derek's rifle. Derek had shot at him a million times, even shooting one of his mom's cigarettes out of his mouth on three tries. But none of that mattered. Now, bending his head in prayer again, his dad's hand strong in his, all that mattered was that one shot. It was his fault, and he was sorry, but that wasn't enough.

"Amen," his dad said, and there was the squeeze, like a reminder.

Later he went out and raked the yard by himself until he saw his mom at her sewing room window looking down at him. She'd bought a huge trash bag that looked like a pumpkin, and he stuffed it with leaves and faced it toward the road so you could see it when you came around the curve. Then he went in and watched the late game, or sat there not watching, startled when Peter called out, "Nice! Nice!"

No one told him it was not his fault. After the dishes, his mom took him into the living room and said he hadn't meant for this to happen. Tucking him in, his dad told him he shouldn't blame himself, that what was done was done. He was a good guy, everyone knew that. Derek knew that, Derek's parents knew it. Okay?

"Okay," Mark said.

His door closed, blocking out the hall light, leaving him alone. He wondered if Derek was awake in the hospital, if he'd gotten a new room-mate. He closed both his eyes and tried to see. Blue dots floated, then shifted when he tried to look at them, drifted like galaxies, little soft stars. He opened his eyes and the room grew back. No, he thought, that wasn't what it was like at all.

It was just one, he still had the other. Peter said that to be mean, but it was true too.

The wind was in the trees. It was only two weeks till Halloween; his mom had already bought candy and hid it where his dad couldn't get at it, set out bowls of candy corn around the house. Would Derek be able to be a Creature? Mark wanted to see him, to say he was sorry to his face. He couldn't remember if he did when he shot him. It was funny: he thought he would never forget it, but already, like his part in the service this morning, the Steeler game, the leaves, the two farmers—like the blue stars under his eyelids, it was all fading away.

The next day his mom picked him up after school and drove him over to church. Father Don had the two suits hung over folding chairs in the parish hall. They were greenish-black, the color of snakes, and sagged like empty skins. They were so fake it made Mark want to laugh. Their claws came to sharp points. On the table sat the two heads, the eyes bugged out under angry brows, flipperlike gills behind the jaw.

"You look out of the mouth," Father Don explained, and fit it over his head.

"Can you see?" his mom asked.

He could, but just a wedge between two even rows of ridiculous fangs. He'd have to remember to tell Derek.

"Okay," Father Don said, "take that off and let's try the body."

It was heavy, and the webbed hands went on separately, like rubber gloves. The feet went over his shoes, kept on with a gumband. It was like wearing armor, he thought, everything covered up.

"How does it feel?" Father Don asked him.

"Good," Mark said.

They had him move around some; it wasn't easy.

"Okay," Father Don said, "get that off and try on the other one. They're supposed to be the same size but it never hurts to check."

So then Derek was going to do it. For some reason, it made Mark afraid the suit wouldn't fit.

It did. Father Don zipped him up, and Mark put the head on and stumped around.

"Growl," his mother said. "Look like you're going to drag someone overboard and take them to your secret cave."

"Graaaahhhh," Mark tried, claws raised, and his mother screamed like she was the girl in the movie. Father Don stepped between them to protect her, and he knocked him aside with one blow.

"Very convincing," Father Don said. "Okay, let's get it off."

Mark wondered if Dracula would have been better. Probably not. It all seemed cheesy now, dumb.

After that they visited Derek. He was awake, drinking ginger ale through a straw. He smiled when he saw Mark. He had a patch over the eye, otherwise he was fine. He turned so his good one was aimed at him. It was brown; Mark hadn't noticed it before.

"Hey," he said.

"Hey," Mark said. "How's it going?"

"All right. Got to miss school. It would have been great but they don't have cable, just the regular stations."

Mark didn't have anything else to say.

"Randy took the gun apart," Derek said. "Did you know that?"

"No."

"He unscrewed all the parts and put them in this plastic bag. He says I can have it back when I'm fifteen."

"Wow."

"Yeah. That's all right, he said we might get a Nintendo 64 for my birthday."

"Cool," Mark said. It was good to hear Derek talk like he always did. It was only bad when he looked at the patch. "Hey, I'm sorry."

"That's okay," Derek said. "Did you know there's a club for people with one eye? Yeah, it's called Singular Vision. A lot of famous people are in it, like Wesley Walker, the receiver for the Jets."

Mark didn't mention that he was retired; Derek knew that. He thought he should say he was sorry again. It was like saying his name; he expected it to do something, but it didn't.

Derek was coming home tomorrow. He could have come home today but they had to fit him with a prosthetic eye.

"It's not glass," Derek insisted. "It's a special kind of plastic they did experiments with on the Space Shuttle. You can drop it fifty feet onto concrete and it won't chip."

"Huh," Mark said.

It was dinner time; a man with a hairnet was rolling a cart down the hall, bringing trays into the rooms. Derek's had plastic wrap over some kind of chicken. Derek's mom peeled the plastic off and steam came up.

"I guess we ought to be heading out," Mark's mom said, and Derek's mom walked them out into the hall. "We'll see you tomorrow, I guess."

"Oh yeah," Derek's mom said. "We're having a little welcome home party for him."

"We'll be there."

"Thanks for coming," Derek's mom said to Mark.

"Sure," Mark said. Because what else was he supposed to say? You're welcome?

He thought about all this in bed—which was dumb, he thought. There was nothing he could do about it then.

Tuesday after school Mark helped his mom hang a banner from the porch. It was one she rented out. It said *WELCOME HOME* and then had a patch where you spelled out the name of the person. Mark handed her the scratchy, Velcro-backed letters from the plastic bin and then held the ladder.

They were all waiting on the porch for him, and then when the Rotas' truck pulled into the drive they all ran down to the yard. Derek was sitting in the passenger seat; he waited until his stepfather came around to open the door for him.

The patch was gone. At first Mark couldn't see because his mom was hugging him, and then Sarah, her hair pulled back in a black velvet scrunchy. Derek's mom was crying a little, and trying to laugh at how sappy she was, and then Derek turned to get a hug from Mark's dad and Mark could see the eye.

It seemed big, maybe because the lid was puffed-up, and Mark tried not to watch for it to move. It couldn't, he thought, but he couldn't be sure, and he didn't want Derek to catch him staring. But it didn't look right.

No, because inside when they sat down to have cake, they sat Mark right beside him, on that side. It was like they did it on purpose, so he had to see what he'd done, and so close it was impossible not to see the eye was plastic, and stuck looking straight ahead, no matter who Derek was talking to. To talk to Mark he had to twist around in his chair and look at him over his nose.

"Good cake, huh?"

"Great," Mark said.

"My mom said you tried on the costumes."

"Yeah."

"So, are they like amazing?"

"They have teeth just like you said."

"Cool."

"Are you boys ready for the big night?" Mark's dad asked. "You got your act down?"

"Oh, forget it," Derek's mom joked. "I'm not going anywhere near that place. I've had my scare for the year, thank you."

They all laughed and pitched in to convince her.

"All right," she said, "but just once."

It was decided; Mark's mom would drop them off and then the rest of them would all go together, even Peter and Sarah.

The next morning Derek and Mark got on the bus together. Derek's eye wasn't as puffed up, but Philip Dawkins across the aisle wouldn't stop looking at him.

"What are you staring at?" Derek said.

"You. Your eye."

And before he knew what he was doing, Mark shot across the aisle and was smashing Philip Dawkins in the face, driving his fist in again and again and growling as Philip's friends tried to drag him off.

"I'll kill you," Philip was saying, but now everyone was staring at him, then looking away, embarrassed for him because blood was coming from his lip and he was crying, even his ears red.

Mark sat rigid in his seat, ready to hit him again if he didn't shut up. He wouldn't say anything, he'd just hit him. And when Philip said it again, Mark did. And then no one would look at him.

"What are you doing?" Derek asked.

"He was looking at you."

"Yeah, so? People are gonna look."

"I didn't like what he said either."

"You didn't have to hit him again," Derek said, and the rest of the way they didn't talk.

"What's this I hear about a fight on the bus?" his mom said when he got home.

"Nothing," Mark said. "Someone was making fun of Derek."

"So you split his lip, is that right?"

"We got in a fight."

"That's not the way I heard it. The way I heard it it sounds like you attacked him."

"It was a fight," Mark said.

"You make it sound like you've been in fights before. Have you?"

"No."

"Then why now?"

"I don't know."

"Well," his mom said, "why don't you go up to your room and think about it, and I'll think about whether you should do your haunted house tonight."

He didn't argue, he just went up and closed the door. It was starting to get dark, the sun behind the trees, turning the sky orange. He thought of the gun in pieces in Derek's basement, in a plastic bag. He still wanted to hit Philip Dawkins, and he would tomorrow if he said anything, he didn't care.

"Well, have you thought about it?" his mom said when she looked in.

"Yes."

"And?"

"And I'm sorry," he said, and this really was a lie.

"You should be," his mom said, "and if you think you're sorry now, you just wait till your father hears about this." She told him to get ready, they were leaving in five minutes.

Derek must have told on him, but on the way over neither of them mentioned the fight. They talked about the Ghost Mine at Kennywood and all the things that jumped out at you, the hiss of air that made your hair stand up just before the end. This was going to be better, Derek said, because there it was the same ride every time; here things could jump out at you from anywhere. Mark was on the side with his good eye but couldn't stop thinking of the other, the wall of black there, not even blue stars, just nothing.

The haunted house used to be the main building of the old hospital. There was already a long line outside, teenagers and parents with little kids. The fence around the parking lot was covered with giant spiders Mark's mom made from black garbage bags and old socks. From the trees in front hung ghosts and grinning skeletons. The porch was done up in cobwebs, and speakers on the roof blasted out eerie laughter. Mr. Jenner waved them through to the back lot with a flashlight. Father Don's mini-van was there, and a bunch of other cars. Mark's mom got out and came in with them to check on her work.

The hallways were wide but the ceilings were low, and they'd crammed in as much as they could. There were bats that flittered on nylon fishing line, and zombies that peered at you from the rooms, and a mummy who swung down from the ceiling. "Whoa!" Derek said. "Man!" There was an operating room in the real operating room where the doctor cut off the patient's head, and a torture chamber with an iron maiden and a victim stretched hideously on the rack—all his mom's work. She bent over the displays, straightening things, touching up. Right now it looked stupid, but in the dark with the dry ice fog sliding along the floor it would be scary, or that was the idea. Last year when they went through, Mark had stayed close to his dad, hoping he wouldn't notice. None of it was really scary, it was all fake; it was just that he didn't like being frightened. It was stupid to be frightened of that stuff, he thought; there were real things to be afraid of.

Father Don was putting on his costume—the lab coat and wire glasses of Dr. Frankenstein. Mark's mom told him everything looked okay and that she'd see them later and left them with him.

"Let me show you where you are," Father Don said, and took them upstairs.

They had a room of their own, made up to look like the ocean, the walls covered in wavy, mirrored paper with a blue light shining on it, an inflatable shark in one corner, fake seaweed and cardboard starfish everywhere. There were mossy papier-mâché rocks with a crack you had to squeeze through to get to the next room; that's where they'd scare people.

"Cool," Derek said when he saw the suits, and Mark wished he'd stop being so stupid.

"Okay, I'll let you two get settled. We should be starting in about ten minutes. There'll be an announcement on the PA."

"Wow," Derek said, and looked around the room, turning in a circle. The foil and the blue light made the room seem bigger. He went to the stairs and then came back. "Check this out," he whispered, and pulled a small white tube from his pocket and handed it to Mark.

It was Vampire Blood; Mark had seen some in the novelty shop downtown, thin runny stuff the color of maraschino cherries.

"What are you going to do with it?" Mark asked.

"We'll put it on, it'll be scarier."

"You shouldn't put it on the costumes."

"Look," Derek said, and pointed to where it said *DOES NOT STAIN CLOTHING.* "Okay?"

"Whatever."

"Whatever," Derek echoed him.

"Shut up," Mark said, and threw the tube at him.

As soon as it left his hand, he was sure it would hit him in the other eye. He didn't mean it; he didn't know why he was angry. Everything.

The tube flew past Derek and skittered under the shark.

"What was that for?" Derek said.

"Nothing. I'm sorry."

"You should be," Derek said, and retrieved it.

They didn't say anything while they hauled their suits on.

"Here," Mark said, and zipped him up, helped him settle the head.

"It's heavy," Derek said. "Can you see anything?"

"Not much."

The announcement came over the PA and someone's dad ran up the stairs and left a bucket with a chunk of dry ice steaming in the corner. Derek held up the Vampire Blood.

"You want some?"

"Sure," Mark said, more to be nice than anything. It would probably look cheesy; all that stuff did.

Derek held the front of the mask and for a minute all Mark could see were his hands and the tube. The lights flickered and finally stayed on, but just barely. With the blue light it almost looked like they were underwater.

"How about your claws?"

"Why not?" Mark said, and held out his arms. He waited inside the suit and then Derek let go of one hand and took the other.

"Well," Mark said, "how's it look?"

"See for yourself." Derek led him forward a few steps and then turned him toward the wall.

There in the wavy mirror stood the Creature from the Black Lagoon, its lips bright with blood. Mark raised his claws and growled, then did it again, leaning closer, and again, till he was inches from it, his breath coming back off the wall. The foil distorted his face, made the Creature's eyes bulge and slither, his fangs grow. Mark tilted his chin until he could see himself inside the mouth, his eyes looking back at the monster that had devoured him. In the mirror, in the dim light, with the fog rolling all around him, Mark thought it looked very real.

DEATH AND DISBURSEMENT

S.P. Miskowski

Isn't it strange, the number of trivial things we can't help remembering, useless phone numbers of dead relatives, songs we listened to in high school? Compare this to the multitude of cherished memories our brains will jettison before we die. I often wonder what purpose memory serves. Are we only collecting, and sorting, bits of information to help us get through another day? Then why is it, at this time of year, when children dress up as ghouls and monsters and their parents worry about the dangerous people they might run into while trick-or-treating, my mind always wanders back to Garrison Reynolds?

I worked at Northwestern Residential Life for six years in a stuffy, file- and paper-strewn office in downtown Seattle. During the first two years I handled Disbursement payments. I have no idea how many accounts I processed during my tenure. Most of the clients must be dead by now.

"No Rest," as we called it, started out as an insurance firm in the 1950s, building a modest reputation during the post-war housing boom. By the '80s, when they decided to branch out, regulations restricting stock investment to brokers had loosened up. Like a lot of corporations with only a sideways connection to portfolio management, No Rest seized the opportunity. Management created a sales team to specialize in retirement plans for K-12 schoolteachers, and the company made a fortune.

By the time I worked there in the late '90s, the heat wave of ridiculous prosperity was winding down. Sales incentives had dwindled from first-class vacations in Bangkok to a weekend of whale watching in Port Townsend. Other signs of trouble were emerging, rumors of financial impropriety coiling upward to the executive level. Most of us didn't care. We were making a living. The rumors only mattered to people who could recall the company's original mission statement, something lofty about hard work paying off.

Many of our clients had difficulty remembering my name. They grappled with health concerns and family issues that had festered over the years. They struggled to communicate through a haze of medication and dementia. In my mind, most of these people are now indistinguishable from one another. Yet I remember Garrison Reynolds and what happened to him with absolute clarity.

That year the Midwest was hit by a freak snowstorm a few days before Halloween. For once I didn't mind living in Seattle, where the rainy season ran from October until early July. Cable news channels covered the escalating storm with on-the-scene reporters bundled in parkas, their eyes squinting almost shut in the blistering cold, voices intoning the latest weather statistics with an underscoring shiver. One reporter was killed when a van overturned and skidded onto the shoulder of the road where he stood waiting for his camera crew to set up. At least a thousand times the network repeated video coverage of the reporter turning and catching only a shadow of the massive white wall sliding toward him. He seemed to be drawing breath, presumably to scream, before he was obliterated by snow.

A few weeks earlier I had chosen Death over Disbursement, and for good reasons. First and foremost, I disliked talking to retirees on the phone all day. It was a job I'd survived for two years with plenty of coffee and too many snacks, and by using a characteristic I'm not proud to admit. Actually it was a skill, one I'd developed while my mother was in the last phase of her illness. When necessary I could withdraw from another person, swiftly and silently gliding backward into the shadows. From there I could peer out at the world and feel nothing. I became a ghost, a presence with no connection to the situation. This made me a prime candidate to deal with the tough cases: the crying octogenarian who insisted her dead sister was stealing her monthly checks; the schizophrenic man who inherited his father's account and called every other month to register a change of address.

People told me I was good at customer service, a real "people person," and I accepted the compliment. But it wasn't true. I was patient and helpful with each client because they didn't matter to me. My aim was to do my job well, not save the world.

At the beginning of my third year, Disbursement hired a new gal, Bonnie, to answer the phones. Bonnie was given the early shift, seven A.M. to three P.M., to cover calls from back east. Another associate handled the nine-to-five shift.

Bonnie was needed because I'd been promoted to fill a gap on the Death team. I tried to conceal my relief. After you've spent a couple of years listening to elderly people gripe about their rotten health and hateful children, it's a luxury to sit quietly in a private cubicle filling out paperwork to make their post-mortem retirement funds the property of those same hateful children. Best of all, no one wanted Death. New associates found it boring. I could pace myself because there was no competition for the job.

High on the list of reasons I was happy to leave Disbursement and take up the surprising backlog of Death was Garrison Reynolds. In many ways a typical client, Reynolds called Disbursement at least four times a month and every call lasted half an hour. No matter how often I reminded him of the due date for his retirement check, the 30th, he would begin dialing on the 20th or 25th. All because his payment had arrived a week early one time and he wanted to know why it wasn't early every month.

His impatience wasn't unusual. Quite a few of our clients led a frugal existence. Some lived desperately, the ones who had failed to invest enough cash before time ran out and they were pushed away by the employers they'd counted on for a living and a purpose.

Reynolds wasn't desperate. His mortgage was paid. He and his wife had no children. He didn't call Disbursement out of need. He called because he had no friends. No one wanted to talk to him. He had no hobbies aside from harassing the people who handled what was left of his money.

"Yes, I understand. I get it, I do." Bonnie's voice carried through the wall to my cubicle. I could hear the strain when she stammered, "We mailed the end-of-month checks two days ago, but we have no control over the weather. Sir? Sir? We're dealing with a very unusual, natural event. Sir? If we replace the payment now, it will just be delayed like the first one. Your best bet is to wait for the original check to arrive."

She paused and I imagined I heard the faint buzz of Garrison Reynolds on the line. In his gruff intonations he was, no doubt, telling Bonnie what she could do with her opinion.

In Seattle the season was in full swing. We'd had four consecutive days of rain. Not refreshing or cleansing but drizzling, a perpetual cosmic leak over the industrial-gray city. On storefront windows the scarecrows and black cats stood out in the glaucous wash. Doorsteps were cluttered with jack-o'-lanterns. At night the streets, ordinarily etched blue-black, were softened by the dull glow of orange lights and candles in windows. The Midwest snow and ice seemed far away, telescoped, a vague human-interest story flickering on TV screens.

"Sir," Bonnie said. Her voice cracked. "Sir, if you're going to speak to me like that, I have no choice. Mr. Reynolds? Mr. Reynolds? I have to hang up now. Sir? I have to hang up."

The next sound was the receiver snapping into place. Cutting off the tirade but not soon enough to prevent a crying jag. I rolled my eyes when I heard Bonnie whip a couple of tissues out of the Kleenex box on her desk and trudge around the corner to my cubicle.

"Katie," she said. Her lips were quivering from the struggle to stay calm. "I'm sorry to interrupt you."

I looked up from the files and forms on my desk, and refrained from laughing. Bonnie was still new. Maybe she would toughen up. Otherwise she would surely have to find another job. Talking to depressed or angry seniors and hearing the stray facts of their ever-diminishing lives would kill her if she didn't put some distance between herself and their misery.

"Bonnie, you can't take it personally," I said.

She drew a halting breath. She dabbed the corners of her eyes with the tissues crumpled in her hand.

"He asked me if I'm retarded," she said. "And. Well, we don't even use that word in my family. Or any of the other words he used."

"That's what I mean by personal," I explained. "It doesn't matter how you feel or what you do in your family. The person on the phone is a client. Nothing he says to you should be taken to heart. Just listen to his complaint and reassure him. If you decide his case warrants a replacement check, forward the details to one of the clerks in Accounting."

"His check isn't due until Thursday," she said, fighting a second wave of tears.

"Great," I told her. "Don't worry about it."

"He's called twice this morning. He said he's going to call every day because he already knows his check is going to be late."

"Because of the storm."

"He doesn't even watch the news. He says his check is late every month and it's my fault."

"All he has to do is look out the window," I said. "The storm's knocked out mail delivery. As of last night, even the FedEx office had to shut down."

"Oh God," Bonnie said. "What am I going to do? Kirk is out sick with the flu. He might not be back all week. Every time Reynolds calls, he'll get me!"

I was still young enough back then to feel a sliver of contempt for Bonnie in her sprawling Eddie Bauer sweater, her olive drab skirt and leggings. When she'd dressed that morning she must have believed herself to be fortified against a world she feared at every turn.

"Fine. Forward his calls to me," I said. "Only Garrison Reynolds and only this week." And because I'd written her off in that instant, deciding she would never succeed in Disbursement, I returned to my paperwork and ignored her blubbery thanks.

On the bus ride home that night, bone tired from all the tedious facets of my job, I stared out the window at wet, black streets. House after house went gliding by, glowing with amber light, decked with festive pumpkins and cartoon witches. The homes looked warm and snug, but who knows what went on inside them.

The smooth hiss of electric cable overhead and the gentle rocking of the bus lulled me. In the dim alleys, neighborhood cats traced a path from doors and gates to trash dumpsters and back. In my nearly dreaming state I imagined the shadows growing long and narrow, then separating into a multitude of dark figures scuttling between muted streetlights.

I almost expected Bonnie to call in sick the next day. But she sat straight-backed and smiling at her desk when I arrived. Apparently my taking over her least favorite client gave her a lift. I said good morning and she waved one hand toward a plate of muffins.

"These are home baked pumpkin spice," she said. "Have one. Have two!"

"Sorry," I told her. "I don't think I can eat one more thing made with pumpkin this year."

I'd barely sat down and arranged my desk for the day when the first call came through, a transfer from Bonnie. As I picked up the receiver I heard her voice on the other side of the cubicle wall.

"Sorry, Katie!"

"Northwestern Residential Life, Death Claims, how can I help you?" I said automatically.

There was a distinct pause on the line. Then came the sputter of an old man clearing his throat.

"What?" He asked. "What did you say?"

"Sorry, Mr. Reynolds," I replied. "This is Katie. I've been promoted to another team. How can I help you today?"

"What kind of a team?" He asked, his voice full of phlegm.

"I'm on a different team now. I've switched from Disbursement to— another team."

"Why don't you call it a department?" He said.

"A team is a department," I said. "It's the same thing. What can I do for you today?"

"Well, if it's the same goddamn thing, why the hell don't you call it the same thing?"

This was his typical strategy. Bait and attack, lure and argue.

"Mr. Reynolds," I said gently and firmly. "How can I help you?"

"What happened to that other girl? She got sick of me, didn't she?"

I was holding the receiver in my left hand. This made it possible to continue filling out forms with my right.

"Mr. Reynolds, you're a valued client. We never get sick of you," I said.

"You're a goddamn liar." He cleared his throat again, a hacking, viscous wave ending in a cough. I waited until he stopped.

"Aren't we all?" I asked.

The hacking noise rose again, and expanded. It could have been wheezing but once it developed a rhythm I realized he was wheeze-laughing like a despicable cartoon character. I waited until he calmed down.

"A liar is lavish of oaths," he said at last. "Where's my check?"

"I've seen the weekly report," I said. "And your payment was mailed on time. I confirmed the date with Accounting."

"So, where is it?" He asked.

"Tomorrow is the 30th," I reminded him. "And the 30th is your due date."

"Don't give me that bunk!"

"Remember when you signed the contract to begin your pay-out?" I said. "The date you chose was the 30th. Since today is the 29th, your check isn't due. If it doesn't arrive tomorrow, please let us know."

A rustle on the line followed by a loud click let me know that Garrison Reynolds was gone. I sat staring at the small ceramic tableau on my desk: a Cadillac containing three manic skeletons dressed in dark clothing, holding down a figure with flailing arms and legs. Meanwhile a crimson Satan with silver horns sat laughing at the wheel. The tableau had been a Day of the Dead gift from an artist my mother used to know, in Austin. It was the only office decoration I ever displayed on Halloween; its bright colors gave me a lift. Something in the devil's expression was strangely amusing.

"Go to hell, Mr. Reynolds," I said under my breath.

The rest of the day was quiet. I was able to hit my average in processing claims, so I treated myself to a Donut Day cruller at afternoon break. The sugar made me dopey. I almost fell asleep on the bus ride home.

On Thursday when I arrived at the office, Bonnie was absent from her desk. I imagined she had spent the first two hours of her day apologizing to Midwest clients for the delay in their payments. Two lines blinked on her phone. The Kleenex box lay on its side near a scattering of M&Ms. I took off my raincoat and hit one of the blinking buttons.

"Northwestern Residential Life, Disbursement," I said. "Would you hold, please?" I put the client on hold before he could speak. I hit the second button and repeated the greeting then placed the second client on hold. Finally I answered the first call.

"Residential Life, Disbursement. How can I help you?"

A damp wheeze identified the caller. He seemed to gather his words from a distance.

"What happened?" Garrison Reynolds asked. "Did you get demoted?"

He recognized my voice. I squared my shoulders. I forced a smile. Clients, my training had taught me, can hear a smile in the tone of your voice. The facial muscles contract even if the expression is false.

"Good morning, Mr. Reynolds," I said.

"It's lunch time where I live," he said. "And there's no check in the mailbox."

"Right," I said, visualizing the address in our database. "Illinois. Wow. You're in the thick of it. How are you doing?"

"I'd be doing a lot better with a check in my hand. You said to wait. You wasted my time."

Something caught my eye and I turned to see Bonnie striding back from the women's bathroom. She was clutching tissues in both hands and her face was a patchwork of pink splotches. She must have been crying for a while. She nodded but avoided making eye contact when she took her seat.

"Mr. Reynolds," I said. "Hold for a moment while I transfer you to my phone, all right?"

I took my time putting away my raincoat and settling at my desk. I saw the button light up when Bonnie forwarded the call. I heard her placating the next client in line. I paused for another couple of seconds, hoping in vain that he might give up and go away.

"All right, then," I said when I picked up the line.

"What's going on there?" Reynolds asked. "A goddamn party? I don't want to hear any more music. Stop putting me on hold."

"Sorry for the delay," I said.

"You can keep your apology. You and that Asian girl you hired to answer the phone."

Among his many charms Garrison Reynolds could count racism. After a knee-jerk impulse to thwart his assumptions by pointing out that Bonnie's family was Norwegian, I decided to ignore the comment.

"I'm sure I can answer any questions you have."

"Good luck!" He said. "Where's my fucking check?"

Somewhere in his original file I'd noticed that he had been a History teacher at a middle school for twenty-five years. I wondered if he'd spoken to students the way he spoke to us. How much was his wretched personality and how much of the salty sailor routine was put on for my benefit? Probably only his wife knew the answer. I pitied her.

"How's the weather in your neighborhood?" I asked.

"What?"

"Is it snowing in your part of Illinois?" I said.

"Hell, yes," he said. "The whole neighborhood's covered in it. What do you think?"

"Well, Mr. Reynolds," I said. "What you can see from your living room window is pretty much the same all over the Midwest at the moment. Even the FedEx office had to shut down for a day. Planes are grounded. Buses have stopped running. And the mail is delayed."

"The mail is never delayed," he said. "What about their motto, about rain and sleet?"

"I'm afraid the postal service has met its match this year."

"What are you telling me?" He said.

"This is a regional, possibly national crisis. It affects everyone."

"So?"

I had to marvel at the self-involvement of the old man. The little tableau of skeletons, holding their captive for the benefit of Satan in the driver's seat, made me smile, a genuine smile this time.

"No one is getting their mail," I said. "If we issued a new payment you wouldn't receive it."

He was silent for a moment. I could hear him murmuring in the background, as if he held his hand over the mouthpiece while he spoke to someone.

"Mr. Reynolds?"

"I'll call you back," he said. And he hung up.

I barely had time to feel fortunate before the light began to blink again. From the other cubicle I heard Bonnie's apology.

"Sorry, Katie, I'm so sorry. He's back," she warned as I answered the phone.

"Mr. Reynolds?" I said by way of greeting.

"Listen," he said, his voice reduced to a deep rasp. "I have to have that money."

"But I just explained…"

"I need it!" He said. "It's mine and I want it right now. Right now!"

"I would help you if I could," I said. "Didn't I replace a check that was lost in the mail, last year? So you know I only want to do what's right."

"Shut up!" He snarled.

"Excuse me?"

"Stop talking and talking," he said. His voice broke. "I don't have time. I need, I need my money right now. It belongs to me and you owe it to me."

"Mr. Reynolds, if there were any possible way…"

"No!" He was shouting again. "I need it this afternoon. Before it gets dark. They're coming back!"

I stopped staring at the little crimson devil with his silver horns and his grin of cruel delight.

"Mr. Reynolds," I said. "Could I speak to your wife for a moment?"

"Why?"

"Oh," I said, mind racing through a series of flimsy excuses. "I was reading your file yesterday and I realized we don't have her social security number listed."

"What difference does that make?"

If his nasty idiosyncrasies had all been a precursor to Alzheimer's maybe his wife should know about these multiple calls and complaints. I decided to lie to him.

"Before I can issue a new check, I'll need to fill in the information gap."

"Why?" He asked. "You've been paying me all this time without it."

"Yes," I said. "But now I know it's missing from the account."

"That's goddamn ridiculous! I want my money!"

"No," I said. Might as well make the lie as big as it needed to be, I decided. "If I can't speak to your wife I'm afraid I'll have to cancel your payment."

"What? What?" He was sputtering. "You can't keep my money. I earned all of it. I spent years and years with those little monsters..."

The line went dead. Bonnie stepped into my cubicle. She had a strange expression, now that her tears had dried.

"What was all that about?" She asked.

"I'm not sure he's lucid," I told her.

"Oh my God." Bonnie shook her head. "Has he had a stroke?"

"Look," I said. "Later on, maybe I'll call his house and try to get hold of his wife. She should know how irrational he's become."

"That's so sad," she said. "Do you think she'll have him hospitalized?"

What a term. The same one I'd used when people asked how my mother was doing, in her final weeks.

"Poor Mr. Reynolds," Bonnie said.

It was irritating to make small talk like this about a client Bonnie couldn't handle. While we gossiped I was losing time I could have spent processing death claims. I started shuffling papers. Bonnie didn't take the hint. She stepped closer, and reached down to touch the Day of the Dead tableau with one index finger.

"You know," she said. "I actually took his first call this morning. About twenty minutes before you got here."

"Why didn't you say so? It would've helped to know he was already wound up."

"That's just it," she said. "I think he was wound up before he talked to me. He screamed at me. So I told him we wouldn't take his call until he calmed down."

"Well, Christ, Bonnie," I said. "Thanks for the head's up."

Her eyes welled with tears. I snatched a tissue from a box on the file cabinet and handed it to her. She sniffled and caught her breath.

"Katie," she said. "He sounded kind of crazy. He said something was after him."

"Who?"

"Not who, I think, not a person. He said it was something hiding in the vacant lot next to his house. It freaked me out and I hung up on him. I'm so sorry!"

For the rest of the day I tried to push those words out of my thoughts. I reviewed notarized proof of identity and powers of attorney from two middle-aged brothers who were having their 80-year-old mother declared incompetent and placed in a nursing home. Placed. That was another one of those polite words.

Reynolds didn't call again all day. I didn't try to reach his wife. I decided to let sleeping dogs lie.

Every time Bonnie passed my cubicle she glanced at me with a ghastly expression I think she mistook for some kind of camaraderie, a sort of "we're all in this mess together" look. She frowned and shrugged at the same time. I don't know what she hoped to elicit with this ugly pantomime. It didn't matter because we didn't hear from Reynolds again that afternoon.

This time I fell asleep on the bus. October in Seattle is a dark night, pitch black under a slate cover of clouds. Condensation collected in the heated bus and ran in snaky streams down the windows. The throb of the electric cables, the too-warm interior of the bus once it filled with bodies, the dark blur of Capitol Hill streets flashing by, acted like a narcotic on my frayed nerves. I only knew we reached my stop, and my head jerked forward into consciousness, because the driver knew my schedule. His shout had caught my ear in the middle of a dream.

The screech of brakes woke me. The driver sat at the front of the bus looking back over his shoulder at me.

"You're here," he said. His voice carried all the way to the back where I sat sprawled between my purse and my canvas grocery bag.

"What are you doing?" He asked.

I sat up straight and for the first time it occurred to me. If all of the passengers were gone, we must be at the end of the line, not at my stop. We must have passed my house an hour ago. I was going to point this out but I was alone and the lights and heat were off. I tried to calculate how long the warmth sealed inside the bus would last, and this made me drowsy.

When I woke up the bus was freezing, and it was moving. Not forward but slightly, minutely side-to-side. Every window dripped with condensation and in the center of each one a pair of hands pressed against the glass, pushing in, rocking the bus like a cradle.

When I woke up, another passenger was poking me in the shoulder with an index finger. She had a malicious grin. The driver waited for me to collect myself and amble up the aisle. It felt like an expedition. I had to use my elbows to shove past several men dressed as devils and witches. They laughed good-naturedly. Someone said, "Happy Halloween, ma'am!"

If I slept at all that night, it was intermittent with frantic dreams of trains and bus stations, boarding houses without doors, and neighbors I didn't recognize drifting through.

Nothing was safe. Every drifter stole something: a trunk full of clothes I kept intending to sort; the hummingbirds that gathered around a feeder on the porch in late Spring; my mother's silver combs; the Japanese maple in the back yard. When my room was empty except for a sheet on the floor, I lay down and tried to sleep but my mind raced with dates and times from a half-remembered itinerary. I was supposed to be somewhere. It was time to go. Any delay would cause me to miss my connection and then the next one. I tried to stand up but my body clung to inertia. The floor absorbed my full weight. It brought back those times at the end of yoga class when I dozed off while lying flat on my back. The ground held me.

The only thing that got me out of bed and into work the next day was the allure of coffee and Halloween cupcakes supplied by management. They never missed a holiday, but as the company's value decreased over the ensuing years the holiday treats would diminish from bakery delicacies to bags of candy purchased in bulk at Costco.

The first call came at nine-thirty. When I heard Garrison Reynolds wheezing I was glad to be so groggy. My sleep deprivation acted as a sedative to take the edge off his words.

"The mailman never came," he told me. He sounded stunned, child-like in the face of something he couldn't explain.

"Yes," I said. "That's because of the snow. You're due for warmer temperatures this weekend, Mr. Reynolds. The ice will melt and you'll probably have your check and the rest of your mail on Monday."

"It's too late, now," he said. "They're coming back. You lied to me."

"Mr. Reynolds," I said. "Would you mind putting your wife on the phone?"

"She's gone. She's outside. There should be a newspaper in the driveway. They stole it."

I couldn't tell whether he was telling the truth or describing what he thought was true.

"When Mrs. Reynolds comes back," I said. "Will you ask her to give me a call?"

"Comes back?"

"Yes. Tell her I have some questions. Will you do that?"

"She comes back?"

"Yes."

"They won't stay outside, now," he said. "You fucked that up." Then he hung up the phone.

All day I anticipated another conversation with Reynolds or his wife or both. I wondered, briefly, if Mrs. Reynolds had finally gotten sick of his temper, or his dementia, and left him. But surely a woman who had coped with this man for over forty years wasn't going to abandon him now. Yet I felt a twinge of guilt when Bonnie wished me good night before she left the office for the weekend.

"Happy Halloween!" She said. "Watch out for ghosties and witches and whatchamacallits. I'm dressing as a vampire when I get home. The kids love it."

"You get a lot of trick-or-treaters, in the rain?" I asked.

"Tons! I bought six bags of candy to make sure I don't run out. They get so mad when you run out."

"Do they?"

"Oh, we've got some little devils in my neighborhood," she said. "You know, I wonder if that's what Old Man Reynolds was yelling about. I bet he hates this time of year."

"He doesn't seem very happy, no," I said.

"Is he okay?"

Again I had a twinge of irritation. Bonnie wore a jack-o'-lantern button pinned to her coat. When she moved the eyes seemed to glow.

"I'm sure he'll get his check on Monday," I said. "And I can't believe any kids will stop by his house in the snow and ice. When I was a kid we all knew the cranky people on our street, and we stayed away."

"Sure."

"What?" I asked.

"I don't know. Do you think we should call the police?"

"Why?"

"To stop by, and make sure he's okay?"

I considered Bonnie's wide-eyed expression and decided to lie again.

"Sure," I said. "I'll do that."

She waved goodbye even though she was standing right in front of my desk. She was smiling like a child who's just been tucked in after a really good fairy tale. Like most people, Bonnie only wanted to be told everything was fine.

Afternoon crept into dark night. I took the bus home. Opening the front door, I was greeted by the familiar combination of patchouli and mildew. It was a scent that had lingered since my mother occupied the house. There were nights when the hint of patchouli tricked me into thinking I heard her voice, the voices of her friends murmuring in another room. Her lifelong pals with their shoulder-length hair and their poems about the city haunted by spirits. How many hundreds of nights I must have fallen asleep to these whispered tales of loss and longing.

Three children came to my door on Friday night, wearing handmade masks. I couldn't tell what they were supposed to be but I controlled the urge to laugh at their lack of artistic talent. Their parents huddled at the curb wearing hooded rain jackets and sheepish grins. When the children stopped giggling and went away with their chocolate treasures, I tossed the bag of barely touched candy in the garbage and went to bed. Twice

I woke up thinking the phone was ringing, only to find the sound had carried over from a dream.

On Saturday I shopped and read magazines. On Sunday the rain stopped for a few hours. Patches of gray and yellow light broke through the clouds. Neighbors appeared on the street, walking dogs or just enjoying the fresh air.

Cable news reported a slight rise in temperatures and the beginning of what they dubbed the Big Thaw. Rain melted what was left of the premature Midwest snow and the rest of the country lost interest.

The following week I worked with hardly a break. Bonnie never transferred any calls and never stopped by to say hello. That month I set a new record for claim processing and felt very pleased with my progress.

Every night I took the bus home, watched an hour of mind-numbing TV, and fell asleep. I dreamed about the bus, many times, and when I woke up I had the sense that I'd forgotten something. The more I tried to recall what it was, the more vague my memory became.

In early December several new claims arrived in the mail. One stood out immediately. Before I opened it I stared at the return address for a long time.

Garrison Reynolds, age 73, deceased October 31st. Cause of death was a self-inflicted shotgun wound to the head. His primary beneficiary, his wife, was deceased on October 30th, an apparent heart attack. The account and its remaining funds would go to a secondary beneficiary, a nephew in Chicago.

I completed the paperwork in less than an hour. There were dozens of claims ahead of this one but something compelled me to bump it up and get it off my desk.

I went home early that day. I drank a cup of chamomile tea. Surrounded by the fragrance of patchouli, I lay in bed all night listening to the cold rain dripping from the roof to the damp ground. Sometimes I thought I heard a telephone, distant and isolated, as if it rang in a vacant house down the street.

All The News

Karen Heuler

A few years ago I started an imaginary newspaper for a small community I join every summer out in the country. Every week or so I
send out an email and comment on the articles I've read about my neighbors in the "Gazette." Some of the articles certainly are legitimate, chatty
stuff. But some of them are pure bluff. The great part is that neighbors
occasionally get into the spirit of things and send out emails about a
column they say they've read in the paper; and sometimes they make
themselves the columnist.

It all got very Garrison Keillor-ish.

But this was really an imaginary *summer* newspaper, and I wanted to
discontinue it over the winter.

The obvious thing, of course, was to kill everyone off for the Halloween edition.

It wasn't an easy decision. Most people don't like to think of themselves as dead, nor do they think being dead is all that amusing. But I

believed it was the right thing to do. If the deaths are outrageous, then there is a gleefulness about it; if they are surprising, then there is a thrill about it. If it's all very glaringly impossible, then there is a good chance we will continue to believe in our own immortality.

Killing your neighbors can be a potentially bonding, life-affirming thing, as long as you keep it from getting too personal.

Although of course making it personal is probably the most gratifying/interesting way to do it.

Writers often use people and personalities they know as a start for a character in one of their stories. Of course we've all been told that in the interests of preventing outrage and lawsuits, we should change how they look or some of the back story so that they won't be recognizable. In this case, I decided to break all the rules of writing. Everyone was identified by name, and I gave them all their own recognizable back stories, and then some.

In fact, the back stories were the best part. One of the perks of writing an imaginary newspaper about your neighbors is that you get to pick and choose what stories about them should be broadcast to the neighborhood. Over time, you begin to develop them as characters whether they like it or not, and over time they begin to become the character you selected for them. It's very simple: just take the thing they like to do and make it into an obsession, and everyone else will see them exactly the way you see them. Put that obsession out of context—say, someone who washes his pickup obsessively only gets mentioned while washing his truck—and even the writer will become suspicious of just what evidence that neighbor keeps washing off his truck.

And if someone says something that pisses you off, why those words become part of a story. That neighbor becomes inseparable from his or her uncharitable words. In turn, they may try to mention imaginary newspaper columns about you, the writer, in their own emails about the newspaper, but that only keeps their latest offense in everyone's mind that much longer.

You kill them, then, gently and with a gleeful, hidden agenda. If they all turn into zombies, then it's important to choose who started it; it's important to give them deaths that relate to them somehow, preferably deaths that relate to how you feel about them. This is the time to get even, to settle scores, to make your digs in the name of humor and loving affection.

For instance, if a neighbor borrows things and forgets to return them, then there's probably death by unreturned item in his future. If another neighbor has dogs who poop in front of your front door, then either those dogs or that poop will be an instrument of death. In a nice, neighborly way, of course.

So I killed them all. And they were delighted.

One of the beauties of this, for a writer, is that you don't really have to worry about how believable the action is. All bets are off, and anything can happen. Even those neighbors who read only nonfiction and who listen relentlessly to NPR can find themselves attracted to horror, suddenly, and will inevitably try their hand at writing horror in return.

It's true, I take great care not to harm them in any ordinary way. I don't want them to feel singled out or targeted, but the bottom line here is that I kill them every year.

And every year, they come right back.

DEAR DEAD JENNY

Ian McDowell

It was Halloween 1972 and Jenny Locklear was dead and I'd never find another girl like her. I guess she was my first girlfriend, although I hadn't gotten around to calling her that when a car hit her while she was walking home alone in the rain, her Bride of Frankenstein wig slipping off her head and makeup running down her face. Maybe she was crying. If so, that also makes me her boyfriend. You have to be that to make a girl cry, unless you hit her or do something else dumbass mean when you're both kids. I never did even when little. She hit back too hard.

What made her special, other than she's the only dead person I ever knew other than Mom? Mom went into the hospital the summer between the first and second grade and never came out and I don't remember the next two years. But I remembered every one of the 364 days since my dad told me that Jenny had been found in the ditch beside Raintree Road, four dark lanes that separated her neighborhood from mine.

I'd known her since kindergarten, a little scabby monkey girl with tangled brown hair and black eyes. She threw dirt clods really hard and, because of her older brothers, was nobody to tussle with. Not just because they'd kick your butt or maybe stab you. At least we all thought they would, them being part Lumbee, as their last name would tell you if you were from this part of North Carolina, where all the Lumbee are either Locklears or Oxendines. Her brothers were as dark as a Sugar Daddy, the Lumbee in Fayetteville supposedly being as much what we then called colored (or sometimes, the N-word) as the Indians they claimed to be, not that you told them that unless you wanted a stomping. She was a lighter caramel, although darker than her blond dough-colored mom.

The dirt clod fights ended when she lobbed one into my left eye so hard I fell down crying, although I was later happy to get a patch like a pirate. Mom drew a skull and crossbones on it and let me wear it longer than I needed to. Then she got sick and died and I don't remember Jenny or much else except being sad until it was the fourth grade and I wasn't so sad anymore and Jenny had somehow become my best friend. She later told me she jumped on the Robinson twins when they were making me eat one of those big green horn worms, but I don't remember that. She said they made me chew instead of just swallowing like the time I gulped down a fat wiggly tadpole on a dare. According to her, mustard-colored goo squirted out my mouth right before she hit David Robinson with a softball bat. I wish I could remember her hitting him, but am glad I can't recall what the caterpillar tasted like.

The first time I remember her doing best friend stuff was when she borrowed a stack of my monster magazines. I'd been reading them ever since Tony, this grownup who did plays with my father at the Fayetteville Little Theater and wanted to be a professional makeup man, lent me a copy of *Famous Monsters of Filmland* with a cool painting of a snarling werewolf on the cover. Big scary letters said this was the Werewolf of London, but Tony explained that the magazine had goofed and it was actually the one from *Return of the Vampire*, a movie which bugged me when I saw it later because I didn't think werewolves should talk.

I guess Tony, who would come over to our house to run lines with my dad when I was younger, and whom I started regularly visiting once I was old enough to go to his place on my own, was the first monster movie fan I knew. I soon became one, too. A few other kids my age had some of the Aurora monster models, but I was the only one who had them all, even the Old Witch and the Bride of Frankenstein. Many of us watched monster movies on *Dialing for Dollars* in the afternoon or on *Sunrise Theater* on Saturdays, but I was the only one whose father let him stay up late on Saturday nights for *Shock Theater* with Dr. Paul Bearer. By the fifth grade, my dad was buying me *Famous Monsters of Filmland* and by the Sixth, *Castle of Frankenstein,* which wasn't really meant for kids, but he didn't know that. I was always afraid he'd look inside that magazine, because sometimes the pictures had tits in them, but he never did.

The important thing is, Jenny liked monsters as much as me. She never got the models, but she played with mine, bringing over her Barbies and making it look like the Frankenstein Monster or the Mummy was carrying or strangling them. She was the only kid I knew who called him "The Frankenstein Monster" instead of just "Frankenstein." Girls weren't supposed to like this stuff. Girls weren't supposed to like comic books, either, but she read them, and I don't mean the Romance ones. Unlike my male friends, she called the big green guy that Bruce Banner turned into the Hulk, not the Huck like Tom Sawyer's buddy on the raft. She didn't care for *Spider-Man* and I didn't like *Wonder Woman* even when they changed her to look like Mrs. Peel on our favorite program *The Avengers,* but we read them together, sitting back to back under the big oak tree in my yard or side by side on the couch with our feet next to each other's heads. We particularly loved the ads. She said she'd heard the submarine was just a big cardboard box but surely the live squirrel monkey wasn't a gyp.

She came over to watch *Star Trek* and, of course, *The Avengers,* and we were sad when Mrs. Peel left and didn't like Tara King. Her folks wouldn't let her come over for late night movies, but we watched plenty of afternoon ones, racing to get home from school in time for *The Attack of the Giant Leeches* or *Gigantis the Fire Monster,* although these were never as good as the Karloff and Lugosi stuff on Shock Theater. Dad dropped us off at Christopher Lee and Peter Cushing matinees downtown and by the Seventh Grade we were getting a lot of "Jim and Jenny, sitting in tree, K-I-S-S-I-N-G," but all we ever did was wrestle. Her brothers acted like they almost liked me and after that neither one of us had to worry about anyone giving us grief.

At the other end of my neighborhood were some old houses that had been divided up into apartments. That's where Tony the makeup guy lived, although I knew him before she did and was the one that asked him to show her his stuff. Tony had been in Vietnam, where Dad said he'd been a combat photographer. I heard he had a scrapbook of photos of real wounds and dead guys but he wouldn't show it to me and changed the subject when I asked him. What he would let me and then later Jenny do was read his amazing collection of monster magazines and books, some older than me. He also had a couple of those really expensive Don Post masks that were advertised in the back of *Famous Monsters*, and some he'd made himself that were just as good, with real hair and everything. He worked in a costume rental place for a living when he wasn't acting or doing makeup at the Fayetteville Little Theater. I'd known him since I could remember stuff again. Dad had really thrown himself into the theater after Mom's death and while I never acted, he would take me with him and I'd hang out backstage where everybody called each other by first names no matter what their age. Tony was the first grownup I ever did that with.

In the Seventh Grade, Jenny and I decided it was the last time we could ask Tony to make us up to go trick-or-treating together, since next year we'd be thirteen and that was too old for it (if not for Devil's Night pranks) and anyway, Tony kept talking about going off to do professional makeup for movies and we knew he soon would. He agreed to make Jenny up as the Bride of Frankenstein and me as the Monster. He said he'd send a photograph of us in to *Famous Monsters*. They were always running photos of kids in monster makeup, some really good.

Halloween afternoon, we went over to Tony's and I sat on his busted up porch and read his magazines while he made Jenny up as the Bride. He painted her face and neck and arms really pale with green highlights and used something called collodion which puckered her skin up to make that scar on her neck. And he'd already made the wig with the lightning bolts in it, saying it was only the second time he'd ever worked with that much hair, the first being when he made the mask for the ape suit in *Cabaret* (the costume was rented but he'd hated the mask that came with it, and made something that looked more like *Planet of the Apes*). He said the hair was real and that it might have come from a dead person, but when Jenny got grossed out he laughed and said no, women sold their hair all the time and Jenny said yeah, we'd read "The Gift of the Magi" in school and the way she smiled at him bugged me. Tony was my hero and like the uncle I never had. But he was a handsome guy, dark and Italian and muscular, and for some reason it bothered me to see him touching Jenny, even though he was twice her age and wasn't doing anything creepy and of course he had to do that to make her up. But I suddenly didn't like it and that's why I took his magazines out on the porch.

Jenny finally came out and she looked amazing, maybe not as great as the Jack Pierce makeup for the Bride in the movie, but at least as good as anything you'd see on a comedy show or commercial. He'd wrapped bandages around her arms and from somewhere he'd gotten a long white dress. She stared at me with those dark eyes and she knew that I was jealous of Tony and she knew that I knew it. "You're beautiful," I said, my face burning as the words came out. She stared at me harder and then she kissed me and time just stopped. I couldn't hear the cicadas or the lawn sprinkler or cars going by or the Moody Blues eight track Tony was playing on his stereo inside. Just my heart beating.

She finally drew back. "Did you like that?"

I did, I did so much, but somehow I couldn't say it. I was afraid to say anything.

It was getting dark and Tony's porch light had come on. Tony was still inside, getting his makeup chair ready for me.

"Jimmy, did you like it?" asked Jenny again.

I looked away, then down at the issue of *Castle of Frankenstein* I'd been reading. On the cover, a Doctor Frankenstein who was supposed to be Peter Cushing (but looked more like a white Greg Morris from *Mission Impossible*) and a Boris Karloff Monster were threatening a blonde in a mini-skirt with really big tits popping out of her top. "What's the matter? You don't like that I don't have those?"

I mumbled something, and wanted to kiss her again, told myself I should just grab her and do it like they did in movies, but I was afraid.

"Nobody has boobs like that," she said.

I tried to make a joke. "I dunno, Natalie Johnson's are pretty big."

She stopped smiling and her black eyes suddenly looked like holes in her green-white face. "Why don't you go trick-or-treating with her, then!" Yeah, like that would happen. Natalie was already dating an Eighth Grade jock.

I knew I needed to say something, but I couldn't think of what. My chance to kiss her back had passed. She stepped down off the porch. "Get Tony to give you a ride home. I'm walking. Don't follow me." It wasn't unusual. We kids walked everywhere back then, even after dark.

The cicadas had stopped and I could hear something hitting the leaves. "It's raining," I said. "At least let me see if Tony has an umbrella."

"Screw that," she said. "Screw that and you."

"Well screw you right back!" I shouted after her.

She began to run. Why didn't I run after her?

The rain started to fall harder and the sky got dark. I watched the rain and waited for Tony but he didn't come out. I went back inside. He was smoking a joint. "Be ready in a few minutes, man."

I didn't know what to say about Jenny. "You don't need to make me up. Just let me borrow that mask you made of Karloff as the Monster"

"It will be kind of big on you. And it will look weird, you in a mask and her in makeup. Where's Jenny?"

"She went home," I mumbled.

He finished the joint. "You guys had a fight." He didn't say it as a question. "I guess that had to happen."

He put the rubber headpiece he'd made for me back on the plaster cast he'd made of the top of my head and got the mask from its display atop his bookcase. He was very proud of it and had never lent it to me before. "You know she's special, right?"

What, did he think I was stupid? "She's the only girl I know who's into this stuff."

"That's not what makes her special, Jim. You better treat her right. If it was your fault, tell her you're sorry. If it was hers, apologize anyway."

"Nights in White Satin" started up again on the eight track.

Tony took me home and I called Jenny's house and her dad said she wasn't there. Later I found out she'd been hit in the early evening but nobody saw her lying there in the muddy ditch for hours. Maybe she was already there when we drove by. Maybe if we'd seen her we could have gotten her to the hospital in time. But no, they later said she'd died right away. I hope that's true. The only thing worse than her lying there dead would be her lying there dying.

But I didn't know that yet. I called her again and her father said she hadn't come home and then he started asking me angry questions and yelling. Dad got on the phone and yelled back and hung up. I didn't dress up as the Karloff Frankenstein. Dad and I sat on the couch and watched something with Dennis Weaver on the *CBS Sunday Night Movie.* I don't remember what it was. Well, he watched and I pretended to watch, and he put his arm around me for the first time in a while. Then he made himself a gin and tonic and drank it and made another one, as he always did on nights he wasn't at the Little Theater. And then he fell asleep snoring, his face red and his glasses down on his nose, his head nodding back into the wall paneling with a dull *thump thump thump.* Something else he always did on nights he was at home. I moved from the couch to the armchair.

Eventually, *Shock Theater* came on. They showed movies all night on Halloween, but the first was *The Mummy,* which is pretty boring once Boris Karloff stops being a real mummy and is just an old guy. I fell asleep.

Shock Theater was playing *Captive Wild Woman* when the cops knocked on the door. Apparently Mr. Locklear had told them I was the last one to see Jenny. They'd found her by now. Dad came to the door and spoke to them outside, where he apparently convinced them they didn't need to talk to me tonight, although they'd want a statement tomorrow. Then he came inside and told me what had happened.

"That's not true," I said, "you're joking." He said he wished he was and hugged me hard and then I was crying. I don't know if I'd stopped by the time I went to bed.

I dreamed Jenny and I were standing out on the street in the autumn leaves she loved. In the dream, it must have been earlier in the evening, because all down the street the jack-o'-lanterns were still lit, although there were no trick-or-treaters. Jenny kissed me and I touched her neck where Tony had made the scar. Her eyes were so black, even more like holes. Instead of collodion and greasepaint, I felt real stitches. They popped open and blood flowed out, down her white neck and white dress, turning both red.

I woke up and sobbed for a long time in the dark.

They never found out who hit her.

I didn't go back to school for two weeks. Dad dropped out of the play he was in and stayed home with me at night. He tried not to drink until I went to bed. For dinner he cooked steaks and burgers, or brought home pizza, no more macaroni or spam or TV dinners, but I didn't care. When I finally went back to school, Leonard, Jenny's older brother who was in the ninth grade (while we called ninth graders "Freshman," they were still in junior high and didn't go off to the high school until the next year) grabbed me and shoved me into a row of lockers and was going to hit me, but then he started crying and hugged me before letting me go and walking away very fast.

He wasn't the only one to hug me. Natalie Johnson did too, and when she did I could feel her boobs against my chest. I closed my eyes and saw Jenny standing there looking like she wanted to throw a dirt clod at me and I pulled away. Natalie's Eighth Grade jock boyfriend Mitch glared and cracked his knuckles, but you don't hit a kid whose girlfriend is dead.

I remembered my mom dying and I remembered it being two years later and me not so sad anymore. Why couldn't everything jump ahead like that now, with me in the ninth grade and starting to think about other girls? Why hadn't I grabbed Jenny and kissed her? Why hadn't I done so a long time before that afternoon? So many whys. Those were my thoughts every night and most days.

We didn't get much snow that winter, but a lot of freezing rain. Spring took its time but summer got really hot. I didn't do much on my summer break, mostly staying in my room, although one time I walked in the woods and carved her and my initials on a tree. Once or twice, I prayed for her and for me. I hadn't been brought up religious. Dad later told me that he'd studied for the seminary but quit when he realized he didn't believe in God, that he was just in love with what he called the theater of the pulpit. Mom had been a Quaker, which Baptists don't consider a real Christian, and she never sent me to Sunday School. I didn't even go to her funeral, as Dad thought I couldn't deal with it. I did go to Jenny's, but never visited her grave after that. Whatever was in the ground, that wasn't her.

The week before she died, she'd given me a green stone the light shown through. It looked like nothing so much as the bottom of a Seven Up bottle. She said her grandma had given it to her and that it was Wish Stone and that if I put it in my pillow and made a wish at night, the wish would come true when I woke up. I thought it was silly when she told me that, but now I sometimes picked it up off my night stand and felt its smoothness, but I didn't make a wish because I already knew how I'd feel when I woke up and it hadn't happened. At least, I didn't make one until the next Halloween.

It was now the Eighth Grade and I was thirteen. Not that I could have stood to go trick-or-treating even if I were still twelve, having done it with Jenny since the Fourth Grade and maybe earlier. I didn't even want to help Dad carve a pumpkin or decorate our porch. He did it by himself and I looked at it and thought even harder of Jenny and ran upstairs.

I had a little black and white TV in my room. Channel 11, one of two I could get with the bent antenna, was rerunning *The Night Stalker*. Not the show that came later when I was in high school, the first TV movie with the vampire. I watched it thinking Jenny would have liked it a lot. Dad knocked on my door. "Jim, you can't go on like this. She wouldn't want you to. It's been a year."

I told him to go away. After a while he did and I could hear Johnny Carson on the big TV that was plugged into the stereo downstairs. Dad was hard of hearing. He hadn't worn his earplugs when he was in the artillery in Korea.

I eventually switched to Channel Eight and *Shock Theater*. I used to love the host, Dr. Paul Bearer, but his jokes seemed so corny now. The first movie was *The Raven*. Unlike the poem, which I'd memorized to impress Jenny, there was no lost Lenore in it. But soon it was a midnight dreary.

I looked over at my night table. The Wish Stone flickered green in the light from the TV. I picked it up and put it in my pillow. Come back Jenny. Even if just for tonight, so I can say I'm sorry, and kiss you again.

I fell asleep before Lugosi started skinning Karloff and the weird looking castle blew up.

My door opened and Jenny came in. Her eyes were more like holes than ever. She was so pale. The blood on her wasn't makeup.

I woke up. Someone was knocking at the front door. I went downstairs and saw Dad snoring on the couch. There was a big orange bowl on the coffee table. Judging from how much candy was still in it, not many trick-or-treaters had been by. Surely none were still out this late. So who was knocking?

I walked to the door and opened it. Jenny stood there. She wore her Bride of Frankenstein wig but it wasn't crooked now. There was no blood or mud on her white dress or her bandaged arms. She was pale, but it was the pale of makeup, and the porch light was bright enough that I could see caramel-colored skin at the hollow of her throat.

"Hi Jimmy." Her voice was that of a live person. She sounded embarrassed. "Trick or treat." She smiled that smile that I just then realized meant everything to me and had for years. "I'm not much of a treat, but I swear this isn't a trick."

My face was wet. I knew I wasn't dreaming. I knew that she was dead. I knew that she was really standing there.

"Are you a ghost?"

She knew she was dead, too. "Yeah, I guess. I'm not all messed up, like the kid the monkey's paw brought back. I feel alive. But I know I'm dead. Just not right now."

I didn't say anything.

"Aren't you going to hug me?"

I did. She was cold, but not too cold. "I still don't have big boobs. I guess I never will."

"I'm sorry," I finally said. That sounded stupid, like I was sorry about her boobs.

But she knew what I really meant. "No, I'm sorry. I'm the one who got mad and ran away."

"I'm the one who was too dumb to kiss you again. Or before. We knew each other so long and I never kissed you before."

"You can kiss me now."

I did. Either her lips weren't as cold as her body or she was getting warm. She rubbed one of her bandages on my mouth, then showed me the black lipstick on it. "Let's go trick-or-treating."

I just wanted to hold her again. "This late?"

"Just one house. There's something I've got to do. Then we can come back here and I can be with you for the rest of the night."

I wondered if she meant sex. That was scary. Not because she was dead, but because sex was scary.

She seemed to know what I was thinking. "Just hold me for a long time. Until I'm dead again."

In the living room, I heard Dad grunt and roll over on the couch. I shut the door behind me, not caring that I didn't have a jacket.

We walked down the street holding hands. Hers was colder than her lips, but got warmer as I held it. Unlike the road where she died, my street was well lit. In the buzzing glow of the street lamps she looked black and white, like the real Bride of Frankenstein. Tony hadn't given her Frankenstein shoes and she was wearing Keds under her dress, but her wig made her seem taller than me. She kicked at dry leaves, sending them skittering down the pavement. I didn't care where we were going and was happy.

She laughed to see someone had toilet-papered the Robinson's house. "Remember what we did after Mrs. Robinson called me a red nigger?" I remembered, because it had happened a couple of years after she'd hit one of the boys. The Robinson twins were bullies and their mom was so big and mean they must have gotten it from her instead of their dad, a meek little guy with a head like a light bulb. Two summers ago, I'd taken my life-size model skull and a veal chop from the fridge and she shredded the meat with scissors and mixed it with Elmer's Glue-All. We spread it on the skull and she got an old cheap black wig from a previous Halloween and glued that on too. Then we climbed our old oak tree and nailed chicken wire over it on a thick limb so no varmint could get it. Once it smelled awful and there were maggots in it, we left it in the Robinson's garden. Mrs. Robinson found it, crawling with flies, when she came out to water her roses. She nearly had a heart attack. The cops took it away and didn't figure out it was fake until it was back in the morgue. Dad knew I'd done it and grounded me for two months, but he let Jenny come over and hang out with me. She thought it was the funniest thing ever.

She still did, and as she laughed, her hand gripped mine very tight. We turned onto Sagebrush Lane, which ended in a traffic circle. At the bottom of it was Reverend Jackson's house. I'd never gone to his church but I didn't like him, as I knew from the paper and the TV news he was always trying to get books taken out of the school library, and he'd tried to organize a protest when the Fayetteville Little Theater did *Cabaret*. For some reason, you never heard him say anything about the nightclubs and strip joints and porno theaters on the 400 block of Hay Street downtown where all the soldiers from Fort Bragg went on weekends.

Jenny led me to his door. Of course there wasn't a jack-o'-lantern. Reverend Jackson didn't like Halloween. Any kids who trick-or-treated here got a lecture about Satan.

Jenny rang the doorbell. I didn't understand why we were here and was nervous. I wanted to spend time with her, not with some angry grownup who'd yell at us and might call my dad.

She had to ring six times before he came to the door in a big fluffy nightgown. He smelled more of booze than my dad ever did.

"You damn kids shouldn't be out this late. You shouldn't be trick-or-treating at all," he mumbled groggily.

"You shouldn't cuss. Or drink and drive," said Jenny quietly.

He stared at her and his expression changed into something more scary than any monster makeup. I think that was him knowing before he knew. "What?"

"You shouldn't have hit me and not stopped."

Whatever else his expression was, it wasn't surprise. I couldn't stand to look at his face, so I looked at hers. Her eyes got really black and I saw they really were holes. Her mouth spread wide, no lips, just teeth. She was thinner. She let go of my hand before hers became mostly bone.

"Jesus save me," he whimpered.

"No," she said.

He fell to his knees and started blubbering. I hoped I hadn't made noises like that when I cried. "I should have stopped. When I heard about you, I should have turned myself in."

"Yes," she said.

"I still can. I will. I swear to Jesus I will."

She tapped his bald spot with her bony hand. He yelped liked a dog. "If you don't, I'll be back."

"I know," he said very softly.

She reached for my hand, hers live flesh again, and started to lead me away.

"Wait," he said. "Were you in Heaven?"

She stopped. "No."

"Were you in Hell? I know that's where I'm going."

She shook her head. "I wasn't anywhere."

"You can't say that," he whimpered. "There has to be a Heaven and Hell. How could you come back if there's not? There has to be a Hell. I have to go there."

Jenny didn't say anything. We walked away, leaving him shaking and blubbering on his knees. Next door, a light came on.

Jenny's hand was colder than before but felt like a hand, not bones. "That's why you came back," I finally said.

We kept walking, the leaves all crunchy underfoot. She squeezed closer and put her arm around me and I put mine around her. She felt warm again.

"No. I came back for you, not him. But this way everybody will know he did it. When they have somebody to blame, nobody can be mad at you again."

Even with her father yelling at me on the phone that night and her brother starting to threaten me, I hadn't noticed people being mad, but I guess they had been. "I shouldn't have let you walk home in the dark."

Her arm around me squeezed tighter. "Never say that again. Or think it. That's my command as a girl and a ghost and you know better than disobey either."

Back home, I opened the door quietly. I could hear static from the living room and Dad snoring. The stairs didn't have any carpet, so I took off my shoes. Jenny's footsteps didn't make a sound.

In my room with the door shut, she took off her wig and shook out her hair, all dark brown and curly. Then she took off her gown. Underneath, she wore a tank top and shorts. In the dim light, her arms and legs and the place where her throat met her chest were darker than her normal caramel color, her face makeup paler. She lay down with me and we kissed a lot. The makeup started coming off, some on me, on the sheets. I kissed her collodion scar, which had started to break up. I rubbed my tongue over it until it was wet and then picked off some of the flakes. She sighed deeply and nuzzled my neck.

I didn't try to get to second base, much less further, even though if I'd ever wanted anyone to be my first time, it would have been her.

"Girls must like you now," she said softly. "We like sad boys when they have something to really be sad about. I did, when you were little and so sad. I wanted to take all that sadness away."

"Maybe you did," I said. "I'm not sad now."

"You can date anyone you want. Even Natalie Johnson."

"I don't want to date Natalie Johnson."

"Really," she said, teasingly drawing out the word. "They really are very big."

"Dammit, Jenny."

She laughed. "See, I can still make you mad."

"I'm sorry." How many times had I said that tonight?

"Don't be. My teasing means I love you."

"I love you," I whispered. "You're the only one I want to date."

"Can't do that, Jimbo," she said looking older than me, even though she was still fourteen and I was fifteen now. "I mean, not unless you dig my body up like a perv, and that's not dating. I can't come back again."

"But you told Reverend Jackson you would, if he didn't turn himself in."

She smiled the saddest smile I'd ever seen. "I guess ghosts can lie. I can't really come back after tonight, not to him or to you, but I won't need to."

"I'll need you to."

She started crying then. "You won't, not any more. But we'll have this. That's enough, even if you don't think so." I used my shirt to wipe her face, leaving a darker patch. "I'll visit your grave every day," I said through my own tears, feeling guilty I'd not done so since her funeral.

"That's sweet, but why? I won't know it. After sunrise I won't know anything ever again."

"You won't know you love me?"

"I know you love me right now. That's enough. When you wake up, I'll be gone and I'll never be back. Cry then if you want, but then don't cry anymore. Promise?"

We said some other things, but after a while I promised. I've even kept it.

We talked some more and I held her tight. We watched some of *Son of Frankenstein*. It's not as good as the first two, but it felt right. Eventually, I slept a bit. I don't know if she did.

I woke up to light shining in the window and Dad knocking on my door. Of course I was alone. Of course I cried. Dad came in and squeezed my shoulder. "I'm going to make breakfast. Please come down and sit with me."

After a while, I got up. There was makeup on my t-shirt, but it was the same one I'd worn a year and a day ago when she kissed me when she was alive, and the makeup smear was small and looked old. There wasn't any on the bed sheets. I changed and went downstairs, smelling bacon frying, and was surprised to find I was hungry. Dad squeezed fresh orange juice and made coffee for himself. He started to talk about counseling, and how it could really help, but I shook my head. "Maybe I needed that before. I don't now." He stared into my eyes for a long time. Eventually he looked relieved.

After eating some bacon and drinking some orange juice, I started to talk about her. He listened without saying anything and I didn't cry and haven't since. But sometimes, in late October when the wind sends lipstick-colored leaves dancing down the street and the skinny bare tree limbs shake, I think I hear her call my name.

WHAT BLOOMS IN SHADOW WITHERS IN LIGHT

Richard Gavin

I. CONCERNING THE KEEPER

The property had long been prone to lightning strikes, cattle mutilations, even a shower of falling stones. Yet no one but its owner—a stout spinster known to the locals as Miss Prudence—was aware of such phenomena. She alone had experienced these diabolical miracles. She alone is cognizant of their purpose.

At dawn Miss Prudence steps out her front door to survey the expanse of her withered farmland. The air is simultaneously mild and chilling as it so often is in October. She shuffles to the edge of the drooping front porch, wrapping her fingers, which arthritis has rendered into plump misshapen stubs, over the railing.

Nothing appears to have been altered during the night. The soil bears neither cloven-hoof print nor trail of shimmering slime; the air is not choked with brimstone; the thin twining of wolfbane and garlic flowers remains intact over her front door. Most importantly, the great grey barn that is slumped in the center of her farmyard appears to be intact, which means that today's work may not be as dangerous as Miss Prudence had initially feared.

She descends the steps carefully and the wood groans under her weight.

Across the dew-soaked grass, over to the barn.

The property has been in Miss Prudence's family for generations. She, like her ancestors, had been raised to be wholly self-sufficient. With the farm being a nexus of unnatural elements, the fields have long been scourged of whatever nutrients they once possessed. The meager crops Miss Prudence manages to harvest are scarcely enough sustenance for herself. She sells any left-over produce to those passersby who pity her enough to purchase a basket of withered apples in the autumn, parched peaches during summer.

It is an archaic way of life, but it is the only life Miss Prudence knows. Had fate been kinder, there would now be adult children ready to take over the sacred family duty of Keeper; a duty that the family had begun to execute with fierce diligence during the Dark Ages, but less maniacally since the Industrial Revolution had sharpened men's minds as well as their material appetites. (Keen thought and covetousness had managed to level most of the superstition that had once thrived in the world.) But Miss Prudence has been so immersed in her Work that time managed to slip by her unnoticed. Now just two months shy of her seventieth birthday, she has no hope of continuing the Keep, no prospects for personal happiness, no indication as to the destiny of the race she has spent her life protecting.

She reaches the barn door and pauses to listen to the slithering, to the growling, to the howling that bounces from rotted wall to rotted wall.

Taking the small sack down from its hook on the door, Miss Prudence begins to sprinkle a fresh salt ring around the barn. She wonders how much longer these bitter little crystals can hold them; all the tentacled things and the many-legged things and the things with arachnid bodies…or worse; no bodies at all. If only she'd had others to help her, she could have then taken the time to learn new techniques, new binding spells, new banishments. Oh, if only…

She begins the opening rubrics to guard herself against the onslaught that will occur at dusk.

II. FROM MEPHITIC ASH, A SAVIOUR

Aptly, the evening sky resembles an inferno; all livid orange and scarlet and ash-grey. Its fuming half-light endows the numerous decorated homes in the town of Greyleaf with a mock-animation. Bed-sheet phantoms snap and bob upon the chill breeze as if struggling to free themselves from their tree limb traps. Plastic gargoyles seem to stir upon their porch step perches, hungrily leering toward some tender prey. Cardboard black cats arch their backs in defiance. Rubber replicas of movie monsters nod in agreement over some unspoken pact.

A tiny shape (only slightly more human than the decorative grotesques that line the street) plods along the sidewalk. A padding of desiccated leaves crunches beneath the soles of his work boots.

The wind carries omens of the coming winter. It penetrates the worn fibers of the figure's coveralls, but the figure is unfazed for tonight is pregnant with potential for men like him; men possessed of shadowy appetites.

Both of the man's hands are full: one clutches the steel lunchbox in which he carts his frugal meals to the plant each morning, the other lugs a cumbersome plastic grocery bag whose overstretched handles dig into the meat of his fingers.

The figure (a small, stout man with a pronounced chin and a balding cranium) was, in youth, called Otto. Age has earned him the more official-sounding title of Mr. Umbra.

Mr. Umbra shuffles up the steps of his front porch. His house is tiny, its contents sparse, its decor painfully utilitarian. The red brick exterior hosts no decorations whatsoever. He balances the grocery bag on his left thigh while he searches through his pockets for his house keys.

Unlocking the front door, he slips into the murky stillness of the empty abode. Shutting the door on the outer world, Mr. Umbra steps gingerly down the hallway, feeling the plastic bag beginning to split, threatening to spill out its precious contents. He enters the kitchen just in time, plopping the shredded bag onto the counter with a thud before hurrying back to lock the front door, to slide the security chain in place.

Mr. Umbra then tends to his duties in the kitchen.

Rummaging through the semi-clean dishes that sit in a rack beside the sink, he selects an appropriate knife and sets it down on the Formica countertop. The remnants of the plastic bag are peeled away, revealing a single package of Halloween candy and a rather poor specimen of a pumpkin. One side of the shell appears to be caving-in from decay. The black-green-orange rind is perforated with wormholes.

"Serves me right for not shopping until October 31st," Mr. Umbra thinks to himself as he jabs the dull kitchen knife into the top of the pumpkin and begins to saw. He hollows the gourd of its pulpy innards, most of which stink of rot. Giving little thought to the design of his jack-o'-lantern, Mr. Umbra opts for a simple design. He slices out two triangle eyes, a lopsided triangular nose, and a sneering zigzag mouth.

Cursing himself for not remembering to purchase a candle, Mr. Umbra resorts to using one of the slender white candles from his blackout emergency kit, which he keeps in a cupboard above the stove.

He empties a cereal bowl of that morning's bran flakes and milk, rinses the dish under the tap, and then fills it with the meagre selection of candy.

With the trappings of his outer temple now prepared, Mr. Umbra readies himself for the second, and far more crucial, inspection; that of his secret inner temple.

He makes a quick jaunt to the upstairs bedroom to retrieve the spiral-bound notebook off his nightstand. This he carries down into the cellar. Weaving through the labyrinth of cardboard boxes, bundles of old newspapers, and pieces of broken furniture, Mr. Umbra finally reaches the hatch-door in his cellar floor.

There is a string that never leaves his neck. It holds the keys for the hatch-door's padlock. Mr. Umbra loops the string around his finger, pulls the keys out over the collar of his coveralls and unlocks the hatch.

The room it opens unto is tiny but equipped with all the essentials: a narrow cot, a standing lamp, an electric fan, a baseboard heater, and firm manacles that are bolted into the stone wall and the floor.

Mr. Umbra opens the notebook and thumbs through the pages that bear his shaky handwriting; squiggles that sketchily chronicle his night-mares. His eyes alternate between the barely-legible notes and his subter-ranean inner temple. Ordinarily his work ethic is slipshod, his attention to detail almost non-existent, but as he gives the inner temple one final inspection Mr. Umbra is warmed by the knowledge that he has executed this particular project with rare meticulousness.

The distant laughter of children becomes audible through one of the blacked-out basement windows. Mr. Umbra hurries (as much as a man like him *can* hurry) upstairs to the kitchen. There he lights the white emergency candle and inserts it into the jack-o'-lantern. He carries it and the tiny bowl of candy out to the porch.

With some difficulty Mr. Umbra props the lopsided pumpkin against the porch railing and eases himself into his battered porch rocker. There he sits, waiting, running his fingers through the psychedelically-coloured candies in his cereal bowl.

Twilight wanes, shadows lengthen. Mr. Umbra waits. Each pack of giggling trick-or-treaters sparks a hopeful excitement in him, but after examining their costumes, their gestures, their demeanor, Mr. Umbra is saddened to discover that the dream-child is not among them. To these undesirable urchins Mr. Umbra sulkily tosses little packets of chewing gum or mini chocolate bars before he shoos them off his porch.

He runs out of candy in less than an hour but he remains on his porch until the white emergency candle has burnt down to a useless blob inside the rotting pumpkin. The night grows winter-crisp, the stars glint like ice from behind woolly black clouds.

It is while Mr. Umbra is preparing to toss the pumpkin into the trashcan at the side of his house that the child arrives, crying out "Trick or treat!"

Mr. Umbra freezes while the pumpkin is still in his hands. He turns to spy the tiny grease-painted ghoul that is sheepishly scaling his front steps. Mr. Umbra grins.

"Trick-or-treat," the monster repeats, softer this time.

A shudder of bliss runs through the plump man.

"I have something *very* special for you, Mr. Grave-robber, sir," begins Mr. Umbra. "Now, if you'd be kind enough to step inside my haunted mansion…"

III. TWILIGHT'S FRAGILE GUARDIAN

Miss Prudence is so grateful to see the first signs of the All Saints' dawn that for a moment she almost believes that the sun's ascent is illusory. She studies the ribbon of orange; a tiny ember glowing at the heart of the darkest night of the year. It begins to dilate, casting wide beams of illumination over the woods and the nearby farmyards.

From her hermetically-sealed barn come yowls of defeat.

Miss Prudence raises the rosary she's been clutching in her crooked fist. She presses it to her lips. This year's banishments had been the most difficult ones she could remember. More than once the barn looked as though it was about to tumble, more than once it seemed that its captives would be freed.

There but for the grace of God…

Drained and teary, Miss Prudence staggers off to her warm bed, muttering ecclesiastical praises.

IV. COLD PROPHESIES

Mr. Umbra glances out the snow-bearded kitchen window, at the February blizzard that stirs and lashes the town. The wind moans. Ice pellets patter against the glass in arrhythmic blasts. Mr. Umbra shivers, pulls the threadbare cardigan tighter around his plump belly. He turns his attention back to the saucepan of turkey soup that is heating on the stove. He gives the milky broth a stir and then pours it into the same chipped cereal bowl he'd used to dispense candy from last Halloween. Mr. Umbra picks the bowl up cautiously, tucks a box of cheese-flavoured crackers under his arm, and makes his way to the cellar.

Weaving between the basement's clutter while carrying an overfilled bowl requires savvy; something Mr. Umbra lacks completely. The hot broth sloshes over the bowl's rim, scalding his hands. He curses under his breath. When he reaches the hatch door Mr. Umbra sets the bowl and the box of cheese-flavoured crackers down on a battered carton containing unused yuletide decorations. He slides his grub-like fingers beneath his shirt collar.

The child hears the fat man beyond the door, fumbling with the lock again. Quickly, defiantly, he tosses the notebook underneath his cot. Perhaps this way the fat man will not ask him about his notes; out of sight, out of mind. Perhaps he would be spared, just this once, of having to recount the horrors of his dreams.

After so many months the child had grown accustomed to living inside Mr. Umbra's inner temple, but he still did not believe the little man's theories about the Saviour, or that the little man had actually dreamed of his arrival; right down to his ghoul costume. Such things seemed foolish to the boy, even though in some ways it did explain why he had never been found by his parents or by the authorities, and why Mr. Umbra had never even been a suspect in his disappearance.

And lately the boy *had* been experiencing dreams of a distant place; a place where unearthly forms were slithering toward freedom, toward dominion.

The lock gives and the fat man staggers into the cell. He is balancing a bowl against his bulging belly. The smell of the soup reminds the boy of his mother's kitchen in a house at the other end of town. He remembers the copper pots that decorated her kitchen walls and his eyes sparkle with fresh tears.

The fat man sets the bowl down gently on the lopsided folding card table that stands at the foot of the cot. The spilled broth forms sickly yellow puddles on the tabletop.

"How are you feeling tonight?" asks the fat man. His voice is disturbingly high-pitched for such a large man.

"Cold," answers the boy.

There is a low whistling sound as the fat man breathes through his nostrils. Is he deep in thought?

"I will bring you some more blankets. I think I might have another space heater too. I'll look for it before I go to bed tonight. Now," the fat man wags his thick hand, "your notebook please."

The boy reaches for the tarnished spoon and his shackles chink in the darkness. He pierces the congealed film floating on the soup and scoops up some of the steaming broth underneath. The spoon is halfway to his mouth when the boy feels the fat man's enormous hand coiling around his wrist.

"Please," the fat man says in a tone that is at once both quiet and forceful, "the notebook."

Hunger pains twist the boy's insides. He drops the spoon sulkily and reaches under the cot, groping about the cold, un-swept stone floor until he feels the gritty cover against his fingers. The boy slides the book out and hands it over to the fat man, who immediately frees the boy's wrist.

The boy gulps the soup up greedily.

The fat man flicks through the ink-tattooed pages just as greedily.

Neither one finds satisfaction.

"These squiggles and curlicues," the fat man announces after a long, oppressive silence, "do they mean anything?"

"Yes," answers the boy.

"Really? What?"

"I dreamt of them, on a barnyard wall. They were written there in an old woman's blood."

The fat man actually moans with delight. "And?" he gasps.

The child shrugs. "They were just symbols, but in the dream I could read them. In the dream they read *'It will unfurl this All Hallows…'*"

The boy can see the fat man's teeth as he grins. They are slick with saliva and are as grey as tombstones.

V. FATE MANIFESTS, DARKLY

It is an unseasonably warm October 31st. Miss Prudence awakens in a sweat-drenched bed. Could the weather be an omen?

Miss Prudence thinks of last night's dream, and shudders.

"Really now," she says aloud, disgusted by her own susceptibility, "really, such dreams." Enough of this grim and bloody dream-stuff; there are preparations to make before tonight's Binding.

Her hands are shaky, her head light. It is going to be a long day indeed.

She makes her way down the hall to the bathroom where she washes her face. Then, downstairs for a cup of boiling water to aid in her bodily purification. She puts the kettle on the range and waits for the water to fume. 'Silver tea' was what her mother had called it whenever she'd served it to Miss Prudence as a child. Sometimes her mother also gave her communion wafers to munch on. Other times she'd serve her select herbs. Those had been happier times.

Miss Prudence shuffles into the sitting room and retrieves one of the large diaries from her bookcase. She carries it back with her into the kitchen and, after pouring her silver tea into a mug, begins to read over the details of her mother's battles with benighted powers.

Flicking through the brittle leaves, Miss Prudence wishes she had a photograph of her mother, though she knows full well that snapping a picture would have thieved her mother's soul. Nevertheless, Miss Prudence is pained by the way her mother's face is beginning to fade from her memory. She suddenly wishes she had maintained notes of the noble conquests she herself had made in the name of the Prudence family. But then, who would read them?

"All things end," sighs the old woman, closing the diary. The distant howling rouses her from her reverie. She rises and begins to prepare for the annual Binding.

VI. INTO WHOSE HANDS?

The bus barely makes it across the final state line before its radiator hose blows, shooting fluid and steam out across the dirt road. At that moment Mr. Umbra temporarily loses faith in the operation.

It is the boy who centers him.

"We can walk to the farm from here," the child explains.

"You sure?"

"Yes."

It is late afternoon. The sky is heaped with leaden clouds. The cold-warm air smells of wood-smoke, tilled earth.

"The old woman has them trapped in a barn nearby," the boy says. His certainty is comforting to Mr. Umbra. "And they're getting anxious," he adds.

The two of them stand for a moment or two, gazing into a skyline that is the color of decomposing flesh. As if on cue, they simultaneously resume walking.

"You know," says Mr. Umbra, "all the things I did I did as an act of service; to you as well as them."

"I know," replies the boy.

"It wasn't something I necessarily *wanted* to do, but strangely enough it was something I *chose* to do. It was a blind choice; deciding to intercept you and allowing your fate to flourish, but I think I made the right decision."

"Did you really dream of me?"

"Yes."

The boy smiles sweetly.

Although she'd been ailing for the entire day, Miss Prudence doesn't experience the actual attack until she spots the child and the man making their way up the road that winds snake-like between two sprawling pumpkin patches. She collapses as something powerful squeezes the tender jelly of her heart. Salt and holy water spill uselessly about her. The captives in the barn squeal with bestial delight.

This cacophony is the music that marks Miss Prudence's passage to the next world.

Mr. Umbra follows the boy partway onto the property and then halts. He is taken aback by the terrible sounds from the barn, but the boy is not; he moves with grim determination.

The wood of the barn door groans. It throbs like a splintery heart. Then it bursts like a boil, spraying wedges of ancient wood and alchemically-treated wax seals out across the desolate fields of the Prudence property. By this time dusk has fallen and the land is washed in a purple-orange glow.

"Free!" the eldritch things seem to hiss. *"Free!"* The slithering things and the scaly things and the things that are but cold fog and maddeningly distant whispers.

The boy sees them. He whimpers with joy, with awe.

Mr. Umbra sees them also and bows his head.

The shapes swim upon the swelling darkness of All Hallows. They clamor up twisted trees, hover on brimstone-tinged smoke, take flight with sprawling wings, burrow swiftly under the scorched earth.

Not even in their blackest reveries could Mr. Umbra or the child have expected the Unbinding to be so glorious.

But it was only the beginning.

"Gone," the boy says breathlessly when he at last joins his companion, "they're all just...gone."

Mr. Umbra is bent and is breathing heavily. His sweaty palms are pressed against his knees. "Yes," he gasps. "Migrating. Just for a little while. Most people aren't ready to greet them yet."

After a time the boy asks, "So that's it then?"

Mr. Umbra shakes his head.

"Not if my dreams are to be believed," he says. "They should have left some things for us in the barn," Mr. Umbra explains as he produces a small velvet pouch from the pocket of his trousers. "We need to go in and collect them."

"And then we burn it?"

"To the ground. But first we have to search, really search."

The child sprints to the barn and obediently begins inspecting every inch of its dark, reeking interior. Mr. Umbra searches also; first inside the woman's house for a flashlight (which he does not find, but does discover a small kerosene lamp which suits his purposes just as well), and then with the boy inside the great wooden fortress. By ambient lamp-glow, the two rescue sprouts of wiry hair from beddings of moldy hay. They pluck the torn leavings of claws and talons from the gouges in the barn door. They peel gelatinous scum from the summit of the loft.

Mr. Umbra then intones quietly, "So it is done. So it shall be." He tugs the drawstring on the velvet pouch.

The child accepts the lamp that is passed to him. He raises it above his head and glances at Mr. Umbra, who nods his approval. The glass casing of the lamp shatters on the barn floor. Thin eels of flame skitter across the hay, along the warped planks.

Mr. Umbra and the child exit the blazing property without comment.

VII. HALLOWED HARVEST

The soil of the tiny lot is flecked with glinting frost as the child and Mr. Umbra prepare to dig on that cold November dawn. They shovel a pocket into the soil and into this pocket they deposit the nail fragments and the wiry hair and the sludge. They cover them, pat down the soil, and mark the area with a chunk of polished hematite.

"And now," Mr. Umbra announces as the boy helps to pull him up from his squatting position, "we wait."

Wait they do; through the remainder of that smoky, leaf-rustled autumn; through the grave-cold stillness of the long, long winter; through the brief, marshy spring and the subsequent searing summer.

The boy stayed cloistered in Mr. Umbra's tiny house. In the daytime Mr. Umbra worked his simple job. Sometimes in the evenings he and the boy would share their dreams with one another or they'd play Scrabble or Mr. Umbra would read his books while the boy watched television.

The two of them waited until the world once more turned greyly dank with shadow.

October. Then and only then did the two of them return to the meadow where they'd planted the remnants.

The tree has grown with unnatural swiftness. Its trunk is large and firm, its branches thick, lengthy. The bark is white as the harvest moon or as fresh bones. It is porcelain-smooth to the touch and smells of rain and charnel house pyres.

The tree's apples grow in great ripe bunches on the boughs. In contrast to the pale limbs it sprouts from, this fruit is onyx-black. The apples shimmer darkly, reflecting the constellations of the night sky.

"Is it like your dream?" the boy asks.

Mr. Umbra finds it difficult to speak at first. "Yes," he replies, "exactly."

Methodically, the two of them collect their harvest.

"Trick-or-treat!" cry the goblins, the witches, the little giggling Father Deaths.

The boy steals peeks at the procession, standing shielded by the living room drapes.

Soon the world will be safe for him to walk freely again. Soon...

Mr. Umbra sits on the porch. A large basket rests upon his lap.

"Aw, an apple," huffs a small red devil when the treat is handed to him.

"Oh, not just any apple," replies Mr. Umbra. He rotates the black fruit slowly before the child's eyes. "This is a very special All Hallows' apple. It's magic."

"There's no such thing," rebuts little Lucifer.

"What a thing for the Father of magic to say!" Mr. Umbra laughs then leans toward the child. "Confidentially, you are absolutely correct, Mr. Scratch. There is no magic. Unfortunately I can't seem to convince any of these stupid children, so I need your help, okay?"

The child nods.

Mr. Umbra continues. "I want you to promise me that you will eat this delicious apple before you go to sleep tonight, so that when you wake up tomorrow morning you can *prove* to all your silly schoolmates that magic is a sham, that apples cannot give a child magnificent nightmares. Do we have a deal?"

The devil-child looks at him bewilderedly, but takes the apple just the same.

The other children do not seem to be as skeptical as Satan. They are all eager to sample the black fruit that can only be eaten (or so they are instructed) *"when you are alone, in the dark, and ready to slip into slumber."*

Later, as the first few snowflakes of the season begin fluttering down and the last few trick-or-treat cries begin to fade, Mr. Umbra blows out his jack-o'-lantern and steps inside. He is actually giddy. He begins to hum an improvised tune.

That night only a dozen or so children actually follow the strange fat man's instructions. But it is enough to begin the Change.

These children, some of which are daring, others merely superstitious, crunch their black apples in the sanctuary of their bedrooms, relishing the candy-sweet pulp as it melts upon their tongues.

Cozy table lamps are then switched off. Novelty skeleton-finger candles are puffed out. Heads recline onto pillows. Fresh minds open unto Nightmares.

And the open-mindedness of these Nightmares allows something *outer* to slip inside the dreamers.

The cycle begins slowly, but not unnoticeably. For how long can a parent dismiss the nightly screams of their child as he or she is ripped from sleep by unearthly images? How long can a rash of diabolic visions documented in tabloid journals and religious tracts be laughed at or discarded?

As all things slip, swiftly and inexorably, toward a new Dark Age, one whose laws are dictated by the vague and nameless forms that occupy the distant margins of the night, two figures wait to hear the heralding howl. For only then can they enter the darkness and lose themselves. Only then can they enter the darkness and be found.

THE JUMP

M. Rickert

I really don't have any Halloween memories except for that time I jumped out of the moving car. I mean, of course I have memories; the Rileys who lived across the street from us used to put a walkie-talkie (remember those?) inside the large Jack O'Lantern on their front porch, creating the illusion of a conversant pumpkin, Mrs. Deheck passed out apples, which was seriously not cool, and one year Mrs. Fischer, the elderly next-door neighbor who was my first (and for a long time) only friend, forgot the date entirely, as she weepingly explained to me later at her kitchen table, returning home to find *witch* written in chalk on her front sidewalk. "Why do they do this?" she asked as if I had any authority at all about people my own age, which I did not; they confused me as much as they tormented her, screaming as they ran through backyards waving toy guns, or walking in pairs so close their shoulders touched. I had been studying them for some time, but when Mrs. Fischer asked why my peers behaved the way they did, I had no idea.

With Halloween's approach, my six siblings and I would bring out the box of costumes that had been recycled over the years: Little Red Riding Hood's red cape—and a particular favorite of mine (I especially remember how much I liked to carry the basket) white pillow cases transformed with scissors and paint, and the orange fabric with holes strategically placed to accommodate legs and arms which, once stuffed with newspaper, became the pumpkin costume I never wore because the paper itched and was also noisy.

We trick-or-treated in the dark with our mother, and I insisted on her presence well past the age for doing so. I also suffer the humiliating memory of having her walk me to the bus stop my first week of *college* because we had recently moved to the city and I was frightened of so much.

When I was older, and well past the point for her to fear its possibility, my mother confessed she thought I would probably live with her forever—this assessment based on my timid nature and appearance. No one noticed when I stopped eating my favorite foods because I was offering them up to Jesus; people just assumed I was naturally frighteningly thin. I also wore glasses to accommodate what might have been the final nail in my unpopular coffin, my crossed eyes.

I did grow up though, and moved far from that small town bifurcated by the railroad tracks I used to stand over and vow would take me from there—all the way to California where, as a young woman I went to my friend's Halloween party. She dressed as a sexy vampire, and I, perpetually out of synch, dressed as a giant Raggedy Anne doll, driving home that night in blissful ignorance of the gas gauge so that when the car began to sputter I was confused until I realized what had happened. And there I was, on the side of the road in the dark. It was Halloween and I was frightened.

Eventually, two guys pulled over and offered to help.

The 'Corn Factory

Benjamin Kane Ethridge

The screaming kept Ruddy up all night when he ran out of pills. It was strange because he would hear the same sounds in the factory throughout the day, but he never really considered the depth of agony until that inconvenient moment before sleep hit. Then it was different. Then, he recalled each struggled shout as though played on a loop at full volume a breath away from his ears.

They weren't human sounds. He'd known that the day management moved him into the central processing area of Clanill's Candy Corn plant. That didn't mean he'd say a word. He'd been canned at the car dealership, laid off at the hardware store and passed over at the bartending gig for a big-boobed lady who didn't know the difference between gin and vodka. Begging for interviews, searching for jobs online and in the paper, it'd been a long, indecorous employment hunt. He needed this damn job. He had to will himself *not to hear* the shrieking and disregard the safety posters fluttering against the walls from the resonance.

Despite his better efforts, one day the damned sounds got the better of him and Ruddy asked the facility manager, Jim Payton, to have a listen. Of course, once his boss stood there near the wall, nothing happened.

"You feeling okay, Taber?" This from an unusually compassionate Payton; the man was an over-caffeinated prick on his best days, a trait intensifying as the calendar moved closer to Halloween.

"Yeah."

"You wouldn't be trying to leave Clanill's on medical? You've only just passed probation, guy. Don't do me like that. 'Corn factory don't need wishy-washy types."

Then it happened. The loudest, wickedest wail of the entire day. An OSHA poster popped off its thumb tack and slipped to the floor. Both men stood there, the regular mechanized sounds of the factory distant and arbitrary. With a low grunt, Payton retrieved the poster and tacked it back to the cork board. He shot a cool glance at Ruddy. "Go work," he'd said.

And nothing more.

Day in and day out, Ruddy suppressed his wonder about what lay beyond the ten foot tall freezer door. His mind just wouldn't let it go though. Not alone in his cheap studio apartment, lying in bed without a woman, no more booze in any of the bottles on the nightstand. Certainly not when the shadows poured over everything and his life became one big tired sigh before passing out on pain killers.

Then he couldn't ignore it any longer. Late into the afternoon, after the screaming had his earplugs humming inside his ears, the freezer's padlock broke with a particularly violent, yet unseen, impact. The screaming thing *wanted* him to come inside, and though he needed to see what was there, he wasn't a fool. He was petrified. Opening the freezer wasn't a good idea. Not at all. But he believed the thing behind the door needed help, and he was the only person who could provide it.

Toeing the padlock out of the way, Ruddy took the freezer's long handle. He detected no refrigeration. Opening the door wider revealed an unlit corridor. There was nothing remarkable about it—all the factory hallways looked identical in fact. Ruddy stepped inside, stealing a glance back to the empty C-Pro area before continuing on. At the end of the hallway, a room opened to a much larger space, like an aircraft hangar. Something metallic stretched there like a lattice or web.

Chains. They were chains.

Several lifted and something larger came into view. A galaxy of bloody eyes gleamed in the wild darkness—and then there was a scream, this one from the same source of others before it, but pitched with a desperate, tormented hope.

Jessica, now that you are finally here, please help me.

The scream sent Ruddy back. He crashed into someone.

Payton gripped him by the elbows, forced him around and shoved Ruddy out of the hallway. He tried to turn around but was shoved again, this time harder.

"Goddamn you Taber. I told you." Payton's bullish face showed not the angry tone of his voice, but instead bloodless fear. "Your last check will be in the mail. Keep quiet and I won't press charges about your intoxication at this job site."

"What? But I'm not—"

"Get the hell out," Payton said and slammed the freezer shut.

His last paycheck from the factory was rather large. Ruddy hadn't figured out the numbers, but it was probably around two years' worth in wages.

Hush money?

Who would he tell though? What he'd seen... what he thought he'd seen, couldn't be described in a serious way. Combine that with the amount of medication and alcohol flowing through his system on a given day, any person with an IQ higher than a wet piece of cardboard would be calling bullshit.

Nope. Being branded a lunatic was the last thing his miserable existence needed.

He shook the last two Oxy into his palm and drank them with some Sprite. Taking another look at that check, he pulled his phone to dial Janice. She gave him shit, questioned the amount of money he'd send, and then did the normal passive aggressive interrogation about which women he was currently sleeping with. When Ruddy asked to speak to Junior, she told him he was with friends, just like every time he called now. He'd appreciate Junior returning his calls once in a while and told her so. She responded that two-faced bastards don't always get what they're *fucking entitled* to.

All in all, the conversation went exactly how he imagined.

Ruddy couldn't feel the effects of the last two pills and with a fresh refill renewal from his doctor hook-up, a trip to the Rite Aid was well in order. He was too tired to walk that far though. He just needed a nap to clear away the junk in his mind.

Closing his eyes, he tried to recall the last few years. None of the women had faces. None of the highs were fond recollections. All he could remember was Janice's uncharacteristic downpour of curses the night everything came out, her voice building to the *get out of our lives, scum.* As he walked out the house, she shattered their wedding portrait with a scream. She'd always claimed to be a forgiving Christian woman, but the sound that came from her indicated nothing of the sort. Janice's scream had been wrought of hatred and expulsion, but that chained thing in the factory called out with longing and inclusion. Ruddy almost could decipher the words therein.

Help me! Take me from this before it's too late. Like nobody before, I will accept and forever understand the real you.

The week before Halloween, each night Ruddy visited the gate outside the loading docks. He listened for the creature but became fascinated with a group of strangers who came at nightfall. A procession of black limos showed in the receiving area without fail. Men and women in dark business attire would stand around chatting and smoking cigarettes in the suspiciously gentle Californian autumn. A few feet from the chain link fence, behind a row of sycamore trees, Ruddy would watch like a curious nocturnal scavenger, careful not to loudly crunch all the brittle leaves on the ground.

Some of the suits would venture into the plant, while others stood around like guards. Around 9PM, trucks would arrive and dockworkers would load pallets of candy into their trailers. At this time, most of the suits departed in their limos. Thereafter, Ruddy could hear the creature's faint screaming. Though the factory walls muffled it, his ears immediately recognized the oscillations. Most passersby would mistake it for some noisy industrial byproduct, but Ruddy knew better.

He popped open his pill bottle. Took six this time instead of five. His Sierra Mist was flat from all the time out there. He wasn't even feeling high. Soon he'd have to give them up or he might check-out in a hotel room like one of those ODing actors.

Well, they'd actually be missed. Ruddy, not so much.

He slipped out his cell phone from his jacket and went to his voice mail. In these times of absolute solitude, his ritual was listening to Junior's last message.

Hey dad…got your text, you know my feelings. I…I don't know what else I can say. I don't know. I'll call back later. We can talk some more. Bye. Love ya, ok?

But whatever love had been inside that original message no longer existed for the teenager. Perhaps Junior woke up the next day thinking, *wait, screw that guy. He's not the person I thought he was. I hate him for what he did to my mom and me.* Who could say for sure? The kid never spoke to him anymore.

Still, the hopefulness in the message was music to Ruddy's ears. It made it seem possible that Junior would someday come back around.

He listened to the recording again.

It was nearly finished playing when a gloved hand clamped around his mouth.

"Come with us, Mr. Taber," said a man. "Quietly now. *Very* quietly."

They put him in a van that smelled musty and alien. There was a mélange of disturbing odors colliding with a formaldehyde smell, which Ruddy could only assume came from the various jars of dark jellies and aquatic-looking animal specimens shelved between surveillance equipment.

"What's this about?" he asked.

The two officials looked like FBI or CIA. A bald black man with vitiligo spots down the side of his face. He acted strong but had vulnerable eyes that suggested the spots might bother him more than he let on. Nevertheless, he seemed less bitter than the tall blond woman with the crew cut. She had contempt in her eyes for Ruddy and maybe even her partner, too, or at least it seemed that way.

"Am I under arrest for something?"

The woman stopped mid-whisper and dropped the file folder against her long leg with a disgusted sigh. Her partner approached Ruddy with his dark hand outstretched. "Rudson Taber, I'm agent Barnes," he thumbed over his shoulder, "that's agent Hughes. Sorry we had to meet like this, but you were in plain sight."

Ruddy nervously chuckled. "Of the factory execs? So what?"

"They aren't executives," said Hughes. She dropped down next to Ruddy. Her body was heavily drenched with lilac perfume, which was familiar and not totally unpleasant, but her nearness was.

"Okay then, so who—?"

"Did you like that check you received?" she asked.

"What check?"

"Don't be silly, sir." Barnes lifted his slacks as he sat on the bench seat across from them.

"I got a severance check. That's my business though."

The two agents exchanged glances.

"That wasn't from the factory," Barnes explained. "That was a check cut from our office. An advance. You should have looked closer at who wrote the check, Mr. Taber. The US of A paid you that amount."

"Federal government doesn't use Quickbooks," Ruddy quipped.

Barnes's mouth twisted before he said, "Well, not the visible agencies anyway."

Ruddy checked the woman next to him. She loomed over him, as though peeking into his soul. He edged away but the space was cramped.

"We know you saw *it*," she said. "We know it talks to you. Why do you think that is?"

Ruddy swallowed a bad taste. In some sense he felt talking about the beast a betrayal; it didn't seem right to break a trusted bond, despite having no certainty that's what it was. He decided the only way to learn more was to share.

"It doesn't want to live anymore. Look, why…why is it in there?"

Hughes looked at her partner with a *should we go on?* look. Barnes pressed his lips together thoughtfully and sniffed. She took this as a cue and said, "The beast is part of the factory's process, of course."

Ruddy got the idea these people only knew part of the story. "Really, agents. No offense, but I'm well acquainted with the factory. It's cornstarch modeling, simple as that. Nothing special or weird about it."

"The high fructose corn syrup—do you know where it originates?" Hughes asked.

Ruddy thought about that. He'd always assumed a vendor delivered the totes like every other ingredient or chemical in the plant, but he'd never actually seen a corn syrup delivery truck, not that that meant anything; he had only been day shift.

"How about health inspections? Ever seen the FDA?"

Ruddy slowly shrugged.

"Rather odd, that. Ya think?" asked Hughes. Before he could answer, she added, "We need to show you something, Mr. Taber."

Barnes stood and put out his finger to a DVD player under a small screen TV. "It's queued, right?" he asked, not turning around.

"Yep," answered Hughes.

The screen went from the generic DVD menu to a grainy silent movie. A woman in a thick hospital gown sat on a bed surrounded by doctors. Her face was angelic, well meaning, the speed of the old film making her nod all too agreeably. She held a roughly two-year-old girl on her lap.

TITLE CARD: "Patient 9 enjoys three days without adverse effects, suggesting success with the new glucose solution."

The next shot showed an outstretched palm with several candy corn resting there. Another hand came into view with other candy corn, which looked more crumbly. A razor cut through the candy to demonstrate the consistency.

TITLE CARD: "New batch is denser, which enhances the salability of the product."

The following shot showed a room heaped in the doctors' corpses. The woman stood in the center of the death, the toddler draped over her shoulder. Dark fluid, perhaps blood, saturated her hospital gown. The woman flashed the camera another well-meaning smile before swaying back and forth, the child's arms waving flaccidly as she moved. A pit hollowed Ruddy's stomach until he saw the toddler pat the woman's cheek, like to tell a pet *well done,* and then that pit filled with ice. The woman bowed, letting the child down, the film skipped forward, and the little girl ambled from the shot.

A close-up showed the woman shove an overflowing handful of candy corn in her mouth, so much it spilled out the sides. Her eyes darted around, empty, and light-years from warmth.

TITLE CARD: "Patient 9 says, 'I've got clocks in me!'"

With a low grunt, Agent Barnes pressed stop.

Disquiet washed over Ruddy. "What *was* all that?"

"Taken in 1865," Hughes explained. "Despite obvious timeline problems with the invention of film and candy corn itself, everything in this account has been verified. It was a hospital in Philadelphia. Patient 9 we ID'd as Elizabeth Baring. She was found dead in the Schuylkill River along with the bodies of three food chemists and—"

"The little girl?"

"Never found," said Hughes. "The organization, or *cult* if you will, used Renniger's Wunderle Candy of Philadelphia as a front for their business. The candy's formula was finally perfected in the 1880s and distribution began. They were able to sell it without psychotic incident."

"You mean the candy made that woman go psycho?" asked Ruddy.

"The sweetening additive, yes."

"As truly diabolical as that sounds, Agents, it would seem that people have safely been eating this stuff for over one hundred years now, without going nuts, so thanks for the arcane history lesson but—"

"Don't blink away what you saw," Hughes warned. "You know the thing in the factory isn't natural. You were paid, so listen, damn it. We've worked at this too long for your flip ass."

With a disparaging sigh, Ruddy laced his hands together in his lap.

"From our research, these reactions, we believe, lie dormant. The manufacturer will let off these bombs on a given October 31st. Could be this Halloween, or next. We cannot confirm, but in the last couple years the company has increased global distribution one hundred fold, including products molded for other holidays. They're gearing up. The time is ticking away to the moment activation occurs."

"I've got clocks in me." Ruddy let out a dry chuckle. "I'll get all your money back, somehow, but I'm not going back into the 'corn factory."

"We know you want to help the thing in there. That's why you come out here every night."

"I don't know the reason behind half the stupid things I do, but I know liars when I see them. The beast isn't reaching out to me and both of you know it."

They stared at him with the same routed expression.

"I didn't know until I saw the video, but I recognized that little girl. I've heard her described in my dreams. The thing in the factory is calling for her, not me. Jessica, right? Isn't it? And you two smug assholes know all too well. Don't you? What aren't you telling me?"

Hughes scrubbed at her forehead before giving a yielding shrug. "The little girl was your great, great grandmother, Jessica Billings."

"Right."

Barnes cleared his throat before standing. "The thing is calling out to her closest relative, and that would be you Mr. Taber."

Hughes stood, joining him. "You *have* to go in there, with us, to-night. You have to help stop production."

"Bull."

Hughes snatched his wrist and her hazel eyes hardened. "You're the only one here who can. So you're going in there."

They left Ruddy in the van for forty minutes to digest everything. Just witnessing the truth had brought back the screams to his mind, those insistent babbling sounds that felt more like emotional notes from a mythical musical instrument than actual words, but this time he translated everything in his memory. The torment reminded him of how he imagined Janice and Junior felt after they discovered the man he really was. The ache to return to a better possible reality, the betrayal of a world standing on its head, and the pain, despair and poisonous strands joining them together.

End me, had said the thing in the 'corn factory.

End me. End me. Endme. Endme.

Before they find out what the candy really does.

That it will never affect your blood. Your family line, Jessica.

Ruddy recalled the little girl in the old film, stubborn resolve in her eyes, but false sweetness stitched into her face with a craftsman's hand.

End me.

End me, before the clocks stop ticking… before everybody sees… before everybody becomes…

The van door opened with a shuddering jerk and Ruddy startled. Agent Hughes stood outside, her smile a wet white smear in the darkness. "Jumpy? I guess you believe now, huh?" She swung her head for him to move.

"Kind of a coincidence," he said, stepping out onto the unseen gravel.

"How's that?"

"I end up working at a factory with a link to my family."

"Not much of a coincidence I'm afraid." Hughes carefully slid the door shut before turning to him, grinning impishly. "You still don't recognize me, do you? I'm not the hard-ass you take me for, though I play one well, and I guess I did have more makeup and longer hair when you last saw me." She absently touched her crew-cut. When she could see he remained clueless, her shoulders dropped. "We screwed for an entire weekend at the Happy Moon lodge. We met at Bahama Mamas at the golfing video game—we went there, got kicked out twice?"

Ruddy faked an expression of recall, but still didn't remember anything about Hughes from before this night. Not that all the booze and painkillers could have helped his ignorance any.

She let out a rough sigh. "You were plowed most of the time, but you enjoyed my company. I told you about the factory job. Tried to beat it into your head. Even tucked a flyer in your knapsack. Guess it worked— might not remember nailing me, but you applied to the factory a couple days later." Hughes moved closer to him. "I was prettier with longer hair. You touched it…a lot."

"Sure," Ruddy replied with a dry swallow.

"After Barnes and I put on the masks in a trial run, we discovered after removal they take your hair off at the root."

"Masks?"

"These, Mr. Taber," said Barnes, rounding the van with something shadowy in his hands. Hughes' demeanor changed with her partner's arrival and she backed away from Ruddy. If Barnes detected anything scandalous he didn't show it. "'Course, I didn't have much hair to lose in the first place." He chuckled. "The factory won't let us in unless they believe we're one of them."

"And they're stupid enough to fall for a damn mask?" Ruddy folded his arms. It was getting colder outside and he needed Oxy.

"These aren't made of rubber," said Barnes. "Here, take a look."

Ruddy ran his thumbs over the mask. Thin and sandpaper rough, it felt more like a fibrous table trivet than something you put on your face.

"Look through it," said Hughes.

Ruddy did, slowly. The mask had no eyeholes and from what he could tell in the scarce light, the scaly surface was blue and translucent.

"I don't get—"

The ends of the material snapped open. Ruddy let go but the mask *leapt* for his face—attached and dissolved into his skin. He twisted around, trying to fix on something tangible, except that the world had become a racing azure star-field. The foulness of saltwater and raw chicken drowned his sinuses. Ruddy gasped, the motion unhinging his jaw, which then re-hinged, the cheekbones expanding. He grasped his face and found it wasn't his face anymore. Not remotely.

"Don't fight it," Hughes said in the outer darkness.

He could hardly hear her over his thunderous heartbeat and gasping breaths. His fingers explored the new face growing over his own. He pried his eyes open to a burning meadow of exaggerated color—too bright and lively for the scarcity of light outside. He staggered to the van and propped himself there, peering into the reflection in the passenger window.

"What in God's name did you do?"

"That would be a tree goblin. In their native world they detach from branches and drift down like leaves, often to attach to a host. Our R&D had success breeding some with no neurological connection. You will still be in control of your body." Barnes held up a zippo lighter. "And stick a flame under its chin for a couple minutes and the whole thing will release. Your hair goes with it, but there's no lasting pain involved."

"You, you fucking people..." Ruddy seethed.

"Just settle down Taber."

Ruddy studied the abomination staring back at him: hooked nose forked with green veins, drooping folds of orange speckled pale skin, bulging black eyes like molasses wells, and a mouth of eager devil teeth. He could sense his own face grimacing behind the organic mask, but the monster grimaced with him. Ruddy closed his eyes—both pairs. Deranged thoughts and dreams flexed in his mind. When he finally turned around, two goblins in suits stood before him. With much less spectacle, Barnes and Hughes had fitted their "masks" on as well. Each shared the same dirty- looking pigment, but the facial features were decidedly distinct; Barnes's features were more angular and menacing, while Hughes had a wilder look with a head feathered in dark purple hair.

"It'll be Halloween in three hours," said the Barnes-goblin. "It's past time we go inside."

Hughes approached, shadows slinking off the wrinkled crevices of her parasitic veneer. "Are you ready, lover?"

Ruddy pressed his hands together to stop their shaking. "Am I ready?" He moved both sets of his eyes down the hill to the factory. "I guess that doesn't really matter now, does it?"

"No," the agents replied.

Ruddy stood just outside the southeast loading dock with his two hideous companions. All of the black suits had retired inside the building and the parking lot was frozen with unnatural calmness. Hughes knocked on the fire exit. Speckled like her goblin face, her hand was longer, with china white claws protruding from nail beds of torn pink meat. Ruddy could tell other parts of his body had also changed with the parasite's attachment, but he didn't have the guts to explore himself.

The door opened halfway. Ruddy gasped when he saw his ex-boss, Jim Payton, dressed in nothing more than a bloodstained sheet. He roboted back and forth, sheet swaying, gaze falling on each of them with anxious appraisal. His cheeks jiggled in an unhealthy, watery motion, a terrain of over-scavenged resources.

"We are ill," he whispered. His tooth sunk into his bottom lip where blood formed.

Hughes straightened and replied, "Ill, we are."

Payton lifted his arm under the sheet, gesturing to the C-Pro area ramp.

Barnes lowered his head in some customary self-admonishment. "Apologies, but we aren't here to package the product. This is about our Beijing interest."

Payton's eyes narrowed and his head canted. "You've been to the 'corn factory before? Know the way?"

"Yes," Barnes said.

Ruddy couldn't look at Payton and instead gaped down at the awful claws that were once his hands.

"Is that one ok?" Payton pointed at Ruddy.

Hughes slipped her arm underneath Ruddy's. "He's completely fine, he only just crossed over yesterday."

For a moment Payton just stood there, staring, and then he waved them on. "Get in, get in," and shut the fire exit, checking it locked.

Payton went to his podium near logistics. Black and orange candles lined the top of it instead of the usual stacks of manifests. Hughes, Barnes and Ruddy quickly descended the ramp and took a left at the railed corridor. The two agents moved as though they knew the factory better than he did. Perhaps that was really the case, because after maneuvering three hallways, Ruddy had no idea where they were. He thought he knew the building well and yet an unfamiliar area opened up, bigger than the main production line by five times.

Hundreds of people in blood-decorated sheets wandered here and unlike Payton, most of their heads were shrouded at the neck with charred cords, making them resemble cheap murder ghosts. Ruddy felt sick looking at them and averted his eyes. Overhead, rather than dull gray paint, the plumbing and electrical conduit in these rafters wound in a black and orange labyrinth. He squinted to the staggering heights above and made out what seemed to be people in black capes, hanging upside down. They were very still and might have been decorations. He hoped that's what they were.

Hughes ushered them through a busy area amongst bizarre machinery—waxy yellow bulbs, spinning iron skulls with clattering diamond teeth, rubber accordion bladders perspiring blood with every contraction—all this on a floor where old women in threadbare robes swept ghastly biological debris off the floor. On their charcoal lips they murmured chants as they worked. Conical black hats rested low on their heads, bent into a blade-sharp point and their ashen hair wound around the hats. Under Neanderthal brows, their tar-blasted eyes shared the same mean spirit.

"Keep walking," Hughes said with an urgency that snapped Ruddy back from his repulsion. "Just up there to the conference room."

He saw where she meant them to head, up a wrought-iron scaffold to an unimpressive office trailer.

A heavy shadow dropped before them and stretched into the shape of a bat-like creature. Ruddy choked on the gasp in his throat. The creature grew taller and unfurled its wings, ready to embrace him. The face wasn't humanoid at all, more of a hybrid bat and insect species. Instead of a mouth and teeth it had an onyx proboscis that reached to its chest. Two perfect orbs of scarlet under a thin smoky membrane, its eyes entreated him to make a move.

Ruddy sensed the government agents shift. He wasn't certain what they'd do, but this thing obviously had no intention of letting them interfere. The proboscis inched forward with frightening authority. The wings bent around him, bringing him stumbling closer.

"*Alain-Xi!*"

Payton was suddenly there. His sheet was askew, revealing part of his torso, a site of open cuts and black-yellow bruises. The bat creature didn't unlock its bloody stare from Ruddy but it halted its folding wings.

"They're here for the Asian market listings and the Valentine corn, what was discussed last fall. Let them pass, old friend. Ill, we are."

A warm, brackish gust blew out with an answer and made Ruddy's goblin face tingle and itch. He resisted the urge to scratch his crawling skin beneath and stood there, trying to control his quivering legs. The bat's wings expanded to insane lengths. Had Payton's message fallen on deaf ears? Ruddy nearly screamed but with one powerful flap, followed by two even more fierce, the bat thing returned to the pipes above.

Hughes seized the next moment and pushed Ruddy up the scaffold. Barnes was in front of them, carefully opening a door just behind the trailer.

"Not locked?" asked Hughes.

"No, we finally caught some luck." Barnes fully pushed open the door to a familiar darkness. Ruddy had seen such darkness when he'd ventured into the freezer before. He could hear the beast calling to his ancestors, to Jessica, to him. *End me. Stop the clocks. End it.*

"Nearly there," Hughes whispered. "It's just inside."

"Those other checks go to my son only," Ruddy told them. "To Junior. Not to my wife, understand?"

Hughes paused, her expression unreadable under the goblin skin.

"I know what this could mean if something goes wrong. I'm not stupid. You'll make sure my son is taken care of. Promise?"

"Of course I promise," she said.

Barnes looked over his shoulder with anxious beast eyes. "I promise, too."

Ruddy stepped into the darkness. "Let's end this then."

Those shining eyes in the freezer hadn't been eyes at all. Ruddy held his breath at the immense network of shifting organs. They were tethered by chains, tendons and colossal blood vessels engorged with fluids of an orange, yellow, and white color. The vessels originated from what resembled the largest ear of red corn in the world—but Ruddy knew this creature in ways he couldn't explain, and this corn-like organ, he knew, was the brain-heart. This was where every scream, wail, plea, and hushed oath had been derived.

And yet now the creature was completely silent. It had been left in such awe with Ruddy's arrival, it took his presence like a gaped-mouth man finding freedom after a penitentiary lifetime.

Hughes handed Ruddy a butane torch. "Burn a hole in all three vessels. You will need to pull out the clot that forms. You're the only person here who can touch the plasmas. With the clot removed, it will empty the vessels and the creature will bleed out. Prepare though, its death might take a toll on your body."

As if he even had to ask, Ruddy voiced a question to confirm his weird intuition, "What are these different blood types?"

"Based from a series of books called the Tomes of Eternal Harvest, the orange is pure *love*, the yellow is pure *hate*—"

"And the white is *regret*," Ruddy finished.

The beast's chains flexed. Ruddy mentally reassured it, but the beast remained anxious.

Barnes's wispy eyebrows lifted on his goblin brow. "You've read the tomes too?"

"No. This beast is tied to my heart. I live its nightmares. I accept my tie to it now. I tried to screw, drink, and drug it out of me, but this is part of my soul. Always has been." Ruddy closed his eyes behind his goblin eyes and meditated on that statement before looking back at Barnes. "You're wrong about what the candy does, but I'll do what needs to be done here."

Both monsters held quizzical expressions that faded into relief as Ruddy approached a low hanging vessel filled with orange.

End this.

I will.

Ruddy pulled the torch's trigger and blue fire hissed from the end. He held the flame to the vessel's transparent tissue. The flesh sizzled and broke away. A deeper orange color immediately collected there. No time to waste, he shoved his arm inside the wound. He could feel the blood attacking but it failed to harm him. His hand caught a gloppy clot and he tugged it through the hole. Orange blood blasted onto the concrete floor. Hughes and Barnes moved to another catwalk to avoid contact.

I love you, thought the corn creature.

Yes.

You are not afraid as your kin was.

I'm not.

Ruddy repeated the process with the yellow blood, with the same results.

"How do you feel?" asked Hughes.

"Fine," Ruddy replied, feeling comfortable with the lie.

"Well go on and finish! You're saving the fuckin' world here!"

Ruddy's soul sagged as he approached the vein of the glowing white blood. He held out the torch and wrapped his finger around the trigger.

Thank you my friend. Thank you.

I'm sorry. Ruddy's head dipped. *So sorry.*

No… please! PLEASE! CONTINUE!

His arm fell to his side. He left the white vessel intact and headed up the catwalk.

Barnes thundered down the grated floor after him. "Hey! You're not done. Get your ass back over there. We had a deal. You're nearly there!"

Ruddy caught Barnes by the throat and the man's monstrous eyes widened.

"Taber, what are you doing?" shouted Hughes.

"You think everybody turns crazy on the Last Halloween? That isn't what happens. It's so much better than that!"

Hughes ran to intercept him, but Ruddy shoved Barnes into her. They collided and dropped with a sickening impact. Ruddy jumped over them and dashed up the ramp. The organs in their cages quivered in revolt. He could almost imagine the arms and legs the creature wished it possessed so it could pummel him for his betrayal.

The two agents gained with terrifying speed. Ruddy fell behind a corner and waited. When they passed he threw himself into them.

He stabbed the lit torch under someone's chin.

Hughes.

All at once, the tree goblin parasite shifted violently left and right, up and down, detaching from her face. Barnes thrust him to the wall, pinning his arm, but the agent's misshapen shoulders buckled and Ruddy fell away to fire the torch into the man's pointed ear.

Wet sounds of borrowed flesh plopping down followed him down the corridor along with angry shouts of disgust. Ruddy made it back to the main hall. Fortunately, the bloody sheets and the witches continued their work, oblivious to the disruption within the creature's chamber. He calmly walked through the processing area as though he still worked in the 'corn factory. By the time he reached the loading docks he heard cries of panic. He turned to look. Twenty or more bat people had descended and made a disturbing crowd around Hughes and Barnes. The agents, frantic and baby-bald, fought a losing battle in the middle of a blood feast orgy. Even though they no longer possessed grotesque goblin features, their faces were the most disturbing thing Ruddy had ever seen in his entire life.

Junior was late, but that wasn't necessarily a bad thing. It had taken Ruddy a while to get used to his real face again and he also needed some emotional unraveling time. With his cheeks and neck raw and red, every last hair gone from his head, he'd occupied himself with cleaning up the remnants of goblin flesh from his car. He'd done a decent job but an aquatic reek lingered in the air as a reminder of the transformation.

The rest of the time he waited for his son he'd munched mindlessly on candy corn. He still had a case in the trunk from when he'd worked at the factory—the intention had been to give it to Trick-or-Treaters. Now he wanted nothing more than to just gorge himself with the stuff, loading his cheeks like some miserly chipmunk. He enjoyed eating the candy now probably more than drinking, drugs or women—just the thought of his genetic fortune got him higher than anything else ever would again.

Junior's orange Honda Civic pulled in and the headlights were killed immediately. He got out of his car, dressed in what looked like a butler costume. There was fake blood splashed on his hands and face. His kid loved murder mysteries, and had once floated the idea of dressing as a butler. Ruddy's eyes stung at the thought of not being there when Junior first tried on the costume.

Ruddy pulled on his Dodgers hat over his naked skull and grabbed a bag of candy corn. He wasn't even out of the car and Junior was already storming over. "Dad! Why are you *here*?"

"Calm down. I needed to tell you something."

"I don't want to—"

"Just listen," blurted Ruddy. Junior took a surprised step back. "Look, I'll be quick. Promise. Really."

"Say it and go."

"Someday you will have a choice, son. The voice in your head, the one that keeps you up sometimes at night, it comes from a factory."

"Jesus! I'm getting mom." Junior turned away.

"It wants you to kill it—I know you've heard this voice. Don't play like you haven't."

Junior froze a step away.

"Everybody has clocks in them. Everybody who tries these." Ruddy leaned forward and pressed the bag of candy into his son's hand. Junior held it without expression. "Well, I should say, everybody, that is, except you and me, and one day, *your children*. The last Halloween hasn't come yet but when it does, the clocks will all strike and these little time-bombs will go off."

Junior glanced at his father. "You sound crazy. You're high, aren't you?"

"You can choose to end it for everybody, save people from themselves. I had my chance tonight, but I didn't take it. You see, the bombs activate something inside a person that makes them see himself, herself, for who they really are, and then they *become* that person. They have no choice. They cannot hide. All of their masks come off. Someone's true nature is on display for the whole world…but we have the greatest gift of all."

Junior clenched the bag and shook his head. "So what's that?"

"We never have to face ourselves, son. We can keep our masks on forever and the entire world's lies will be on display. We will be the only liars left alive, accountable to nobody, the only secret-holders in the masses. Wouldn't that be great? Wouldn't that just, just…be bliss? One day, when you're confronted with this, remember what I told you tonight. If you kill that creature in the factory, you're giving away a gift beyond all other gifts, perhaps better than the gift of life itself. So please think about it. Take care of yourself, and do the right thing for our family."

"You done?" Junior asked, his eyes haunted.

"Yes, I'm going."

Junior stood there on the moonlit sidewalk as he returned to his car.

That felt right enough, and Ruddy thought he might somewhat be at peace now. He didn't know where he would be going next, what or who he would find when he got there, but he knew the drive would be extraordinarily long.

And the candy, sweet.

On a Dark October

Joe R. Lansdale

For Dave Silva

The October night was dark and cool. The rain was thick. The moon was hidden behind dark clouds that occasionally flashed with lightning, and the sky rumbled as if it were a big belly that was hungry and needed filling.

A white Chrysler New Yorker came down the street and pulled up next to the curb. The driver killed the engine and the lights, turned to look at the building that sat on the block, an ugly tin thing with a weak light bulb shielded by a tin-hat shade over a fading sign that read BOB'S

GARAGE. For a moment the driver sat unmoving, then he reached over, picked up the newspaper-wrapped package on the seat and put it in his lap. He opened it slowly. Inside was a shiny, oily, black-handled, ball peen hammer.

He lifted the hammer, touched the head of it to his free palm. It left a small smudge of grease there. He closed his hand, opened it, rubbed his fingers together. It felt just like…but he didn't want to think of that. It would all happen soon enough.

He put the hammer back in the papers, rewrapped it, wiped his fingers on the outside of the package. He pulled a raincoat from the back seat and put it across his lap. Then, with hands resting idly on the wheel, he sat silently.

A late model blue Ford pulled in front of him, left a space at the garage's drive, and parked. No one got out. The man in the Chrysler did not move.

Five minutes passed and another car, a late model Chevy, parked directly behind the Chrysler. Shortly thereafter three more cars arrived, all of them were late models. None of them blocked the drive. No one got out.

Another five minutes skulked by before a white van with MERTZ'S MEATS AND BUTCHER SHOP written on the side pulled around the Chrysler, then backed up the drive, almost to the garage door. A man wearing a hooded raincoat and carrying a package got out of the van, walked to the back and opened it.

The blue Ford's door opened, and a man dressed similarly, carrying a package under his arm, got out and went up the driveway. The two men nodded at one another. The man who had gotten out of the Ford unlocked the garage and slid the door back.

Car doors opened. Men dressed in raincoats, carrying packages, got out and walked to the back of the van. A couple of them had flashlights and they flashed them in the back of the vehicle, gave the others a good view of what was there—a burlap wrapped, rope-bound bundle that wiggled and groaned.

The man who had been driving the van said, "Get it out."

Two of the men handed their packages to their comrades and climbed inside, picked up the squirming bundle, carried it into the garage. The others followed. The man from the Ford closed the door.

Except for the beams of the two flashlights, they stood close together in the darkness, like strands of flesh that had suddenly been pulled into a knot. The two with the bundle broke away from the others, and with their comrades directing their path with the beams of their flashlights, they carried the bundle to the grease rack and placed it between two wheel ramps. When that was finished, the two who had carried the bundle returned to join the others, to reform that tight knot of flesh.

Outside the rain was pounding the roof like tossed lug bolts. Lightning danced through the half-dozen small, barred windows. Wind shook the tin garage with a sound like a rattlesnake tail quivering for the strike, then passed on.

No one spoke for a while. They just looked at the bundle. The bundle thrashed about and the moaning from it was louder than ever.

"All right," the man from the van said.

They removed their clothes, hung them on pegs on the wall, pulled their raincoats on.

The man who had been driving the blue Ford—after looking carefully into the darkness—went to the grease rack. There was a paper bag on one of the ramps. Earlier in the day he had placed it there himself. He opened it and took out a handful of candles and a book of matches. Using a match to guide him, he placed the candles down the length of the ramps, lighting them as he went. When he was finished, the garage glowed with a soft amber light. Except for the rear of the building. It was dark there.

The man with the candles stopped suddenly, a match flame wavering between his fingertips. The hackles on the back of his neck stood up. He could hear movement from the dark part of the garage. He shook the match out quickly and joined the others. Together, the group unwrapped their packages and gripped the contents firmly in their hands—hammers, brake-over handles, crowbars, heavy wrenches. Then all of them stood looking toward the back of the garage, where something heavy and sluggish moved.

The sound of the garage clock—a huge thing with DRINK COCA-COLA emblazoned on its face—was like the ticking of a time bomb. It was one minute to midnight.

Beneath the clock, visible from time to time when the glow of the candles was whipped that way by the draft, was a calendar. It read OC-TOBER and had a picture of a smiling boy wearing overalls, standing amidst a field of pumpkins. The 31st was circled in red.

Eyes drifted to the bundle between the ramps now. It had stopped squirming. The sound it was making was not quite a moan. The man from the van nodded at one of the men, the one who had driven the Chrysler. The Chrysler man went to the bundle and worked the ropes loose, folded back the burlap. A frightened black youth, bound by leather straps and gagged with a sock and a bandana, looked up at him wide-eyed. The man from the Chrysler avoided looking back. The youth started squirming, grunting, and thrashing. Blood beaded around his wrists where the leather was tied, boiled out from around the loop fastened to his neck; when he kicked, it boiled faster because the strand had been drawn around his neck, behind his back and tied off at his ankles.

There came a sound from the rear of the garage again, louder than before. It was followed by a sudden sigh that might have been the wind working its way between the rafters.

The van driver stepped forward, spoke loudly to the back of the garage. "We got something for you, hear me? Just like always we're doing our part. You do yours. I guess that's all I got to say. Things will be the same come next October. In your name, I reckon."

For a moment—just a moment—there was a glimmer of a shape when the candles caught a draft and wafted their bright heads in that direction. The man from the van stepped back quickly. "In your name," he repeated. He turned to the men. "Like always, now. Don't get the head until the very end. Make it last."

The faces of the men took on an expression of grimness, as if they were all playing a part in a theatric production and had been told to look that way. They hoisted their tools and moved toward the youth.

What they did took a long time.

When they finished, the thing that had been the young black man looked like a gigantic hunk of raw liver that had been chewed up and spat out. The raincoats of the men were covered in a spray of blood and brains. They were panting.

"Okay," said the man from the van.

They took off their raincoats, tossed them in a metal bin near the grease rack, wiped the blood from their hands, faces, ankles and feet with shop rags, tossed those in the bin and put on their clothes.

The van driver yelled to the back of the garage. "All yours. Keep the years good, huh?"

They went out of there and the man from the Ford locked the garage door. Tomorrow he would come to work as always. There would be no corpse to worry about, and a quick dose of gasoline and a match would take care of the contents in the bin. Rain ran down his back and made him shiver.

Each of the men went out to their cars without speaking. Tonight they would all go home to their young, attractive wives and tomorrow they would all go to their prosperous businesses and they would not think of this night again. Until next October.

They drove away. Lightning flashed. The wind howled. The rain beat the garage like a cat-o'-nine-tails. And inside there were loud sucking sounds punctuated by grunts of joy.

THE REAL DARKBORN

Matthew Costello

All right, a few caveats and explanations before you begin reading this.

First, and most importantly, everything you are about to read is true. Everything I will write about happened. You have my word on that.

At the same time, when I have finished this brief, um, memoir, I will tell you about the fiction the event gave birth to and—as Coleridge wrote in his epic poem—you, too, will be sadder and wiser.

Well—maybe not that sad. Or wise. Let's just say...informed? Entertained?

Good—so to begin.

This did not occur on Halloween. It *did* occur during Halloween week.

When I was in high school—for this is a high school tale—Halloween could easily occur on a Monday. Tuesday, dull school nights heavily laden with the workload the good Jesuit fathers doled out to us Brooklyn Prep kids preparing us for the future. To be:

Captains of Industry!

Masters of the World!

Legendary Football Coaches!

And...or...

Abject failures. Kids who would face both personal demons and those demons the world can arbitrarily summon and send without a word of warning of such things when we are growing up.

And yes, I do realize I am asking for some reading between the lines here. But—isn't that what those spaces are for?

So, it was that week. I had spent the summer in France studying French in Grenoble. I had been well under 18, and enjoying the wine, the food, the world-view, which I strongly recommend to any and all.

Then, back to Brooklyn, to reality.

And somehow, among my group of friends the four...or five of us (not sure, you see, and I am trying to stick to the truth here), we had this *idea*.

Maybe—knowing me, my interests—*I* had this idea.

Sounds absurd. Now. But here it was the idea. That we 16-year-old boys, men to be, would attempt to put the tenets of our ancient and mystical Catholic faith to the test.

In this way: we would attempt to summon a devil. Or (at the risk of triggering a bit of mirth) one of his minions. Demons. Spirits. Little wobbly on the nomenclature.

(And you know, since this is all true, if you find this at all unsettling, you can certainly stop reading ASAP. I won't mind. *Honest...*)

And how exactly did we do that? Old-school, my friend. We went to the main New York Public Library, two or three of us, to find one of the mammoth and oh-so-old arcane volumes buried in their musty reference room.

Where we found this giant, frayed, leather-bound book that had exactly what we were looking for.

How to draw the demonic pentagram.

Where to place the symbols.

And oh yes—those all-important words to say.

We were able to photocopy the relevant pages—and back then, it was indeed a *photo*copy, thick, a sepia-toned picture of the page with the images and incantations.

We were ready.

Now, for the place.

And that was easy. We often gathered on the rocky coast of a place called Manhattan Beach, the word "beach" a misnomer. It's down from the then-decayed amusements of Coney Island and the day-fishing boats of Sheepshead Bay, a great jumble of rocks designed to keep the sea waters at bay.

One has to wonder how it's been dealing with that sea lately.

Then, as with any good summoning, an elixir of some kind was needed. To quote Jim Backus, from *It's a Mad, Mad, Mad, Mad World*, we required "booze." In this instance, bourbon.

We started swigging straight from the bottle. Night. Stars out. The great Atlantic crashing against those rocks, a repetitive, almost hungry sound. (Sorry-slipped into writer mode there. I will restrain myself...)

We drew the pentagram. Think we used the same chalk that we used to put in socks on Halloween, smashing it against the street and then using said weapon to "peg" other kids with a colorful splash of electric pink, lime green, or a ruddy brown.

Guess—that doesn't happen anymore?

And then, the symbols were chalked into each polygonal section of the pentagram. The air a bit chilly—was October after all. The bottle being swapped. Maybe—another opened.

And then, we were ready. Five friends. Five corners to the star, each of us on a point. Maybe a bit wobbly, standing on the slanted rock that we selected as our "altar" for this activity.

Thinking about it now, the craziness, I'm actually surprised that we didn't bring a goat, or chicken, or a good old Brooklyn rat to sacrifice.

Then—the words. Calling on this being, then other beings. Think we had to pledge ourselves to work on his team. Or something. (It was a long time ago. I know more about contracts now.)

All of us saying the words, as we waited...

More waves crashed. Another breeze off the (adjective deleted) ocean.

No one else there.

When—well…

What do you think happened? Nothing at first.

Then: our great experiment in the realm of the supernatural ends with us teetering on the star points of our pentagram, now just wanting some more of the warming bourbon.

Which is what we did. The formal summoning over.

I took the photocopy, which I kept for quite a while. Don't know where it is now. Rain or the ocean would ultimately wash away our chalk drawing.

And just two codas to this true tale.

First, since I had been in France unlike the others, I had learned how to drink as the French do—in moderation. My disappointed pals never saw me buzzed. So good old peer pressure was used to get me to kill one of the bottles.

And after that, I remember stumbling on those rocks, with their sharp edges, before doing a nose-dive onto one of them. Blood all over. Still have the scar on my chin.

(And I won't share the outrageous tale I told my parents about what happened. Suffice to say, it wasn't my finest moment…but it did show some good story-telling potential.)

And there is this other, darker coda…what happened to the five of us.

The part that's eerie. Scary, even. That—perhaps—could be shrugged off. Things happen right?

But I'm afraid I can't share that with you. Not, here, not now.

But if you do see me, an old horror writer, sitting at some classic bar—say Keen's in NYC—you buy me that second martini, right? And I might, voice lowered, share that with you.

And, oh yes. It all led to a story. A novel. *Darkborn.* My third for the wonderful Ginjer Buchanan of Berkley. It is I believe, in some ways, my best. Certainly the best—satisfying, moving, *unexpected*—ending I ever wrote. And, he said, head inflating, maybe one of the best I ever read.

You can get that as an ebook now. We live in a wonderful world, no?

You can read about the event turned into fiction, the fatal journey to the bizarre closed and classic amusement park Steeplechase—that never really happened.

Little did I know, a quarter of a century ago, how my fiction would, in some weird way, mirror, predict fact.

And if I ever do get to share that with you, *mano a mano*, huddled, whispering it to you, then you *too* will wake up in the dark of night screaming...

Well, no. Sorry. I never did that.

And boo! 'Tis just a Halloween memoir after all. So, no middle-of-the-night screams, no waking up in a sweaty fear.

But in the fictional world, in a story, tonight? Why, of course that's *exactly* what you would do.

We writers wouldn't want it any other way.

The October Game

Ray Bradbury

He put the gun back into the bureau drawer and shut the drawer.

No, not that way. Louise wouldn't suffer that way. She would be dead and it would be over and she wouldn't suffer. It was very important that this thing have, above all, duration. Duration through imagination. How to prolong the suffering? How, first of all, to bring it about? Well.

The man standing before the bedroom mirror carefully fitted his cufflinks together. He paused long enough to hear the children run by swiftly on the street below, outside this warm two-story house; like so many gray mice the children, like so many leaves.

By the sound of the children you knew the calendar day. By their screams you knew what evening it was. You knew it was very late in the year. October. The last day of October, with white bone masks and cut pumpkins and the smell of dropped candle fat.

No. Things hadn't been right for some time. October didn't help any. If anything it made things worse. He adjusted his black bow-tie. If this were spring, he nodded slowly, quietly, emotionlessly, at his image in the mirror, then there might be a chance. But tonight all the world was burning down into ruin. There was no green spring, none of the freshness, none of the promise.

There was a soft running in the hall. "That's Marion," he told himself. "My little one. All eight quiet years of her. Never a word. Just her luminous gray eyes and her wondering little mouth." His daughter had been in and out all evening, trying on various masks, asking him which was most terrifying, most horrible. They had both finally decided on the skeleton mask. It was "just awful!" It would "scare the beans" from people!

Again he caught the long look of thought and deliberation he gave himself in the mirror. He had never liked October. Ever since he first lay in the autumn leaves before his grandmother's house many years ago and heard the wind and saw the empty trees. It had made him cry, without a reason. And a little of that sadness returned each year to him. It always went away with spring.

But, it was different tonight. There was a feeling of autumn coming to last a million years.

There would be no spring.

He had been crying quietly all evening. It did not show, not a vestige of it, on his face. It was all hidden somewhere and it wouldn't stop.

A rich syrupy smell of candy filled the bustling house. Louise had laid out apples in new skins of caramel; there were vast bowls of punch fresh-mixed, stringed apples in each door, scooped, vented pumpkins peering triangularly from each cold window. There was a water tub in the center of the living room, waiting, with a sack of apples nearby, for dunking to begin. All that was needed was the catalyst, the inpouring of children, to start the apples bobbling, the stringed apples to penduluming in the crowded doors, the candy to vanish, the halls to echo with fright or delight, it was all the same.

Now, the house was silent with preparation. And just a little more than that.

Louise had managed to be in every other room save the room he was in today. It was her very fine way of intimating, Oh look, Mich, see how busy I am! So busy that when you walk into a room I'm in there's always something I need to do in another room! Just see how I dash about!

For a while he had played a little game with her, a nasty childish game. When she was in the kitchen then he came to the kitchen saying, "I need a glass of water." After a moment, he standing, drinking water, she like a crystal witch over the caramel brew bubbling like a prehistoric mudpot on the stove, she said, "Oh, I must light the pumpkins!" and she rushed to the living room to make the pumpkins smile with light. He came after, smiling, "I must get my pipe." "Oh, the cider!" she had cried, running to the dining room. "I'll check the cider," he had said. But when he tried following she ran to the bathroom and locked the door.

He stood outside the bathroom door, laughing strangely and sense-lessly, his pipe gone cold in his mouth, and then, tired of the game, but stubborn, he waited another five minutes. There was not a sound from the bath. And lest she enjoy in any way knowing that he waited outside, irritated, he suddenly jerked about and walked upstairs, whistling mer-rily.

At the top of the stairs he had waited. Finally he had heard the bath-room door unlatch and she had come out and life below-stairs had re-sumed, as life in a jungle must resume once a terror has passed on away and the antelope return to their spring.

Now, as he finished his bow-tie and put on his dark coat there was a mouse-rustle in the hall. Marion appeared in the door, all skeletonous in her disguise.

"How do I look, Papa?"

"Fine!"

From under the mask, blonde hair showed. From the skull sockets small blue eyes smiled. He sighed. Marion and Louise, the two silent de-nouncers of his virility, his dark power. What alchemy had there been in Louise that took the dark of a dark man and bleached and bleached the dark brown eyes and black hair and washed and bleached the ingrown baby all during the period before birth until the child was born, Marion, blonde, blue-eyed, ruddy-cheeked? Sometimes he suspected that Louise had conceived the child as an idea, completely asexual, an immaculate conception of contemptuous mind and cell. As a firm rebuke to him she had produced a child in her own image, and, to top it, she had somehow fixed the doctor so he shook his head and said, "Sorry, Mr. Wilder, your wife will never have another child. This is the last one."

"And I wanted a boy," Mich had said, eight years ago.

He almost bent to take hold of Marion now, in her skull mask. He felt an inexplicable rush of pity for her, because she had never had a father's love, only the crushing, holding love of a loveless mother. But most of all he pitied himself, that somehow he had not made the most of a bad birth, enjoyed his daughter for herself, regardless of her not being dark and a son and like himself. Somewhere he had missed out. Other things being equal, he would have loved the child. But Louise hadn't wanted a child, anyway, in the first place. She had been frightened of the idea of birth. He had forced the child on her, and from that night, all through the year until the agony of the birth itself, Louise had lived in another part of the house. She had expected to die with the forced child. It had been very easy for Louise to hate this husband who so wanted a son that he gave his only wife over to the mortuary.

But—Louise had lived. And in triumph! Her eyes, the day he came to the hospital, were cold. I'm alive, they said. And I have a blonde daughter! Just look! And when he had put out a hand to touch, the mother had turned away to conspire with her new pink daughter-child—away from that dark forcing murderer. It had all been so beautifully ironic. His selfishness deserved it.

But now it was October again. There had been other Octobers and when he thought of the long winter he had been filled with horror year after year to think of the endless months mortared into the house by an insane fall of snow, trapped with a woman and child, neither of whom loved him, for months on end. During the eight years there had been respites. In spring and summer you got out, walked, picnicked; these were desperate solutions to the desperate problem of a hated man.

But, in winter, the hikes and picnics and escapes fell away with leaves. Life, like a tree, stood empty, the fruit picked, the sap run to earth. Yes, you invited people in, but people were hard to get in winter with blizzards and all. Once he had been clever enough to save for a Florida trip. They had gone south. He had walked in the open.

But now, the eighth winter coming, he knew things were finally at an end. He simply could not wear this one through. There was an acid walled off in him that slowly had eaten through tissue and bone over the years, and now, tonight, it would reach the wild explosive in him and all would be over!

There was a mad ringing of the bell below. In the hall, Louise went to see. Marion, without a word, ran down to greet the first arrivals. There were shouts and hilarity.

He walked to the top of the stairs.

Louise was below, taking wraps. She was tall and slender and blonde to the point of whiteness, laughing down upon the new children.

He hesitated. What was all this? The years? The boredom of living? Where had it gone wrong? Certainly not with the birth of the child alone. But it had been a symbol of all their tensions, he imagined. His jealousies and his business failures and all the rotten rest of it. Why didn't he just turn, pack a suitcase, and leave? No. Not without hurting Louise as much as she had hurt him. It was simple as that. Divorce wouldn't hurt her at all. It would simply be an end to numb indecision. If he thought divorce would give her pleasure in any way he would stay married the rest of his life to her, for damned spite. No, he must hurt her. Figure some way, perhaps, to take Marion away from her, legally. Yes. That was it. That would hurt most of all. To take Marion away.

"Hello down there!" He descended the stairs, beaming.

Louise didn't look up.

"Hi, Mr. Wilder!"

The children shouted, waved, as he came down.

By ten o'clock the doorbell had stopped ringing, the apples were bitten from stringed doors, the pink faces were wiped dry from the apple bobbing, napkins were smeared with caramel and punch, and he, the husband, with pleasant efficiency had taken over. He took the party right out of Louise's hands. He ran about talking to the twenty children and the twelve parents who had come and were happy with the special spiked cider he had fixed them. He supervised pin the tail on the donkey, spin the bottle, musical chairs, and all the rest, amid fits of shouting laughter. Then, in the triangular-eyed pumpkin shine, all house lights out, he cried, "Hush! Follow me!" tiptoeing toward the cellar.

The parents, on the outer periphery of the costumed riot, commented to each other, nodding at the clever husband, speaking to the lucky wife. How well he got on with children, they said.

The children, crowded after the husband, squealing.

"The cellar!" he cried. "The tomb of the witch!"

More squealing. He made a mock shiver. "Abandon hope all ye who enter here!"

The parents chuckled.

One by one the children slid down a slide which Mich had fixed up from lengths of table-section, into the dark cellar. He hissed and shouted ghastly utterances after them. A wonderful wailing filled the dark pumpkin-lighted house. Everybody talked at once. Everybody but Marion. She had gone through all the party with a minimum of sound or talk; it was all inside her, all the excitement and joy. What a little troll, he thought. With a shut mouth and shiny eyes she had watched her own party, like so many serpentines thrown before her.

Now, the parents. With laughing reluctance they slid down the short incline, uproarious, while little Marion stood by, always wanting to see it all, to be last. Louise went down without help. He moved to aid her, but she was gone even before he bent.

The upper house was empty and silent in the candle-shine.

Marion stood by the slide. "Here we go," he said, and picked her up.

They sat in a vast circle in the cellar. Warmth came from the distant bulk of the furnace. The chairs stood in a long line along each wall, twenty squealing children, twelve rustling relatives, alternately spaced, with Louise down at the far end, Mich up at this end, near the stairs. He peered but saw nothing. They had all grouped to their chairs, catch-as-you-can in the blackness. The entire program from here on was to be enacted in the dark, he as Mr. Interlocutor. There was a child scampering, a smell of damp cement, and the sound of the wind out in the October stars.

"Now!" cried the husband in the dark cellar. "Quiet!"

Everybody settled.

The room was black black. Not a light, not a shine, not a glint of an eye.

A scraping of crockery, a metal rattle.

"The witch is dead," intoned the husband.

"Eeeeeeeeeeeeeeeeeeee," said the children.

"The witch is dead, she has been killed, and here is the knife she was killed with."

He handed over the knife. It was passed from hand to hand, down and around the circle, with chuckles and little odd cries and comments from the adults.

"The witch is dead, and this is her head," whispered the husband, and handed an item to the nearest person.

"Oh, I know how this game is played," some child cried, happily, in the dark. "He gets some old chicken innards from the icebox and hands them around and says, 'These are her innards!' And he makes a clay head and passes it for her head, and passes a soup bone for her arm. And he takes a marble and says, 'This is her eye!' And he takes some corn and says, 'This is her teeth!' And he takes a sack of plum pudding and gives that and says, 'This is her stomach!' I know how this is played!"

"Hush, you'll spoil everything," some girl said.

"The witch came to harm, and this is her arm," said Mich.

"Eeeee!"

The items were passed and passed, like hot potatoes, around the circle. Some children screamed, wouldn't touch them. Some ran from their chairs to stand in the center of the cellar until the grisly items had passed.

"Aw, it's only chicken insides," scoffed a boy. "Come back, Helen!"

Shot from hand to hand, with small scream after scream, the items went down, down, to be followed by another and another.

"The witch cut apart, and this is her heart," said the husband.

Six or seven items moving at once through the laughing, trembling dark.

Louise spoke up. "Marion, don't be afraid; it's only play."

Marion didn't say anything.

"Marion?" asked Louise. "Are you afraid?"

Marion didn't speak.

"She's all right," said the husband. "She's not afraid."

On and on the passing, the screams, the hilarity.

The autumn wind sighed about the house. And he, the husband, stood at the head of the dark cellar, intoning the words, handing out the items.

"Marion?" asked Louise again, from far across the cellar.

Everybody was talking.

"Marion?" called Louise.

Everybody quieted.

"Marion, answer me, are you afraid?"

Marion didn't answer.

The husband stood there, at the bottom of the cellar steps.

Louise called, "Marion, are you there?"

No answer. The room was silent.

"Where's Marion?" called Louise.

"She was here," said a boy.

"Maybe she's upstairs."

"Marion!"

No answer. It was quiet.

Louise cried out, "Marion, Marion!"

"Turn on the lights," said one of the adults.

The items stopped passing. The children and adults sat with the witch's items in their hands.

"No." Louise gasped. There was a scraping of her chair, wildly, in the dark. "No. Don't turn on the lights, oh, God, God, God, don't turn them on, please, please, don't turn on the lights, don't!" Louise was shrieking now. The entire cellar froze with the scream.

Nobody moved.

Everyone sat in the dark cellar, suspended in the suddenly frozen task of this October game; the wind blew outside, banging the house, the smell of pumpkins and apples filled the room with the smell of the objects in their fingers while one boy cried, "I'll go upstairs and look!" and he ran upstairs hopefully and out around the house, four times around the house, calling, "Marion, Marion, Marion!" over and over and at last coming slowly down the stairs into the waiting breathing cellar and saying to the darkness, "I can't find her."

Then…some idiot turned on the lights.

FEAR OF FALLEN LEAVES

James Newman

"Autumn is the most difficult, for obvious reasons," she said. "God, how I dread the end of summer. Some mornings it's all I can do to make myself leave the house."

The others offered their usual looks of sympathy. A young lady whose name she could never remember dabbed at her eyes with a tissue. Marilyn thought the sweater she was wearing should have been a crime: candy-corns and pumpkins in a gaudy checkerboard pattern.

"I hate this time of year. Hate it."

Even now, she imagined she could hear the source of her distress outside: rustling, sighing, crackling. Like the flames of the constant struggle burning inside of her.

And then she was done talking. She shrugged. "I know they can't hurt me. I know it's crazy."

"No one's here to judge," said Evan, the leader of her support group. "I once met a man who had an irrational fear of ladybugs. Remember, you're talking to a guy who's terrified of *tall people*."

They all laughed—*with* him, never *at* him. Especially Markus, who stood six-foot-nine and had to duck to get through the door. His phobia was big shaggy dogs, Marilyn remembered as their eyes met across the room. She quickly looked away. She found him incredibly handsome, and such thoughts disturbed her. Bryan hadn't even been in the ground a year.

She stared off toward the refreshments table at the back of the room: coffeemaker, packets of non-dairy creamer, a few stale donuts on a paper plate. Someone had donated a ceramic jack-o'-lantern full of mints since their last meeting. It seemed to be staring right at her.

She noticed it sat on a bed of fake autumn leaves.

That was disrespectful.

Evan checked his watch. "We have about ten minutes left. Who would like to share next? I see a new face or two...."

A chubby woman in a Keith Urban T-shirt held up her hand, introduced herself as if needing confirmation: "My name is Celia? And I'm afraid of spiders?"

"Welcome, Celia," said the others.

Everyone except Marilyn. She wasn't listening. She was already dreading the walk outside to her car.

She wondered if she could slip out the back door, so she wouldn't have to pass by the man with the leaf-blower again.

"*Two more days 'til Halloween, Halloween, Halloween*," sang the jingle on the television. Some silly horror flick her ten-year-old was watching. She caught a snippet of it on her way through the living room to get the vacuum cleaner out of the hall closet.

Don't remind me. Marilyn was sure the song had been composed to taunt her personally. *I'm trying to forget, as if that will make it go away.* She wished she could just crawl under her bed, stay there until October 31 was just another "X" on the calendar and it was time to start preparing for Thanksgiving. But the thought of disappointing Joey was too much to bear.

"*Two more days 'til Halloween....*"

"Honey, turn that off," she said. "You know scary movies give you nightmares."

Once upon a time, that hadn't been true. He used to watch them with his father at every opportunity. After what happened, though, it wasn't just Joey who had trouble sleeping when he watched that crap.

"But, Mom! This old dude's using masks to kill all the kids! They put 'em on and snakes and spiders and all kindsa' gross stuff come out—"

"Scary movie. Off. Now. Don't make me tell you again." She rubbed at her temples, felt a headache coming on. "Why don't you go play in your room? Build something with that Lego set you wanted so bad for your birthday."

She didn't dare suggest he play outside. And not just because of the chill in the late-October air.

She softened her tone, didn't like snapping at her son: "Please, honey? If you'll do that for me, I'll fix your favorite for lunch in a little while. Peanut butter and jelly sandwiches?"

"Fine." An exaggerated sigh. He turned off the TV, stomped down the hall.

She smiled as she watched him go. He was a good boy.

Her smile disappeared at the knocking sound overhead. A muffled smoker's cough, followed by a hint of male laughter. A metallic scrape, a *thud* (what were they doing up there, *wrestling?*). All morning it had been like this, as if her home itself were alive. She had hired two local men to clean out her gutters (and almost fired them before they got started, as she didn't care for the way one of them looked at her when he said *getcha cleaned out good n' proper*; in that moment she missed Bryan with an ache that nearly brought her to her knees). Now, three hours in, she wondered how something like this could possibly take so long. She didn't dare peek outside to check on their progress. Wouldn't even allow herself to get too close to the windows until their work was done, lest she witness brown horror raining down from above, inches from her face.

They couldn't get the hell off her property soon enough, taking with them the waste from her gutters. But even the thought of the damned things burning somewhere—blackening, withering, curling in upon themselves like dying spiders—made her feel no better.

Sometimes Marilyn wondered if everyone else in the world knew of her affliction, and were trying their best to rub it in her face....

Driving to the grocery store on Halloween morning, she stopped at a pedestrian crosswalk in the center of town. A young man with a buzz cut and a bad case of rosacea strutted past her Camry. He wore an oversized "CANADA" jersey that matched the color of his face. An invisible ice cube slid down Marilyn's spine. The symbol of his favorite country—a monstrous maple leaf—might as well have been an ugly smear of blood on his chest. A gory handprint left there by the victim of a brutal murder.

That made her think of Bryan. She squeezed her eyes shut, cursed beneath her breath.

"You shouldn't say bad words," Joey said from the backseat.

The drive home proved no less stressful. She felt a panic attack coming on, thought she might need to pull over and empty one of the grocery bags into the seat beside her, use it to keep from hyperventilating. *They* were everywhere, impossible to ignore....

Other people stepped over them, swept them aside, found the wretched things *beautiful,* even (some folks took photos of them, or drove great distances to visit her state just to watch them change color, something she would never comprehend as long as she lived!). But for Marilyn they were russet nightmares skittering across every sidewalk, hideous papery shapes stuck like parasites to the hood of every vehicle, remains of a dead season crammed like the casualties of a suburban apocalypse into every drainage ditch.

As she turned into Sycamore Terrace, her neighborhood, she spotted a skinny teenager working in the front yard of his split-level home. He brandished a rake like a lazy warrior halfheartedly swinging his weapon around; judging from his sullen expression, he wasn't out here because he wanted to be, but he'd been at it for a while. Behind him, like sated ticks squatting in the grass, sat three black bags pregnant with the proof of his labor. She imagined the bags bursting, spilling forth their contents, and bile rose in the back of her throat.

She took a right onto her block, saw Ray and Paula Quinlan's boys jumping into piles of leaves that had fallen from the grand oak at the edge of their property. The youngest had already donned his Superman costume as if he couldn't wait a few more hours for the festivities to begin. Watching the twins plunge willingly into those vile brown heaps made Marilyn's skin crawl as if her clothes were infested with bugs.

Three houses down from the Quinlans', Craig Cannon knelt under his carport, filling a leaf-blower with gasoline. He wore an orange T-shirt that read THIS *IS* MY HALLOWEEN COSTUME. He waved at her as she passed. She would have returned the gesture, but when she saw the countless leaves covering Craig's driveway like a rust-colored quilt stitched together from her worst nightmares, she gripped the steering wheel so tightly her knuckles turned bone-white. If she didn't hold on to something, she feared she might fall right off of the world.

When she passed Tom and Teresa Huston's property a few houses down from her own, she swerved, nearly striking a tomcat sitting on the curb. For a second she was sure she saw a pale face leering at her from within a drift of maple leaves beneath the Hustons' new deck...her *late husband's* face, entombed in a deciduous cocoon. A second look, however, showed her that it was only Tom Junior's soccer ball. Nothing more. Just a half-deflated soccer ball.

Leaves. God, how she loathed them.

As she pulled into her driveway at last, she glanced in her rearview mirror to make sure none were chasing after her.

She knew it was stupid. She didn't care.

The kitchen smelled of sugar cookies and pumpkin-spice-flavored coffee. On the radio atop the counter, a cheesy commercial filled with cheesy horror-movie sound effects advertised an (undoubtedly cheesy) local haunted attraction called "The Fear Farm."

Marilyn turned the radio down. Her finger left a smear of orange frosting on the knob.

"Joey, honey, could you come in here for a minute?"

He came running into the kitchen. "Cookies! Awesome, Mom!"

"I am an awesome mom," she said.

He reached for one, but she gently slapped his hand away. "Not so fast. Gotta wait till they cool down. Plus, I'm not quite done. Still adding the final touch."

She was only about halfway done with painting little Halloween-themed pictures on them, using the tubes of frosting set beside the stove.

"We've got vampire bats…ghosts…here's an *eyeball*…this one's supposed to be a goblin but it didn't turn out so well."

"It looks like a big green booger," Joey said. "No offense."

"*You're* a big green booger!" She whirled around, pretended like she was going to squirt him with one of the tubes.

He giggled, ran away.

"Hey, come back here!" she said. "I'm not done with you."

He returned to the kitchen, shifted his weight impatiently from one foot to the other as he stood in the doorway. A lock of straight blond hair fell across his forehead. He looked so much like his father.

"Do me a favor, honey. Go look in the hall closet, you'll see a bag from Laymon's Grocery. Bring it to me, please?"

"Sure."

He came back a minute later, tossed the bag onto the table next to the set of tools they would use to carve a jack-o'-lantern later.

"Open it. There's something inside for you."

He reached into the bag, pulled out what she had bought for him.

"Frankenstein! Cool! This is the exact costume I wanted!"

"Of course, I knew that," she said. "And it's Frankenstein's Monster, remember. Frankenstein was the guy who made him."

"Good one, Mom."

Where most kids couldn't wait to dress up like Batman, Spider-Man, or the Hulk for Halloween, all her son had talked about for the last month was transforming himself into Dr. Frankenstein's creation. Bryan would have loved that.

"So, Mom, does this mean we're going trick-or-treating?"

"We are."

He ran to her, threw his arms around her. "Yayyy! You changed your mind?"

"I guess I did."

"But aren't you afraid?"

She held him close, and her eyes grew wet with tears. "I'm always afraid, honey. But I can't let my phobia control my life. It's why I go to those meetings every month. I have to keep telling myself that there's nothing to be afraid of. Maybe one day I'll believe it."

"Because they're gone, right?" he said.

"They're gone. Right." She hesitated only a second or two before adding, "They can't hurt us anymore."

The events of a year ago would haunt her forever, and had done nothing to help with her foliphobia.

At the time, they lived in Loomis, a small town in North Carolina. Population: two thousand and four. While it wasn't quite a "one-stoplight town" (more like a half a dozen), Loomis was the kind of place that could have disappeared overnight and the rest of the world might never even notice.

In fact, that's exactly what happened.

The holiday had always been Bryan and Joey's thing. Ever since the age of eight or nine, the last time her own parents had taken her trick-or-treating—before her father left and her mom quit trying, and she was forced to grow out of such things sooner than most kids—she didn't care one way or the other about Halloween. She could take it or leave it. Thanks to Bryan, though, October 31 was their son's favorite day of the year.

No one would have known it to look at her husband, with his professional haircut and corporate lawyer attire, but as long as Marilyn had known him he loved monster movies and slice-and-dice slasher flicks. The cornier the better. Most attorneys she knew decorated their walls with photos of themselves shaking hands with politicians, or shelves full of leather-bound books they would probably never read. Bryan's prized possessions: a framed first-edition *Invasion of the Body Snatchers* poster on the wall behind his desk, and a vintage Mole Man model in a glass display case in one corner of his home office.

For better or worse, Joey had inherited his father's love of scary movies. It caused occasional arguments between them, as Marilyn felt Bryan was too liberal in regards to what he allowed their son to watch (Godzilla destroying Tokyo was one thing, college kids chopped up by a machete-wielding madman was another). God, how she wished she had it all to do over, though. If she could turn back time, she would join him on the sofa for days, would gladly sit through whatever B-movies he begged her to watch with him. She would fix them up a gigantic bowl of popcorn, enough to feed a family of twelve, and Joey could watch whatever he wanted. As long as they could have his daddy back.

How could any of them have known, on that fateful day one year ago, that their lives would soon become a horror movie, that Bryan would end up just like the victims in those monster movies he adored so?

Joey had insisted on going trick-or-treating dressed as a "rotting zombie." He was his father's son in every way. Marilyn had asked him more than once in the days leading up to Halloween if he wouldn't prefer something less gruesome, like the Lone Ranger, a scary pirate with an eye-patch, or maybe Buzz Lightyear ("Mom! How old do you think I *am*?" he scoffed at that last suggestion). She knew she had lost the battle when Bryan bought an old flannel shirt and a pair of ripped jeans at a thrift store on his way home from work, proceeded to "dirty them up" in the backyard with Joey's help.

"It'll be perfect." He grinned from ear to ear as if he'd scored the winning Million Dollar Lotto ticket instead of someone's musty-smelling secondhand clothes. "Tell me the kid won't look like he just crawled out of the grave!"

"Yeah," Joey giggled, "it'll be perfect!"

"Sure," Marilyn said, giving up. But even as she rolled her eyes, she couldn't help but smile.

She wondered more than once who was more excited for the holiday, the boy or Bryan. As always, Daddy dressed up too. Ultimately, she was the one responsible for applying their makeup: fake blood, cracked yellow teeth, green flesh oozing with latex sores. When all was said and done, she was actually quite proud of her work. She squealed with mock terror as the decaying twins lumbered after her to Bryan's Volvo.

"Braaaains!" the tall one grunted, and the short one followed suit.

"Don't forget your trick-or-treat bag, kiddo!" she called over her shoulder.

They set out a couple of hours before dark. The streets of Loomis were filled with miniature superheroes, vampires, ninja turtles, Grim Reapers, Disney characters, werewolves, and adult chaperones of the same. Jack-o'-lanterns grinned from porches beneath strands of blinking orange lights and motion-activated skeletons that mocked their victims with canned stentorian laughter. Bryan and Joey lurched down the sidewalk from house to house as Marilyn followed in the car. Each time they approached a home with its porch light on—the universal sign that the people inside welcomed trick-or-treaters—she pulled over to wait at the curb.

Bryan's love of Halloween wasn't the only reason she stayed in the car while he did the footwork with Joey. As she cruised down the block, the abundance of fallen leaves everywhere she looked did set her on edge more than a little. They were everywhere this time of year, and she was constantly aware of them, like a bullied child forever on the lookout for her tormentors. Marilyn's pulse quickened when she spotted a lone yellow dogwood leaf dancing along the sidewalk behind her son, as if it were chasing after him. Gooseflesh broke out on her forearms any time she saw a bunch of them raked into a neat pile like a burial mound in the middle of someone's yard. Still, she pushed her fear to the back of her mind, forced herself to enjoy this evening with her family as much as possible.

Before long, Joey's trick-or-treat bag was nearly overflowing with so much candy it would take him months to eat it all. As she rolled to a stop in front of a Cape Cod with a "FOR SALE" sign in the front yard, she thought she might ask Bryan if they were ready to call it a night after this one. She'd been listening to a collection of Elton John's greatest hits as she drove; she paused the CD now so she could hear her husband's reply through the open passenger-side window.

That's when she heard the first scream.

Bryan and Joey heard it too, as did the stooped old man who had just dropped a handful of Tootsie Rolls into Joey's candy bag.

"What in tarnation was that?" The senior citizen stepped out onto his porch, rolling a small oxygen tank behind him.

Marilyn peered through the windshield into the twilight. The air had an odd pinkish hue, making the scene before her appear even more surreal….

At the end of the block, about three hundred feet in front of the Volvo, an obese woman flailed about beneath a giant oak tree, swinging her arms and screaming as if performing a maniac's dance. The three children with her—a chubby vampire, a miniature witch, and a pint-sized Hulk—started bawling in terror and confusion as they watched.

From where Marilyn sat, it looked as if the woman was being attacked by a swarm of *leaves*. A chill shot through her body as if she had just stepped naked into a snowstorm.

Bryan and Joey ran across the yard, back toward the Volvo.

"Dad? Dad, what's wrong with her?" Joey asked.

"I don't know. Get in the car, son. I'll be right back."

Marilyn leaned across the seat, popped open the passenger-side door.

"Mom, I'm scared," Joey said, climbing in. "What's wrong with that woman?"

"Bryan, where are you going?" Marilyn called to her husband.

He ran past the car, toward the screaming woman at the end of the block. "She needs help, honey—I'll be right back!"

"Bryan!"

She gave the Volvo too much gas. It shot forward. She slammed on the brakes. The tires squealed. Everything was happening too fast. She couldn't make sense of it all. She eased her foot off the brake, idled toward the intersection at the end of the block, and called out to her husband again.

Something to her left caught her attention. Helena Tennant—a lady Marilyn spoke to often, as she was the head of the P.T.A. at Joey's school— thrashed about on her front porch, screaming. Those...*leaf things*...were attacking her too. They flitted around her like a flock of small brown birds possessed by demons. In her terror, Helena knocked a massive jack-o'lantern off of the porch railing. It smashed onto the ground in a gooey orange mess. She followed it a few seconds later. Her ankle turned, and she went down face-first onto her concrete walkway.

The creatures covered her instantly, darkening her flesh like living shadows.

"Oh, my God," said Marilyn.

Joey started to cry. "Mom? What's happening?"

More screams echoed throughout the neighborhood.

Another group of trick-or-treaters—two young women and six or seven small children—ran across the street further up. At first glance, it looked as if they were all trying to rip their own hair out. A mother in a glow-in-the-dark BOO! shirt batted at her face and breasts as she was attacked. Another lost her pointy witch's hat as she fled from the creatures in pursuit. A toddler in a baggy Spider-Man costume tripped and fell in the middle of the road. One of the things darted under his mask with twitchy, bat-like movements. Another boy in a Captain America costume tried to help the toddler to his feet, but a moment later he was rolling about in agony too as the little monsters converged upon both of them.

Again, from where Marilyn sat, she thought they looked like *leaves*. For a moment she forgot how to breathe.

She heard gunshots from the next street over. Three, in rapid succession. A man's voice shouted hoarsely from somewhere behind her, "Jesus! Look out, Martha! *Look out!*"

The man's screams ended in a grotesque gurgle, as if something had crawled down his throat.

Trying her best not to panic, Marilyn eased the Volvo to a stop beside Bryan and the crowd under the oak tree. The fat woman and her young wards were now dark shapes crumpled on the grass a few feet away from a faux cemetery erected in someone's side yard. Their bodies undulated ever-so-slightly, as if covered with a living blanket. Otherwise none of them moved.

"Bryan!" Marilyn cried. "*Please* get in the car!"

"Daddy!" Joey shrieked.

And then the things were on Bryan too.

They were a dark rust-color, almost but not quite star-shaped. Not much bigger than the hand of a human adult. Something about the way they moved reminded Marilyn of flying squirrels. Or stingrays. The way they glided effortlessly through the air from one victim to another.

But mostly they looked like *leaves*. It was as if her phobia had come to life...and it had grown fangs.

Two of them stuck like flying leeches to each side of Bryan's face, another to his neck, and yet another wrapped around his left wrist. He swatted at them, knocked one away, but it was replaced by three more. He fell to his knees. Their flat brown bodies swelled as they sucked his blood. Marilyn had never heard her husband scream before—she was struck by the incongruous realization that his high-pitched scream sounded as if it came from a little girl.

She screamed with him as she watched him die.

"They got Dad!" Joey cried. "We have to help him!"

Tears streamed down her face. It was too late for Bryan, she knew. She had to protect her boy.

"Roll up your window, Joey."

When he didn't respond, she reached across his seat and did it for him.

One of the creatures slammed into the window, inches from Joey's face. It left a thin smear of blood on the glass where it stuck, the blood of one of its victims, but it was obviously still hungry. In the center of its maple-leaf-shaped body, its furiously-working mouth: round, lamprey-like. Ringed with hundreds of teeth no bigger than grains of rice, but all of them as sharp as needles.

Then, just as suddenly, the thing was gone. As if it had lost interest in them.

"What are they?" Joey wept. "Monsters?"

She didn't reply. She just peered through the windshield, her vision blurred with tears, and saw that Bryan's body was covered with them now. He lay on his stomach, half-in and half-out of the road. He twitched once, then lay still.

"I'm sorry," she said. "I'm sorry...."

She slammed her foot down on the gas. No clue where she was headed. Just had to get away from here. Away from those hellish things.

They were everywhere. Anyone who had not found shelter was food for the invaders. They floated down from the heavens by the hundreds, descended from the trees, attacking men, women, and children on both sides of the street. Marilyn saw Frank Parker, Bryan's boss, thrusting a snow shovel at a swarm of them as they cornered him against the storage shed out back of his place. A young couple dressed like Dracula and a sexy gypsy fell beneath the monsters on the front lawn of their three-story home; amidst the elaborate Halloween decorations on their patio, a flickering strobe-light gave their demise an eerie silent film quality. In another yard, a muscular man in a Gold's Gym tank-top was able to pry one of the things from his face, but his flesh came with it. Another leaf-creature crawled under his lacerated cheek, slid behind his features and across his skull. Marilyn saw his eye sockets turn brown.

She suspected the things hunted by sight, as the only people who survived their attack—at least for now—were those who found shelter by fleeing into their home or jumping into a vehicle. The beasts seemed to lose interest immediately, once there was any barrier between them and their prey. She watched as a skinny kid in a Darth Vader costume pulled a plastic swimming pool on top of himself to get away from a quartet of the flying bloodsuckers. Instantly, once he was hidden beneath it, they abandoned their pursuit, soaring across the street to attach themselves to other victims.

"We've got to call for help," said Marilyn. "Hand me my cell-phone, baby. In my purse."

Joey's hands trembled as he dug it out and handed it to her.

She heard the wail of the siren a second before she rolled through the intersection, and the ambulance struck them on her side.

The door crumpled in on her left arm, and the Volvo was thrown violently to the right. They spun around—once, twice, she lost count—and from a million miles away she heard Joey scream with her. Broken glass sprayed across her face and lap.

They finally stopped spinning when they hit another car parked against the curb.

Something hissed under the Volvo's hood. She was pretty sure her left arm was broken. She couldn't move it. Her head felt as if it had been stuffed full of cotton. She smelled blood and burned rubber. Heard voices, incomprehensible murmurs, like music heard through water.

"Joey," she moaned. "Oh, God…Joey…honey…are you okay?"

"I think," he said, blinking.

They fell into one another's arms. Joey was obviously dazed, and blood trickled from a small cut on his cheek, but he didn't appear to be seriously injured. Thank God. He started bawling, but that meant he was okay. By force of habit, he had buckled his seatbelt as soon as he climbed into the Volvo. *Good boy.* He was such a good boy….

"Ma'am, are you okay?" said a deep male voice. She flinched, turned to the source of the voice. Her entire left side felt as if it had been doused in gasoline and set on fire when she did that.

Two paramedics were looking in on her, trying to open her door. One of the men had a thick black beard with blood in it, the other barely looked old enough to drive.

And then the paramedics weren't there anymore. They were on the ground, covered with those leaf-creatures. Their white uniforms were varying shades of rust. *Moving* rust.

"Mommy," Joey cried, "what are we gonna do?"

"We have to run for it," she said. "We have to get help."

She winced as she fought to open her door. It wouldn't budge.

"Try yours."

"Stuck."

"Try the back door. On your side. Can you do that for me?"

He climbed over the seat, opened it with some effort. She followed. Every movement was agony, but she had to…couldn't fail him now….

They ran. Through a small park at the edge of a dying neighborhood. Past a picnic table, across a basketball court—the corpses of three young men lay beneath one of the goals, their bodies covered with masses of bloated bloodsuckers, as if the wages of losing a game here was violent death—and past the far boundaries of the park.

Right away, Marilyn wished they had stayed in the car. They were exposed out here, vulnerable. But then, they wouldn't have been safe for very long in the Volvo, with its busted windows. Those things might have gotten inside. Then they would have been trapped. She had to find help, find someone who knew what was going on, someone who knew how to deal with this…this *whatever it was*….

She risked a look back, over her shoulder.

At least a dozen of the creatures flew through the air toward them in a deadly phalanx. They were less than thirty feet away, closing fast.

She had brought them to a dead end. They were cornered.

A split-rail fence marked the edge of the park. On the other side of it, a copse of trees lined a small ravine. At the bottom of the ravine was a thick bed of dead leaves, perhaps as deep as Joey was tall.

She swallowed a lump in her throat, said, "Jesus."

The drop appeared to be twelve, fifteen feet at the most.

It was their only chance. She recalled how the one creature had lost interest when Joey rolled up the window. As if, once the glass was between them, it no longer knew they were there. She thought of the kid crawling beneath the plastic swimming pool, and how the things seemed to forget about him once he was out of sight (if they hunted by sight at all)....

She took his hand, and they climbed over the fence.

"We're gonna jump," she told him. "Think you can do that?"

He stared up at her with wide, terrified eyes. "Into the…leaves? Mom, are you sure?"

"I'm sure. I can do this. We have to do this. Ready? One, two, three, *go!*"

They leapt into the ravine.

As soon as they hit bottom—harder than she'd intended, and if her left arm wasn't broken before, there was no doubt in her mind that it was shattered now—she started pulling them on top of her with her good arm. Hundreds of *leaves*. Hiding herself and her son from the creatures in the air…covering their bodies completely as if burying themselves in their own grave.

Darkness consumed her. Her greatest fear tickled, scratched, poked, and scraped at her face and arms, filled her nostrils with the smell of dirt and compost. She could *taste* them.

She was drenched in sweat, but a frigid chill wracked her body from head to toe. Her guts roiled.

She shivered, said a silent prayer to a God she wasn't even sure she believed in. She pleaded with Him to let them live through this. Let them survive this ordeal with her sanity intact....

Later, when she thought back on everything that happened, she would be thankful that He had answered at least the *first* part of her prayer.

She didn't know why she'd told them. She sure as hell hadn't planned it. Maybe it had something to do with the almost intoxicating sense of self-confidence she had felt since facing her fear, since she'd taken Joey trick-or-treating one year later after thinking she couldn't do it. Perhaps she believed she had finally found a family as screwed-up as herself, a safe place where people wouldn't judge her. She expected—no, *demanded*—unconditional sympathy here, in this room full of men who trembled in terror at the sound of someone snoring, women who broke down sobbing at the sight of an escalator, and couples whose debilitating fear of germs brought them to each meeting with rubber gloves on their hands, their faces hidden behind surgical masks.

"There was never a word about it in the media," Marilyn explained. "They covered it up somehow. It was like Loomis was just wiped off the map, and those of us who survived it...they did something to us, to make us forget. But it didn't take with me. I don't know why. As far as where those...things...came from? Maybe it was pollution, chemicals in the air from the factory on the edge of town. I don't think knowing would make it any easier."

When she finished sharing, the other members of her support group just sat there staring at her.

Evan's lips parted, but he didn't say anything for a minute or more. The expression on his face resembled that of a man trying to assemble something complex but he just discovered the instructions were written in another language. Toward the end of Marilyn's story, he had taken a piece of hard candy out of his pocket, unwrapped it and popped it in his mouth. She could see it sitting on his tongue like a pumpkin-colored tumor.

Donna G. and Donna P., the quiet lesbian couple who always sat in the back, whispered something to one another and snickered. A senior citizen in a silvery tracksuit who often shared stories about his aversion to aerosol cans cleared his throat in an exaggerated manner. Markus, the tall guy Marilyn suddenly didn't find so attractive anymore, covered his mouth with one hand as if fighting an urge to break the awkward silence with a deafening guffaw.

"Umm...okay, then," Evan finally said. The candy clicked against his teeth.

Marilyn gathered up her purse and excused herself, knowing she had said too much.

She didn't need a therapist or some high-priced shrink to help her figure out where her fear of leaves had originated. She had always known. It started with an incident that occurred when she was six years old. Her parents had left her in the care of her older brother, Billy, for a few hours one morning. When she accidentally broke one of his toys he had held her down, shoved handfuls of muddy leaves into her mouth. She had swallowed some of them, and was subsequently sick for days, little bits of leaf and grit coming out of her body from both ends every time she ran to the toilet. Billy was long dead now, buried in a grave upstate that she had visited only once after his O.D. on pain pills when she was in high school (she imagined him lying beneath a thick brown blanket of the things that scared her the most, and she felt no guilt for appreciating the poetic justice of such a scene). Thirty years later, the assault was her most vivid memory of him.

As bad as her foliphobia had always been, it was worse than ever since the night Bryan died. Her greatest fear lurked on every lawn, darkened every ditch, blew across every backyard as if they were gathering one by one to outnumber the human race. She knew the leaves hadn't killed her husband, of course. Still, at first glance, the demons were identical to the shed foliage of innocent oak trees, beatific maples, and the namesake of her neighborhood. Their camouflage was infallible. The monsters that took Joey's father away, they had looked just like the autumn leaves.

So the question was never far from her mind: What if it happened again, here, in this town where she had attempted to pick up the pieces and make a new home for her and Joey? What if they *came back?* A second wave, hungrier than the first....

It's why Marilyn remained vigilant.

Call it unbalanced, or even crazy. She called it being *safe*.

If she had no choice but to leave the house and go out among the fallen leaves, she would keep watching. Waiting. Just in case.

When the world turned green again...vibrant, reborn, alive...she could relax.

Only then. And only a little.

COSTUME

Melanie Tem

I was twelve, probably no more prone to making malformed utterances than any other young adolescent. But this one was so mortifying that I still cringe when I think about it, even though I've since been absolved by the person I thought I'd hurt.

That morning in seventh-grade home room the teacher was leading a discussion about what we were going to "be" for Halloween. Maybe she was trying to encourage us to "be" *something*. Maybe she meant to head off some outrage she'd gotten wind of, or was hoping to encourage a little variety for a change. Or maybe she was just keeping us occupied till the first-period bell.

On the dusty blackboard she made two columns: "Boys" and "Girls." Half-turning to us, she cheered us on to call out ideas.

My mother was making an elf costume for me. She was having trouble getting the points of the green felt shoes stiff enough to stay curled. I wouldn't realize till much later how I loved the costumes she made, and the fact that she made them for me and worried over the details. But that's another story.

Girls were swooning about their princess and prom gowns; the teacher wrote "princess," "prom queen," and, though nobody'd said it, "fairy" in the "girls" column. A few giddily described dresses potentially right on the edge of scandalousness; the teacher wiggled her chalk-holding hand while she considered what to write, finally settling on "flapper."

Boys were boasting about going as hunters with real bows and presumably unloaded guns (in this rural place, schools *still* close on the first days of buck and doe seasons) and farmers (which many of them actually were) and soldiers and hobos. All these, plus the teacher's contributions of "policeman" and "fireman," went under the "Boys" heading.

Sharon sat to my right and a little behind me. She wasn't saying anything. Sharon was what people called a tomboy. Small, wiry, strong, athletic, she never had a boyfriend; she never had a girlfriend, either, as far as I know, but at that time and place we *wouldn't* have known.

"A bride," announced one frilly girl, and I thought it was odd that a bridal gown would be considered a costume. "Lots of lace. All satiny." The girls nodded and clasped their hands at their nascent bosoms. The boys guffawed. The teacher wrote "bride" and "bridesmaid" in the "Girls" column.

"A nurse," offered a more serious girl. Even then, I vaguely wondered why she didn't say "doctor."

Sharon wasn't saying anything. I wasn't saying anything, either; "elf" was both too wonderful and too embarrassing to bring up, partly because I didn't know which column it would go in.

Sharon was being left out. I could imagine her in a police uniform a whole lot more easily than in a princess gown. I had to stand up for her. I raised my hand. When the teacher called on me, I actually stood up and, even more clumsily, turned to look at Sharon when I said, with emphasis, in what I can still feel in my throat as a clarion tone, "*Some* of us girls don't like princesses and nurses and bridesmaids. *Some* of us might want to be a baseball player or a fire—" I hesitated—"fighter."

The instant the words were out of my mouth, I knew I'd done something terrible. In an attempt to defend my friend's right to be whoever she was, I'd called her out, put her on display.

I have no memory of anyone's reaction or of what happened next. Doubtless the bell rang and we went to class. I think I might have spent much of that school day in the nurse's office, sick to my stomach and unable to face anybody, but I don't know if that's an accurate memory or an attempt at redeeming myself. I don't know what Sharon was for Halloween.

A good forty years later, at a high school reunion, I sort of lay in wait for Sharon and blurted out an apology. She said she didn't remember the incident at all, even when, foot in my mouth once again, I related it in considerable detail; she said she didn't know what she'd been that year.

I remember the elf costume, the green felt boots with the curly toes. And Sharon's sharp, wary look when I insisted on telling her I was sorry.

DANCING WITH MR. DEATH

Kealan Patrick Burke

L ike many of us, when I was a kid, I spent a lot of time at my grand-mother's house. She lived, then as now, in a mountainous, sparsely populated rural village in the south of Ireland. After my parents separated, my mother decided it was a healthier environment for her son, while she figured out which direction her life should take, and how to find it. The time I spent in this village shaped in many ways the adult I would become. With its solitude, peace and quiet, and incredible mountain vistas, not only was it a sanctuary for a confused child, it was a creative nirvana. With so much time and so little distraction, I was free to wander the endless fields that surrounded my grandmother's house, feed the horses, sheep, and cows that roamed it with me, fish in the lakes and streams, and putter around the chaos of my grandfather's storage shed, where cats snuck in to have their kittens. It was there, on the large, discarded wedges of wood left behind by my carpenter father that I began, with magic markers and pencils, to replicate my favorite book and album covers, my first tentative steps toward the design work I do today.

I could write a book about my memories of that place and the impact it had on my childhood, adulthood, and creative life, but that's not why any of us are here. This is, after all, a celebration of Halloween, so let me pick through the mental files from that village and select a more appropriate memory.

It was my eleventh Halloween, and rather than spend it trick-or-treating with my school friends at home, I found myself, as was so often the case in those turbulent years, staying at my grandmother's house. My grandparents are to be credited for never looking upon me as a burden or a nuisance. If anything, they celebrated the presence of youth in their home, even if sometimes the exuberance expected of a child was tempered by a morose preoccupation with familial abandonment. On every holiday, they threw themselves into the traditions associated with each one and spared no expense in adorning their home with festive accoutrements solely for my benefit. It was difficult not to be overwhelmed by the spirit they installed in their house. Had I somehow managed to ignore the extravagant lights and decorations, attempts to avoid succumbing to their pervasive enthusiasm was an exercise in futility.

The biggest Christmas trees, the brightest lights, plain walls bursting with dazzling lights and drapery.

At Easter, egg hunts and mountains of boxes, all manner of chocolate delights nestled within.

My birthday, the house crowded with children and adults alike, none of whom I knew, all of them from the village, stacks of presents and an oversized cake.

I was spoiled and I loved them for it, functioning as it did as a direct counterpoint to my poor and broken home, the irony being that they too, were poor. It just failed to matter whenever an occasion arose to make a lonely child feel wanted.

Halloween, then, was no different. The house virtually exploded with candy. Skeletons and ghouls festooned the walls, and the air smelled of candle smoke and pumpkin guts. There were plastic tubs filled with water in which green apples bobbed. Suppertime saw generous helpings of Halloween barnbrack, a kind of dense and delicious fruit-and-raisin bread with a prize tucked inside. The prize, whether a tiny plastic bicycle, a coin, a ring, or some other innocuous little trinket, was said to be a sign of imminent good fortune (and often, chipped teeth.) Unsurprisingly, the ring foretold marriage, the more immediate result being a good-natured ribbing and rampant speculation regarding which fine young lass was destined to be your betrothed.

On this Halloween night at my grandmother's house, while I basked in the joy of celebrating the night with my cousins, one of the films from the *Halloween* series was airing on the small portable TV in the corner of the kitchen. It was muted—not that we'd have been able to hear it over our raucous din, but my eye was frequently drawn to the creepily masked Michael Myers all the same. This led me to wonder why none of the children from the village had come trick-or-treating to my grandmother's door. All the houses were close, and I had seen those children scuttling around in their homemade costumes before the sun had gone down. I wondered if perhaps none of them were allowed out after dark. Then, almost as if the wondering had summoned them, there came a sharp hard knock at the front door.

"Why don't you go see who it is?" my grandmother asked, depositing a load of candy into my hands as she ushered me into the hall. Then she shut the door behind me and I found myself in near dark. The front door was half wood, half frosted glass, and through it, backlit by the yellow light on the porch, I could see a tall dark shape, too dark, I thought, to be a child, barring an impressively elaborate costume. I felt a twinge of fear, no doubt enhanced by the spirit of the season, my glimpse of Mr. Myers, and the gloom into which I had abruptly found myself deposited, the cheer that had buoyed me to this point now muted behind the kitchen door. I waited a moment, debating whether or not it might be wiser to summon either my grandmother or one of my cousins to assist in countering my irrational but no less insistent dread by greeting the visitor with me. But as I counted defiance among the attributes adopted prematurely by virtue of my circumstances in those days, I decided to be brave and handle the situation myself, whatever the outcome.

Shifting the candy to one hand, I went to the door, held my breath and opened it, just wide enough to get a better look at the visitor, not wide enough for him to yank out my soul should he prove to be some emissary from Hell.

My initial impression, the one that froze me in place and caused my mouth to drop open and emit a sound not unlike a stepped-on cat, was that the latter impression had been the correct one. It wasn't a demon though, not in any traditional sense. No vampire, ghoul, ghost, or monster stood upon that stoop. Only Death.

I backed away, my bladder quivering with the promise of letting go, and the candy fell from my hand. Part of me insisted that I was validating some elaborate prank and that at my age I should know better. Hadn't I been forced to question the validity of realer and substantially crueler things of late? But as those bony fingers reached around the jamb and forced from either the door or its own ancient joints a low, drawn-out creak as it pushed its way in, adjusting its scythe so that it would not catch on the wood, I unequivocally believed in horror, in nightmares made real, in the supernatural. I believed the worst thing imaginable was standing before me, here to claim my life. I should have screamed, should have run, but all I could do, as the candy rained to the floor from my stricken fingers, was stare in abject terror as that hunched, black figure with its moldy yellow face slid into the hall. He grinned at me and my bladder voided itself. His breath made a sound like someone dragging a body over gravel. Around him, the air smelled of smoke.

"Don't," was all I could say.

He mumbled something and his skull-jaw shifted sideways without opening. The teeth in that death's head grin did not part. The scythe wobbled liquidly as he reached up a hand to scratch the side of his head.

I swallowed. "Wh-what?"

"Boo," he said, and I ran so quickly and without thinking, my face collided with the unyielding wood of the kitchen door before any other part of me could think to stop it. I went down in a haze of swirling lights, groaning, mercifully oblivious to Death, wherever he was. The kitchen door swung open and shadows descended upon me. Bright lights hurt my eyes and I shielded them with a trembling hand.

A voice. My grandmother: "Oh, for Heaven's sake, Ned."

She helped me up. "Are you all right?"

I nodded, knowing she wouldn't have needed to ask such a question if Death were still present. She had chased him away, as she had so often chased away my troubles. The lights were on. She was there. My cousins were there, all of them gazing down at me with concern writ large on their faces. My heart abandoned the idea of exploding.

I sat up, the confusion abating enough for me to formulate my story. But when I turned my head toward the door to check that the horror was gone, I saw Death had not left after all. He had simply removed his face and replaced it with my grandfather's. My body's instinctive decision to bolt was halted by eleventh-hour realization. And then I felt like a fool.

"Sorry," my grandfather, Ned, said. "'Twas just a joke. You all right, boy?"

At the sight of the rubber mask dangling flaccidly from his right fist, my cheeks caught fire. I might have wept at my own gullibility, save for the lecture that came streaming out of my grandmother's mouth, aimed at her husband. Sheepishly he retreated into a room to change back into himself. Even as Death, he couldn't better my grandmother when she had her ire up.

"He's such a child," my grandmother said, and for a terrible moment I thought she meant me. But then I saw her cock her head and knew better. "You'd think he'd grow up."

I stood, forced a laugh to show I was the good sport I didn't feel I'd been at all, and went to get cleaned up. The Halloween party moved back into the kitchen to await my return. My cousins went back to gorging on candy and divining their futures from a loaf of raisin bread. I stayed in the bathroom for a long time, angry at myself. Eventually my grandfather came to find me and he apologized for the scare, despite his sly inference that it was not only entirely justified, but *necessary*. After that I felt even worse because I knew he had been doing what he did every season: getting into the spirit of things. At Christmas, he dressed up as Santa Claus even after I stopped believing in him, because it seemed the thing to do, the kind of procedure you must follow when you have a child to entertain. Halloween was the season of ghosts and scary things, so he had dressed appropriately, and now he was going to have to endure my grandmother's scorn for the rest of the evening.

We made our peace, and by then, I felt it, the idea of Death appearing at the door going from unimaginable to absurd. I rejoined the party, which some hours later culminated in another memory that would never leave me. My grandfather, dressed now in his trademark navy sport coat with leather elbow patches and equally worn slacks, his narrow face crowned by a tidy oiled-down swath of hair that looked for all the world like a careful painter's brushstroke, gathered us all around the long kitchen table. He had us light candles, which we placed before ourselves, and then he quenched the overhead lights. I felt a thrum of excitement in my chest, the warmth of it welcome after the ice that had only recently vacated it in the wake of my encounter with Mr. Death. My grandfather took his place at the head of the table, the candlelight filling the network of wrinkles in his face with deep shadow. It aged him further, gave him the aspect of a man who had lived a thousand years, and had heard as many stories.

And there, on Halloween night, he shared them with us.

I have yet to encounter a night, a scene, a place, or a storyteller, who did for my creative soul what my grandfather did that night, both via his terrifying practical joke or the stories with which he drew that night to close. If forced, I believe I would admit that I became a writer in that moment.

The village has changed quite a bit in the decades since that night. There are more houses, more stores, more people, fewer farms. Modernity has infiltrated, and the once moonlit streets are now bathed a fluorescent orange. My grandmother lives there still, but her mind is starting to go. My grandfather passed away many years ago. On his deathbed he asked how the storyteller was doing over in America. He called me by my father's name.

It wasn't the first time.

On that night back in 1987, as I lay in bed replaying the events of the evening, there were no streetlights through my bedroom window. Only the moon. And when at once, a tall, hunched shape passed by the window and threw its shadow across the floor, I told myself it was my grandfather again, trying for one last scare before the clock struck midnight.

I've spent the last twenty-six years pretending I believe it.

SCARECROW

Roberta Lannes

Cristian's mother stopped visiting him just before he turned fifteen. On her last visit, two weeks before Halloween, she left him four large brown paper bags. Inside, an orderly found a worn and battered burlap jacket two sizes too large for Cristian, faded denim overalls, a moth-eaten Old West style cowboy hat, a red and white bandana, a corn-cob pipe, and a bound wodge of straw. Someone other than she had written SCARECROW COSTUME FOR CRISTIAN ALLEN in black crayon on each bag. Inside the bag of straw, she'd included two twenty-dollar bills and a handwritten note. In simple sentences, again written by another, it read that Lupe Allen had gotten married to a man who couldn't take care of her son and he was taking her out of the state. She asked the doctor to inform Cristian that his mother and father were dead, though she had no idea where her ex-husband was. She was sorry.

As a result, Cristian became a ward of the state to receive basic board and care, plus minimal treatment for what the clinical staff determined was "Undefined Mental Retardation."

Helen Dunn read Cristian's story the week of her March arrival at Hammond Sanitarium. Given the redacted charts of her prospective students, she recognized there was only enough information to help her handle them in a studio setting. The list of her first group included two Down's Syndrome women aged 21 and 26; a man of 27 with Klinefelter's Syndrome, a woman aged 22 with Turner Syndrome, and Cristian, now 30. Each patient, considered a high-functioner, would thrive in an art and crafts program.

The art program, along with writing, dance and music programs, was created with funding from patients' wealthy parents who insisted their throw-away children, now adults, receive more benefits than others. Helen learned Cristian had earned the privilege by, over the years, becoming an integral part of staff projects, Hammond's plant care, and designing and making holiday decorations for the entire sanitarium.

From his first day in class, Cristian struck her as so remarkably normal, Helen reread his chart. After speaking with staff, Helen learned they also found Cristian to be a somewhat shy, compliant, yet wholeheartedly determined original. As a slow learner, he had adequate intellectual capacity to get a high school diploma at eighteen. Helen also noticed his Enrique Iglesias-good looks. He had a childlike manner at times, so when he gave her side-long glances, his slow grin growing into a smile, she regarded it as his nature. The truth was, those looks made her flush the same as when any proper man paid her extra attention, and woke her sleeping sense of girlishness.

Helen thought herself average in appearance, yet knew that with the help of cosmetics, she could be rather attractive. At least that was the feedback she got from guys in bars, the occasional suitor, and her last employer. The mottled mirror in her dormitory quarters, probably as old as Hammond's vaguely threatening neo-gothic architecture itself, had lost most its reflective quality. So, filled with intention, she bought a cheap wall mirror in town at Buy Mart, then put in some serious effort. The response was immediate. Staff to whom she'd been invisible now took long looks, smiled and nodded their appreciation. As did her students.

Helen knew it was inappropriate to have a *teacher's pet*, but Cristian had her heart from the start. Not only did he excel in drawing, painting, sculpting and design, he helped the others in class, patient and adroit as a teacher. When she asked Cristian to stay after class, help her set up for the next day or work up a new project, he did so with a boundless enthusiasm and creativity. During those hours, they had illuminating conversations about life, people, and every area of the arts. His naïve views, peppered with fresh perspectives delighted Helen. And when she spoke of her life, her losses, he listened, his eyes never leaving hers. Though she wasn't sure he understood her completely, it felt as if he did.

In the first several months, that he treated everyone with equal regard escaped her. Doctors, nurses, staff had great affection for Cristian, but managed a professional distance. Helen felt she'd become far too insulated living on the grounds, that she was lonely, should work at growing friendships with colleagues. But, the way Cristian seemed to fill her up despite his limitations, plus a sexual tension she sensed was reciprocal, made her lose interest. She couldn't have dreamed she'd be drawn into a romantic fantasy, pushing ethical boundaries with a student; a patient in an asylum, no less. But, it happened.

On Helen's studio wall, September's calendar had been highlighted in Cristian's fat orange lettering: *HALLOWEEN PLAN—START NOW!* Because this had been his job now for fifteen years and he was very good at it, he wanted to begin immediately. He brought Helen a stack of photo albums from each year showing the various holidays and celebrations for which he'd designed and constructed the themes and decorations. In some photos Cristian stood cradling a Valentine's Day centerpiece, pointing at a huge, intricately painted Santa with his face cut out allowing people to pop their head in for pictures, or holding American flags made of crepe paper rosettes. And in each Halloween photograph, he was present, beaming as the scarecrow from *The Wizard of Oz*. That day Helen fell a little deeper under his spell, his keenness infectious.

As they walked a path down towards the duck pond on the sprawling grounds after class, Helen felt the subtle weather shift from the humid days of summer to the cool breezes of fall. Beside her, Cristian chatted on about his Halloween ideas, this year his most ambitious. He wanted a haunted house. His pal Jasper, the eldest orderly at Hammond, showed him a 1959 movie called *House on Haunted Hill* that scared him and inspired him.

Cristian's deep voice shifted with subject and mood. Excited, he pushed past the occasional struggle to stick to a thought; a childlike lift inflected his speech.

"If I start now, I can draw out a...floor plan. Jasper and Deke will help me...put up walls in the sun room. Dividers? No...ceiling. That's okay! If they turn off the lights, it'll be...*scary* like if there's a ceiling, but I... Will Dr. Rudge let us do that?"

Helen put her arm in his. The gesture calmed him. "I think you should do a three- room floor plan. Make one room for games, one room for scares, and a lobby, like in the movie. Everyone can enter there."

He mused over the idea. "Oh, with tall...stairs?"

"Well, we can't build a stairway. But we can paint it on the wall to look real. Hugh can help. He's getting better at painting shadows." Cristian grasped her hand. Her cheeks glowed red.

"Ya, ya! And Margaret and Angela can make...um, frames for creepy pictures? They made good ones for the art show." He nuzzled her with his shoulder. "Nurse Lopez and Nurse Holquist want to make the...a drapey stuff like webs again. You seen the

Pictures! That was *so* cool!"

Helen glanced back up the path to see if anyone was following. Watching. The slope down to the pond provided some seclusion. They were alone.

She nudged him toward a covered bench. Ducks hurried out of the water anticipating food. Cristian pulled a baggie stuffed with pieces of bread from his pocket.

They sat together, touching. She brushed his cheek with the back of her hand.

He broke up the bread and began tossing the lumps at the quacking throng. "Look! Lots of new babies! Here you go duckys!"

His hair had grown longer, the breeze pushing it onto his beatific face, obscuring his smile. Helen leaned against him, feeling his warmth. She pulled her arm from his, snaking her fingers under his shirt to his back, his skin as smooth as his hands, arms. Helen swooned. Cristian went still, his face going slack. As she'd anticipated, they shared this bliss!

"Is this okay, Cristian?"

"Ya, ya!" He leaned closer, smiling. "Nice!"

He enjoyed their closeness; occasionally putting his arms around her waist, touching her hair, her back. Once he smoothed her apron down over her breasts when he thought no one was looking. His face went blank as his groin stiffened, the arousal exhilarating and confounding him. Helen knew from the nurses that Cristian had been adamantly discouraged from acting on his hormone-driven urges. As an impressionable boy, Cristian took the words of the repressive staff as orders, and as time passed blithely suppressed his sexual self.

How she wanted to help him find it! Yesterday in the empty studio, she'd hazarded a long, brazen embrace and wet fumbled kiss, during which he pressed himself against her over and over until he gave a soprano grunt. He rushed out saying, "Sorry. Sorry!" over his shoulder. Today, she'd wanted to ask him if he ever touched himself 'down there'. She fanaticized him in bed, thinking of her, his long exquisite fingers moving over his erection. She'd shivered at the thought.

A gardener came over the ridge pushing a cart. She yanked herself back to reality. Halloween.

"That scarecrow outfit is really old. Will you get a new costume this year?"

He pulled away. "No. Mrs. Slattery...washed it...last year and I...I painted the dirt back on just right. Jasper even found me...more straw."

"Do you keep it because your mother gave it to you?"

He shrugged. "No. She's dead." He stared at the tree line where the willows danced. "I don't know what else...to be. I like making other people look...like witches...monsters and stuff." He tossed out more crumbs. "What about you?"

Helen hadn't thought about it. Halloween wasn't one of her holidays. She was a Christmas girl. Valentine's Day girl. "I don't know. The last time I dressed up for Halloween, I was in college. I think I was a sexy cat!" She laughed.

Cristian squirmed. "I think you're a sexy…teacher." He gave her the sly sidelong glance and smiled. "But, you have to at least wear a mask." He set the baggie of bread on the bench. His hands moved as if fabricating something before her eyes. "I'll design you a good mask! Make it out of papier-mâché characters. We can paint it. Whatever you want!"

She wrapped her arms around herself, the breeze turning chilly. "Can I think about it?"

Cristian got up and paced, hands gesticulating, scattering the hungry ducks. "Ya, ya. What about a…Harli-queen? Oh, oh, cat woman!"

Helen smiled indulgently; explaining she didn't like wearing a mask. They were claustrophobic. Makeup, maybe. And after all, a teacher should be recognizable to everyone. His smile disappeared.

"Ya, ya…I get it. But…it's *Halloween*." He rarely whined. It reminded Helen that Cristian was in many ways still like a ten-year-old boy.

Cristian looked away to hide his disappointment. Averting his eyes from hers, he grabbed the baggie and angrily emptied it onto the lawn. Petulantly, he stepped through the ducks back onto the path to wait for her. Helen wondered what the hell she was doing.

"Okay, we'll go. I'm cold anyway." She stood, noting the breeze had gone and the late afternoon sun was reflected in the glassy pond.

On the walk back, Cristian stared out over the rolling hills, into the clouds moving overhead, gasping at a flock of birds moving in unison, then breaking into wild arcs. She loved how he absorbed everything, allowing it to dissipate his darker feelings. She wished that worked for her.

Slowly, his mood shifted, grew brighter. By the time they reached the main building, he was chattering on happily about the new flowerbeds, explaining what grew in fall, preparing for winter. Helen had sunk back into her fantasies, longing for him to take her to his bed, embrace her. Make her forget the ache of loneliness.

Over the next month, Helen let Cristian appropriate the arts and crafts students, pull in staff, and begin directing his highly choreographed series of projects. The more he took on, the more they worked together. As Helen's admiration and respect for self-assured Cristian increased, so did her passion. A kind of blindness crept up on her, as if the world the two of them inhabited gradually blurred at the edges until there was only shadow. Conversely, Cristian radiated light and joy, inviting everyone around him to partake of it. Selfishly, she began to resent sharing him at all. Her ardor had begun to edge into the realm of madness.

During a meeting with staff about the Halloween extravaganza, Dr. Rudge sat with the team flipping through Cristian's gorgeous renderings of his vision for the haunted house, the pumpkin patch, and decorations for the sanitarium. Helen sat doodling in her sketchpad, lost in thought. Nurse Holquist kicked Helen's ankle and she started.

"Miss Dunn, you have some input here, yes?" Impatience tinged Dr. Rudge's voice.

Helen blushed. "Uh. We're talking about scheduling?" She sat up, looking into each of the waiting faces.

"As I was saying, we've approved Cristian's images, we've signed up for our roles in this, but we all know that scheduling isn't Cristian's strong suit. We have less than a month. You gave us the list of things already completed, so how do you envision our participation over that short period of time?"

She hadn't worked up a schedule but was getting good at thinking on the spot.

"Okay, Cristian has us figured into teams. There are the builders, fabricators, painters, the set-up crew, and then finishing-touches group. The fabricators and builders have everything they need. My students and some staff are the painters. Set-up combines all the groups." Everyone looked at each other.

Dr. Rudge ran his plump hand over his balding pate, adjusted his glasses. "Can you give us a time frame? A schedule? We're all quite busy."

Helen swallowed hard. Yes. A timeline. "Let's meet back here in a week at this time and I'll have a complete program with names, places, jobs and times as exact as I can figure. How's that?" Pretty competent-sounding, she thought.

Nods all around. "Agreed. Thank you, Miss Dunn. Oh, and Nurse Lopez wanted a word with you before you left." He stood and the staff scattered like cockroaches when the lights go on.

Anya Lopez, a short, matronly Hispanic woman, approached. In her fifties, Nurse Lopez had risen to head nurse a decade before Helen's arrival and had been Cristian's surrogate mother as long as he'd been at Hammond.

"Hi Helen. *Don't* get up." Helen felt immediate panic at the tone in Anya's voice. Anya sat down beside her.

Helen steeled herself. "Okay. What's this about?"

Anya smiled tightly. "Cristian." She clasped her hands on the table, her knuckles white. "I'm not going to lecture you. You're what...thirty-five? You've worked in hospital settings before? Done art therapy with adults having diminished capacities, yes?"

Helen nodded, though she wanted to correct her age. Thirty-one.

"Cristian's unique in our community. He's very competent, reliable. It's easy to see him as a staff member instead of a patient. Maybe you don't realize this, but your behavior with him is getting...questionable." She sighed. "Do you know what I'm talking about?"

Helen wouldn't say what was truly happening between her and Cristian. No one would understand, least of all his surrogate mother. She grabbed the edge of her seat and held on tight.

"I might if you told me your concerns." She felt as though she was about to fall through the floor into a vat of writhing snakes.

"All right." Anya sighed, barely concealing her distaste. "Cristian started calling you his girlfriend this summer, not Miss Dunn. Not even Helen. I've corrected him, explained you're his teacher and that's all. He explained that he loved you and wanted to marry you. *Have babies.* I asked him where he got these notions, and he said you told him it was what you wanted, dreamed about. He might confuse that to mean *with him.* I know he gets baffled with concepts. But adding the way you look at him sometimes and touch him...flirt...

"While Cristian's a good boy and he knows right from wrong, he also has a man's body. Need I say more?"

Before Helen could stop them, tears fell over her cheeks and her hands went over her face. Anya could have saved her words and simply slapped Helen a few times. The shame would've overwhelmed her either way. Helen had erred beyond reckoning.

Once composed, Helen admitted that her loneliness, her isolation, her ease with Cristian must have thrown her off course. The admiration, even love she'd developed for him had taken on mortifying proportions. She recognized the need to redraw the boundaries before they were beyond repair.

Anya remained correct, proper. "We all feel that way about Cristian. It's the…"

Helen shook her head, adamant. "I know. Inappropriate behavior. I've got it."

"I haven't said anything to Dr. Rudge, though there is talk around here I can't help but hear. You must take control and fix this, or I'll have to say something." She grasped Helen's wrist, stared into her eyes. "You're expendable, Helen. Cristian isn't. We're his home as long as he lives, and if need be we can hire another art teacher."

Helen nodded meekly. "Understood."

Nurse Lopez stood, straightened the tunic of her scrubs and walked away. A minute later, Helen followed her out on wobbly legs.

That night, unable to sleep, Helen ruminated on diplomatic ways to make the necessary changes. The opportunity to explain things to Cristian was ripe before her. But, with Halloween approaching, his focus and enthusiasm so necessary, she decided to implement adjustments in increments. She'd first curtail her affection, reel in expressions that went beyond those she'd offer other students, and say "no" to any temptation, even when every nerve in her screamed "yes!" She hoped he'd be too busy to notice. Then, after Halloween, she'd explain everything. Slowly but eventually, he'd adapt.

She wouldn't allow her mistakes, though *she'd* been the one to misconstrue or romanticize a man's inappropriate behavior, to end her employment as they had before. She loved this job.

The moment she entered her studio, saw him sitting at his table with a bowl of flowers and his open smile, her heart began to break. She wanted to throw her arms around him, tell him all she wanted was to take him away with her. But, tragically, they weren't meant to be. She'd made a promise to Anya Lopez. To herself.

She could barely breathe. Feigning neutrality turned her fingers to ice and made her blood run cold. How did she speak to others?

She stared at the flowers. "What do you have there?"

"Flowers for you. I cut them. Put...them in the bowl I made. Your favorite colors!"

He held his wonderful hands out around the bowl. Like flesh wings.

"Don't move! I want to take a photograph." She rushed to the safe and retrieved her digital camera. *Go with a distraction.*

Cristian kept his hands still, his smile frozen as she moved around him shooting the fuchsia, red and purple flowers. His precious, talented hands. Like a mantra she repeated the words *keep it professional* over and over.

"Done." She set the camera on the table. "Okay, let me tell you about the meeting."

She sat across from him, pushing the sketchbook with her notes to the middle of the table. She babbled the minutes of the meeting like a reporter. Once, when she got fixed by his gaze, she felt her heart open. Terrified, she shut it down. Then, just before the others arrived, filing into the room, she reflexively opened her arms to him. Stricken by her slip, she turned away, grabbed the camera off the table and moved it to the safe. She went to her desk, and stared out the window, drowning in anguish.

He went to her, crestfallen. "Did I do something wrong, Miss?"

No eye contact. "No, Cristian. Why?" She glanced at his smooth hands, held in prayer at his chest.

"I don't know. I feel...it hurts here. My belly's cold." He described her pain. She wanted to run, get drunk under a cold shower, and sleep a year away.

"Are you sick?"

"I don't know!" He stepped backwards, then turned and hurried out.

Helen wondered if she could end this. She'd started it, stoked the heat of it, and Cristian got stuck with flames she'd had to dowse with frost.

Somehow, through a state of shock, she kept the students working. They asked where Cristian went, but once involved in their projects, forgot their concern.

Late that evening, the cold shower stunned her despite downing half the bottle of whiskey she'd kept in her closet. Then, she relished the penance of it. Naked and shivering, she went to her window overlooking the path. For a moment she thought she saw a scarecrow standing under a lamppost staring up at her. She put her hands over her eyes; let her head hit the sill. Without looking out again, she turned to her bed, aching for sleep.

Helen kept up the façade of detachment as Cristian grew sullen and distracted a little more each day. His mood infected the others. Their efforts waned. Jasper stopped her on her way to lunch to say he was worried about Cristian. He'd never seen him so *bummed*. She frowned at him and suggested Cristian talk to a doctor. After all, this *was* a sanitarium. Jasper called her a bitch under his breath. When she passed Nurse Lopez in the halls, she roiled with regret.

Returning after lunch, she found a jar on her desk. It looked like a nail jar from the woodshop downstairs. Inside was a wodge of cotton with a raisin-colored stain. She opened it and peered inside. The smell of copper rose up. The stain was blood. She slapped the lid on and tossed the jar into the trash.

As her students resumed work on the joinery for the cardboard skeleton parts, she pushed aside the disgust mixed with morbid curiosity. Then, mid-afternoon, Helen caught Cristian standing over the trashcan, arms at his sides.

Margaret shouted at him, awaiting help to keep the shoulder bone connected to the neck bone.

"Cristian! We need you! Over here!"

Helen chastised her. "We don't shout, Margaret."

Cristian ambled over. He pushed the brad through the cardboard wincing, and Helen saw then that he'd cut his hand. Gauze encircled his knuckles.

She reached out and touched his wrist. His head snapped up, his eyes wide as if she'd just held a live wire to his arm. "How did you hurt your hand?"

It took him a few moments to collect himself, his eyes holding her gaze. "On the wire. Making the plaster spiders." He'd been working on them with Deke and Jasper in the woodshop.

"Sorry. Hope it gets better quick." She turned to work out which bone attached to the thigh bone.

The next morning before class, as Helen checked that the witch silhouettes had dried, she noticed a small white box on her desk. Still haunted by the jar, she left it there untouched the entire day. Cristian checked on the box a few times to see if it had been moved or opened, his eyes darting to her then back. This gift. It was Cristian's. She bit back a grin. He'd always given her things; flowers, interesting stones, pictures cut from magazines, but this? She waited until everyone left before she opened it.

Exhausted, she slumped into her chair. Her stomach growled. Tonight was another meeting for the 'Halloween Haunt' as it was now called. She hoped she had time to run to the dining room and get a huge hamburger and fries. Be back in time.

Pulling the top off the box, she steeled for more bloody cotton. Tissue had been meticulously folded into a neat envelope. She lifted it out. Nearly weightless. She unfolded it slowly, then shrieked, dropping it on the desk. A crinkled brown scab fell out, encircled by neatly clipped toenails. A revolting sun. She pushed the box, the tissue and *gift* into the trash. An involuntary shudder coursed through her.

Cristian. Why *this*? So confoundedly unlike him! Should she speak to Dr. Rudge? No, then she'd have to tell him the entire story. Anya! She'd speak to Anya Lopez at the meeting tonight. No one knew him better.

But, Anya wasn't at the meeting. Dr. Rudge mentioned a family emergency. Shaken, Helen forced herself to keep with the agenda, hand out the schedules and give the expected progress report. After the meeting, she offered a folder for Anya to Dr. Rudge, asking him to get it to her. She hoped he didn't open it and find the post-it note that said: *FIND ME—IMPORTANT WE TALK.*

When Anya hadn't returned by late October, Helen sought Nurse Holquist out to find out if Nurse Lopez was ever coming back. She found her in the break room looking bothered, but asked about Anya anyway.

"The last anyone's heard, she flew to New Mexico, or wherever her people are. Someone died. Now, I'm doing her job *and* mine. We need to hire another nurse!" Nurse Holquist continued carping about her plight as Helen found the butterflies in her belly had grown razorblade wings.

The gifts had worsened in size and grotesqueness; dirty bandages, cotton balls soaked with puss or jizz, finger and toenail clippings and clumps of curly hair she suspected were of the pubic variety. In the event Cristian was watching, she feigned detachment at finding a new gift. Then, after they'd all gone, she wrapped whatever had been left there in a plastic bag and stored it with the others in the safe because Cristian had taken to searching the trashcan at the end of the day. Once again, he gave her sidelong glances, his grin now menacing; blood draining from her face instead of flushing it.

Later, alone in her quarters, she realized Cristian wasn't much different from the beginning. Her perspective had changed. Her sadness and remorse were replaced by revulsion. In fact, Cristian's sullenness had disappeared after the third gift. He laughed again, sought Helen's approval, which she had to give him—his work was excellent. A few times, Helen noticed the injuries on his arms that produced his presents. She told him she was happy he'd kept his hands beautiful. But, be careful. This pleased him and his fervor grew.

Cristian's change in mood impacted the others as well. He initiated conversations centered on Halloween, its origins, what scared people, and he speculated about ghosts.

With her entire gang now fully engaged with Halloween now only a day away, Helen surrendered wholeheartedly. When Cristian reached out to touch her, nudge her to see what he was doing, only then did she flinch.

On Halloween, as with every big event at Hammond, parents, the curious and unafraid, as well as local journalists came in the afternoon to swarm the grounds. The staff and patients had created a truly remarkable spectacle.

Helen accompanied Deke to the pumpkin patch he'd supervised. She'd not yet seen it and gawked at the sight.

"These carved pumpkins are going to look amazing lit from within tonight."

"Oh, yeah! Thanks!" He grinned at her. "You decide your costume for tonight?" Deke already wore a clown get-up without the wig or makeup. He waved at his head. "I've got to finish mine later."

"I've been too busy to do anything special. I borrowed an old style nurse's uniform Mrs. Slattery found in the back of the linens storeroom. It fits perfectly. Pathetic, isn't it?"

He raised an eyebrow at her. "Really? Nobody *expects* to see a nurse here?" Helen giggled, a hand over half her face.

Deke looked out at the sawdust laid down over the fake cornfield where the pumpkins sat on crates. "Crap. I suck at subtlety." He laughed, kicking at a corn stalk, then turned to her. "So, after the festivities tonight, you want to go into town and watch the mayhem the sane folks get into?"

"Are you...asking me out?" She'd never considered Deke. After months of insanity, something so ordinary struck her as strange.

He stared into the darkening sky, nodding. "Aye. That I am. Looks like that storm they said was coming in tomorrow may be early."

He had an accent. English? Aussie? And kind eyes. She grinned. "Where should we meet?"

"I'll find you. You'll be the only person dressed as a nurse who isn't one. I'll ditch the clown act before we go, but please...keep the uniform on." He chortled, pointing to his face. "This mask'll suit me just fine."

Helen supervised the finishing touches when she couldn't find Cristian, glad and annoyed at the same time. At seven, the haunted house thrummed with activity. Though less than a third of sanitarium patients were allowed to participate, the forty plus gathered there, nearby, eager for new frights, treats, and fun. She enjoyed guessing at the staff's identity beneath a mask or makeup. Dr. Rudge arrived, dressed as a judge with a gavel and law book under his arm.

"Where's our special Halloween director?" His rheumy green eyes scanned the sunroom.

Helen shrugged. "Saw Cristian around four when he took the last of our spiders to the scare room. Have you been in to see it?"

He shook his head. "I'm sure it's frightening, but I want to keep my eyes on a few of my patients I paired up, then…" He frowned. "And here I go!" He rushed over to two rag dolls, one old and skinny, the other fat, fighting over candy.

There, in that moment, she felt proud and happy with the results. But her feet hurt in borrowed nurse's shoes. When she leaned over to loosen the laces, a tap on her shoulder made her jump.

Standing before her was a short, grinning clown. She couldn't make out who it was and looked puzzled.

"Helen, its *Anya*." She put her hands on her hips. "I got your message."

Helen threw her arms around her, but she recoiled in surprise. Helen backed off. "Sorry. I just got worried when I heard…When d'you get back? How are you?"

"Okay, considering. My daughter-in-law was in an accident and my son is doing a tour in Afghanistan. I had to take care of my grandkids." She turned to watch the drama with Dr. Rudge. "I got back yesterday."

"Have you seen Cristian? I bet he'd like to see you. He's asked about you every day since you've been gone."

Anya eyed her up and down. "*Nurse* Dunn…" Anya smirked. "No, not since dinner. I was surprised to see him so…*up*. He was pretty shaken when you cut off the romance. Good job, by the way."

"So you talked? I'm glad. Do you know about the gifts, then?"

She squinted. "Gifts?"

Helen surveyed the room and decided it was under control. "Come with me to the studio. I've got some things to show you." Anya hesitated, then followed.

As they passed a gaggle of revelers, Helen explained what had gone on since Anya had disappeared. She wished Anya hadn't painted her face; her expression got lost beneath the rubber nose and drawn arched brows.

There was a sudden din of haunted house sounds and eerie music.

Anya shouted, "This is so out of character for Cristian. Like a different person! Do you think he's maiming himself on purpose to create these…things?"

"Maybe. In a twisted way, I thought maybe he imagined he was giving me a piece of himself. A pretty horrific concept. But, I didn't think he could form that kind of…"

Anya stopped her at the top of the stairs. "¡Dios mío! I just thought of something." She drew Helen towards the wall of the landing. "Just before I talked to you about your *thing* with Cristian, he told me he wanted to give his girlfriend a new present. I knew he meant you. I thought about his artwork. Told him that you'd most appreciate something that came from him, by *his* hand. Something he created himself. If he warped that into…this? Maybe we all underestimated our boy."

"I can't think. Come on." Helen stopped at the half-open door to the studio, then turned to Anya. "I locked it."

Anya pushed the door open and switched on the light. "So many people have keys to the classrooms. Janitors, orderlies. Come on, show me."

Helen felt her legs turn to jelly as she approached the safe. Opened it. Anya stood aside, taking the baggies as Helen handed them over. "See? Some of the jars and boxes…he turned into bugs, little animals." Helen quaked.

Anya clucked. "I'd never have guessed he did these. He's the most pure, genuine…" She shoved the bags back at Helen, then began to walk away. Over her shoulder she said, "He was a complete innocent before you. I should've said something during summer. I didn't think…"

"Oh, *no!*" Helen looked at her desk, the large corrugated box with orange pumpkins painted on the sides. A huge bone knife on the floor. The window, open. Blood on the sill. Dark pools on the linoleum floor. Her vision went dim and she fell to her knees.

"Anya?!"

Cristian, she wanted say. *Another gift. Look! Look out the window!* But a scream came out instead, queerly high pitched. Anya followed Helen's eyes as they jittered from her desk to the floor to the window.

"I'm getting security!"

Don't leave! Please don't leave me alone! Helen meant to shout the words, but her screaming continued. She crawled to the desk, then pulling herself up by the table leg, stood over the open box. The screaming stopped.

Nestled in a snowy bed of cotton balls was a graying hand. Cristian's hand. Severed at the wrist. Somehow she managed to shuffle to the window, her white nurse's shoes pulling the blood into brushstrokes. Helen plopped her hands onto the windowsill beside the bloody prints. Her legs went out from under her, her chin smacking the sill, rattling her teeth. She didn't feel it.

As the sounds of heavy footfalls on linoleum filled the room, she looked down. Leaning halfway against a lamppost, his hat on the lawn and straw strewn about like golden exclamation marks, was a scarecrow. His legs were skewed in preposterous directions, and he cradled a bloody burlap sleeve in the most beautiful hand Helen had ever seen.

STRANGE CANDY

Robert McCammon

"Now *this*," I said, "is a piece of strange candy."

"Yeah, I've seen it," Carol answered. "Jenny saw it too, and she said no way she was eating it. She put it right back in there. Said you could have it." Carol smiled faintly, saying *if you dare*. A faint smile was about all she could muster this Halloween. It had been a tough year.

"Hm," I replied, looking more closely at what I'd just taken from the bottom of the bag of treats. It was a small hand, five-fingered and ghostly-white. It sparkled, as if covered with small grains of sugar, but instead of being grainy it felt very smooth. "Weird," I said. "Do we know where we got this from? A haunted house, maybe?"

"No idea." Carol cuddled up next to me on the sofa. "I do know it's not wrapped, so I wouldn't let *anybody* eat it."

"Beware the poisoned hand." I dropped it back into the bag, which our eight-year-old had decorated with colorful stickers of bats, black cats, owls and witch's hats. Jenny had done her work this night, dressed as a fairy princess along with a brigade of neighborhood zombies, ghouls, Batmen, vampires and walking pumpkins, and gone on to bed pretty much exhausted. Leaving me and her mom to prowl through the trick-or-treat bag, after Jenny had taken out the best "loot", as she called it, the little individually-wrapped candy bars, the small bags of M&Ms and the Reese's cups. Smart kid we had. She put everything she wanted in a smaller plastic bag on the kitchen counter, and I was sure she'd know if anything was missing. Therefore, no looting through the "loot" tonight.

We lived in a small town. Not too small. But a place where there were not too many streets and not too many houses and not too much stuff to get in the way of life. It was a good town, and we lived in a good neighborhood. I had gone out with my wife and daughter tonight and walked many streets in search of the prime loot. Of course you always got strange candy that seemed to collect at the bottom of the bag, and no kid would touch it and no adult ought to. That was part of Halloween, as well.

It had been, as I said, a tough year. It seemed colder this Halloween than it did last year. A little darker too, and for sure it was quieter. Maybe I should say, more solemn. The family photographs in our house were diminished. It was the way things were.

Carol and I talked about our day tomorrow. A Saturday. We could take things easy. We had nowhere to go, and no particular plans. It was supposed to rain early in the morning, and get chilly. Winter was on the way. I thought of bleak days and trees without leaves, and I realized I wasn't ready to think about those things yet.

It was nearing midnight. Time for my horror movie. Yes, that's what I did near midnight every Halloween. I watched a horror movie, usually an old one, from my DVD collection. And I had a bunch. Carol was tired, and she wasn't a big fan of horror movies anyway, so I kissed her and said goodnight and when she went upstairs I looked through my collection for the flick I had in mind. There it was: *The Haunting*, the first version, 1963, in glorious and spooky black-and-white. I'd seen it before, several times. Last year I'd watched it. It was familiar.

I put the DVD into the player, settled back on the sofa and started the movie. I heard the wind blow past the house, like a keening cry. Yeah, suitable for Halloween all right. Except Halloween was almost over, all the witches and black cats and ghoulies and ghosties of the night either already asleep or headed to dreamland.

When did I reach into that bag and take out the sparkly white hand?

I don't remember, but I did take it out. Maybe it was when you got your first view of Hill House, that beautifully gothic pile of fright. Maybe. But I was suddenly looking at the strange candy, and I wondered who had dropped it into the bag. I sniffed the thing.

Pepperminty.

Eleanor…Eleanor…it knows my name…

A great movie. But I had the strange candy in my hand—a ghostly hand in my hand—and I begin to think that not only was it beautiful, with its long tapered five fingers…and that it smelled good…but that maybe it tasted good too. Not poisoned at all. Just…different. Unique. I'd never seen anything like it before. So…well, I mean, I didn't want to die, but…still…it was just a piece of candy, shaped like a hand. What was the big deal?

Man or mouse? Kind of ridiculous to be afraid of it. I mean, I wasn't afraid of it. So I bit off one of the fingers first. Crunchy. Definitely… peppermint? No, not quite. Minty, yes, but…a little cinnamon in there too? Oil of clove? I thought it tasted like something I'd had a long, long time ago: a pair of wax lips. The taste of that was memorable, and yet… unexplainable.

No harm done. I ate the whole thing. Crunchy crunchy. Now back to the drama, and the black-and-white fright, and the suffering spirit in Hill House who walks alone.

It was nearing midnight, as I said. Midnight, almost. A few ticks of the clock away, and then Halloween would really be gone.

Only I was no longer in my living room watching a movie on the bigscreen.

No.

Not there.

Had it happened when I blinked my eyes? Had it happened when I looked away from the screen to check the clock? Had it happened sometime between the beats of my heart?

No longer in my living room. I was standing up, in another room. Was there in this room the faintest odor of gunsmoke? It was a small room, like a hotel room. Dark. Sad. The windows had their blinds pulled down and closed tightly, like old wounds stitched up but not quite healed. The windows looked like they had not let light and life into this room for a long time.

And sitting in a chair before the darkened windows and the closed blinds was a man, about middle-aged, with gray hair. A lock of hair hung over his forehead. He glanced at me, incuriously, and then away again. His face remained in shadow. He spoke.

"Tell Maggie that she is *not* responsible," he said. "Tell her I loved her, but that I was weak. I could say it was the gambling. I could say it was a lot of things, but it was really only me. She tried to be strong for both of us, and that was a blessing I failed to see. Tell her that, will you? Tell her she is *not* to blame for what I did…that was my choice. She is Margaret Ballard, at 309 2nd Avenue South. Will you tell her?"

"Yes," I said. Or think I said. Margaret Ballard, 309 2nd Avenue South. "Yes, I will."

And suddenly the man and the chair and the room and the windows were no longer there. Suddenly I was standing in the middle of a curving road, with woods on either side. The wind moved around me; the wind pushed me forward in the dark. And standing there on the side of the road were two figures, a young boy and young girl, maybe sixteen or seventeen. They were holding hands, and they were smiling because it was obvious they were very much in love.

"Hey!" said the boy, who had curly dark hair and the fiery look of someone who enjoyed being a rebel. He looked like he could bite the wind in two and ride on a shooting star. The girl hugged close to him, and he pulled her even closer until they were nearly one.

"Tell my Dad and Mom we're okay," he said. "It was over real quick. I was dumb. Took that curve way too fast. But we wanted to get away, so bad. So awful bad. Tell them not to be so sad, okay? Tell them we were in love…really in love, like everybody says you ought to be. We couldn't just *stop* being in love, could we? And tell them we're still in love, and we'll always be. Okay? That would be Mike and Ann Frazier, at 622 Overbrook Road. You tell them, and you should tell Lynn's folks too. Gerald and Kathy Bannerman, at 4114 Millview Street. And tell them... maybe they could bring some flowers out here? You know...just to show they heard us."

"All right," I said, as the wind moved and turned and twisted, and I saw behind the lovers the scars on the trees and the foliage still broken. 622 Overbrook Road and 4114 Millview Street. "I'll tell them," I said, and I saw the boy kiss the girl's forehead very tenderly, and I thought *yes you will always be in love.*

And then I was standing on a corner downtown, and as far as I could see the traffic lights were green and yet there was no traffic for it was nearly midnight on Halloween and our town was asleep.

Except for the little boy with light brown hair who stood in the street, and he smiled at me as if he knew me, and maybe I knew him too but I couldn't quite remember his name, and maybe I had heard about this tragedy sometime in May.

"Tell my mom I'm sorry I can't be the man of the house anymore," he said. "But tell her she has to stop being so alone, and she's got to get out and find people again. It didn't really hurt when the car hit me. It was an accident. I was running where I shouldn't have been. But tell mom I want her not to give up, and not to want to follow me. Tell her I said I always wanted to fly in a plane, but I never got to...but...when it happened...it kinda felt like flying. Tell her I love her, and I said go live your life like you should. And to go start playing bingo again, maybe she'll win another jackpot! She's Mary Waldron, at 744 Clark Street. You'll have to knock real hard, 'cause she stays in the back."

"I will," I told him. 744 Clark Street. "Yes," I said.

Just that fast the scene changed. I was standing in Midpoint Park, with all the lamps aglow, and an old man with white hair was sitting on a bench. He was wearing a dark suit and a white shirt with a thin black tie. He looked very comfortable, his legs splayed out before him.

"Well, well," he said, and he sighed. "The passage of time. Oh, mercy me. What a life!" He glanced at me and smiled. "I had me one," he confided. "Now you go tell Teddy that his Grandpa Nicholas will *never* forget him. Not a chance of it! He's such a young boy, he doesn't understand, and John and Amy have tried to make him understand…but he just can't. You go tell Teddy that his Grandpa Nicholas wants him to grow up and throw that football a country mile. The football I bought him. He'll know. Tell him I'm happy, that I miss him and I'll never *ever* forget him, and things are as they should be. Oh, tell John and Amy I think they ought to put the swimming pool in, Teddy would like that. John and Amy Phillips, at 2561 Viceroy Circle. Got that?"

"I do," I answered. 2561 Viceroy Circle. *Got it.*

"You're done now," he told me. "Go home."

Did I wake up? Did I come to? Did I return home from a far distance?

I don't know, but I was sitting on my sofa looking dazedly at the image on the bigscreen. Halloween was over. It was maybe seven ticks past midnight. I heard the wind keen again outside, and I guess I thought I ought to get to bed, because I turned off the TV and the DVD player and I went upstairs. And on my way up I was thinking about this weird dream I must have had…and I remembered vividly all the addresses I was given, and what to say, and to whom. And weird…very weird… was the fact that I could still taste the strange candy in my mouth, and I thought I had met one spirit for every finger of the ghostly hand.

I checked in on Jenny. She was sleeping soundly, even as rain began to tap at the windows. I looked in on the empty room, just out of habit. Then I went to the bedroom where Carol slept, and I was so weary I only took off my shoes before I got into bed. She nestled her body up beside mine, she sighed, and I got to sleep a little while later after thoughts of the ghostly hand and the five spirits had faded.

What time did the doorbell ring? Early. Just after seven o'clock.

I got up, and Carol sat up groggily and said, "Who can *that* be?"

"I don't know," I said as I staggered out when the doorbell rang again, "but whoever it is better have a *real* good reason."

At the door was a slim man in his thirties, with reddish-blonde hair and a determined expression. It was raining lightly, and he was wearing a dark green jacket that made the water stand out in beads on its fabric. His glasses were flecked with rain.

I opened the door, a little bit angrily I guess, and I asked, "What is it?"

"Chris Parker?"

"Yes. Can I help you?" I was aware of Carol coming up behind me, yawning and rubbing her eyes. A great way to start a lazy Saturday, for sure!

"Mr. Parker," said the man, "she says she's doing just fine. She says she's not hurting anymore…and she wants you to know how much she loves you. Both of you," he added, glancing at Carol.

"What?" Carol asked. "*What?*"

I listened. I was stunned. But I listened.

"She says it really was no big deal when she lost her hair. No biggie, she said. And…she wants to say to Jenny…she hopes she got some good loot."

"*What?*" Carol grasped hold of my arm. Tears bloomed in her eyes. I put my arm around her, and held on tightly. We became one, as I had seen two other lovers recently become. In that moment we needed each other, and maybe I needed her more than ever.

We had lost Beth, our fifteen-year-old, to cancer in April. A sad springtime. It had been a tough year. Our family photographs were diminished by the loss of one member.

"That's all, I guess," the man said, and he started to move off the porch and down the steps to the street where his car was. But he paused in the rain and looked back, and he said, "Oh…one more thing. She says…where she is…no one walks alone."

Then he went on to his car.

And I let him go.

I let him go without asking if from his child's bag of treats he had taken last night a piece of strange candy, and thought it smelled like peppermint. I let him go without asking if he had eaten that strange candy, and what number on the fingers I might have been.

He got into his car, and drove away.

Carol had her head against my shoulder, and she was shaking because though she didn't understand, she knew we had just received a message from a spirit who had come through some kind of passageway between the living and the dead on Halloween, with the intent not on fright but on freeing their loved ones from pain, sadness, loss and doubt, if just a little bit.

I remembered very clearly all the addresses I'd been given, and all the messages I had to deliver.

I kissed Carol's forehead, very tenderly. *We will be in love forever,* I thought.

Then I told her I had some places to go visit this morning, some very important places, and she and Jenny could go with me if they liked, and on the way I would try to explain as best I could about the night and about the strange candy.

And I would tell her as best I could about the mission I had been called to complete. A mission of the heart and the soul. A mission of mercy. A mission of love that knew no boundaries, to five different houses on five different streets, in our little town where there was not too much stuff to get in the way of life.

The Road Not Taken

Harry Shannon

It took me a while to realize what I wanted to write about October 31st, my very favorite holiday. It turns out that it's not about one specific event so much as a long learning curve about the very human struggle Halloween represents—life and death, darkness and light, choosing wickedness or learning how to love.

I am an old man now, in my 66th year. I loved Halloween as a kid, because even though I spent my childhood in personal turmoil, that one magic night always spelled freedom. In costume, I got to be one of those happy boys in a Ray Bradbury story, racing down the dark fall streets sweating colored greasepaint, clothed in a torn white sheet, packing my pillow case with hundreds of pieces of those dime store purchased chocolate-flavored constipation-generating little candies. Reno was a great place to be young, but by the time we moved to Pomona, California, my family had begun to disintegrate. Alcoholism and addiction and divorce ultimately claimed us. As for me, I morphed into a six-foot-tall,

165-pound, 13-year-old. On Halloween evening of 1962, when I went out to play monster one last time, I got mocked by an adult for being too old, for even clinging to such silliness. Humiliated and stung, I went home to lick my wounds. Unfortunately, home was not a fun place to be that night. Enough said.

By the time Halloween of 1963 rolled around, I'd started hanging with a very bad group. I guess we thought we were James Dean in *Rebel Without a Cause*. We smoked Camels, trashed things, drank beer and beat on each other now and again, mostly just for the hell of it. That Halloween, my best friend, another kid from a troubled home, persuaded me to replace Halloween treats with trickery. We downed a six pack, manufactured a life sized dummy of a boy in jeans and a work shirt with a string tie and a cowboy hat, and went down to squat by a blind turn in a nearby road.

I'll bet you can see the rest coming. One lone driver left the freeway and took the dark corner too fast. Just as he broke through the trees we tossed the "body" out into the road. The man stomped on squealing brakes, struck the fake child anyway, and ran his vehicle up onto a dirt embankment, very narrowly avoiding causing a serious wreck. I still remember his twin beams pointing up at an angle, as if aimed at the moon. He jumped out waving his arms and screaming. When he got close enough to see the boy was a dummy, he understandably went ballistic.

My friend and I sat in the weeds, listening as he cursed us out and threatened to have us arrested. Eventually, he threw the dummy in his back seat and drove away. My friend kept on laughing and laughing about our successful prank. I tried my best to join in but I was just faking it. Even though no one had gotten hurt, something inside me genuinely visited to the dark side that night. We'd both crossed some kind of a line, and I knew it.

High School had started and a lot of trouble followed. Soon the year-round darkness we occupied was no longer just a harmless amusement. It became a disturbing reality. Felonies happened, though most of them without my even realizing that I'd participated. Some more serious fights took place. One hell of a lot of drinking went down. My life went places it shouldn't have gone. The two of us tried to hot wire my father's old Ford one night, and he chased us down the street in his underwear, smashed out of his mind, screaming, "Stop, thief!" My brother remembers it, but Dad died without ever knowing it was me.

To make a long story short, by my senior year, I'd kind of gotten my act together, mostly due to the intervention of some damn good teachers. Still, many years passed before I allowed myself to celebrate Halloween. If I was home, I left the lights off and didn't answer the door. I was on the road performing much of that time anyway, but in my early twenties, around 1974 or so, I lived in a little guest house in North Hollywood. When that fall came I felt the old spirit returning. I bought a bunch of candy, and that set me off. Impulsively, I hung rows of orange and red lights outside and hid two stereo speakers in the plants and played creepy haunted house sounds on my record player. I made gravestones and bought some plastic skulls and left turned dirt in the yard, with faux hands sticking up. The kids loved all this of course, and I found the long-forgotten ritual oddly reassuring.

That following year, I went even further, got dressed as a werewolf and scared the crap out of all the neighborhood children. The holiday lifted my spirits yet again, as the little boy in me came out to play, after a long time underground. The joy of October blessed my life again. This was Halloween back on the treat side, the fun side, the thumbing your nose at fear side. The real life horror had retreated back into the shadows. In short, my life began to work.

Around that time, I later learned, my old boyhood friend got sentenced to something like twenty years in prison. I think it was for armed robbery. In any event, we never spoke again.

As for me, I struggled with my demons for well over twenty years, but finally put the bottle down for good back in 1986. And now, I never miss a Halloween.

When my teen daughter was old enough to understand the prose, I read her Ray Bradbury's The Halloween Tree, a few pages before bed each evening. She just ate it up. Now I do that as a ritual every October, starting on the first of the month and running all the way through the most magic of nights. Every year, Pip and Jim and Mr. Nightshade live again. Damn, I love this holiday, and I just adore The Halloween Tree. For me, that is a very spiritual book. See, as far as I'm concerned, Halloween is the one night we get to dance with the devil and walk away unscathed. And that is just what I did way back when, though I was just lucky enough to end up on the right side of the shadows.

At Halloween, and all year round, I remain grateful for that.

THAT WHICH DOESN'T KILL YOU

EARNS YOU CANDY

Nate Southard

The first Halloween I remember began with tears. Don't worry. It ended in wonderful, candy-bellied fashion, but I made sure to kick things off with a good, ugly cry. We won't mention how many new experiences in my life start with a bucket of tears before I realize I'll survive the ordeal. It's possible I need to work harder on my stress-coping skills.

This was supposed to be about Halloween, right? Sorry about that. Moving on…

I was three years old, and I was excited as all get out to go trick-or-treating. My parents might have toddled me house-to-house a year earlier. I was raised in the Midwest, after all, where stuffing candy down a two-year-old's mouth isn't uncommon. I don't remember anything from my terrible twos, though. As far as I know, my first time trick-or-treating took place when I was three.

Weeks before, my parents had taken my brother Matt and me shopping for costumes at Murphy's Mart, a local department store I'm relatively sure was owned by somebody named Murphy. Matt chose one of those ridiculous costumes that was only possible in the early 1980's. It was black and yellow and involved a giant inflatable spider as a hat. When I saw it, I got jealous in that way little brothers do. If he was going to be a spider man, I wanted to be a better spider man. I didn't know how I was going to pull off that particular trick until my parents led me another six feet down the aisle and I saw the costume. Not just the costume, but *the* costume. *My costume.*

If Matt got to be a spider man, then I was going to be Spider-Man. The official Spider-Man costume was glorious in its awfulness. More than thirty years ago, they didn't make superhero costumes that bulged with fake muscles. What my parents bought me was a baggy suit made from some weird pseudo-plastic material and a plastic mask that stayed on via rubber band. So what? I was gonna be Spider-Man!

For two weeks, I pulled out that costume and admired it every day. Okay, so I probably asked my mother to pull out the costume so I could look at it. Somewhere between annoying my mother and staring at that plastic monstrosity and wondering if it would really let me shoot webs, this nugget of an idea formed in my mind and heart: this was my *first* Halloween. No matter what, it was going to be special.

In retrospect, it seems I manage personal expectations roughly as well as I handle stress.

The night finally arrived. October 31st! Halloween! Bring on the candy, and pour it down my face-hole! I watched with excitement as my father, who'd probably smoked two packs that day, valiantly fought to inflate my brother's spider hat. Then, I watched my sister paint Matt's face in black and yellow. I climbed into my costume that was made out of who knows what. Finally, it was time to put on my mask. Spider-Man's here, ladies and gentlemen!

One problem: for some reason, the mask now terrified me. I don't know what had changed. Maybe it was the way my family had hyped up the holiday as the spookiest night of the year. Maybe I was just a real pain in the ass. All I know is that suddenly that plastic Spider-Man mask was the scariest thing I'd ever seen. I burst into tears at the thought of wearing it, the kind of big, ugly, lip-quaking sobs a child usually reserves for a skinned knee or lima beans. I hid behind the couch. I ran from that spot and hid under my parent's bed. Matt, being the kind of helpful soul all older brothers are, started shouting that I was ruining Halloween. That's when my frightened cry became more of a guilty cry. Even at such an early age, I had an impressive repertoire of cries.

I'm pretty sure it was my sister Sheryl who talked me down. Even now, more than thirty years later, she has a miraculous ability to bring me back from whatever edge I've decided to perch myself on (you caught the earlier thing about my stress-coping skills, right?). Well, once she got me to stop blubbering, she came up with an idea, the kind of idea that probably makes any adult smirk, but sounds like the perfect bit of sense to a three-year-old.

My sister, a teenager who probably just wanted to finish up taking her little brothers trick-or-treating so she could make out with her boyfriend, summoned up her patience and ingenuity and then took an eyeliner pencil and drew Spider-Man's mask directly onto my tear-puffed face.

I'm willing to bet I looked idiotic. A three-year-old running around happily, pretending to sling webs in a baggy plastic costume with web lines drawn on his face. The neighbors probably thought my family had scrounged the costume from a dumpster. None of those thoughts occurred to me, though. I was three years old, and I was Spider-Man, and I had a pumpkin-shaped bucket full of candy! How can life ever get better than that?

By the time we got home, I wasn't afraid of that plastic mask anymore. I probably wore it again that night. I'm sure I wore it for weeks after, right up until the rubber band broke. Then, I cried again. Some habits are hard to break.

PuMPKiN

Robert Bloch

Night came early in the country.

The sun disappeared into the woods and shadows started slinking out from between the trees. Twilight brought a chill wind whipping across fallen leaves and in the distance the huddling hills were hidden in autumn haze.

That's when David began moving through the farmhouse, locking the doors and windows.

It was a regular ritual now, but tonight Vera rebelled.

"For heaven's sake, must you close things up so early? We'll suffocate in here without fresh air."

David didn't answer. Instead he opened the kitchen cabinet, pulled out the vodka bottle, and poured himself a shot.

"Please, David," she said. "Couldn't you wait until after dinner? I'll have it on the table just as soon as Billy shows up."

David was staring out the window, squinting at the woods across the road, but now he turned and his eyes widened.

"I thought he was in his room," he said. "How often do I have to tell you I don't want that kid outside when it gets dark?"

"But he's just across the way—"

David turned so quickly that Vera got only a momentary glimpse of his face, but what she saw frightened her because he looked so frightened. And now he was hurrying to the door, flinging it open, rushing out.

As Vera moved to the window she could see him running across the road and into the tangled, weed-choked remnants of the vegetable garden beside the old Holloway place. Then he was swallowed up in the dusk and Vera lost sight of him.

I lost sight of him a long time ago, she told herself. *Ever since we moved here to the farmhouse.*

Perhaps it started even earlier than that, back in town, when David was terminated just before Easter.

"Terminated, hell!" he'd raged. "Bastards fired me, that's what they did. Ten years working my butt off for the company and now they're giving my job to a lousy computer!"

"It's not the end of the world," Vera said. "There must be other openings for comptrollers and you know a lot of people in the business. The thing to do is start making some calls, get out a résumé."

So David called around and circulated his résumé. He had several promising interviews, a few nibbles, and no firm offers. By Labor Day they'd run through his severance pay, and it was then that Vera suggested moving to the farm.

"You're out of your mind," he said. "I'm an accountant, not a manure spreader."

"No one expects you to work the place, darling. But it's only forty minutes from town on the turnpike and if you get a job—"

"*If?* I'll land something, just be patient."

"I am patient," Vera told him. "But we're already digging into our savings. And here you have a perfectly good piece of property your uncle left you, standing idle all these years, where we can live rent-free."

"That's crazy," David said. "The whole place is run-down; cost a fortune just to fix it up halfway decently."

Vera shook her head. "We've got our furniture and the appliances. Maybe we'll have to spend some money on minor repairs, but the house is sound. I'm sure we can manage on far less than we're paying here. Besides, it'll be good for Billy, living in the country. And it will be good for you too, getting away from this rat race."

"I don't want to go there," David told her. "And that's final."

Only it wasn't final. Vera went right ahead on her own and made all the arrangements. Their lease on the apartment was up at the end of the month and by then she'd gotten the painters and carpenter and the electrical contractor working against the deadline. Just as she thought, it was no big deal.

The big deal turned out to be persuading David to make the move. But she kept after him, and when it came to facing the hike in the new leasing agreement he finally saw the light.

They'd moved in at the beginning of October and even David had to admit she'd done a wonderful job transforming the old farmhouse into a comfortable home. Billy lost a few weeks of school but for an eight-year-old it wasn't important, and he liked his new surroundings—ten full acres to run wild in, plus the woods behind the abandoned Holloway place across the road.

But right from the start David put his foot down. He didn't want Billy playing anywhere near the deserted farmhouse with its caved-in roof, and he served notice that the woods were strictly off limits; in fact Billy wasn't permitted to cross the road at all.

Vera could understand about the farmhouse because it was boarded up, and there was no telling if the structure was safe. What she couldn't understand was why Billy couldn't play in the yard or the wooded area beyond.

"Private property," David said. "No trespassing. Folks out here are funny about such things."

Vera tried to reason with him. "There's nobody living within a mile of this place. And Billy isn't going to harm anything."

"That's not the point. I don't want anything to harm Billy."

"What do you mean?"

David didn't answer her. But it was then she began to notice the way he acted every night as darkness came, locking everything up. Vera believed in taking precautions—after all, you never knew who might be driving around nowadays, looking for a place to break into—but he started so early, even before twilight, and if he found anything left open by accident he blew his stack.

But it was the drinking that bothered her the most. Back in town they usually had a cocktail before dinner to help him unwind when he came home from work. Now there was no work and he wasn't sharing a martini with her; he was drinking straight vodka and going through as much as half a bottle a night. He'd gotten into the habit of sleeping in all morning and watching television all afternoon. Funny, he'd always hated soap operas before. Maybe he still did because he never commented on them, just sat staring at the tube with a sort of glazed look in his eyes. But when Billy came home on the school bus, David turned off the set and the glazed look disappeared. He watched the youngster like a hawk if he went out to play and chewed Vera out for not doing the same.

It's David I should have been looking at, not Billy. Vera frowned, peering through the window. *Where did I lose him?*

She found him now, moving forth from the deep shadows across the road and pulling Billy along by the collar. As they neared the house she could hear the muffled sounds of sobbing.

Now David's voice rose as Vera opened the door. "I warned you, remember? Why didn't you keep away from there like you were told?"

Billy raised a tear-stained face. "Honest, I was only—"

"Never mind the excuses! I give the orders here and don't you forget it. I want you to march upstairs to your room and go straight to bed."

"But, Dad—"

"You heard me. Now get going!"

Shoulders shaking with suppressed sobs, Billy made his way up the staircase as his parents stood watching in the hall, avoiding each other's gaze. The sound of his footsteps faded and they heard the bedroom door closing in the hall above.

Vera turned, speaking softly. "Really, David, must you? The poor kid hasn't even had his dinner."

"It won't hurt him to miss a meal. And he's got to learn to obey the rules. I don't want him going over there."

Vera took a deep breath. "You keep saying that, but you never give any reasons. Just as long as he keeps away from the house I don't see—"

"You don't see anything," David said. "Come on, let's eat. I'm starving."

But when she served dinner David didn't seem hungry. He scarcely touched his food; instead he got up and poured himself another drink, bringing the bottle back to the table with him.

"Want some coffee?" she said.

"No, I'm okay." He gulped the drink, then refilled his glass.

Vera took another deep breath. "You're not okay."

David shrugged. "Have it your own way. I've got no job and no prospects. Winter's coming, we're stuck out here in the middle of nowhere and God knows what happens next year when we run out of savings. Is it any wonder I'm uptight?"

"That part I can understand. But since we came here you act as if you were afraid of something—"

"Afraid? You're imagining things."

"I think you're the one who's imagining. That look you had when I said Billy was across the road tonight. And other times, when you just stare out the window."

David scowled. "I told you I never wanted to live here in the first place. It gives me the creeps."

"What does?"

He lowered his glass. It was empty, and so was the expression in his eyes. "All right. I didn't want to say anything but it's probably better than letting you think I don't have both oars in the water." He sighed and leaned back. "If you must know, this isn't the first time I've come to live here."

"David—you never told me that—"

"I never told anyone. But a long time ago, when my mother took sick after the divorce, I spent a summer and part of the fall with my aunt and uncle in this house. I was just about Billy's age then. So you see, I know."

"Know what?"

"About the place across the road. The first thing Uncle George did was warn me never to go over there, because the old man didn't like strangers."

"Who was he talking about?"

"Jed Holloway. He lived on the property all alone, ever since anyone around here could remember. Uncle George moved in here right after he and Aunt Louise were married, but he said that even then Jed Holloway was an old man. God only knows how long he'd been there or what he did to keep going. Maybe he raised enough food from his vegetable garden, because nobody ever saw him at the stores in town. Folks said he had a wife once, and after she died he never left the place, just boarded up all the windows like they are today. If salesmen or anybody else showed up he'd run them off the property with a shotgun."

"Didn't anyone ever do anything about it?"

David shrugged. "Like what? It was his place. If he wanted to cut off the water and electricity that was his own affair. He had an old well and an outhouse in back, and he must have used candles in the house because some nights you could see lights flickering from cracks between the boards on the windows. It wasn't as if he was breaking any law—just an old coot who went off his rocker when he lost his wife. Maybe he lost a kid too, because she was supposed to have died in childbirth. That would explain why he hated children so much.

"I know he hated me. Playing in the yard here, sometimes I saw him puttering around in his garden, mumbling to himself. I'd never seen anyone talking to empty air before and it scared me. The way he looked was pretty scary too—tall and skinny, with long white hair down to his shoulders and a beard that hid all of his face except the eyes. That was the worst, those eyes of his, glaring at me when he noticed I was playing outside. I'll never forget it, him standing there dressed in rags like some kind of scarecrow come to life, a scarecrow with little red-rimmed eyes staring—"

David broke off and reached for the bottle again.

"So that's why you didn't want to come here again," Vera said.

David finished pouring and raised his glass. "There are other reasons. Oh, I never believed those stories floating around about Holloway getting into magic and practicing witchcraft. That stuff about him putting curses on people and making spells to wither their crops and kill off cattle sounded pretty wild even then, and nobody ever proved anything. I probably would have gotten used to how he looked and acted if it hadn't been for Halloween."

David drank, then sat back. From the hall beyond the ticking of the grandfather's clock echoed through the silence.

Vera leaned forward. "Aren't you going to tell me what happened?"

"Jed Holloway left the house," David said. "That's what happened. Two other kids and myself, we were playing out by the barn after supper and we saw him come out and start walking into the woods behind his house. He was carrying an armful of candles and something that looked like a big book—black, with metal bands around it.

"These kids I was playing with, Tom and Terry, were older than me, and I guess they'd heard all those stories. Tom told us Holloway was going down into the woods to pray to the devil. That's what witches and wizards did on Halloween, they prayed to the devil and conjured up ghosts and demons.

"Terry didn't buy that. He said there were no such things as witches or ghosts and Jed Holloway was crazy as a bedbug. The way he acted, chasing kids and yelling at them and all, maybe it was time to teach him a lesson. So later that night, after dark, he did it."

"What did you do?"

"We tipped over Jed Holloway's outhouse."

Vera started to laugh, but David's face was grim.

"You think it's funny?"

"Of course it is!"

David nodded. "So did we, at first. I remember the way we kept giggling when we sneaked across the road. It was a moonless night, everything dark and still. Not quite everything, because far away through the trees we could see little glimmers of light. Tom said Jed Holloway must be off in the woods down there lighting his candles, and sure enough we did hear a voice that sounded like someone saying a prayer, very solemn and deep.

"That sobered us a little, that and the way the shadows seemed to move in the darkness around the outhouse up ahead. Then we set to work and forgot about being scared. The outhouse was old and rickety and quite small, but prying it loose from the foundation with a shovel was a big job for kids our age. And when we did the next problem was how to tip it over without making a racket.

"Only noise wasn't that much of a problem after all, because all at once a cold wind began to whistle through the trees. It seemed to come from somewhere back in the woods and Terri said we were in for a storm. Sure enough, the sky was pitch-black overhead and we could hear thunder growling off in the hills.

"But we didn't mind, since it drowned out the creaking when we started to lift the outhouse and tilt it over on its side. Then, just as we got ready to ease it down, lightning turned everything green and there was a clap of thunder so close and loud it almost deafened us.

"One thing for sure, it scared the hell out of Tom and Terry. They let go of their hold and took off for the road, leaving me standing there trying to balance the damned thing all by myself. I guess I was too startled to move. Then the lightning flashed again and I looked up over my shoulder.

"Jed Holloway was standing there at the edge of the woods, and he *was* the lightning. It was playing all around his body like green fire, playing around his hair and beard and his little red pig eyes. Only it wasn't just around: the lightning seemed to be coming *from* his eyes. Then he opened his mouth and the thunder boomed right out of his throat.

"I let go of the outhouse and it dropped back into place on its foundation. At least I think it did, but I didn't wait to see. I turned and ran and the lightning followed me, stabbing into the ground at my heels. I swear one bolt came so close it grazed the hairs on my neck.

"The next thing I remember was blubbering in my bed, with Uncle George and Aunt Louise trying to calm me down. Of course they didn't believe what I told them. They even dragged me over to the bedroom window so I could look for myself. By this time the storm was howling and the rain kept coming down in buckets, but I saw that the old farmhouse was completely dark and Jed Holloway had disappeared.

"They tried to tell me he'd never been there, that it was all just my imagination, but I knew better. And when they realized I wouldn't go outside to take the school bus the next day or the day after they finally decided to pack me up and ship me back to my mother in town." David forced a smile. "So that's the way it was."

"*Was,*" Vera said. "Not *is.*" She met his gaze. "Look, David, I understand, really I do. Living with that traumatic experience bottled up inside you all these years must have been a terrible thing. But it's over now and you've got to realize that. You're not a kid anymore, and Jed Holloway is long dead and gone."

She rose briskly, glancing at her watch. "Look at the time! We'd better get to bed."

David's hand curled around the bottle. "I'll be up later."

Vera hesitated. "Sure you don't want me to sit with you a while longer?"

"Of course not. I'll be all right now that I've gotten this out of my system. Thanks for being such a good psychiatrist."

"Come up soon." Vera smiled. "I may be able to offer you another kind of therapy."

Vera's smile faded quickly once she got upstairs. She'd done her best not to let David see how his story had disturbed her—not what he said, but the way he said it. Maybe telling all this would really help him; she hoped so.

Of course there was nothing to be alarmed about, but just the same she looked in on Billy before going on to the other bedroom. He was sound asleep.

That relieved her, and by the time she'd undressed and slid under the covers the tension began to ease. Now, if only David would come up...

The grandfather's clock tolled the hours in the hall. Windows rattled in reply, and somewhere a door groaned on rusty hinges. Vera snuggled back against her pillow, fighting a sudden childish impulse to bury her head beneath it.

No wonder David had a hang-up about returning here. To a small boy, suddenly being torn away from his home and family was a disturbing experience; living here in this lonely old house must have been an ordeal for him.

Vera sighed, shifting her head on the pillow. Thank heaven Billy didn't seem to have that problem—

"Mommy!"

Vera levered upright in sudden shock, alarm propelling her out of bed and into the hall.

"Mommy—"

The shrill cry rose again as she raced into Billy's room. Crouching amid the tangled covers he turned to her, eyes alive with terror. Vera sank to the side of the bed and he buried his contorted face against her breast.

"There now, it's all right." Her fingers smoothed tousled hair, soothed trembling shoulders.

"That's better," she said. "What happened?"

Billy moved back on the bed, eyes darting around the room. "Where is he?"

"Nobody's here, nobody but us. You can see for yourself."

The boy stiffened. "No, he's coming; can't you hear him?"

And she did hear something, the sound of footsteps from the hall. For a moment Vera panicked, then relaxed as David entered.

Billy looked up. "Dad—did you see him?"

"See who?"

"That man. The one who was looking at me through the window."

David strode across the room and stared out into the night. "Nobody's outside," he said. "Look—the window's locked."

"But he was here." Billy's lower lip quivered. "He was standing right there, outside."

"Now you know better than that." David turned, shaking his head. "We're upstairs here, on the second floor. So how could anyone be standing outside?"

Vera held Billy close. "It was only a bad dream," she said.

"No!" The boy pulled away. "I saw him! This old man—he had long white hair and a beard and little red eyes staring at me—"

Seeing the fear in Billy's face was all Vera could bear. Luckily for her, she couldn't see David's.

D avid's face was haggard in the hazy afternoon sunlight filtering through the parlor window. No wonder he was beat today; it had been a rough night before they got Billy calmed down and back to sleep again, and there'd been little enough rest for him afterward.

Vera was probably right about the nightmare; what else could it have been? She said the description of the face wasn't even a coincidence, really; most kids tend to be afraid of old men and it's only natural when they show up in their dreams.

Natural or not, David didn't want to think about explanations now because other things were more important. Bad enough that this place bugged him, but if it spooked Billy that was the last straw. He'd made up his mind this morning: they had to get out of here. Monday he'd drive back to the city and make the rounds and this time he wouldn't be so choosy, just take anything he could get, as long as they could move away before winter.

Right now the thing to do was revise his résumé, play down all that executive-experience stuff that might turn off employers who were only looking for somebody to fill an ordinary accounting job. A pay cut didn't matter; what mattered was getting out.

But it was hard to concentrate, hard to figure how to rewrite the damned thing. Maybe Vera could help; she was good with words.

David looked up and called. "Honey—can you come here for a minute?"

No answer.

"Vera—"

Still no reply, only the tick-tock of the grandfather's clock.

He pushed back his chair and rose, striding down the hall to the kitchen. He could have sworn he saw her go there, only a few minutes ago, but the room was empty now. Where had she disappeared to?

Peering across the room he saw that the kitchen door was ajar.

It was fear that forced him forward. Hinging the door wide, he moved out into the yard, calling her name. Before he realized it he was at the edge of the road.

For a moment David hesitated, glancing off into the purple haze haloing the ruined house, the weed-infested garden patch and the treetops rising darkly from the slope below. He wanted to stop but he couldn't, because he knew. It hit him the moment he saw the open kitchen door.

Crossing the road he raised his voice in a shout. No response came, and desperation drove him past the huddled house and the windswept weeds, his feet churning dead leaves as he stared at the dead limbs of the towering trees beyond.

Then he did halt, heart hammering. Something was moving down there below between the twisted tree trunks—moving and emerging.

"Vera!"

She came toward him, hair disheveled, her housedress splotched and stained. But she was smiling.

"I thought I heard you," she said.

David stared at her, numb with relief. "Are you all right?"

"Of course. Why shouldn't I be?"

"But what were you doing over here?"

She reached out and took his hand. "I'll show you."

Before he could resist she was leading him forward, down into the woods, into the forbidden forest, while the voices rose. *"No—don't go— keep away from there, you hear?"* His aunt's voice, and his uncle's, dead voices echoing over the years.

Now Vera's voice, here and very much alive. "After last night I couldn't help it. Oh, I knew there was nothing to worry about, but I had to make sure. And I did find something—here."

She halted in a little clearing deep down under the trees, pointing to a cluster of matted grass and wilted wildflowers which sprouted from an oblong mound. "You know what this is?"

David blinked, silent and uncomprehending.

"Can't you guess?" Vera smiled again. "It's a grave."

S he stooped, parting the tangled growth at the far end of the mound and disclosing a weathered wooden slab. It bore neither dates nor inscription, only the crudely carved lettering of a name.

Jed Holloway.

"You see?" Vera nodded toward the mound. "Now we know there's nothing to be afraid of. He's been dead and buried here for years."

Nothing to be afraid of. David nodded automatically and again she took his hand, leading him away from the dead man's grave, past the twisted trunks of the dead trees, up the path between the skeleton of the dead house and the ruined remains of the dead garden.

But the garden wasn't entirely dead. A flash of vivid color caught his eye in the rays of the setting sun and then he saw it clearly—the orange outline, rounded and resting amid the weeds. Vera saw it too.

"Look, a pumpkin!" Her smile broadened. "Just what we needed."

"Needed?" David frowned.

"Don't tell me you've forgotten. Tonight's Halloween." She stooped, reaching toward the pumpkin, but David yanked her away.

"Leave it alone."

"But, David—"

"Leave it alone, I said!"

A sudden blast of sound interrupted Vera's reply. The two of them turned, glancing toward the road at another orange object—the school bus, halting before their yard.

They crossed over to it just as Billy got out. The bus moved off, trailing a cloud of exhaust, and he turned to them, his face flushed with excitement.

"Guess what?" he cried. "We had a Halloween party at school. Miss Zelisko gave us a whole bunch of colored paper to make masks and black cats and witches and ghosts and we had a cake and orange soda and boy was it ever neat—"

"Take it easy, young man," Vera said. "If you don't slow down you'll trip over your tongue."

They moved across the yard to the back door. "You should of been there," Billy said. "All the kids, they're getting ready to go in town tonight for trick or treat. Can you drive me Dad?"

"Sorry, son, I've got work to do." Anticipating the next question, David continued quickly. "And don't ask your mother. I'm going to need her help."

Vera glanced at him. "Maybe for just an hour, if we went early—?"

David shook his head. "I really do need you. I'm stuck in the middle of that damned résumé."

The boy's smile withered, then suddenly blossomed anew. "Okay. But I can have a jack-o'-lantern, can't I?"

"A what?"

"Don't you know about jack-o'-lanterns? Miss Zelisko made one and brought it to class for the party. It's a big pumpkin, only you carve a face on it. Then you squish out the insides and put in a candle to light up the face."

"Now I remember." David nodded. "We used to put one in the window on Halloween night when I was a kid."

"Can I do it tonight, Dad? If we put it in the front window it would look—"

"Real neat," David said. "Trouble is, we don't have a pumpkin."

"Yes we do." Billy beamed happily. "I saw one yesterday—a great big one, too. It's across the way in that old garden. We can get it right now—"

"No."

"But it's just an old pumpkin." Billy's voice took on a shrill edge. "Nobody even lives there, so it's not like stealing. Why can't I have it?"

"Because I say so, that's why." Ignoring Vera's look, David took his son's arm. "It's getting dark. Time to go inside."

Billy gazed up at him in mingled disappointment and defiance. "What's the matter, Dad—you afraid of ghosts or something?"

"There are no ghosts," Vera said.

But she wasn't talking to Billy.

Nobody was talking to Billy now. He could hear Mom and Dad in the front parlor, arguing about the resumay, whatever that was. Something you showed people when you wanted to get a job, like. Anyhow he hoped it wouldn't work because then they'd have to move back into town and he liked it here. This place was neat and even school was better than that old dump in the city. The only thing wrong was Dad, the funny way he acted lately. Like yesterday, when he caught him sneaking across the road, and tonight, not letting him have the pumpkin.

No fair, that's what it was. Other kids were going trick-or-treating, getting money and candy and good stuff like that. But he couldn't even have a plain old pumpkin lying right there on the ground across the way. What good did it do to leave it? When the frost came it would only spoil. And it would make a real neat jack-o'-lantern too, sitting there in the front window for kids to see when they came driving past with their folks on the way to trick-or-treat in town.

But what did Dad care? All he cared about was this resumay thing and now he was yelling at Mom again, real loud this time. So loud that he wouldn't even hear if somebody went out the kitchen door.

Two minutes is all it would take. Two minutes to sneak across the road and get that old pumpkin. Nobody would notice, not if you were quiet.

Just to prove it Billy came downstairs slow and careful. Sure enough, both of them were sitting in the parlor at the table under the lamp and they kept on arguing without looking up.

And the lock on the kitchen door opened easy.

It was almost dark outside now, dark and sort of chilly with a lot of clouds in the sky and a big orange moon coming up over the trees. Orange like the pumpkin across the road.

Billy crossed real fast and headed for the garden patch. He could hear the leaves scrunching under his feet and the wind blowing through the trees down there in the woods. When he got to the garden it was all shadows and he couldn't see the pumpkin lying under the weeds. The wind was sort of wailing now.

But Billy wasn't afraid of the shadows. And he wasn't afraid of that old house no matter how spooky it looked, because nobody lived inside. If the boards creaked that was just the wind. He was all alone here with nobody to see or stop him.

Now he saw the pumpkin next to a vine where the weeds were hiding it. Billy bent down to reach out for it.

And felt the cold hand gripping his shoulder.

I shouldn't have scared the kid, David told himself. Sitting there in the kitchen with only the bottle for company he stared out into the moonlight and poured himself another drink.

How was he to know the kid would be so shook up? He'd been shook up too when he noticed Billy was gone, and running across the road to get him was the natural thing to do. It wasn't as if he really feared for Billy's safety, but somebody had to teach him to follow orders. Why couldn't Vera understand?

But she didn't understand, any more than Billy. Instead she took his part. "Never mind that stupid old pumpkin," she told him. "How about you and I driving into town for trick or treat?"

Stupid pumpkin. *Stupid David,* that's what she really meant, and it hurt. Did she think he was wigging out? All he wanted was to protect the boy, teach him a little discipline.

Instead she rewarded him for disobedience. Naturally Billy was overjoyed and the two of them left happily together. Left him without another word, left him alone there feeling like a fool.

David raised his glass, watching it turn orange-gold in the moonlight streaming in from the window. The whiskey was orange-gold, too, and as he drank it kindled a golden glow inside, warming and expanding.

He set the glass down with a sigh. *Maybe I am a fool.* Was it the liquor talking or did he really feel that way? He wasn't quite sure, but now he was able to face the possibility as his anger ebbed.

Perhaps he'd overreacted. After all Billy was just a kid and his excitement was normal for his age. It wasn't his fault David felt the way he did about Halloween and something that had happened twenty-five years ago.

Vera was right; he was a grown man now and Jed Holloway was in his grave. Why keep him alive in his own mind?

David bought himself another drink. Bottle getting empty, he was getting full. But the whiskey was helping, helping him to think straight for the first time in months.

When you came right down to it, what did he really know about Jed Holloway? Seen through a child's eyes he'd been pure evil, but as a reasoning adult David knew nothing is completely pure or entirely evil. That talk about witchcraft was just local gossip, but even if it had been true, all it meant was that an eccentric old man got mixed up in superstitious nonsense.

There was no proof he'd actually harmed anyone, not even David himself. The events of that long-ago Halloween night had been colored by a child's imagination. Nothing actually happened except that Holloway had run him off his property.

Besides, he was dead now and David didn't believe in ghosts. So why was he acting this way? He'd only end up harming himself, and perhaps harming Billy too. No, Vera was right and he was wrong. No sense passing along his own foolish fears to the youngster.

Maybe it was already too late now, but at least he could try to undo the damage. He owed it to Billy, and to Vera. And there was a way.

David lurched to his feet and opened the top drawer at the side of the sink. His fingers fumbled, then closed around the handle of a big butcher knife. Pulling it out, he headed for the kitchen door. *By God, if my boy wants a jack-o'-lantern he's going to have one.*

Stumbling across the road, David felt no fear. He wasn't afraid of the night, not even when the moon hid behind a cloud. Perhaps the moon was afraid of the wind and the way the shutters banged against the boarded-up windows of the old house, but David didn't care. The woods down below were black as ink and he could hear the groaning of dead branches rubbing against the gnarled tree trunks, but that didn't scare him.

He weaved across the weedy garden, searching for the dark outline of the pumpkin on the ground below. When he found it there was nothing frightening about that either. Perhaps this was why people got the idea in the first place—carving a harmless vegetable into a hobgoblin face just to show they weren't afraid.

David knelt beside the pumpkin, wrenched it free from the rotting vine, and lifted his knife. Drink made his fingers clumsy at first, but they steadied when he went to work. Squatting in the darkness he hollowed out the inside, then sliced away at the surface. First he cut two triangles for eyes, then one for the nose below.

Now the moon came out from behind the clouds and David wielded the knife quickly, forming the mouth into a grinning gash. The result was a perfect pumpkin head and he stared at it with a smile of satisfaction.

Suddenly the face of the pumpkin disappeared in shadow, looming from behind.

Then David turned and looked up into the *other* face.

It was a wonderful surprise, seeing the face in the front window as Vera drove into the yard.

Billy saw it too and he bubbled. "Look, Mom—the jack-o'-lantern!"

Vera nodded. Gazing at the pumpkin resting against the window ledge inside she felt as though a weight had been lifted from her. The candle within the hollowed-out pumpkin danced merrily behind the eyes and nose and mouth as the jack-o'-lantern smiled its warm welcome.

Her own smile warmed as she realized what its presence meant. David had come to his senses and from now on all would be well.

She cut the lights and motor, then emerged from the car. Billy's door was already open and he slid out from the seat; he was so excited he dropped his trick-or-treat bag, and its contents spilled across the ground below.

"Pick that stuff up," she told him. "I'm going in."

The front door was unlocked and she entered quickly, not even stopping to turn on the light. The parlor was dark, but over at the window the jack-o'-lantern cast its friendly glow.

"David, where are you?" she called.

There was no answer, nor any need of one. For as she moved to the window she saw what rested beneath it.

David was slumped against the windowpane. And the jack-o'-lantern wasn't on the ledge. Instead the pumpkin was perched between David's shoulders.

On the stump where his head had been.

Somehow Vera found the strength. The strength to keep Billy in the yard while she called the state police, the strength to tell them what had happened when they came, the strength to lead them down into the woods to Jed Holloway's grave.

It had been disturbed, its surface uprooted, the earth mound yawning open so there was scarcely need to dig. But setting down a lantern at the graveside, they did. A trooper offered a sympathetic shoulder and Vera pressed against it, averting her gaze as the other two officers wielded their shovels.

One of them spoke now. "Hey, look at the coffin; the lid's all splintered."

He slid it back, then gasped.

It was his gasp that caused Vera to look up, then run forward and peer down into the grave, into the open coffin and the moldering outline of what lay within: a fully articulated skeleton, the skull mouth frozen in a ghastly grin.

Cradled in its bony arm was David's head.

MR. AND MRS. WEREWOLF

Whitley Strieber

Everything was competitive. Even where your desk was located in relation to Nick's desk was competitive. Nick liked holidays—Halloween, Thanksgiving, Christmas—so holidays were competitive. Christmas, you gave Teslas and Maseratis or you were an asshole. Thanksgiving was turkey, sure, but stuffed with caviar and chased by Château Latour. Halloween was costume time, and that was always a challenge. Nick was capable of spending fifty grand on his. If you couldn't do at least as much, you were marked as a failure, and if you weren't making enough money to throw it away, you were on your way out.

You did wild things, wildly expensive, gutsy things. Jane and Rob Harper, who were the biggest producers on the floor, also did the wildest things. They hunted endangered species, they collected stolen art, and through one of their shell companies, they were making a fortune a month in the thriving middle eastern slave trade.

Endangered species collectors were a subculture of the extremely rich and powerful and bitter. Here in New York, there was Rob and Jane, plus Henry and Tilda Leisen who had collected gorillas. Two years ago, they had disappeared under circumstances that still hadn't been completely understood. Animal rights activists were suspected. Joe Ford in San Francisco had amassed a magnificent collection of endangered snakes, and he'd disappeared, also—in fact, on a buying junket. He'd landed at JFK, that much was known. Then nothing.

But the other collectors were just fine, and both Ford and the Leisens had been into all manner of ugly businesses. So who knew.

It was now late October, and the office was wild. The markets were headed up and Roper, Magnus was pushing Enviromedical into the stratosphere. In boom times like this, if you didn't ring the million dollar bell at least twice a week, it was time to cut your own throat.

Jane and Rob were company stars. Between them, they hit the big red buttons on their desks on average once every twenty-four hours. When the bell rang, it meant that you'd sucked a client to the bone and were ready for more leads. If you didn't keep sucking the clients, keep the money moving, Nick would foretell your future: just die.

Jane and Rob were running hard but lately Jane was running harder. Rob hadn't scored a big placement in two days. He was torching the phone, promising the personal intervention of God to the marks while Jane was kicking back, pushing the button so frequently that brokers across the office were having the dry heaves.

She was just plain rolling. Nick had her name at the top of the Swingin' Dicks chart, way up there where the eight-figure dollar players lived.

That was bad enough, but what was worse, as far as Rob was concerned, was that she had some kind of a line on a major costume for the upcoming party. There were four days left and right now he was coming in a Lone Ranger mask and a sharkskin suit.

Last year, he'd been rolling, pulling cash out of his clients like a milkmaid with high-speed hands. He was moving so fast you couldn't see him. He'd gone to the party as the Gilded Man from Four Color 422 and yes the gold body paint was damn real. Not to mention the eagle feathers, obtained at significant cost from one of the dealers in endangered species who supplied them with trophies for their houses. The secret gun room in their palatial Turtle Bay brownstone contained, along with its bald eagles and the spectacular narwhal that Rob had nearly gotten himself killed catching, their ultimate prize: an entire pack of wolves, pups included. They'd shot them from a helicopter in Alaska, and the most delicious part of it was that the hunt had been absolutely legal.

When you opened the front door of their house, the first thing you saw was the wolves, all magnificently preserved, staring right into your face. The illegal heads were kept deeper in the house. The gun room was closed to all except other endangered collectors.

Their next hunt was going to be in the Russian Primorye. There were about twenty Amur leopards still back in those deep forests. The plan was to take two, get the taxidermy done in Russia, then smuggle them home. When you entered the gun room, they would be waiting for you, ready to pounce.

Magnificent.

A big part of the pleasure of all this was the process of corrupting people. Watching the rubes drool over peanut bribes, taking things that it was illegal to take, spitting in the face of the law—it was just plain fun, all of it.

On planet Earth, money rules, not the law.

As these thoughts passed through his mind, Rob found himself gazing at Jane. She was as pale as powder, the softest, most blond woman he had ever met. Beautiful innocence. When she smiled, you thought little girl, you thought saint.

That was her power.

On the phone, she sounded like a sex kitten with a genius-level grasp of the markets. She was a genius, all right, you had to be to work here. A genius at separating marks from their cash.

Rob listened to her working, the hypnotic rise and fall of that voice, so moist with sex that the guy on the other end of the line was going to get a hard-on no matter what she was saying.

She spouted numbers, great numbers. True, too, in a sense. Like all their false companies, Enviromedical looked like something. If you went to its office in Greenwich, you found real people. If you investigated its balance sheet, you found real money. Because the profits it was making were entirely real. But if you went to the factory in China where the drugs were manufactured, you found just two machines in a filthy, rat-infested warehouse. Between them they turned out a million fake chemotherapy capsules a week for the African market. As long as they weren't sold at home, Chinese regulators didn't give a damn. As long as they didn't come into the US or the EU, no real drug authorities would ever inspect them. So the profits rolled in and the marks bought the stock.

Eventually, when the marks owned all the stock and Roper was short a couple of billion shares, Chinese regulators would be paid off to shut the outfit down. All of the profits now in clients hands would flow right back to Roper.

That's how they did it, and there was basically no way anybody was ever going to see the crime. A couple of Chinese managers went to jail, sure. Who cares?

She hung up the phone, hit her red button and rang the bell.

Damn her.

"Whatcha wearing this year," he asked, trying to seem unconcerned by her success.

She fixed her steel blue eyes on him. She smiled. "Go fuck yourself," she said.

Last year, she had lost Halloween big time. She'd been Marie Antoinette and tried to pretend that her tiara had actually belonged to the queen. Bullshit. She'd been snookered by a fake jeweler, a real expert called Pierre Gilland. The instant Rob had heard the name, he knew that she was in trouble.

He'd waited until the party was in full swing, then had taken the thing off her head and sunk it in the punch.

What had come back was wires and rubble.

For Rob, it had been a moment of purest triumph.

They hated each other. She was his worst competitor. They loved each other. She was his best friend.

You'd see them in the late night, walking home from dinner together hand in hand, young lovers rich enough to own a twenty million dollar house.

Ah, youth! They would shake the world in their bed at night. Then they'd fight in the office for every scrap of sucker meat, two tigers circling, as ready to slash one another's throat as they were to deball the next client.

Her phone rang. She snatched it up, listened for a moment, then hammered her fist down on the red button.

Nick yelled, "she's hackin' balls, guys, so where the fuck are you?"

Rob had to find out what she was doing for a costume. She'd been making mysterious trips somewhere on the subway, which meant only one thing to him. They had to do with the costume. She wouldn't be caught dead in a subway unless she was working so hard to keep a secret that she wouldn't even risk letting her driver know where she was going.

At last the markets went to night volume and the office stripped out, and Rob said to her that he was working late. She left, her hips swaying, her eyes blank with the indifference of the victor. She had to be going for a fitting, and he had a plan.

As soon as she left, he leaped up from his desk and headed for the stairwell. Running like a burning cat, he made it to the lobby just as she was disappearing into the street.

Ignoring her waiting limo, sure enough she went down into the subway.

Waving his own car off, he followed her, taking the steps six at a time, fumbling for his little-used Metro Card.

He rode in the car behind her out to the wilds of Brooklyn, past the Heights, even past Park Slope, deep into Sunset Park. Finally, she stood up. He was far down his car, huddled beside a bum who smelled like a dead bum. The doors rattled open, but she didn't leave. Just stood there.

Obvious ploy. He got ready to dash.

As the doors clicked, getting ready to close, she stepped out. He dove out of his door, immediately throwing himself down beside a long-abandoned newsstand.

The train roared away.

He listened to the silence. No sound of footsteps on the stairway. She could be hiding near the old ticket booth, but that wouldn't be like her. She was too aggressive to hide, it wasn't her style.

He gambled. Moving fast, he mounted the steps and went out into the cold and windy streets of Sunset Park on a winter's night.

After a moment he saw an unmistakable figure moving swiftly along 45th Street. She was headed under the Gowanus toward the water. She loved cold, and had left her long black panther coat open. She claimed that it was *faux*, of course, but the pelts were real. She was wearing six hundred thousand dollars down what looked like a damn mean street, but that was Jane. She did it her way and she expected to win. Absolute confidence. She also carried a very lethal little AMG .32, a small gun with major stopping power. That, at least, was legal.

The way the coat flowed and flapped in the wind, it made her look like the angel of death.

The last light glowed in the sky, the bare trees rattled, a tang of smoke sharpened the air.

She stepped into a basement door and was gone. He went up to it. Nothing to see, just a typical door under the front stoop of one of the dingy old brownstones that crowded the street.

He waited at the end of the block. Waited an hour. Another. Finally, she came out, moving like a ghost, swift in the night wind. She made her way back up the street toward the subway station.

He went to the brownstone, to the door. No mark on it, no name, just weathered black paint.

He knocked. Waited. Knocked again. Waited more. He had turned away and was mounting the steps when the air around him seemed to change, to grow somehow darker, somehow colder. A creeping loneliness filled his heart, emotions that seemed to come from nowhere. A sense of space behind him told him that the door was now open.

Inside, he could see a hallway, or rather, a path made through great piles of books, newspapers, old clothes in heaps and on racks, cloche hats and rotting crinolines, button shoes so old they were crisp, and books and books and books. *Sartor Resartus,* Seneca's Plays, *Cujo, Naked Lunch,* hundreds of titles in crazy stacks.

He threaded his way toward a dim light he could see ahead, finding at last a tiny space lit by a single light shining down from the rafters. On the left was a wall of books. The right side was occupied by a railroad kitchen. A kettle boiled on an old stove. The air was dense with the smell of cabbage and blue with cigarette smoke. Directly ahead, a darkly clad figure hunched over a clattering sewing machine. The figure was running what looked disturbingly like skin through it, stitching two limpid, flesh-colored slabs together.

Beyond the figure was a wall of glass that must lead into a dark back garden. Hanging from hooks along this wall were what appeared to be bodies. They were so realistic that he gasped. He stopped.

They were costumes and they were amazing.

Dracula, his eyes glaring as if alive, seemed ready to come down off his hook and latch onto Rob's neck. Priss, the furious female replicant from *Blade Runner* looked about to cartwheel over and get him into a deliciously painful headlock. Jesus appeared as if he'd just emerged from the tomb, his long hair and beard glowing, his lips parted as if he was just about to utter a word of wisdom.

Arnold Schwarzenegger was there, and Barack Obama. Jennifer Lawrence in a pink cocktail dress, Amy Adams in an SS uniform.

And then there were the animals. Endangered species, superb examples. A panda, a gorilla, an orangutan. Wonderful fun to go in the costume of something you secretly possessed.

No wonder she'd come here. She was going to blow him out of the water.

Not.

Without turning around, the figure at the sewing machine croaked, "What?"

It was a female voice, old but sharp with demand.

"Uh, I guess I'm here for a costume."

The figure stopped, turned. "One hundred thousand dollars. Cash. Now." She held out her hand.

Rob had passed big cash many times, and you weren't going to put a hundred grand in anybody's hand. The largest US bill now in circulation is the C-note, so you need a thousand bills, which makes it a briefcase deal.

"I don't have that kind of money with me right now."

"How did you find me?"

"I heard about you from a friend."

"No."

"People talk."

"Not about me. I kill yappers."

Uh-oh, crazy person, time to get out of here. He turned around, intending to leave the way he had come, but found the figure barring his way.

"No."

How in hell?

"You want a costume." It wasn't a question.

The light was behind the figure, which was clad in a black monk's robe. The cowl cast the face into deep shadow, but Rob could see eyes, calm and steady, unconcerned, even a little bored.

"Not for a hundred grand."

"Fine. Then it's free." Thin arms rose, skeletal fingers pushed back the hood.

Rob found himself looking at a very old woman, tight lips puckered from smoking, nose as narrow as a blade, white hair neatly bunned. She smiled, drawing the lips back past a row of sharpened teeth.

Godawful creepy.

"Come on," she said, her voice warm now.

Still uneasy but too fascinated to try again to leave, he followed her back into her work space.

She gestured toward the dangling shapes. "For money, you have your choice," she said. She went to an old dresser that was almost hidden back among the books. "But for free, we do this."

She opened a drawer. Inside was a misshapen figure, folded in on itself. Its face looked like a withered pumpkin.

"What is it?"

She reached in and drew the slack figure out, cradling it in her arms.

Now the face became clearer. He gasped, took an involuntary step back, then choked back a small, awed sound. He mustn't let the old woman know that this was by far her best costume. The eyes glared, gray and intractable, the teeth shone like pale knives behind the cruel lips.

"It's what—a werewolf?"

"Sure. Do you like it?"

His heart skipped a beat. He gave no indication of his excitement. "It's ok. Thank you."

She laughed a little, deep in her throat. "I've discontinued it. Doesn't sell. This is the last one."

Perfect!

"Oh, I'll take it off your hands."

She reached up and ran her fingers along his cheek. Her touch was cold. Vaguely sickening. "These costumes are made with an organic base. You'll need to get in it about two hours before you go out. Lie still, you'll feel it gradually getting tighter. Think of it as kind of baking in. Gradually, you'll stop feeling a border between your skin and the costume." She paused, then smiled with her dagger teeth. "That's when you're cooked. Ready to go out and have fun!"

"What about taking it off?"

She shrugged her shoulders and shook herself. "Shake out of it."

It would be the best costume anybody had ever seen. It would hit the party like a damn tsunami. *And* he was beating the old fool out of the damn thing.

Bee-you-ti-ful!

She told him to keep it in the fridge like meat until he was ready to use it. She showed him how it split down the back, revealing a complex interior colored in moist hues of pink and red and pale gray.

It looked so much like animal fat that he reached toward it, thinking to touch it and see just how organic it was.

Instantly, her fingers enclosed his wrist. They felt like wire. "No, no," she said, "if you touch it, you activate it. You'll need to put it on and run through a cycle. Takes six hours."

He wanted to ask her how the hell it worked, but if he showed too much interest, she might change her mind about the cash.

"OK, got it, no big deal," he said, careful to sound noncommittal. If his sheer joy so much as peeked out from behind the façade of his face, she was liable to ask for some money, even if it wasn't a hundred grand.

Jane had undoubtedly paid for what she'd gotten, and he wanted to be able to crow at the party about how he'd gotten his for free. For nothing. The most incredible costume ever seen.

She wrapped it in butcher paper, put it in a shopping bag and sent him on his way. As he walked up the long street in the freezing wind, he wished mightily for a cab, but there were no cabs in Sunset Park at this hour.

He was relieved to get to the subway, glad when the R train came clanging and shrieking into the station, and almost bubbling with glee as he was whisked from station to station, the miracle costume safely in the bag he carried on his lap.

She had probably paid the hundred grand for some inferior costume. Arnold Schwarzenegger. She'd go for that. She'd want to be a man. Or Hitler. The old lady probably had one hell of a Hitler packed away somewhere.

When he got home, the house was silent. A light glowed from back in the kitchen. Faint music told him that Jane was upstairs in bed. Good, hopefully asleep. He didn't want to confront her just now. She might read his triumph in his face. She was skilled at that sort of thing.

"You've been at that goddamn whorehouse, you bastard. If you can't get it up, I'm gonna whip your ass."

She emerged into the front hall from the darkened living room. She wore only a belt and boots. On the surface, she was every inch the dominatrix, but he had been married to her for enough time to know that this was just that—the surface.

Stuffing his bag into the understairs closet, he went to her, took her in his arms and lifted her up. He kissed her, pushing his tongue in, forcing her head back, holding her against him until she was gasping.

With a flick of his wrists, he pushed her away, causing her to fall to the floor in a heap.

Then he was on her, pulling his pants down around his knees, forcing her legs apart, then blasting into her with the fury that she adored. Her enjoyment depended on this. If he wasn't aggressive, she couldn't let go and if she couldn't let go, the river of her passion would not flood.

She cursed him, she clawed his chest, she tried to bite him, she called him a rapist. None of it mattered, as he well knew, and he plunged on into her heat and her desire, and when he expended himself she came in unison, crying out like some shrieking bird of night.

He sank down onto her. He said, "I was with Josie, if you must know. We did all kinds of shit."

"Tell me."

"Sixty-nine. Then she tied me up and made me kiss her boots."

"Kiss mine, you bastard, kiss my boots."

"I can't."

"Why the hell not? I'm your wife and she's just a damn whore."

"You're barefoot."

"Oh, yeah."

They lay together. Far away somewhere a siren wailed. The wind moaned in the eaves.

"Wanna toke?" she asked.

"You got what?"

"I scored some Kush on the way home."

They went upstairs together, took out their pipes and smoked together. They were gentled now, the furies in their souls for the moment at rest. Rob and Jane, married in love and hate.

When they made love this time, there was a leisurely quality to it that lovers advanced in their relationships sometimes enjoy, when desire has survived familiarity. Perhaps it was because she saw the feminine in him and he the masculine in her, for there was something ambiguous in their sexuality, which was perhaps why this impossible marriage, full of competition and rage, continued to grow—like a weed, yes, but also like some sort of dangerous flower.

Late in the night they went naked down to the kitchen, threading their way through their prized wolf pack in the front hall, and ate caviar out of tins and drank champagne. Around them, New York slept, its roar diminished to a sigh. Each in his own secrecy thought about their costume and the triumph to come.

The next day, the office was sullen and expectant. This was because Nick had come clanking in already costumed at eight in the morning. He'd taken his golden-winged helmet off and now sat at his desk resplendent in the original armor of the Qianlong Emperor. How he had obtained it, whether on loan or stolen from the Musée de l' Armée in Paris he wasn't saying. In any case, he was wearing the first ever multimillion dollar costume, and most of the Lone Rangers, Draculas, and Mickey Mice were devastated. Sure, you had to let the boss win, but this was ridiculous.

Jane and Rob kept their own counsel. Neither of them had the slightest intention of revealing their costume until they actually swept into the Rainbow Room, which had re-opened just last year and was now, on the 65th floor of Rockefeller Center, once again one of the world's most splendid social venues.

The two of them had agreed to go to the party in their separate cars. Rob had understood from hints that Jane had dropped that her costume was incredible. As well it might be. He could see her going as Priss from *Bladerunner*. That had been a hell of a costume. They were all great. But none was even close to the one he'd gotten for free. The werewolf, and how perfect, given that their wolf pack was the dominant decorative element of their house.

On this day, the million dollar bell was quiet, and even Nick didn't mind. Over time, the Halloween Party had become the firm's central event. Their year ended with the blowout on All Hallows.

Rob pretended that he had a sucker lunch, but actually went back to the house, got his costume and took it to the suite he kept at the Waldorf. Two bedrooms, fridge stocked with incredible food, wine cellar with ancient vintages. Here, he romanced clients and other men's wives. He had a need to take not only money from other men, but also their women. He raped lives, and loved every minute of it.

Jane also pretended that she had a sucker lunch, but actually went to her suite at the Sherry, where she already had her costume laid out and waiting. In this suite, she screwed anybody she needed to screw, for whatever reason. She liked to screw clerks for free clothes from Bergdorf's and Bonwit's, or to get a discount on the exquisite antique jewelry at A La Vieille Russie downstairs. She liked kinks, and did her thing up here, playing out her fantasy of being a lady wolf in a sty full of terrified hogs. The sweetness in her had been hurt a lot when she was a kid. Her dad, her older brother, her priest. You name it, they could not resist Jane candy.

She got hers back with a whip. Not on Rob, though she'd considered it. No, he was her one master. With Rob, she was the melted female.

Not up here, though, no way. She'd had the place well soundproofed, so once her mark was tied up, he discovered a few things she maybe hadn't known before about pain. The ones that came back were the best. She took their bodies, their money, their souls, everything, then spat them out like chewed plug.

She and Rob both opened their costumes at about the same time, and looked down into the strange, fatty interiors. Kind of moist and thick. Not uncomfortable, though. On the contrary, as they slid their bodies in, it felt like being embraced by a lover with a soft and intimate touch.

They followed instructions to the letter, and by the time evening was falling, the costumes had taken.

Rob gazed across his wide view to the north, taking in the twinkling beauty of the night city through his werewolf eyes. They were sort of like contacts, not entirely comfortable, perhaps, but you got used to them quickly enough.

He went into the kitchen and got a glass of water. To his annoyance, it poured out the sides of his long snout. Finally, he solved the problem by putting it in a bowl and lapping it up. The costume's extended jaw made it impossible to drink or to eat in any normal manner. At least Nick wouldn't expect him to bob for golden apples this year. Every year, people got their teeth busted doing that, which made Nick roar with laughter. They wanted the apples, though. Each one contained a couple of ounces of real gold in its skin.

The party started at seven. At six forty, he called down for his car and went into the hall. He was alone on his floor, but an elderly couple got on the elevator a few stops down. They practically choked, and he loved it.

Silence followed him across the lobby, and he loved that, too.

"Mr. Farley?" Jake was grinning hard, holding the Bentley's door open.

"I'm in here, Buddy."

Jake took a step back. "Excuse me?"

Rob cleared his throat. The costume seemed designed to swallow his voice and make it into a growl. Cool touch, but not real convenient. "It's me, Jake," he said carefully. "We're off to the Rainbow Room."

Jake peered at him. "That's damned amazing."

He smiled, causing Jake to jump back. "Fuck!"

Rob laughed. "Let's get this show on the road."

When Rob had been a kid, the Rainbow Room was something you read about as a place of legend, an outpost of Valhalla. Like almost everybody else at the firm, he'd grown up blue collar. In his case, on Staten Island. Jane had been raised in Flatbush, same as Rob. You grow up looking across at Manhattan, you want that. The floating jewel.

He noticed that he got a few glances in the lobby. Excellent. He was alone in the express elevator to the 65th floor. It seemed an age before the doors opened. He stepped out into the sky lobby, then turned toward the room itself. From inside, he could hear the frantic wail of voices, people watching, evaluating, speculating, lives being ruined and reputations made.

Ahead of him, Tommy Burt was turning in his coat. He was dressed in a toga, poor guy. A *toga*, Jesus. What was he planning to do before work tomorrow, kill himself? He had all of fifty bucks on his shoulders.

There was no need to wear a coat in this costume, not with all this fur. Wonderful stuff, undoubtedly real wolf.

As he passed the coat closet, the kid burst out laughing. Rob gave him a growl, but he only laughed more.

Seconds later, he realized why. Across the room attempting to lap punch was of all the god damned things another werewolf.

"Shit!"

Toga Tommy laughed at him. He was joined by Hitler and Rapunzel, one of the pros brought in by Nick, who also paid for their costumes. Traditionally, you could recognize them by the fairy tale themes.

The other werewolf rose up from the bowl, turned and glared at him.

That damn thieving old bitch! He was gonna go back out there and tear her throat out. How dare she!

The other werewolf dropped down onto all fours. It was snarling, foam eddying along its lips as they curled away from its teeth.

Rob fought the urge to go down himself, but then could not fight it. It was better this way. Felt better. There was going to be a fight, and he felt way more in control like this.

Around them, Mad Hatters, Hitlers, Rapunzels, Goose Girls, Hansels and Gretels, a great, flopping Pterodactyl and the Qianlong Emperor made a circle. Everybody knew what was going to happen, the same thing that always happened when two morons showed up in identical costumes. From the look of these outfits, the fight was going to be lots of fun.

Priss was there all right, looking contented. Jane had gone in exactly the direction he had expected and now she was watching Rob get his ass handed to him and loving it, damn her.

If the other werewolf was anybody Rob could fire, he was done.

He glared into the face. Who the hell was it?

The other wolf leaped at him. It was damn fast and damn strong, and he was sent flying. He scrambled to all fours and found himself going for the neck.

They mixed it up, tearing at each other. The other one was a little smaller but faster than a striking snake. Damn strong, too.

He sank his jaws into a foreleg. There was a snarl, filled with agony and rage, but he heard not only those tones, there was also something else, a sound that surprised him, then didn't.

The hell with Priss standing there grinning out of her dark and evil eyes, the other werewolf was his own wife. He'd heard Jane's voice in that growl.

The moment he realized who it was, the other werewolf reared back. It tried to stand up, but dropped back down to all fours. They stood panting at each other, circling again.

"Bo-*ring*," the Qianlong Emperor yelled. "We want blood!"

The others shouted and clapped, "Blood! Blood! Blood!"

Rob managed a distorted growl. "Let's get outa here, babes, this is a catastrophe."

She drooped, then looked toward the door.

Screw this. They loped out.

"Whoever you are, you're fuckin' fired," the Qianlong Emperor jeered. "Fuckin' *fired!*"

Priss followed them, but nobody noticed that. She went into the ladies room, but no costumed figure emerged.

They got to the sky lobby. An elderly man joined them. Not from the party, therefore nobody important. He stood waiting for the elevator, seemingly unconcerned by the two wolves who paced the floor behind him.

Jane said something that Rob couldn't understand.

"You sound like a damn animal trying to talk."

"What?"

"We gotta get out of these things, they're shitty!"

Her reply was an indistinct growl.

"Stop that! Talk!"

"Stop that growling, asshole."

The express sped them down to the ground floor. The old man smiled, but they didn't see the familiar teeth. In any case, they were entirely concentrated on their own problem: get the hell out of these damn things.

The thing to do now was to get one of the cars.

In the lobby, people screamed. "Hey," Rob shouted, "take it easy."

This caused an eruption of shouting. A man swung at him with a shoe.

"Relax, this is crazy."

Something hot got poured on his back. "Don't do that," a woman's voice cried, "wolves don't hurt people!"

"We're not wolves," he explained. "These are Halloween costumes."

"It's snarling, it's going to attack."

"Nine one one, we have an emergency," the doorman's voice intoned. "Two animals, apparently wolves, have been released in the lobby of thirty Rockefeller Center, we need animal control officers right away." He stepped into the middle of the lobby. "OK, folks, back off and stop bothering them. It's obviously some kind of Halloween prank, I'm sure they're harmless."

The hair rose on the back of Jane's neck and she growled. Rob could hear the menace in it. She was seriously furious and he didn't blame her. No wonder the old biddy had been giving away free costumes, they were so good that they were terrible.

The cops would solve this. Help them get out of these things. Maybe a fine, then get the hell out of here. He was headed back to Sunset Park with a gun, just speaking personally.

Two officers came in the front door. Couple of kids. When they laid eyes on Rob and Jane, they went white.

"We need help," Rob said.

"OK folks, just back off. We want all of you off the floor soon as you can. Just take it easy, back away."

Rob could hear the kid breathing. He could smell the salt of his blood. Smelled good, and he took another deep pull of it, sucking the air through his long nose. He was damn hungry, matter of fact.

Four more cops came in. They had nets.

"Hey, hold on, here," Rob said. "These are Halloween costumes." He tried to stand up.

"It's gonna pounce!" a voice cried.

"Shoot it, somebody's gonna get their throat torn out."

The next moment, Rob was in a net. He fought, he tore at the strands with his teeth, but he was dragged away out the main door and past a crowd that had gathered on Fifth Avenue. He was dumped into a big cage on the back of a truck. Jane was beside him, methodically gnawing at her own net.

They were taken to the Central Park Zoo. Trapped in one of the small cages, they found themselves pacing away the hours of the night. They shook and shook, but the costumes did not come off. In fact, they didn't feel like costumes any more at all.

Dawn came, and with it a zookeeper with slabs of half rotted meat. Brisket? Some even cheaper cut?

They gobbled it, and Rob was amazed had how good it tasted.

They tried to work the lock with their paws.

Fail.

People passed the cage with dull, disinterested eyes. Sad men and women, kids who never looked up from their phones.

A day passed without making a dime.

As evening fell, Rob cried. He actually cried. Or rather, he felt like he was crying. The wolf that he had become drooped a little, hung its head and drooled.

Every day, they were thrown meat, and the meat was good, they ate it all.

At night, they screwed and lingered butt to butt like dogs do, panting and waiting for their bodies to release, remembering the wonderful lives that had been theirs, the food, the drink, the fabulous possessions and the deliciousness of greed.

Over time, the police entered their house. The State of New York was their only heir, so their possessions were sold at auction—not the illegal stuff, of course.

The wolves were not there, but nobody knew that except old Annie Ross and her team, warriors against all that people like Rob and Jane stood for. Annie's genius was sewing, and perhaps a little magic. Or, more accurately stated, forgotten science. Somewhere behind the old stories of shape-shifting, of werewolves and such, after all, there is a lost truth. Annie knew it. Here and there in the world, others knew it. High magic, high science.

At the zoo, the sun rose and fell on the cages and the pacing, swinging, staring animals. Winter came and the blowing snow, then spring and the blowing blossom. On the air, Rob and Jane caught scent of the distant forests, and their hearts joined the longing of the other hearts in the zoo.

Every so often, the old woman would come and watch them, a cigarette hanging out of the side of her mouth. She brought them big dog biscuits. The zookeepers looked the other way. She had been feeding certain of the animals for years.

Rob and Jane gobbled the biscuits and hated themselves for it. But they were wolves now, and so always hungry. They liked their meat best not just raw but bloody and a little rotted. They were still connoisseurs, but their tastes had changed.

The gorillas followed Anne with their eyes, beads of hate, tears falling like rain. One of the snakes, the biggest of the pythons, utterly despised her, and coiled and hissed when she passed through the little reptile room.

Rob and Jane lived by their noses, scenting the distant forest and dreaming of great woods in the moonlight and running deer, and other things of which wolves may dream.

They lived for many years in that cage. One morning, Jane, now gone gray around the eyes and soft of muscle, did not come out of her hutch. The zookeepers took the body away, and with it Rob's heart. He languished for another couple of months, but then death in its mercy took him, too.

At least they weren't gunned down from a helicopter.

RESCUER?

Nicole Cushing

I was scared, and I didn't like it. That, in itself, should let you know how odd and—well—*dangerous*—that night was. Because I, like most other horror writers, actually *like* being scared. *Especially* around Halloween. Fear is as much a part of the season as candy corn and costumes. People pay haunted houses for the *privilege* of shrieking in terror, right? (Although, sure, *giggles* travel in the wake of such shrieks).

But that night, the fear was visceral. Bordering on panic. Not a giggle to be heard. Because there was a young woman walking down a deserted stretch of road, toward the river. And I was pretty sure that she was going to drown herself.

Let me set the scene for you. It's late October, 1994. I'm a senior psychology major at St. Mary's College of Maryland (a small, public liberal arts college resting on a bluff high above the St. Mary's River, near the Chesapeake Bay). I have two friends who live at the far end of campus (in Calvert Hall, the dorm closest to the river; the *only* dorm on the river, actually).

It is—quite possibly—the most picturesque part of a highly picturesque campus. In addition to having a river view from the balcony, Calvert Hall is right next to an Episcopal church with a large, old graveyard. It's also close to a historical site where volunteers re-enact life in colonial Maryland.

I hang out with my friends in Calvert Hall quite a bit. We get drunk a lot. But that night, we don't. That night, we watch movies. Probably horror movies, given the season and our proclivities toward the genre, but maybe not. After the VHS double feature ends, I start my walk back to my dorm on the other end of campus. This entails traveling for about five minutes on an isolated road before picking up one of the main campus paths.

There's dense fog outside. I'm talking textbook, trope, Universal horror movie style fog. In the midst of that fog, a young ghoulish-looking woman staggers towards me.

Her face is slathered with ghastly white makeup. She's obviously coming from a Halloween party. She wears one of those goth chick costumes along the lines of what we might today call the sexy witch look. You know the drill: ripped, black fishnet hose. Revealing top. That sort of thing. It looks out of place on her. She's skinny, bespectacled and looks almost too young to be in college. Has freshman written all over her.

The whole thing's surreal. She lurches like a Romero zombie (or, given her outfit, perhaps more like Vampira in *Plan 9 From Outer Space*). But she's not pretending to be one of the undead. She's drunk. She's drunk and *bawling* and tottering toward a mostly-deserted part of campus. Does she, like my friends, live in Calvert Hall? I've never seen her around there before.

Something's wrong.

She walks toward me and I walk toward her and as we approach one another, I speak up. I ask if she's okay. I ask if she needs help.

"I don't want help," she replies. "I want the river."

The words burn into my brain. *She wants the river.* Sure, I'm a psych major, which probably makes me more attuned to these sorts of things, but it doesn't take Sigmund Fucking Freud to figure out that she's going to try suicide.

And this, dear readers, is where I feel *fear*. Not the brief fear of a jump scare at a haunted house, but something more visceral. Something that induces a sort of moral vertigo.

Because, really, who wants to *get involved* in something like this? What are my options? Should I try to physically restrain her? Should I write the whole thing off as drama? (After all, if she'd *really* wanted to drown herself, she wouldn't have told me about her plan, would she?) Should I call campus police?

I choose the latter. It just seems like the right thing to do. There's a call box outside the dorm (yes, kiddies, this is before the mass adoption of cell phones—Mama Cushing's a relic). I use the call box to contact the operator, and ask her to connect me with campus police. I tell them what's going on, as best as I can. They say they'll be on their way. What follows are several of the most nerve-racking moments of my life. I want to keep an eye on the ghoulish girl, to make sure she's safe, but I want to lag behind her a little, to keep an eye out for the campus police, so *I can lead them to the girl* when they arrive. If I get too close to the girl, the campus police won't find us. But if I lag too far behind, the girl might get what she wants.

And this is where the night gets even *more* bizarre. Because this suicidal sexy witch decides she's going to take the scenic route to oblivion. She runs through the historical site, following a path that travels down the bluff and to the river (there's a replica of a colonial ship docked there). The campus cops finally arrive. No time for formal introductions: we're all running through the fog, after the ghoulish girl.

The fog worsens the closer we get to the river, enshrouding us, making the paths of the historical site seem like the snowy topiary maze at the end of *The Shining*. Ultimately, we find her, just as she stumbles into the water. She's sobbing. Two or three campus police wade into the river and grab her. She's detained. Safe.

Afterward, there's paperwork to fill out. There are questions about where she may have gotten her alcohol. (Her ID confirms what we already knew—she was underage). That seems to be what the campus cops are most concerned about, actually. "She doesn't *really* want to kill herself," one of them assures me. "It's just the alcohol talking."

A nd so this is the part where I'm supposed to look back, twenty years later, and give you some moral to the story. Maybe offer an epigram that will sum up deep life lessons learned from this misadventure. That's the human instinct—to find meaning in things like this.

Maybe I could point out the fact that Halloween, in folklore, is the time when the veil between life and death is the thinnest. Maybe I could discuss how that's appropriate, because the margin between life and death was so thin in this instance. If I got exceedingly carried away, I could even cite this as proof that an omnipotent, invisible force moves us all around like chess pieces, and chose to place me at just the right place and time to intervene.

I *could* take any of those paths to completing this remembrance. It would probably make for a crowd-pleasing exit, too. But I *won't*.

You want a spooky Halloween story? *Here's* a spooky Halloween story, culled from Mama Cushing's vast life experience: for every instance of apparent serendipity, there's at least one (if not five or ten) heartbreaking missed opportunities.

I know this because I have those sorts of stories, too. A little over ten years out of college, I gave an acquaintance a ride to a gathering of our mutual friends. Two weeks later, I found out she'd blown her head off shortly thereafter. Outside of my own experience, there's the heartbreaking 1980 death of English musician Ian Curtis. A friend in another city suspected he was going to kill himself, and tried calling others who were close by so they could stop him. But all the people who were close enough to do anything were all away from their homes, at the same wedding, and none of them received the call.

As Alanis Morissette, once concluded (using somewhat incorrect language): "Isn't that ironic, don't you think? A little too ironic."

As Harlan Ellison once concluded in an interview with Stanley Wiater (using somewhat more precise language): "The universe is neither benign or malign. It doesn't know you're here, kid."

You want to hear a spooky Halloween story? How's this: one day, the ghoulish girl is going to die. Maybe she's already dead. Maybe she managed to drown herself the Halloween after I graduated. Maybe she got hit by a bus two years later. Maybe she succumbed to an accidental drug overdose five years later. Maybe she felt an incurable lump in her breast fifteen years later. Or maybe she still lives.

But one day, she (and all the rest of us) are going to arrive at that place beyond the reach of any serendipity—that last five or six feet of space we occupy. Either in a gutter or hooked to machines. Alone or surrounded by loved ones. In our car or in our bed. By the criminal's bullet or by the state's needle. Doped to the gills or in terrible pain. In the end, no matter *how* we die, the end result is the same.

How's that for a spooky story?

Boo!

THE NIGHT BEFORE

Ray Garton

In 1969, when I was not quite seven years old, Halloween fell on a Friday. This was insignificant to most trick-or-treaters, but not to me. We were Seventh-day Adventists and observed the Sabbath, which began at sundown on Friday and ended at sundown on Saturday, just like the Jewish Sabbath. During that time, there was no TV, no radio, no secular music or literature, no buying or selling, and certainly no trick-or-treating.

Halloween was mostly frowned upon in the church, but in a sort of shrugging way. Most parents seemed to keep their disapproval to a minimum because the kids loved it so much, and it was the holiday's origins that they didn't like rather than the holiday as it was presently celebrated. But I had a few Adventist friends whose parents didn't let them go trick-or-treating or celebrate Halloween in any way.

My parents knew how much I loved the holiday and made sure I had a fun Halloween celebration every year. They were very good to me in that respect. The church also strongly disapproved of horror movies, but my parents let me watch them on TV because I loved them and, weirdly, they made me happy. Their religion was crazier than a rabid weasel, but they made some concessions for me because they loved me and wanted me to be happy. They even did their best to make sure I had a Halloween in 1969. They meant well.

They decided that my celebration would take place the day *before* Halloween, on Thursday, and it would include trick-or-treating. I was ecstatic about that because, at the age of six, you don't think ahead much to consider what you might be getting into.

The night before Halloween, just after dark, they took me trick-or-treating. Once we got out there, I began to realize that trick-or-treating on the night *before* Halloween probably wasn't going to work.

At six, I was no trick-or-treat veteran, but I knew that on Halloween night, the sidewalks were crawling with kids in costumes carrying bags of candy. That was not true of the night *before* Halloween. The streets were desolate, and somehow, that was magnified by the wind snickering through the trees, and the shadows of the branches cast by streetlights dancing over everything. And there I stood, on the sidewalk in some costume (I don't remember what), with a plastic pumpkin waiting to be filled with candy, completely alone in what looked and felt like an abandoned neighborhood. On the night *before* Halloween.

I don't remember Mom being with us, which means she probably was working at the hospital. Dad drove along the curb, staying with me as I went from house to house. He had a loaded handgun under the seat. I have no idea if it was registered, but I know he didn't have a permit to carry it in the car. He always wanted to be prepared should unexpected circumstances make it necessary for him to blow the shit out of somebody.

At the first house, the woman who answered the door was nice. When she asked why I was trick-or-treating the night before Halloween, I told her, quite nervously and with some embarrassment, "Friday night is the Sabbath."

"Are you Jewish? You must be Jewish. Let me open the Halloween candy."

She disappeared into the house and came back a moment later with a big bowl of candy. She scooped out a fistful of bubble gum, lollipops, and miniature candy bars and dropped them into my pumpkin. Then she grabbed another scoop and said, "Here, maybe this will make up for the people who aren't going to be ready for you," and she dropped another fistful of candy into my pumpkin, wished me a happy Halloween with a smile and closed the door.

And I assumed that was how the evening would go. Wrong.

"You're a *what*?" the next woman said.

"Seventh-day Adventist."

"I don't understand. Does that mean you won't go to doctors?"

"Friday night is the Sabbath."

"But I—*oh*, so you can't go trick-or-treating, I see. Let me see what I can find."

She turned and went into the house as a man shouted, "Who is it? What do they want?" They talked quietly for a moment, then the man said, "Oh, they just want canned food. They were just here."

Stomping feet grew louder and the man appeared in the doorway.

"I just gave all our canned goods to the people who were just here!" he said angrily as he looked around behind me for an adult.

I don't know if they still do it, but back then, Adventist churches always had a canned food drive in the fall.

I turned and hurried away from the house.

Every house I went to, I met confused people who couldn't understand why I was trick-or-treating the night before Halloween, and a couple of them were pretty annoyed that I'd disturbed their evening. I finally gave up and got in the car with Dad.

When I explained to him what had happened, he got angry and asked which houses people had gotten annoyed so he could take care of them. Dad was always prepared should unexpected circumstances arise that made it necessary for him to beat the shit out of somebody.

I convinced him to go home. The whole thing had been rather depressing. But there was a horror movie on Channel 2's *Eight O' Clock Movie* that night—if I remember correctly, it was Robert Wise's *The Haunting*—and I quickly pushed the whole thing out of my mind. But it has always remained as an embarrassing memory.

Great Pumpkins and Ghost Hunters:

Halloween on TV

Lisa Morton

People all over the world love Halloween. And television is a large part of the reason why.

Those two statements aren't meant to be mere attention-grabbing hyperbole; on the contrary, they're quite sober and true. Since the start of the new millennium, Halloween's popularity has exploded beyond just English-speaking countries (and, even though it lacks the autumnal association in the southern hemisphere–where it's spring in October–it's starting to catch on in Australia and South Africa). Two decades ago, most of Europe, Russia and Asia had little to no awareness of or interest in the holiday; in some cases (chiefly the European countries) they already had their own celebration on November 1st (the more somber and reflective All Saints' Day) and viewed Halloween as a glib imperialist festival.

But no one should underestimate the cultural power of American exports, especially our entertainment. The world consumes American movies and television series at an alarming rate, and our sitcoms in particular are popular nearly everywhere. *The Nightmare Before Christmas* may have been a global success story that introduced many non-English-speaking audiences to Halloween, but even more successful were shows like *The Simpsons*, which is poised to become the most lucrative syndicated television series ever.

So, while many Americans grew up with the Simpsons' "Treehouse of Horror" as a yearly Halloween tradition, that experience is now being shared around the globe. Everyone enjoys a grinning jack-o'-lantern, costumed kids, and a playful scare...once they know about it via our television shows, that's it.

Halloween and television have a rich and intertwined history. Both came of age at roughly the same time—in the post-war 1950s, as American prosperity grew and trick or treat finally spread across the country. Halloween, of course, had been around before television, but in a form so different that few modern kids would recognize it; it was a time devoted to fortune-telling, games, and prank-playing (the latter was certainly well represented in radio, where the 1938 Orson Welles production of *War of the Worlds* terrified millions of listeners and is still considered possibly the single most successful Halloween prank in history). It wasn't until World War II ended and production moved from war machinery to luxury goods—including candy and costumes—that Halloween and its most beloved ritual, trick or treat, were firmly established.

Looking at Halloween through television provides a telling look at how the holiday has changed and evolved over the last sixty years. What follows is by no means a comprehensive list; that would be a book-length project, with thousands of entries, especially considering that Halloween episodes have brought in such high ratings for many programs that they've established a yearly tradition of producing a new Halloween episode each October. For the purposes of this overview, I've opted to create a list of twenty key programs, running from 1952 to 2013; these particular works aptly demonstrate the prevalent attitudes toward Halloween at the time. I'm only including programs that specifically mention Halloween and feature real Halloween content, meaning you won't find here, for example, that episode of *Xena: Warrior Princess* that went for a scarier-than-usual story to broadcast in late October. I have tried to include a wide range of program types—everything from sitcoms to sci-fi, from one-time TV movies to classic episodes—and I've chosen only works that are relatively easy to find. It's not my goal to drive you crazy by telling you how great that lost Halloween episode of *The Honeymooners* is.

So, let's put on our costumes, grab our candy collectors, and step up to the first house on our Halloween journey, this one inhabited by the family behind the longest-running live-action sitcom in American television history:

THE ADVENTURES OF OZZIE AND HARRIET–"HALLOWEEN PARTY" (1952)

What It's About: It's the day before Halloween, and while youngest Nelson Ricky plans for trick or treat and older son David works on a school party, Ozzie decides to throw his own Halloween party without Harriet's help. Convinced that he can plan a party better than his wife, Halloween night arrives and Ozzie discovers just how wrong he is.

Why It's Interesting: This early look at Halloween on television also suggests how trick or treat has changed over the last fifty years (it's also worth noting that this same year—1952—saw the theatrical release of the famed Donald Duck cartoon *Trick or Treat*, meaning trick or treat was a big deal in '52). Although the plot of the episode centers on an adult Halloween party, Ozzie repeatedly utters his belief that Halloween is really just for children; and indeed, the adult Halloween party includes virtually no games or activities specific to the holiday, with only two of the adults (Ozzie and the next-door neighbor Thorny) even costumed. Ozzie and Ricky both have fairly elaborate costumes—a devil and a skeleton, respectively—so we know that mass-manufactured Halloween costumes were in place by this time.

And a disclaimer: This show is pretty hard for a modern viewer to stomach, entrenched as it is in '50s lifestyle and production values. Recommended only for Halloween completists.

THE *ADDAMS FAMILY*–"HALLOWEEN WITH THE ADDAMS FAMILY" (1964)

What It's About: It's Halloween night at the Addams house; as Grandmama takes the children (Wednesday and Pugsley) trick-or-treating, Morticia and Gomez prepare to hold a party. When their first two guests arrive, they don't know that Marty and Claude are actually robbers fleeing the scene of their latest crime; and when the criminals see that Gomez has a drawer stuffed with money, they feign interest in the party. After hearing Gomez's Halloween poem (a mangled version of "'Twas the Night Before Christmas"), and playing a painful game of "bobbing for the crab" (with a live specimen), the two robbers decide they'd rather take their chances with the police.

Why It's Interesting: By 1964, monsters were hotter than ever–Universal's syndicated package of its old horror pictures was running constantly on television sets all over America, and a magazine called *Famous Monsters of Filmland* had debuted six years earlier and garnered a sizable following. Kids who were drawn to monster films and magazines naturally felt instant kinship with the gleefully macabre Addams family, and when the Addamses claimed Halloween for themselves, it probably felt like a rallying call to all those baby boomers who didn't yet know they were the nerds of the future. Notice, for instance, the huge explosion of canned laughter when Gomez calls Halloween "our favorite holiday!"; obviously that cut-in reaction is meant to tell the audience that it's perfectly okay for your peers to laugh at your affection for dark things, because the Addams family is *cool* and they're being laughed at. This might have been one of the first times on television that Halloween's more ghoulish side was both acknowledged and celebrated. Plus it has Don Rickles as one of the robbers, and is still vastly entertaining.

BEWITCHED–"THE WITCHES ARE OUT" (1964)

What It's About: Halloween is approaching, and at the same time that Samantha and her witch friends are bemoaning the ugly, wart-covered stereotyped image of the witch, Samantha's ad executive husband Darrin is being asked to design a horrible witch to promote a new Halloween candy. After Darrin is fired for refusing to honor the client's request, the witches pay a nocturnal visit to the client and succeed in convincing him that the image of the long-nosed, awful witch is obsolete and inappropriate. Darrin is re-hired, and the campaign is hugely successful.

Why It's Interesting: Not only does this delightful show play with the classic Halloween icon of the witch, but it even flirts with civil rights (certainly a hot topic in 1964), as the witches openly discuss how they are discriminated against, were burned in the past, and are a minority who need to engage in protests to change their image. And within the evolution of Halloween, this may also be the first television production to openly discuss the marketing of the holiday, which was certainly in full swing by 1964.

IT'S THE GREAT PUMPKIN, CHARLIE BROWN (1966)

What It's About: On Halloween night, Linus and Sally sit in the pumpkin patch waiting for the mythical "Great Pumpkin", whom Linus has written to and believes will arrive. Meanwhile, the rest of the "Peanuts" gang go trick-or-treating, and Charlie Brown gets a rock instead of a treat at every house. After trick or treat, the kids hold a party; later on, Sally leaves the pumpkin patch, angry at Linus for making her miss both trick or treat and the party. Linus eventually falls asleep in the pumpkin patch, but is taken home, disappointed and cold, by his sister Lucy; nonetheless, he vows to wait for the Great Pumpkin again next year.

Why It's Interesting: *It's the Great Pumpkin, Charlie Brown* is the only item in this list that actually impacted the holiday and not the other way around. It's hard to overstate the importance of this animated special, which is still broadcast every year and has spawned DVDs, retrospectives, figurines, and, most recently, apps. But above all else, *It's the Great Pumpkin, Charlie Brown* opened the floodgates for children's Halloween books; surprisingly, prior to the show's broadcast, there were few popular children's books for Halloween. After the 1967 release of the book version sold well, children's Halloween books began to appear at an ever-increasing rate (now, of course, there are literally thousands in existence, with new titles published every year).

STAR TREK—"CATSPAW" (1967)

What It's About: While in orbit around the planet Pyris VII, the Enterprise loses communication with its advance scouts. When one of the men is found dead, Captain Kirk, First Officer Spock and Doctor Mc-Coy beam down to the planet to search for Scotty and Sulu, who are still missing. They encounter fog, witches, a castle, a black cat, and skeletons, all of which they compare to trick or treat and Halloween. They finally meet Korob, who is apparently a sorcerer, and his cohort Sylvia, a witch; however, they soon realize that the power wielded by this pair stems from a device called the "transmuter", and when Kirk manages to destroy the transmuter he frees his crewmen and reveals that Korob and Sylvia are actually dying aliens from another galaxy.

Why It's Interesting: "Catspaw" is not only one of the first serious, adult representations of Halloween in a television program, it's also possibly the first actually written by a noted horror author–Robert Bloch, the creator of *Psycho* (oddly, earlier genre series, including *The Outer Limits* and *The Twilight Zone,* did no episodes with specific Halloween content). While "Catspaw" is a not-entirely-successful attempt to blend horror and science fiction–it's not frightening enough for horror fans, but its reliance on Gothic imagery and magic isn't in keeping with science fiction, and the story features numerous lapses in logic–it's nonetheless colorful and entertaining. Speaking of logic gaps, "Catspaw" continually suggests that trick or treat is still a popular activity three hundred years in the future; while I'd like to believe this might be possible, Halloween's history has demonstrated that this is a holiday constantly in flux and future trick or treat is sadly unlikely.

THE PAUL LYNDE HALLOWEEN SPECIAL (1976)

What It's About: In this variety special, America's favorite master of sarcasm Paul Lynde does stand-up, appears in sketches, and even sings and dances. His guests include Margaret Hamilton (the original Wicked Witch from *The Wizard of Oz*) and Billie Hayes ("Witchiepoo" from the cult children's show *H.R. Pufnstuf)* as sister witches, comic performers Betty White, Billy Barty, Tim Conway, Florence Henderson and Roz Kelly, and musical guests KISS. Halloween bits include a "haunted discotheque" number, Lynde in a black-and-orange sequin tuxedo, and the two famed witch actresses dressed as their respective characters.

Why It's Interesting: Back in those halcyon days before *American Idol* and *Dancing With the Stars,* even before MTV (when it actually focused on music), variety shows were a staple of network programming. Sonny and Cher, Donny and Marie, and the Smothers Brothers all had their own series...but surely *The Paul Lynde Halloween Special* must be the absolute most bizarre marriage of variety show and Halloween ever videotaped. There's Lynde mugging in a skit about long-haul truckers, KISS (in their first national television appearance) lip-synching (badly) to three songs, and musical numbers performed by a horde of dancers in spandex and bright orange fright wigs. It was 1976, so disco and truckers were hardly surprising...but this nevertheless odd olio still proves that Halloween can surely adapt to *anything*.

CHiPs–"Trick or Trick" (1978)

What It's About: It's Halloween in the City of Angels, and CHP Officers Ponch and Jon deal with five concurrent story lines: 1) after an encounter with Ponch, a trick or treater runs away to hide in a haunted house, where he remains until the officers rescue him; 2) a woman dressed as a ghost pulls off a series of robberies until she's caught red-handed by the officers; 3) a middle-aged woman stealing trick or treat bags turns out to be searching for a missing engagement ring; 4) a pair of women on a Halloween scavenger hunt invite Ponch and Jon to a party; and 5) Ponch and Jon pursue and nab a pair of middle-aged pranksters stealing a neighbor's sod. There's also a scene involving a van full of black cats, and a running gag about Ponch's belief in superstitions.

Why It's Interesting: I hope you're not expecting me to declare that an episode of *CHiPs* is either high art or a Halloween must-see; instead, I've chosen this to represent the way Halloween has been used in action series. While many action shows have included some more outré or frightening subject matter around the time of Halloween, some also found ways to work the holiday into their plots. In this episode of *CHiPs*, for example, we have car chases that are interrupted by egg-throwing pranksters, a foot chase involving a woman dressed as a ghost, and a confrontation between Ponch and a father who is angry over the way a cop scared his kid (Ponch jokingly told a juvenile prankster that he'd put him in handcuffs). The episode is enjoyable anyway for the disco soundtrack and those blow-dried '70s haircuts, but the way it incorporates Halloween imagery and activities demonstrates just how far the holiday's tropes can be reshaped and twisted.

TALES FROM THE DARKSIDE–"HALLOWEEN CANDY" (1985)

What It's About: Mr. Killup is a mean old man who is constantly hungry and who hates Halloween. His son pays him a visit on Halloween night, brings candy, and begs his father to ward off pranksters by giving out candy instead; instead, the cantankerous senior hurls insults at the trick or treaters and keeps the candy to himself. At the stroke of midnight, Killup answers a knock on the front door to find a diminutive goblin standing there; when the goblin performs several impossible feats, Killup realizes this is a real creature. The night continues in terror, as time stops at midnight, cockroaches overrun the house, and the goblin pays a return visit. The next day Killup is found dead, and police tell his son that the old man died of starvation.

Why It's Interesting: And finally, a Halloween television show that's actually meant to frighten. Here in 1985–more than thirty years after Halloween's first television appearances–here's a depiction of the holiday that's not whimsical, humorous, or bent to other uses like action. Written by famed horror writer Michael McDowell, "Halloween Candy" is a short exercise in October darkness; it employs bugs, the witching hour, and monsters to scare the pants off viewers, and although it was obviously challenged by a small budget (the goblin isn't always completely convincing, to put it mildly), it still manages to pack in a few jolts, and remains fondly remembered by many horror fans, who consider it to be a stand-out episode of *Tales From the Darkside*.

ROSEANNE–"BOO!" (1989)

What It's About: The working-class Conner family is obsessed with Halloween; husband and wife Dan and Roseanne love trying to scare each other, and together with their three children they decorate their house as a "Tunnel of Terror" for trick or treaters. When the night ends with Roseanne convincing Dan that her mother is coming for a lengthy stay, she is the acknowledged master of fear.

Why It's Interesting: "Boo!" comes at a transitional time for Halloween, and reflects how the holiday's identity was shifting. In the first scene, Roseanne's sister remembers prankplaying as an integral part of trick or treat, and Roseanne's teenage daughter is plainly surprised by the stories of soaping windows and egging passing cars. But most interesting is the extent of the home haunt that the Conners stage for Halloween. In 1989, major professional haunted attractions weren't found in every shopping mall or abandoned warehouse; there were still very few companies manufacturing the complicated props and set pieces that are readily available now, and so home haunters were forced to rely on their own ingenuity. "Boo!" reflects this, by offering a mad scientist's lab cobbled together from drinking glasses and tin cans, a kitchen of props obviously made of aluminum foil, and patently fake gore effects. "Boo!" also does a fine job of conveying the holiday's gleeful, mischief-loving side–due, perhaps, in some part to a story editor named Joss Whedon.

THE SIMPSONS–"TREEHOUSE OF HORROR" (1990)

What It's About: America's favorite animated sitcom celebrates Halloween with three ghostly tales, being told by brother and sister Bart and Lisa in their treehouse on Halloween evening: The first segment, "Bad Dream House", parodies ghost stories and haunted house movies; the second, "Hungry Are the Damned", plays on the famous *Twilight Zone* episode "To Serve Man", as the Simpsons are kidnapped by aliens Kang and Kodos, who are ominously intent on fattening them up; and the final piece is Poe's "The Raven", with Homer standing in as the narrator and Bart appearing as the eponymous bird.

Why It's Interesting: "The Treehouse of Horror" was so successful that it spawned a yearly installment (even though these episodes are notoriously more difficult to produce than an average *Simpsons*). All (to date) 24 installments have featured the three-story structure, the references to and parodies of various horror films and themes, and the aliens Kang and Kodos. There is perhaps no better exploration of the cross-ties between Halloween and horror than the "Treehouse of Horror" shows, which have played on everything from *The Exorcist*, *The Shining* and *Sweeney Todd* to EC Comics, urban legends, and even *It's the Great Pumpkin, Charlie Brown*. For the 2013 episode's "couch gag" (or the opening credit sequence, so-called because it ends with the Simpsons landing on their couch before the television), the series brought in feature film director and horror aficionado Guillermo del Toro, who provided a 2 minute and 45 second mega-tribute, cramming in literally dozens of references to horror authors and films (including his own *Hellboy* and *Pan's Labyrinth*).

GHOSTWATCH (1992)

What It's About: It's Halloween, and the BBC is running a live special as an investigative crew is sent into a supposedly haunted house while an in-studio parapsychologist observes and phone calls are fielded from viewers. The reporters, led by Sarah Greene, at first think they've discovered the source of the poltergeist activity when they spot the Early family's teenage daughter Suzanne banging on a wall, but they soon realize that the ghost, "Mr. Pipes", is a real entity, and via the television crew has escaped the confines of the Early house and spread throughout Great Britain.

Why It's Interesting: Here is the television equivalent of the famed Orson Welles' radio prank, *War of the Worlds*. As written by Stephen Volk and directed by Lesley Manning, *Ghostwatch* was so successful in convincing viewers that it was real that the BBC received 30,000 phone calls in an hour, and the show has never been aired again in Great Britain. Where *War of the Worlds* depicted a Martian invasion, *Ghostwatch* makes specific use of Halloween, setting it up as a night of particularly intense paranormal activity. *Ghostwatch* (which is available on import DVD and YouTube) has spawned both a documentary, 2012's *Ghostwatch: Behind the Curtains*, and a sequel in the form of a 2006 short story ("31/10") by Volk. Viewed twenty years after its initial airing, *Ghostwatch* remains genuinely unnerving, and seems to predict the rise of such later films and series as *The Blair Witch Project*, *Paranormal Activity*, and *Ghost Hunters*. This is Halloween horror at its very best.

THE HALLOWEEN TREE (1993)

What It's About: On Halloween evening, young Pipkin, who loves Halloween, goes missing just as he's about to start trick-or-treating. When his friends search for him, they encounter an enigmatic figure named Carapace Clavicle Moundshroud, who takes them on a journey through the history of Halloween, beginning with the ancient Egyptians; they also experience Samhain with the Celts, the macabre elements of the

Dark Ages, and the Day of the Dead in Mexico. The boys learn the meaning behind each of their costumes and of their favorite holiday, and when they return home they find that Pipkin is in the hospital recovering from an emergency appendectomy.

Why It's Interesting: *The Halloween Tree* is the most beloved fictionalized history in all of Halloween literature. If its history occasionally strays from fact, Bradbury's poetic storytelling succeeds in capturing what's at the heart of the festival: "Night and day. Summer and winter, friends. Seedtime and harvest. Life and death. That's what Halloween is, all rolled up in one." *The Halloween Tree* began as Bradbury's response to *It's the Great Pumpkin, Charlie Brown*, which angered him because it never showed the Great Pumpkin (in a 2004 interview, he claimed to be so angry that he "kicked the TV set"). After talking with animator Chuck Jones the following day, they decided to launch their own Halloween project, and a few months later Bradbury had a draft of *The Halloween Tree* in screenplay form. Unfortunately the script wasn't produced, so Bradbury turned his screenplay into a book, which was published in 1972 (with illustrations by Joseph Mugnaini). It would take more than twenty more years before *The Halloween Tree* was finally produced, by Hanna-Barbera. Featuring a screenplay and narration by Bradbury and with the voice of Leonard Nimoy as Moundshroud, the film is faithful to the book and overall a lovely animated film, with especially evocative, glowing backgrounds. Bradbury was awarded the Emmy for Outstanding Writing in an Animated Program, and the film was nominated for Outstanding Animated Children's Program.

Buffy the Vampire Slayer–"Halloween" (1997)

What It's About: Buffy has been told that Halloween is the one night a year when vampires and other monsters stay quiet, and so she doesn't object to being stuck chaperoning a group of costumed kids as they make the trick or treat rounds. What she doesn't know, however, is that a vindictive sorcerer, Ethan Rayne, has placed a spell on Sunnydale's costumes that will cause the wearers to transform completely into whatever their costume represents. All the kids dressed as goblins and devils abruptly become real creatures, but Buffy–who dressed as an eighteenth-century lady to lure her love Angel–is rendered useless when she becomes an archaic damsel-in-distress. Her vampire nemesis Spike nearly kills her, but fortunately her watcher, Giles, breaks the spell at the last second and Buffy, once again the Slayer, sends Spike running.

Why It's Interesting: Leave it to *Buffy* to surprise its viewers by inverting all expectations. First it suggests that monsters aren't interested in Halloween, typically viewed as the most monstrous night of the year; then it flips the strong, resourceful Slayer and turns her into a whining parody of femininity. "Halloween" offers up one of our most entrenched Halloween fantasies–that we are empowered by wearing a costume–and suggests that power may come with a downside. The episode also features some genuinely unnerving action–Xander becomes a real, heavily-armed soldier, but can't shoot the monsters and demons, who are really costumed children under a spell–and a horde of excellent monsters, running wild in the nighttime streets of Sunnydale. *Buffy the Vampire Slayer* offered up two more Halloween episodes (*Fear, Itself* in 1999, with a Halloween haunt that turns real, and "All the Way" in 2001, in which younger sibling Dawn has a particularly frightening Halloween date), but this is the one that's a minor classic.

THE HAUNTED HISTORY OF HALLOWEEN (1997)

What It's About: The History Channel presents a documentary on the history of Halloween, complete with experts discussing the holiday, illustrations and vintage photographs, and footage of contemporary Halloween and Samhain events.

Why It's Interesting: By 1997, Halloween was popular enough to merit its own documentary, one dedicated primarily to the history. *The Haunted History of Halloween* features such acknowledged Halloween experts as Lesley Bannatyne (author of the first modern history of the holiday, *Halloween: An American Holiday, An American History*) and folklorist Jack Santino (editor of the first major collection of academic essays, *Halloween and Other Festivals of Death and Life*); it also includes footage of contemporary parades and trick or treaters, and a modern pagan Samhain ritual. There have been a number of Halloween documentaries produced since, and filmic documentaries have also appeared on such shows as the Military Channel's *America: Facts Vs. Fiction* and the supplements on the Blu-ray release of the feature film *Trick 'R Treat*. *The Haunted History of Halloween*, by the way, also reflects certain common errors about the holiday's history, including the notion that the holiday derives in part from a Roman harvest festival called Pomona (it doesn't, and there was no such festival).

HALLOWEENTOWN (1998)

What It's About: It's Halloween night, and Gwen Piper's three children are once again disappointed that she doesn't let them trick or treat. When their eccentric grandmother arrives for a visit, 13-year-old Marnie overhears a conversation in which her grandmother and mother discuss her training in the family arts of witchcraft (which Mother is opposed to). When Grandmother returns to Halloweentown, an alternate dimension where witches and monsters co-exist peacefully, all three Piper children follow her; they soon discover that Halloweentown is under attack by an evil force, and only their newly-awakened magical powers can stop it.

Why It's Interesting: One can only imagine the development meetings at The Disney Channel behind the creation of this one: "Halloween's big, and we need a franchise...now we've got *The Nightmare Before Christmas*, but it's too expensive to do stop-motion animation once a year, so..." So, the executives lifted a few elements from Tim Burton's 1993 Disney hit–including the name "Halloween Town" and the idea of an otherworldly town populated by Halloween icons–flipped the plot around from Halloween Town's mayor coming to our world to three kids going to the Halloweentown mayor's world, and *voilà*! A Halloween franchise is born. *Halloweentown* did indeed spawn three sequels, all starring most of the original cast (including Debbie Reynolds as Grandmother), although other spin-off merchandising hasn't moved much past DVDs. The first film is reasonably charming, although it suffers from a painfully small budget (many of Halloweentown's residents are obviously wearing simple masks–compare to the frightening creatures of the above entry, *Buffy the Vampire Slayer*'s "Halloween") and uneven acting. Those who viewed the films as children seem to retain fond memories, although adults should probably proceed with caution.

GHOST HUNTERS–LIVE HALLOWEEN SPECIAL AT THE STANLEY HOTEL (2006)

What It's About: In their second Halloween special, TAPS (The Atlantic Paranormal Society) heads to the Stanley Hotel in Colorado for their first live investigation; during the six-hour broadcast, viewers are invited to call in with suggestions and tips. Famous to horror fans for inspiring Stephen King to write *The Shining*, the Stanley supposedly hosts a number of well-known ghosts, including Flora Stanley, wife of the hotel's builder and possibly the spirit said to haunt the hotel's ballroom, and a pair of mischievous children who play in the hallway on one floor. Using equipment to record electromagnetic fields, room temperatures, infrared video, and audio, the team attempts to contact ghosts and provide some proof of their existence.

Why It's Interesting: Although *Ghost Hunters* aired their first Halloween special in 2005, it wasn't until 2006 that they fully utilized the date by offering both their first live investigation and the opportunity for viewers to participate via call-in or text messages. In her non-fiction book *Halloween Nation*, Lesley Bannatyne suggests that the growing popularity of Halloween may have resulted in increased interest in the paranormal; she calls the cross-over effect "Halloween culture". Surely there's no better demonstration of this "Halloween culture" than this 2006 special. Does it prove the existence of ghosts? Of course not...but the use of a near-constant low, throbbing musical score, the investigators' apparent earnestness ("can you talk to us?" is frequently muttered into dark corners), and the use of pseudo-scientific equipment and explanations makes for undeniably compelling television. Fourteen years after *Ghostwatch* created a fictitious "national séance" on Halloween, here's the real thing. Welcome to Halloween culture.

AGATHA CHRISTIE'S POIROT–"HALLOWEEN PARTY" (2010)

What It's About: Mystery writer Ariadne Oliver is visiting a Halloween party in rural Woodleigh Common. When a young girl is found drowned in the apple-bobbing tub, Ariadne calls in her friend Hercule Poirot, the world-renowned detective, to help solve the case. Poirot uncovers a chain of murders in the small village going back generations, and all centering on Michael Garfield, a charismatic landscape designer.

Why It's Interesting: Agatha Christie's original novel of *Hallowe'en Party* is probably the most famous mystery novel to make use of the holiday, despite the fact that it's generally considered to be a lesser work by the world's bestselling mystery author. The television adaptation, which moves the action from the 1960s to 1936, actually works in even more Halloween references, including Poirot's oblique mention of All Saints' Day, which he far prefers to the more macabre Halloween. The adaptation (by Mark Gatiss, directed by Charles Palmer) is in fact very good, with a warm, rich depiction of a quaint children's Halloween party, which includes possibly the only filmed depiction of the game "Snapdragon" (it's unlikely that a party in a rural part of England in 1936 would have had access to pumpkins, especially in the large numbers shown, but it's a sweet visual and I'm willing to forgive the anachronism). There's also a mention of Guy Fawkes Day and a quick suggestion of fireworks, along with excellent production design and a fine turn by actor David Suchet as the beloved Poirot.

TRUE BLOOD–"AND WHEN I DIE" (2011)

What It's About: The fourth season of HBO's popular vampire series concludes on Halloween night…or Samhain, as the season's Wiccan villainess Marnie notes. Marnie, now in possession of the body of regular character Lafayette, sets out on a vendetta against vampires (vampires and witches have been feuding since the Inquisition) that leads to bloodsuckers Bill and Eric tied to a stake on Halloween night as fires are lit around them. Sookie, Tara and Wiccan Holly are able to use the night to call forth the spirits of their ancestors, who exorcise Marnie from Lafayette and convince her to accompany them to the afterlife.

Why It's Interesting: Here's one of the first real uses of Samhain in an episodic television series, used as an evening when the veil between worlds is lifted and the dead can cross over. It's unfortunate that *True Blood*'s plethora of subplots lose the Halloween/Samhain angle throughout much of this episode, and even more unfortunate that the Wiccan characters all persist in pronouncing it "sam-a-hayne" (I suspect most of you reading this know it's really "sow-en"), but it is worthwhile to note that by 2011 Halloween's Celtic ancestor is well-known enough to merit inclusion in a popular television show.

AMERICAN HORROR STORY: MURDER HOUSE–"HALLOWEEN" (2-PART EPISODE) (2011)

What It's About: Prior to this episode, the Harmon family, battered by father Ben's affair with a young student, have left the east coast for a love-ly American Craftsman-style mansion in Los Angeles. What they don't realize is that the house is haunted by the unhappy spirits of all who've died there, going back to the 1920s abortionist and mad doctor who built the house. In the two-part Halloween story, the Harmons have decided to sell the house, but know that in this poor economy they'll need all the help they can get, so they hire a pair of gay "fluffers", or decora-tors, to spruce the house up for potential buyers. The decorators–who owned the house before the Harmons and died there–style the house for Halloween. But when the night comes, the dead souls in "Murder House" are particularly active, revealing terrible secrets and frightening away both trick or treaters and potential buyers.

Why It's Interesting: *American Horror Story*–which offers a differ-ent story line every season–has dealt with Halloween every year, but in its first year, when it revolved around "Murder House", it managed to combine traditional Halloween television episode tropes (trick or treat, decorations, costumes, ghosts) with contemporary issues (the economy, the way queer culture has co-opted the holiday, a dysfunctional family) in a way that felt completely fresh. The episode also slyly comments on urban legends (when teenage boy Tate tells his girlfriend Violet the story of Charles Montgomery, the mad doctor who tried to restore his own murdered child to Frankenstein-like life, she feigns interest until telling him she thinks the story is "bullshit"), teens who are too old to trick or treat, and Halloween-as-marketing-tool. Although *American Horror Sto-ry's* third season (*Coven*) offered a spectacular Halloween show that riffed on zombies, *The Evil Dead*, and feminine power, this season's holiday of-fering is more serious, multi-layered, topical, and, by the end, strangely poignant, as Halloween night ends and the various ghosts of "Murder House" are drawn to return to it.

YOUTUBE VIRAL VIDEOS (2013)

I know I'm cheating slightly with this final entry, but let's be frank: For the last few years, the networks and cable stations have been losing rat-ings as viewers have moved to online media, so to ignore this dimension of televised entertainment is to ignore both the future and the present. Venues like YouTube have given everyone with a camera and internet access the ability to become a content provider, and many of these new content providers are Halloween fans. Although it's still just guesswork at this point, my hunch is that these sites are contributing to Halloween's explosive growth around the globe, as home-grown Halloween celebrations are now available to anyone, anywhere. Given the proliferation of Halloween-themed shorts online, I'm going to choose just a few that have gone viral (which I'm defining here as drawing more than a million views) within only the last year. Some are professionally made, but most are the result of a Halloween lover with a videocam built into a smart phone. All were found on YouTube.

"YouTube Challenge: I Told My Kids I Ate All Their Halloween Candy 2013" (over 27 million views)–In 2011, talk-show host Jimmy Kimmel asked his viewers to tell their kids they'd eaten their Halloween candy and tape the tots' responses; Kimmel then edited the best bits together into one big montage of screaming, crying, and tantrum-throwing. He continued this new tradition in 2012 and 2013, and here's a look at the spoiled, entitled underbelly of Halloween in America.

"Baby LED light suit halloween costume preview" (over 21 million views)–Clocking in at 22 seconds, this video shows nothing but a toddler in darkness wearing a Halloween costume made of LED lights that make him look like a walking stick figure. Most of the comments think this is just "soooo cute." Yes, Halloween does have a cute side. Sorry.

"Andy and Amy's Haunted House" (over 6 million views)–Comedienne and talk show hostess Ellen DeGeneres is a serious Halloween fan, and each year she celebrates with everything from outrageous costumes to pranks. For the last few years, she's sent staff writer Amy through a Southern California haunted attraction with a video crew on hand to tape Amy's terrified and very funny responses. For 2013, she sent Amy and a second staffer, Andy, through Universal Studios' Halloween Horror Nights' *Walking Dead* maze, with equally hilarious results. By the way, haunted attractions are a big deal on YouTube; although few of the filmed walk-throughs go viral, many rack up hundreds of thousands of views, and make it easy for anyone (including those of us who abhor lines and crowds) to get some sense of the Halloween haunted house experience.

"Mr. Pumpkin - Halloween (SA Wardega)" (over 4 million views)–This SA Wardega fellow seems to be a Polish performance artist, and in this video he pops up from a stack of jack-o'-lanterns to frighten passersby in a park…before launching into a series of ludicrous dance routines to pop songs. Here's proof that Halloween's mischievous spirit is alive in Poland, a European country that has traditionally preferred its own sober All Saints' Day rituals. The times they are a-changin'.

"Halloween Light Show 2013 - The Fox (What Does the Fox Say)" (over 4 million views)–The technological advances made in LED lighting and home computers now allow home owners to stage their own elaborate outdoor displays, and every year you can find several of these illuminated savants displaying their expertise to a holiday classic ("This is Halloween" from *The Nightmare Before Christmas* is a hot choice) or the current megahot novelty song, like "What Does the Fox Say" by Ylvis. The song may be stupid (okay, strike that–the song is *massively* stupid), but the lights really are impressive, and a very creative alternative to home haunters in rubber masks with shaky makeshift mazes.

"Play Doh Halloween Pumpkin Jack-o-Lanterns Play Doh Halloween Decorations Toys" (over 3 million views)–As you might well imagine, there are a lot of Halloween how-to videos online, showing you how to do useful things like create makeup or put together a costume…and then there's this. Yes, it's a four-minute tutorial on how to make tiny Play Doh jack-o'-lanterns. And it's gone viral.

"Lego Halloween" (over 2 million views)–This is a well-done little stop-motion animated film featuring Lego's Halloween and monster figures. Filmmaker Michael Hickox has crafted an amusing tale of trick or treat comeuppance in five minutes. Here's a YouTube offering that truly captures Halloween's creative side, to say nothing of the spirit (no pun intended) of the holiday. Happy Halloween, everyone.

The Pumpkin Smasher

Al Sarrantonio

Jersey Jack was what used to be called a wise-ass. His twenty-four-year-old face even gave it away immediately: a wry, cynical grin under squinting, pale-brown eyes (as if he was always looking straight into the sun) and a mop of longish, uncombed, dull-brown hair. He dressed like a juvenile delinquent out of a 1950s movie, albeit a disheveled one—cracked, black leather jacket, open-collared shirt (complete with gravy stains), hip-hugging black denims with a too-wide silver-buckled belt, and a pair of scuffed boots that had seen better days, including a loose heel that made a *click-swish* sound when he walked.

Click-swish they said as he stepped off the bus in front of the small station in the middle of Orangefield, New York, the self-proclaimed Pumpkin Capital of the World.

Jersey Jack smiled, his cynical grin widening to its fullest.

He cracked his knuckles and continued to smile, taking another step—*click-swish*—to let an impatient old woman get off the bus behind him.

"Such a rude young man!" she said, ambling away, shaking her head, and Jack ignored her, although usually he would have turned and said something profound, apropos a wiseass, like "Eat me."

Today, his attention was elsewhere, on the hundreds of pumpkins that decorated the shops along Ranier Ave., across from the park.

He looked left, he looked right, and saw nothing but fat orange fruit lining the sidewalks in front of shops.

His grin became the widest it had ever been.

Jersey Jack *was* a juvenile delinquent.

One of the most unique ever.

He loved to smash pumpkins.

In fact, was the best at it *ever*.

It had gotten him thrown out of Hoboken, New Jersey, where he been known as "The Pumpkin Smasher," emphasis on the word "The."

"I can't believe this," he whispered under his breath, like a tot locked in a candy store after an earthquake.

He cracked his knuckles, still smiling, and began to saunter, *click-swish, click-swish,* up the street.

By that evening, long after the sun had dropped behind the October horizon like a disappearing jack-o'-lantern, Jack had most of his plans in place. His room in the Adler Hotel was not a good one—in fact it was about the worst in town—but that didn't matter. All he needed was a base of operations, a place to eat junk food and candy bars and drink the cheapest beer he could afford—in this case something called Canadian Ace, which came in plastic, half-gallon jugs and tasted like it. The cable TV, bolted crookedly to the wall, was on—no pay-porn channels, alas—but he wasn't paying attention.

He was putting on his ninja outfit.

Bad boots replaced by black rubber-soled shoes, the black denims remaining but the silver belt buckle removed, leather jacket zipped to the throat, black ski-mask with tiny slits for nostrils and eyes, only a breathing circle for mouth. Black leather gloves that formed to his hands like a coat of paint. There was a crooked and dusty mirror screwed into one badly cracked wall and he checked himself in it—perfect.

He looked like part of the night itself, which is what he wanted.

That, and his natural speed, which had never let him down.

It had done him well in getting out of Hoboken, and Trenton, and Dumont, and Cresskill, and all the other towns in his native New Jersey, just ahead of a jail cell.

But this was a whole new ballgame, this upstate New York town that had beckoned to him like Shangri-La after he saw an article about it in a newspaper.

The Pumpkin Capital of the World, indeed.

Not for long!

He quietly locked the room door behind him, crept down the junk-strewn back stairs of the building, and stole out into the night.

A s was his habit, he enjoyed his exploits at arm's length, by reading about them in the local newspaper.

VANDAL DESTROYS OVER TWO HUNDRED PUMPKINS! The headline in The Orangefield *Sentinel* screamed, and under it was a badly written story about how, mysteriously, every single pumpkin along Ranier Avenue in front of every single shop and building had been smashed during the night. No one had seen or heard anything, except for one citizen suffering from insomnia who had opened his window a crack to relieve his over-heated apartment and thought he heard a quick series of squishing noises receding down the block. The strange noises had been accompanied by nothing—not the sound of footsteps, not a cough or sneeze or wild laughter or any other sound.

The Mayor was outraged, of course, as was the Chief of Police and the sanitation contingent that had to clean up the public streets. The good citizens of Orangefield were properly shocked, just like the good citizens of every other town Jack had partially decimated.

But this, of course, was only the beginning, which the good citizens of Orangefield were blind as Halloween bats to.

Just the beginning.

In his cheap room, with his cheap beer, Jersey Jack threw back his head and laughed, a cackle that seemed to perfectly match his deeds.

Waiting outside the fence of an elementary school was not a good idea these days—but Jack was no child molester. He waited in the deep shadows of an alley across the street with a pair of binoculars, scouring the schoolyard at recess.

And then he found what he wanted: a young, short, mirror-image of himself, a budding punk with a turned-up collar, mullet haircut, and swagger to match. He was shaking down one nerd after another for lunch money, with an occasional punch to the arm to make his point.

Jack lowered the binoculars, grinning his crooked grin, and waited.

Just as he thought, the punk didn't take the bus home but swaggered down the street away from Orangefield Elementary. It didn't take long to catch up with him. And the punk was quick—he turned around, producing a switchblade (talk about retro!) with a smooth motion from his own leather jacket, this one newer and shinier than Jack's, but just as j.d.

Jack curled up a corner of his mouth, dropping his hands to his side. "You got me, kid. Sure, I was following you."

The punk's eyes narrowed. "Why?"

"Because I like your style."

The eyes got narrower. "Whattaya mean, style?"

Jack laughed, as the punk slowing closed the knife, like a cat retracting its claws.

"The way you shook down those geeks during lunch. That's the way I used to do it."

"You mean when dinosaurs ruled the Earth?"

Jack laughed again. "You're just like me—a wiseass."

The kid was enjoying this now. He put his hands on his hips. "So what does it get me?"

"It gets you a job, with me. And all the fun you can handle."

Again the eyes went to slits. "Anything hinky?" he asked. "I don't do hinky."

"Nothing like that. I'm gonna teach you everything I know about smashing pumpkins."

The slits opened up to wide eyes. "You mean you're the guy busted up everything on Rainier Avenue?"

Jack curled a thumb at his chest. "The same. And that's only the beginning. I want to bust up this whole town. And I want you to help me."

"What's in it for me?"

Jack showed surprise. "What's in it? Didn't you ever want to break up a whole lot of stuff, right in the faces of all the stuffed-asses who run this town, and get away with it?"

"Well—"

"Let me finish: didn't you ever want to dress up in a way-cool outfit, sneak right under the noses of the cops and the mayor and the good citizens, and do something they can never pin on you? Didn't you ever want to feel omnipotent, like a god of destruction, and completely get away with it?"

"Well, yeah, I guess. But still—"

"Yeah, I know, I know: what's in it for you. Well here's what's in it—all that, and fifty bucks, too."

The punk grinned. "Now you're talking."

"And ten for any other punks you can get together, sort of into a gang. I want five of you altogether."

"No problem," the kid said, and now he laughed. "This is better than lunch money. And then I can hit the rest of them for their sawbucks."

Jack nodded in admiration. "That's just what I'd do, kid. What's your name?"

"What's yours?"

"Just call me Fagin."

The kid nodded. "And call me Dodger. Yeah, I do pay attention in school sometimes. At least when it's not lunchtime."

They met in the depths of Ranier Park at six o'clock, by the now-empty picnic tables in the pines, as arranged. The sun was just hanging on, giving an autumnal, two-days-before-Halloween glow to early evening. Jack was waiting for them in his ninja outfit, and soon five shadows bobbed into view, resolving into five distinct punks.

Dodger did the introductions. "This is Pat," he said, punching a short blond kid in dark clothes next to him. "Pat's a jerk, but he does as he's told. And this other one," he continued, grabbing a skinny kid two hands taller than himself and yanking him into Jack's view, "is Skeeter.

He doesn't talk much, and looks at the ground most of the time, but he's fast as a rabbit. And this," he said, pushing a huge kid in front of Skeeter, "is Tank, for obvious reasons. No Einstein, but he blocks like a linebacker. And finally," he went on, pushing everyone aside, revealing a sprite who might have been a boy or a girl, "is Twitter. She's my girl-friend. Devoted to everything I do."

Twitter stepped forward, bowed, at which point her ski cap fell off revealing a tussle of long brown hair, which fell over her eyes when she straightened.

"Pleased to meet you," she said in a surprisingly high girlish voice, and then stepped back into the crowed, which closed around her.

"So?" Dodger said, taking lead point. "What do we do now?"

"You listen," Jack said, and then he began to lecture.

That night they only smashed fifty pumpkins, in a neighborhood just east of Ranier Park. The road formed a circle, with two cul-de-sacs, and they cut a straightforward arc through it, blitzkrieg-style, three on one side of the street and three, including Jack, on the other, smashing every pumpkin in their path. They started at eleven-fifteen and were fin-ished by eleven-twenty-eight.

They reassembled near the picnic tables in Ranier Park, under a half moon that made the pines look like ghostly dancers in the chill wind.

"You did pretty good tonight," Jack said, which brought a swell of pride. "But we have plenty more to do, and not much time to do it. To-night was a practice run. Tomorrow's the day before Halloween, and we go all out in the other neighborhoods. And then on Halloween we save the best for last."

"What's that?" Dodger asked.

Jack grinned widely. "You'll see. Special. Coup de grâce."

"Cootie wha—?" Tank asked.

"Cherry on the icing."

"Oh."

"Now listen up," Jack said. "The cops will be looking for us now. So we each leave a different way. And come separately and meet up tomor-row after school. I scoped out a pumpkin field that still had some ripe ones in it, right out of town. It's called Riley's Pumpkin Patch. There are some techniques I want to teach you. You, Tank—"

"Huh?"

"Not too wise to just stomp them while they're on the ground. You gotta be more creative."

"Oh." Tank looked ruefully at his pumpkin-gut-covered boots.

"And the rest of you could use a few lessons from the master, too."

The gang nodded, as one.

"Disperse," Jack ordered, and they went their separate ways.

The next day was colder, and gray. Definitely Halloween weather, with Winter right behind. As he waited in the almost-barren pumpkin field, row upon rutted row of furrowed dirt covered with masses of still-green vines and the occasional curiously unpicked bright orange pumpkin, Jack shivered and held the top of his leather jacket closed.

"You should shiver, my friend."

The voice came out of nowhere, and the temperature seemed to drop another twenty degrees in an instant. Jack whirled around to see something right out of a horror comic—a swirling black cape topped with the whitest face he'd ever seen. The eyes and nose were black slits and the mouth was a cherry-red line that looked like it should be dripping blood.

"Holy shit."

The mouth curled into the faintest of smiles.

"I'll make this short," the specter said in a whisper that seemed louder than a shout in Jack's ears. "I want you to stop what you're doing."

"Who the hell are you?" Jack managed to get out, though he felt as if he was about to pee himself.

"Someone who wants you to leave Orangefield. In a way I…own this town."

Jack was getting some of his wiseass bluster back. "What are you, some kind of projection? A hologram? A thing on a stick?"

"My name is Samhain, and I'm asking you only once, and politely, to leave."

"I'll leave when I'm done," Jack said, and reached out to the specter, but it was gone.

The temperature rose to merely chilly.

He rubbed his eyes, and now saw the five members of his little gang approaching him from five different directions.

"Hey, Fagin!" Dodger shouted, waving.

Jack took a deep breath, regained his composure, and decided to say nothing about the illusion he'd just seen. It just wouldn't be cool.

By the time they assembled in front of him, he was his old self, making fun of each of them in turn and demonstrating how to twirl a pumpkin on one hand before turning it over and driving it into the ground, how to balance another pumpkin on your head before stepping out of the way to let it smash itself, how to toss it backwards over your head and push it with the heel of your boot, giving it momentum so that it skidded into the ground, cracking like an egg, how to drive two pumpkins together without getting so much as a seed on your hands, and a dozen other tips.

"You're the best, Fagin!" little Twitter said, shaking her brown locks loose from her cap.

"You bet, squirt," Jack said, turning to strut off.

"Tonight," he added over his shoulder.

That night, at midnight, they smashed almost every pumpkin left in Orangefield. Twitter was late, because she got caught climbing out of her window and had to wait until her parents went back to sleep. But she did her part, and before long they had quietly and stealthily made their way through one development after another. They worked in pairs and, when told by Jack, alone. The gray had left the sky, showing a fattening moon feathered by scudding clouds. They smashed so many pumpkins that the streets gave off a sickly sweet odor like baked pies. Three times a patrol car drove near, but each time Skeeter, posted as lookout, gave a signal and they disappeared into side yards until it left. Then the cop inside seemed to grow a brain, and stopped just where they had, halfway down a long street, with a stretch of broken pumpkins behind him and a line of protected ones in front. He stayed for more than an hour, but Jack had taught the gang well and they merely waited until he finally left.

They waited an extra fifteen, during which Skeeter scouted the next block over, and then reported back in a whisper, "He's gone!"

"Donuts," Jack laughed under his breath. "Cops gotta have donuts."

They resumed their work and, exhausted, met up in Ranier Park at four in the morning.

"You guys did great," Jack reported. "And it's time for you to get home before your mommies and daddies wake up. There's just one more thing.

"Tomorrow the cops will be nuts looking for us, so we have to make sure we're not seen together. So everyone works separately. And we're gonna hit the gated community. Where the chief of police, the school superintendent, and all the other muckie-mucks live." He pointed at Dodger. "And you get to hit the biggest mucky of them all—the mayor."

"All right!"

"And what about you?" Skeeter asked.

"Me? I'll be out of here. My work, as they say, is done."

"We'll miss you," Tank said, in a dull voice.

"I'll miss me too." He gave them their assignments. "Now get outta here."

They scattered.

Jack woke up late the next morning, yawning and stretching. It was Halloween in Orangefield. Even the sun seemed to know it, rising fat and pumpkin-orange to scatter the chill dew. In the afternoon he sauntered down to the corner store to buy a copy of the *Sentinel,* which proclaimed: HAVOC IN ORANGEFIELD! PUMPKINS SMASHED WITH ABANDON! POLICE HAVE NO SUSPECTS!

Jack laughed, propping his feet on the windowsill of his room. Outside the schools were letting out, and already trick-or-treaters were beginning to appear—robots, little Sherlock Holmes figures, ballerinas, old-white-sheet ghosts, the inevitable tramps. The late day smelled like rotting pumpkin, and the sun dropped toward the west horizon, heralding evening.

Then, suddenly, it smelled cold, like a meat locker, and, his heart freezing, Jack pulled his feet from the sill to the floor and turned around.

Samhain was there, his cape swirling without a hint of breeze.

"I told you to leave Orangefield," he said, in a sepulchral whisper.

"I—" Jack began.

"Hush," Samhain said, his blood-red slit of a mouth almost smiling, and Jack was quiet.

The world went dark for him.

It was Halloween night. The nine o'clock curfew had taken effect, and the streets were quiet.

But Jack heard the click-clack of boot heels.

And saw Dodger, a grin of anticipation on his face, approaching.

It was warm, and orange, and when Jack blinked he couldn't blink but only looked out from triangular eyes. His nose, he saw, was a triangle too, and his mouth was a crooked long slit with three teeth carved into it. He smelled fresh pumpkin.

He tried to scream, but nothing came out.

He saw Dodger getting closer, hungrier.

"NO!" Jack cried, with his smiling mute mouth.

"All right!" Dodger said, and Jack felt himself being lifted high into the air.

"Flip, dip and crash!" Dodger said, kicking Jack high into the air.

And then—

SMASH!!!!!

The House on Cottage Lane

Ronald Malfi

The Toomeys, who lived in the house next door, were always taking in weirdoes. My father repeatedly scolded me about using such a word, but that was the truth of it: the kids were weird. There had been the boy who sat in the yard all day trying on different women's hats, which he carried around with him in an old brown shopping bag from the A&P. There had been a girl of seven or eight who never came out of the house, though she would keep her pale white ghost-face pressed against one of the upstairs dormer windows, staring out at Luther Avenue with melancholia in her eyes, reminding me of fairytales about princesses held captive in stone towers. Last summer, the Toomeys brought home a girl of about eleven or twelve—my age—who seemed normal enough at first. She even came over to play a few times, and we would either go out into the yard and dig up larval ant-lions or play badminton (we have a net) or we would just stay inside and watch TV. But then one afternoon, while we were out digging in the yard for nightcrawlers, she bit me high up on my bicep for no reason. It was hard enough to draw blood. After that, my father said I didn't have to play with her anymore. When I asked him why she had done such a thing, my father's face grew dark, as if clouds were passing overhead, and he said, "Not all kids in this world are as lucky as you, Brian." He seemed saddened by my delight at not having to bother with the girl anymore. When she was finally sent off to some other foster home—or to wherever kids like her go—I was pleased.

The kids were weirdoes, all right, but that meant that the Toomeys were even weirder. What sort of couple brought kids like that into their home? I couldn't understand it. Jeremy Beachy's mom was constantly threatening to send Jeremy, her own flesh and blood, off to boarding school, yet Eric and June Toomey continued to take these strange kids into their home and pretend, at least for a little while, to be their parents. The Toomeys had no kids of their own, so I assumed this was their way of faking it. It was like an assembly-line: when one weirdo left, another one would show up. Over the years, I had lost count as to how many had come to stay at the Toomey house. My mother seemed to regard the Toomeys with an air of suspicion, but my father said they were good people and that they were doing a very good thing helping all those troubled kids. To me, they were weirdoes; to my dad, they were always "troubled kids." I failed to see the difference.

Their newest kid arrived two months ago. He was short and thin for a boy, and I originally guessed him to be a year or two younger than me. Turned out, he was exactly my age, and it wasn't long before my father started in with his not-so-subtle hints that I make an effort to befriend the kid. One afternoon, I went over to the Toomeys' house with a stack of comic books tucked under one arm. June Toomey's face lit up when she opened the front door to find me standing there. She quickly ushered me inside, and introduced me to the new kid. His name was Oliver, and he possessed the big face and widely spaced teeth of a jack-o'-lantern. Despite his slight frame, his clothes seemed too small. A large booger waved in and out of one nostril in rhythm with his respiration, like the hinged valve on a pipe. I asked him if he liked comic books and he just rolled those bony little shoulders of his. His shyness that afternoon would have driven me mad had I not decided to spread out on the Toomeys' living-room floor and read my books while Oliver, sitting Indian-style on the couch across the room, did nothing but stare out the windows.

At my father's behest, I ventured over to the Toomeys' on a few more occasions. Sometimes I brought my comic books, other times I took over my videogame console, which Eric Toomey gladly hooked up to their TV, a smile on his face so stretched out of proportion that it looked like he was trying to hide something. Oliver sometimes played the videogames with me, but he was so awful that it took much of the pleasure from it. Like pack animals, kids know when they're in the presence of a weaker member, and that was certainly the case with Oliver. I could sense his passivity like a stink coming off his flesh. In turn, I think my awareness of our hierarchy drove him into greater submission. I wasn't mean to him, wasn't a bully, but I couldn't help bark at him aggressively on the occasions when his timidity pushed me over the edge.

A week before Halloween, as I was about to sprint out the door to meet up with Jeremy Beachy and Cyn Cristo to play baseball in the park, my father suggested I see if Oliver wanted to join me. So I went next door, was greeted by June Toomey's strangely shocked smile, and ultimately asked Oliver if he wanted to come along. To my surprise and dismay, Oliver agreed to come. He didn't have a glove, so I ran back home and grabbed my old one for him.

At Shoulder Park, I introduced Oliver to Jeremy and Cyn, my best friends, while Oliver stared at his sneakers. Cyn said, "Hello," and spent the rest of the afternoon watching the strange new kid from the corner of her eye. Less understated than Cyn, Jeremy fired a barrage of questions at the boy—where did he come from? What happened to his parents (and were they dead)? Did he go to school? Had he seen June Toomey naked coming out of the shower?

Oliver's baseball skills made him look like a videogame wizard. He couldn't catch, couldn't hit, and he ran with the hobbled gait of someone learning to walk again after a markedly bad automobile accident. Jeremy was relentless in his torment, and never missed an opportunity to criticize. Cyn said nothing, but continued to stare at Oliver as if expecting, at any moment, his head to pop right off the skinny stalk of his neck. Later that night, over dinner, I commented on Oliver's maladjustments to my father. "There's nothing wrong with that boy, Brian," he said to me after I'd finished relaying how the kid had actually shrieked and ran away from a pop-fly. "Do you think everyone was born to be an athlete? I can't shoot a basketball to save my life. And as I recall," he said, winking at me while lowering his voice to a conspiratorial tone, as if he didn't want my mother, who was seated right beside him at the table, to overhear, "you were no Babe Ruth when you first started playing, either."

Given all this, it came as no surprise that my dad had me invite Oliver trick-or-treating on Halloween. I spent the afternoon assembling my werewolf costume, epoxying fake fur to my face and also to the flesh-toned T-shirt I planned to wear beneath a tattered flannel shirt. I had just finished coloring the tip of my nose black with a grease pencil when my mom called from the front hall to tell me Cyn had just arrived.

"Oh," my mother fawned over us both. "You two look fantastic! Let me get my camera."

Cyn was done up as Dracula, her face powdered white, rivulets of dried blood leaking from the corners of her mouth. Her dark hair was pulled back into a long braid, which she tucked down into the collar of her black satin cape, forming an impressive widow's peak at the center of her forehead. When my mom returned with the camera, Cyn popped in her plastic vampire teeth and growled as the flash went off.

We handed out candy to some of the younger kids while we waited for Jeremy to show up. When it started to get dark, I went into the kitchen and called his house. The phone rang and rang and no one answered. Irritated, I hung up. When I turned around, there was a terrible face framed in the center of the kitchen window—a peeling green zombie face. I cried out then relaxed as, on the other side of the glass, Jeremy broke out in bawdy laughter. He ran around to the front of the house and came swooping in through the front door, nearly trampling some little kids coming up the walkway in the process.

"That was priceless!" he howled. His face was done up in a base of green paint upon which he had affixed bits of rubbery latex that, when glimpsed through a window, looked remarkably like real loose-hanging flesh. "You should have seen your face! Oh my God!"

"Hilarious," I said.

Cyn poked her head over the half-wall that overlooked the foyer. "We gonna go or what?" she said around the plastic vampire fangs.

"Yeah," I said, grabbing the freshly washed pillowcase my mother had slung over the back of one of the kitchen chairs. "But we gotta stop next door first."

"Oh, no," Jeremy groaned, his ghoulish face suddenly going slack. "Don't tell me that little faggot is coming with us."

"My dad's making me."

"What horseshit."

"We don't have to hang out with him all night," I said. "He'll probably get tired early on and head back home. Then we can do whatever we want."

"You get more candy if you go to the door with less people," he hypothesized.

"You can go by yourself," Cyn said cheerily from over the half-wall, and Jeremy gave her the finger.

"Hey," growled my dad, passing through the hallway and catching the gesture. "Be nice, Jer."

"Sorry, Mr. Ganelin."

"And be nice to that kid next door."

"We will, Dad," I promised him, and hurried out of the house with my friends.

Next door, the three of us stood on the porch while I knocked. Jeremy took out his trick-or-treat bag and held it open. When I glanced at him, he shrugged and said, "What? Might as well make the most of it, right?"

The door opened and Eric Toomey's plastic smile greeted us. He held a Tupperware bowl in one arm. "Oh. Is that you, Brian? With all the fuzz on your face?"

"Yeah."

"I guess you're here for Oliver, huh?"

I nodded.

Eric Toomey turned and shouted into the house for Oliver. Then he faced back around, noticed Jeremy standing there with his trick-or-treat sack held open, and pulled a handful of pennies and toothbrushes out of the Tupperware bowl. He dropped the items into Jeremy's sack just as a shape moved in the gloominess of the hallway behind him.

"Oh," said Eric Toomey, stepping aside. "Your friends are here, Oliver."

Oliver was dressed as a ghost. A single white sheet covered his body, with two holes punched out for eyes. Along the sides of the costume I noticed strips of reflective material, like the kind of reflective strips you see on construction workers' vests. June Toomey had probably pasted them onto the sheet to ensure Oliver wouldn't get hit by a car. Oliver shuffled forward, thumped one shoulder against the frame of the door, and ultimately needed to be guided out onto the porch by Eric Toomey. "Okay," Eric Toomey said, that plastic smile never leaving his face. "You kids have fun, and be careful." He closed the door on us.

"Can you see in that thing?" I asked.

From beneath the sheet, Oliver shrugged his narrow shoulders.

We walked down the lawn and filed in among the other trick-or-treaters on Luther Avenue. Jeremy turned his sack upside down and emptied the pennies and toothbrushes into the gutter. "Those fuckin' whackos," he mused. "Seriously? Fuckin' toothbrushes?"

I gave him a quick kick to the shin and a look that told him to keep his voice down.

"Hey," Jeremy said, turning to Oliver, who bumbled along the sidewalk like a drunk. "Your foster parents are real cuckoos, you know that?"

Oliver turned his head and stared at Jeremy through the two holes in the sheet. He didn't say a word.

"Come on," Cyn said before we reached the intersection. "Let's start here. Mrs. Gisondi always gives out those supersize candy bars."

We hurried up the walk toward the Gisondi house, Oliver bringing up the rear. By the time Mrs. Gisondi answered the door and dropped a jumbo Mr. Goodbar into each of our bags, Oliver had just joined us on the stoop. He fumbled around beneath his sheet while Mrs. Gisondi smiled patiently at us. Finally, Oliver's small white hands appeared from beneath the hem of the sheet, holding open a plastic Ziploc bag.

"Oh," said Mrs. Gisondi, dropping a jumbo Mr. Goodbar into Oliver's bag. "That'll fill up quickly."

The four of us hit the remaining houses along Luther Avenue, then hooked a right at the intersection onto Watchtower Street. Dusk had darkened the sky and the cool, crisp air was redolent with the smell of chimney smoke. Witches and trolls cackled as they passed us on the opposite side of the street. One house had a cauldron spewing clouds of dry ice on the porch, and a few of the neighbors had propped up fake tombstones in their front yards. At the Miners' house, prerecorded ghost-sounds issued out of hidden speakers. A troupe of ballerinas stared at us as we marshaled up Watchtower.

"Hey," Jeremy said, elbowing me in the ribs. "Check this out." He handed me a Tootsie Roll that looked just slightly thicker than normal.

"What is it?" I asked.

Jeremy laughed. "I wrapped up cat turds in old Tootsie Roll wrappers!"

"Gross!" I chucked the wrapped turd over a hedgerow decorated in orange pumpkin lights.

"Hey, Oliver," Jeremy called over to the walking white sheet. "You want a Tootsie Roll?"

Cyn and I laughed. Oliver stopped walking, his tattered sneakers sliding to a stop along a patch of wet black leaves. Those two eyeholes again fell on Jeremy.

"Ooh," Cyn crooned. "Cripple fight…"

"Shut up," Jeremy said, chucking another turd-wrapped-Tootsie at her. "Come on, Ollie. I'm just busting your balls."

Oliver said nothing. He didn't move.

"Dude, let's *go*," Jeremy groaned.

I nudged Oliver's shoulder. "Come on, man. There's more houses to hit."

Those two little eyeholes fell on me. Then Oliver faced forward again and continued down the street with us.

By the time we reached Chestnut Street, it was coming on full dark, and Oliver was showing no signs of tiring. Even when his Ziploc bag filled up, which didn't take long, he continued going house-to-house with us. At one point, when he stopped to lace up his sneakers, Jeremy and Cyn gathered around me. In a hushed voice, Jeremy said, "Let's ditch the freak."

"We can't ditch him," I said. "My dad'll kill me."

"Well, he won't kill *me.* "

"Yeah," I said. "But if you leave me alone with him, *I'll* kill you."

"Let's pretend we're tired and we're all going home for the night," Cyn suggested. She had a lollipop in her mouth. "When he goes home, we can all go back out."

"But he'll follow me home," I said. "And by the time I walk all the way there and then back out here, I'll miss all the good houses."

"Well, we gotta do *something,*" Jeremy said, picking some of the dried latex off his face.

I looked back over at Oliver, who had apparently stepped in someone's discarded chewing gum. He kept lifting his foot higher and higher off the ground, the gum stuck to its sole stretching like a tendon.

"I've got an idea," I said. "If we scare him enough, he might go home on his own."

"How do we do that?" Jeremy said, bringing the piece of latex to his nose and sniffing it.

"We take him to the house on Cottage Lane," I said.

It was a crumbling old A-frame, partially sunken into the earth and surrounded by woods. Beyond the trees and in the dark distance, the lights of the Naval Academy's communication towers pulsed red. The house had been vacant for the entirety of my lifetime, and it stood at the end of Cottage Lane in solitary confinement, cut off from the rest of the town. There were other houses on Cottage Lane, but they were huddled together closer to the newer developments at the bottom of the hill, separated from the crumbling old A-frame by several acres of black woods.

The four of us hit some of these houses at the bottom of Cottage Lane before I suggested, in a tone that sounded admirably spontaneous, that we check out the old abandoned house farther up the hill. Jeremy and Cyn pretended like it was a great idea. The two black holes in Oliver's sheet surveyed my friends before coming to rest on me.

"You'll love it," I told Oliver as the four of us proceeded to walk up Cottage Lane, leaving the well-lighted houses and the cacophony of trick-or-treaters in our wake. "It's creepy as hell."

"Like something from a horror movie," Cyn added.

"Tell him about the serial killer, Brian," Jeremy said.

"Oh, yeah. That's right. See, a guy used to live there. Like, a hermit, you know? Kept to himself, didn't have a wife. That sort of thing. Really weird."

"Weird like the Toomeys," said Jeremy.

"Quiet!" Cyn scolded him. "I want to hear this."

"Anyway," I continued, "it was a few years ago, in the weeks just before Halloween, when some of the neighborhood kids started disappearing. No one knew where they went, or if they'd just decided to run away."

"Paul Torvall tried to run away when he shit his pants in school and got embarrassed," Jeremy said, laughing to himself. "You guys remember that?"

"I said be quiet," Cyn reprimanded him again.

Jeremy frowned. "Sorry. Go ahead, Brian."

"Well," I said, moving in step with Oliver now, "kids kept disappearing all the way up to Halloween night. No one knew what the heck was going on, not even the cops. So all the worried parents and some of the cops started driving around the neighborhood, looking around to see if they could find clues as to what happened to all the kids. When one of the dads drove past the old house at the top of the hill, he noticed all these kids' costumes and bags of candy lying around on the front porch and in the yard. So he got out of his car and went up to the house. It was mostly dark inside, but he looked in one of the windows. And that's when he saw it."

Oliver sucked in an intake of breath and paused momentarily in his stride.

"The guy was inside the house, and he had his whole dining-room table set like he was gonna have a big party," I said. "Only instead of food on all the plates, there were all these kids' heads. The killer had stuck Halloween candy in their eye sockets and in their mouths, too. The dad, he runs back to the car and gets the police. When the police show up, there's like a shootout or something…and when they break into the house to apprehend the killer, they find that he'd escaped."

"Holy shit," Jeremy said in a small voice.

"Yeah," I went on. "And they never did catch him."

"There it is," Cyn said, and we all stopped in the middle of the street. The old house stood before us, blacker than a cave on the moon, slouching toward the earth as if terminally exhausted. Its windows were boarded up and there were great frilly hawks' nests in the eaves. Beyond the trees, the red lights at the tops of the communication towers throbbed.

"Pretty scary, huh?" I said.

Oliver stared at the house...then turned toward me. I waited for him to speak but he didn't. When he looked back at the house, I could hear his wheezy respiration once more.

"I dare you," I said, "to go inside."

Oliver's sheeted head turned back around to face me. He shook his head furiously.

"We all did it," Jeremy said. "You gotta go right in the front door, straight through the house, and come out the back. That's how we'll know you're brave."

"It would be the coolest ever," Cyn added, flashing a rare smile that hinted at her burgeoning femininity.

Oliver continued shaking his head.

"If you're too chicken," I said, "that's cool. But if you want to hang out with us, you gotta do it. Okay?"

Oliver looked back up at the house. I could tell his hands were fidgeting beneath the sheet, and his breath was coming in exaggerated gasps now. The reflector strips on his costume glowed in the moonlight like lines on a highway. One pale white hand appeared beneath the hem of his sheet, but then slipped back beneath it.

"We'll wait here for you," I told him.

Oliver nodded...then slowly made his way up to the house. The porch was overgrown with weeds, the wooden planks themselves rotted and cracked. He managed the stairs with little difficulty, but then paused when he reached the front door. When he turned back around to face us, I waved him forward. He turned back to face the front door. He pressed his hands against it, pushing.

"Shit," Jeremy said beside me. "It might be locked."

But it wasn't; apparently, even a pipsqueak like Oliver could manage to shove it open, if just several inches. A vertical strip of blackness seemed to ooze out. At that moment, I knew Oliver was going to chicken out, and we'd have to tote him along with us for the rest of the night…

Oliver's white sheet passed through the opening in the doorway, and went into the house. I glimpsed a final reflection of moonlight off his reflector strips before he was swallowed up by the darkness.

"Wow," Cyn said. "He did it." She looked at me, her eyes comically wide in her white-powdered face. "I wouldn't have done it."

"I'm gonna go around back and scare the shit out of him when he comes out," Jeremy said, and before anyone could say another word to him, he was jogging around the side of the house.

We waited.

"That was a cool story," Cyn said after a time.

"Thanks."

"Did you, like, make that up as you went along?"

"Yeah, I guess."

"Wow."

Crickets chirruped in the overgrown grass while the boomerang shape of bats arced across the face of the moon. A few blocks over, I heard the shrill, joyful cries of trick-or-treaters. They suddenly sounded very far away.

Something like ten minutes later, Cyn said, "What's taking so long?" I shook my head.

"Maybe Jeremy's with him?" she suggested, sounding hopeful.

But at that moment, Jeremy appeared around the side of the house, his arms splayed out in a *what gives?* posture. "Where is he?" he asked as he joined us in the street.

"Don't know," I said. "He didn't come out the back?"

"Would I be here asking you where he is if he came out the back?"

"It's an old house," Cyn said. "Maybe he fell through some floor-boards or something."

"I didn't hear anything," I said.

"But still," she said. There was panic rising in her voice now.

"Shit," I said, chewing fake werewolf fur off my lower lip. I handed over my pillowcase full of candy to Cyn. "Hold this. I'll go see."

"You're going *in* there?" she said.

I didn't respond. Slowly, I approached the house. Up close, the floor-boards of the porch looked even more dangerous than they had from the street. Some were missing, revealing dark slats of space at intervals across the porch. I avoided these spaces and went right up to the door, which still stood slightly ajar. A smell like the interior of an old barn wafted from the opening, and I instinctively wrinkled my nose. *There are dead things in there.* The thought hooked me out of nowhere and refused to let go. *Dead animals…and maybe other things, too.*

"Oliver!" I called in through the open doorway. I could see nothing inside—just pitch blackness. "Hey, Oliver! Are you in there? Are you okay?"

My voice echoed off the walls inside the house, but then faded to nothingness. I listened. Not a single sound came from within that house…

I turned around, gripped by terrifying certainty that Jeremy and Cyn had fled, leaving me all alone. But there they were, standing together in the middle of the street, looking up at me. I hurried down off the porch and over to them, my heart strumming feverishly in my chest. "I called but he didn't answer," I said, frightening myself even more by the reedy, whiny quality of my voice. "I don't know what happened."

"What do we do?" Cyn asked, her eyes volleying between Jeremy and me.

"Maybe he's messing around with us," Jeremy said, though he did not sound convinced. "Like, maybe he's in there hiding, waiting for us to come in so he can jump out and scare us."

It didn't seem likely.

"We need to go home and tell my dad," I said finally.

Jeremy's eyebrows knitted together. "That's a bad idea."

"You got a better one? You wanna go in there and look for him?"

"No…"

"Then we've got no other choice." I snatched my pillowcase back from Cyn, who jumped at the suddenness of my action.

The three of us headed straight for Luther Avenue, not stopping along the way, and cutting through people's backyards when we knew the shortcuts. It was closing in on nine-thirty when we finally reached my house. The streets had grown empty at this deepening hour, and there were bits of candy strewn about the sidewalks and on people's lawns. As I opened the front door, Jeremy said, "I'm not going in."

"What are you talking about?"

"I'm going home."

"We gotta tell my dad what happened!"

"You tell him. It was your idea about the house anyway, Brian."

"You wanted to ditch him," I protested.

"Doesn't matter. I'm going home." He cast his eyes down then slumped off the porch. He lived only two blocks over, not far, but when he hit Luther Avenue, he started to run.

I exchanged a look with Cyn. "You wanna go home, too?"

"I don't know." Her voice was small.

"Go, if you want to."

I turned and went inside, calling immediately for my father. He came down the hall and into the foyer, wearing a sweater with black cats on it. He was smiling until he saw the panic in my face. "What is it, Bri?"

"We lost Oliver," I blurted.

"What do you mean you lost him?"

"He went into that old house on Cottage Lane, but he never came out. We waited around and I called to him but he never came out."

My father's eyes flitted past me and toward the front door. I spun around, hoping to find Oliver standing there in his sheet, but it was only Cyn. She looked too frightened to move from the stoop. My father waved her inside then told us to sit down on the couch. My mother appeared over the half-wall, plastic spiders pinned into her hair. She asked what was going on.

"Call the Toomeys and tell them to come over," said my father. Then he came over to the couch and said, "Maybe he went home."

"Yeah," I said, hoping it was the truth, but not believing it. We would have seen him leave the house. Jeremy had been watching the back door. Nonetheless, I held out hope.

Yet this hope was dashed the moment Eric and June Toomey filed into the house without Oliver. June looked frantic and Eric had a stoic, medicated look about him. He came over and sat down between Cyn and me on the couch, but he didn't say a word.

"What happened?" June said, first to my father and then to my mother. "Where's Oliver?"

My father relayed what I had told him. When he'd finished, June looked at me. She was visibly shaking. "He doesn't know the neighborhood," she said. "He's probably lost, wandering the streets."

"I'll call the cops," said my mom, who departed for the kitchen.

"Why in the world would he go into that house?" Eric Toomey said.

My father looked at me. I held my gaze on him for perhaps two heartbeats before I had to turn away. My face felt suddenly very hot.

Less than ten minutes later, two police officers showed up. They asked questions of my father and then of the Toomeys. When they asked what Oliver had been wearing, June Toomey said flatly, "A bed sheet. A goddamn white bed sheet. He was a ghost."

In a softer voice, Eric Toomey said, "The boy has problems. He's got special needs." His dead eyes looked over at the police officers. "You should know that, I think."

"We're gonna head out to the house," said one of the officers to my dad. "I'd like to take one of the kids with me, talk to them, if that's okay with you."

"Sure," my father said, his eyebrows arching. "Should I come, too?"

"No problem," said the other cop.

My father waved me up off the couch. "Come on."

"What about me?" Cyn said.

"You stay here with me, sweetheart," said my mom. "We'll call your parents."

Sedately, Cyn nodded.

My father and I followed one of the cops out to the patrol car, while the other cop stayed inside and asked more questions. The cop opened the passenger door for me. "Why don't you hop up front so we can chat? Brian, right?"

I nodded and climbed inside. My dad got in the back.

Once we had pulled out onto Luther Avenue and were headed toward Watchtower Street, the cop asked me to tell him again what had happened. I started to tell the same story Cyn and I had told back at the house when the officer cut me off in midsentence. "So you're saying your friend Oliver just decided to go into the house by himself? You guys weren't daring him or anything like that?"

"Well…," I said.

"I need to know the truth if we're going to find your friend," said the cop.

I looked out the passenger window, and at the glowing jack-o'-lanterns on all the porches as we drove by. The older kids were out now, safety pins in their shirts, black makeup over their eyes, tattoos. Some sat on cars parked up on lawns, drinking soda and smoking. They pointed to the police car as we drove by.

"Okay," I said, and told the truth.

When we reached the house on Cottage Lane, the officer took a flashlight out of the glove compartment and got out of the car. He went up to the house, completed a full circuit around the property, then went in the front door. I saw the flashlight's beam come slanting through the boards that had been nailed up over the windows.

I glanced up and saw my father's reflection in the rearview mirror. His jaw was set and his mouth was nothing more than a lipless gash just below his nose. When his eyes met mine, he looked quickly away, ashamed of me. He said nothing for the entire time we sat in the car together.

The cop returned a full ten minutes later. Sighing, he tossed the flashlight back into the glove compartment then geared the car into Drive. "There's no one in that house," he said. His demeanor had changed.

By the time we arrived back home, Mrs. Cristo's convertible Sebring was parked outside. As I got out of the police car, Cyn came out of the house, followed by her mother, and marched over to the Sebring without casting even the quickest glance in my direction. My mom stood in the doorway, her arms folded, looking cold and very thin. Apparently, the Toomeys had gone to the police station to fill out some paperwork. It promised to be a long night for them.

I went into the house and straight up to my room, where I dropped down on the bed and buried my face in my pillow. My father's voice ghosted up through the heating vents as he spoke with the police officer in the foyer. Once the cop left, it was my mother's voice that dominated much of the conversation.

After a while, I heard my dad creaking down the hallway toward my room. He opened the door and poked his head inside, where he remained for sometime. I still had my face buried in the pillow, but I could sense him there like a spirit at my back. Eventually, he came over and sat down on the edge of the bed.

"Roll over," he said. "Look at me."

I rolled over and looked at him. My vision threatened to double.

"That story you told in the police car," said my dad. "Never in a million years would I have guessed that my son…" Disgusted, he let his voice trail off. It wasn't necessary for him to complete the thought. I felt horrible enough as it was. "Have you told the police everything?"

I merely nodded, not trusting my words.

"If there's something else, you better tell me now."

I shook my head.

"Speak," said my father.

"There's nothing else."

"All right." The bedsprings squealed as he stood up. "We'll talk more about this in the morning. You better pray they find that boy," he said, and left.

But they didn't.

They didn't find that boy.

I was questioned several times by the police, each time more thoroughly than the previous times. Cyn and Jeremy were questioned, too. Intimidated by the cops' authority, they did not bother lying. In the end, we all told the same story. We all told the truth.

The house on Cottage Lane was searched more thoroughly, too. The cops used dogs, and my parents, along with the Toomeys, joined in the search. But it was futile. There was no evidence found that even suggested Oliver had ever gone into the house. He certainly wasn't still there, hiding.

One Sunday, as we drove home from church, my mother said out of nowhere, "You should have never forced him to play with all those kids."

My father, who was driving, glanced quickly at her, a look of surprise on his face. Then he turned back to face the road.

"They're all problem kids," said my mom. "What did you expect?"

"They were just kids," said my dad.

"He could have just run away. Did anyone ever consider that?"

"It's possible," my father said.

"It's the Toomeys' fault, too," my mom went on. "This is a nice residential neighborhood. Who do they think they are, bringing children like that onto our street?"

"Geri," said my dad, his tone placating.

"Don't give me that," she spat. "There's enough blame to go around. No one's hands are clean in this, Roger."

My dad's eyes met mine in the rearview mirror. A confusing mix of compassion and disappointment greeted me.

"Maybe he'll show up eventually," said my dad as we pulled into the driveway.

But like I said, he never did.

Unless...

There's that old chestnut—a verbal crutch of sorts—that goes, *I told you all that to tell you this,* and I suppose that's the point we've reached in this story. I've told you all that to tell you this:

That a year has passed since Oliver disappeared in the house on Cottage Lane. In that year, I have changed quite a bit. For one thing, I no longer hang out with Jeremy Beachy. We hadn't spoken since that night, when he left Cyn and me standing on my front porch to face the music on our own. I'm sure he was scared and acting out of impulse, and in truth I don't really blame him for it; but the sight of him sickens me, because I see myself reflected in him. I see the way I may have provoked that girl into biting me on the arm, and how I teased the kid with all the hats in the A&P bag until he would cry. I remember one afternoon, troubled by that blank ghost-face peering down at me from the dormer window of the Toomey house, when I gave that little girl the finger. Most of all, I see the way I teased Oliver and tricked him and tried to scare him. Funny, how he wound up scaring us instead.

I still see Cyn at school, but she doesn't come over to the house anymore. Perhaps she sees herself reflected in me the same way I see myself reflected in Jeremy.

The Toomeys still live next door. Since Oliver, they haven't brought in any new kids. I hope they do eventually, because I could use the opportunity to absolve myself by changing my behavior. Maybe some of it is what happened with Oliver; maybe some of it is just a part of growing up. I'm thirteen now. I'm responsible for the stone I throw and the windows I break.

And then there's my dad. I won't be dramatic and say that, since that incident, he has looked at me differently, because that's not the case. True, I had disappointed him. True, it took some time to earn his trust again. But I *did* earn it back, and we share a good, strong, close relationship. My father is a good man, and it's funny how it took all these years to understand what that means.

So here we are, one year later, Halloween night. I didn't go out this year. I'm too old for that. Instead, I stayed home to hand out candy while my parents, dressed as Popeye and Olive Oyl, went to a party a few blocks over. Around ten-thirty, well after all the ghosts and witches and goblins have made their final rounds and ventured back home, I heard a knock at the front door. There was some candy left in the bowl, so I answered it.

A ghost stood on the other side of the door. It was a person just slightly shorter and thinner than me draped in a single white sheet with two eyeholes cut into it. The sight arrested me, and I stood there without moving, the bowl of candy gradually growing heavier in my hand.

A hand emerged from beneath the sheet, holding open an empty plastic Ziploc bag. The fingers of the hand were small and white, but there were crescents of black grit under the nails. There were specks of dirt on the plastic bag, too.

Finding my momentum again, I reached into the candy bowl, snatched up a handful of goodies, and dumped them into the ghost's bag. Apparently satisfied, the bag retreated back beneath the sheet. Yet my visitor did not move away from the porch. I stared at those two dark eyeholes, dark as roofing tar. Listening, I could hear the visitor's respiration, thin and wheezy, behind the sheet. I opened my mouth to speak, but no words came out.

The ghost turned and padded down off the porch. I watched it cross the yard and head down the driveway. When the sheeted figure reached Luther Avenue, I expected it to blink out of existence, but it didn't. It continued up the block, the reflective tape shimmering with moonlight on the sides of the costume, in the approximate direction of Cottage Lane.

OPERATION GHOUL

Tim Curran

October 1972. I remember that Halloween better than most because of what happened that night and what probably didn't happen at all…save in the overactive imaginations of three boys.

My friends—George and Dave—and I pretty much went through the same ritual every year. For weeks and weeks, beginning sometime in September, we would discuss what we were going to be that year for Halloween. By October, our plans had gone from simple costumes to elaborate monster makeup creations to enormous B-movie monsters that were complicated beyond reason (all for a few hours of candy begging, mind you). One year, for example, we had sketched out a giant papier-mâché monster that would be supported by a cardboard framework which could be lowered over the three of us who would be on bicycles. We never discussed how we would see out of the thing or how we would get up onto porches to get our All Hallows' offerings.

You get the picture. We dreamed and fantasized the weeks away and by the time the end of the month loomed in sight, we were woefully unprepared. Then we had to accept the fact that our complex ideas were impractical and we were going to have to come up with something simple. *Fast.* That meant a jog downtown to Woolworth's and the Halloween aisle.

In 1972, Halloween meant *masks.* Not the cheapo plastic Ben Cooper types. Those were half-head masks with a rubber band that snapped around the back of your head and pulled your hair out. No, those marked you as a rank amateur right off the bat. They were strictly for little kids and *girls.* And definitely not the Don Post calendar masks you could order out of the back of *Famous Monsters* and *Creepy* magazines. Good lord, those things would put you back thirty-some bucks and that was a lot of dough in 1972. Nobody could afford those. But there was an acceptable middle ground put out by a company called Topstone (I didn't know their name then and have just recently learned the fact). Their masks were pretty cool—the teenage werewolf, the ghoul, caveman, girl vampire, male vampire, shock monster etc. If you grew up in the late sixties or early seventies, then you'll remember these masks.

So there we were, digging around in the mask bin, trying to figure out what to do. I had already used the mummy and teenage werewolf masks other years, the caveman, too, I think. And although the One-Eyed Cyclops mask (this to differentiate it from the two- and three-eyed varieties, I guess) was pretty cool, I'd already used it as well. We never could make up our mind and went back home with whatever ridiculous things we could lay our hands on—wax witch lips, plastic vampire fangs, rubber noses, Scar Stuff—none of which got us anywhere.

Then revelation hit.

We knew what we were going to do. It was inspired. It was perfect. We were all going to go as The Ghoul. Not the ghoul as in the ghoul rubber mask, but *The* Ghoul, our king and leader. Back in the early seventies, cable had finally reached our neck of the woods and with it had come Channel 50, WKBD TV from way down yonder in Detroit. Each Saturday night at 11:30 we were treated to *The Ghoul Show.* The Ghoul wasn't our only horror movie host, but he was our favorite. We also had a dude named Alexander who came from Green Bay late Friday nights with a show called *Eerie Street* that showed the Shock Theater package of classic Universal screamers. Alexander played it straight with his vampire cape and plywood coffin…but not The Ghoul. He was a riot and an absolute cult figure in our town. The Ghoul showed mostly cheap B-movies like *The Indestructible Man* and *Fiend Without a Face*, but during commercial breaks he performed skits, blew up things with firecrackers, tormented a rubber frog, and played lots of good rock music. His costume was simple: fright wig, Coke bottle glasses with one lens blacked out, fake goatee, and lab coat. Easy.

In two days we were ready. Operation Ghoul was a go.

On Halloween, the three Ghouls went a trick-or-treating. Since we couldn't find any decent fright wigs, we used string mops for wigs. It worked. Off we went. No kiddie plastic pumpkins for us, we used pillow cases. The crazy thing was, we hadn't been out fifteen minutes when we ran into another kid from the neighborhood, Danny, who was The Ghoul, too. Now there were four Ghouls charging neighborhood to neighborhood in a mad quest for treats. We were professionals. We hopped fences, cut through yards, leaped hedges—we had no respect for private property. We were bound and determined to fill those sacks and nothing could stop us.

Halloween in Upper Michigan is a chilly affair. The wind screams, it often dumps cold rain on your head and sometimes it even snows—our parents were fond of telling us about the Great Halloween Blizzard where kids fought through three-foot snow drifts and subzero winds to get their candy. But that year, as I recall, it was perfect. Cold? Yes. Windy? Yes. But no rain or fabled snow. The trick-or-treaters were out in force. The leaves were blowing down the streets and bare tree limbs were scraping together overhead. Pumpkins were lit on porches and skeletons and witches taped in windows.

Perfect.

We never noticed the temperature with all our running and porch-climbing. By the time trick-or-treating ended at about eight that night, our sacks were two-thirds full and only the hardcore revelers were still making the rounds in the dark. We barely had enough time to run home, sort through our candy (people actually handed out popcorn balls and apples back then, go figure), and get dressed-up again to make it to the school Halloween carnival on time. In fact, we were late. No matter. It was mostly kid's stuff anyway. Cake walk. Fish booth. Spook house. Duck pond. Treasure chest. We snagged a couple hot dogs and bumped into our friend Rick who'd really gone all out. For his space alien costume, he had his brothers wrap him entirely head to foot in Reynolds Wrap. It was all taped together and even had the obligatory antennas and two narrow eyeholes. He could barely walk in that get-up, but it sure looked cool.

It was about this time that George got this idea. "Why don't we go check out the haunted house?" he suggested.

I think we were all afraid it was going to come up as it did every year. The haunted house was an abandoned farmhouse out in the woods with trees growing up through its roof. It was only fifteen or twenty minutes away and by moonlight amongst the dark trees…well, it was a guaranteed Halloween treat. But it took guts. I wanted badly to do anything else, but there was no way to back out without looking like a sissy. So we went. We left Rick shambling about, complaining about how hot it was in his costume.

A little sidebar here.

Although the idea of a lonely abandoned house in the woods sounds not only Lovecraftian but downright clichéd, the house existed and it was well-known to most of us kids who had visited it at one time or another…just not at night. The school sat dead center of a subdivision that was of recent vintage in 1972, having come together in the early 1960s. When I was in first grade, the woods came right up to the edge of the playground. Now there are baseball diamonds there. We were warned not to venture beyond the playground, but, of course, we did. Heck, there was a stream out there and hills and frogs and you name it. During recess in first grade, we ducked into the woods and found a skull. The skull of an animal, not a human. It was all tangled in the grasses and we had a hell of a time digging it free. But we did and brought it back, quite proud that we had unearthed the skull of some nameless beast of yore. Our teacher—Mrs. Hebert, old school all the way—wasn't too happy about us sneaking off, but she turned a bad thing into a good thing. A little investigating and she turned the entire affair into a history lesson for us. The skull was that of a cow and apparently, she'd learned, the entire subdivision sat in what had once been pastureland. There had been a collection of family farms out there, all abandoned before the 1920s. So our "haunted house" was the last relic of a bygone time. The orchards and fields had grown over with trees and brush and all that remained were some piles of gray splintered lumber in the woods, a few cairns of stones, the haunted house...and the cow skull.

1972 again.

The three Ghouls—Danny had not joined us at the carnival since he was older—set off across the playground, crossing 21ˢᵗ Street and into the woods. It was a windy, moonlit night, very atmospheric. We located the footpath and wound our way through the clustered thickets in the dark. The crunching of leaves underfoot was impossibly loud. I think long before we got to the house we were probably uneasy. The blowing leaves. The skeletal trees. The reaching shadows of the dark woods. All of that in addition to the fact that no one even knew where we were if something...*awful* was to happen and as we moved through the trees, I think we believed that something would. A dark street is spooky at night, but a lonely tract of woods is ten times worse. Your primeval fears come knocking at the door and you hear things and think you see things and you want nothing better than to run.

Finally, we sighted the peaked roof of the haunted house framed by moonlight and it was enough to dry the spit up in your mouth. I didn't really think anything would happen, but I wasn't entirely sure. If we got away with it, we'd have stories to tell and bragging rights and I think that was what pushed us on.

Had it been daylight, we would have seen evidence of the house long before. Like some great onion whose layers were slowly peeling away, the house had been falling apart for many decades, flaking away, and bits and pieces of it were scattered through the woods—roofing tiles, sheets of tarpaper, rotten planks, you name it. I remember we found a stone birdbath once and an old tub another time that birds were nesting in, both some distance from the house itself.

Standing in the shadow of that leaning mausoleum, we weren't as brave as we thought. It was no Victorian monstrosity like in a good horror story, but a typical two-story Midwestern farmhouse. It was a ramshackle old place that looked like it was ready to fall. It had no windows. Pipes jutted from the walls like old bones. There were gaping holes in the walls and roof and if you pushed real hard on the walls, the whole place felt like it moved. Tree branches grew out of the windows and crows roosted on the roof during the daytime. It was bad enough on a sunny afternoon, but on Halloween night it was a tomb of shadows.

In we went.

Inside, it was unbelievably black. George had matches, but the old place was so drafty they wouldn't stay lit for more than a few seconds. We were very careful because there were holes in the floor and if you went down the hallway to the back of the house, the floor was gone entirely and there was nothing below but the cellar which was flooded with black water and floating leaves. Just the idea of falling down into that cobwebby, dirty wet blackness was enough to give you the shivers. We went up the rickety staircase and it creaked and moaned and trembled, trying badly, I suppose, to pull away from the wall itself. We sat in one of the bedrooms up there— there was no furniture and most of the woodwork had been stripped away like in the rest of the house.

My memories become a little blurry at this point.

I remember that we sat there, cross-legged, three Ghouls telling each other worn-out old stories like the babysitter that cooked the baby and what not. The wind was blowing and it made the house groan and moan and sway in the wind. The place was a deathtrap and about as close to a *real* haunted house as I could have imagined. We could hear leaves blowing in the woods and sticks cracking. We were all on edge, each praying the other would suggest leaving. About that time, George let out a little cry and said something touched the back of his neck. Maybe it was one of the tree branches growing through the wall. I heard the floor creak behind us. I know that much.

Regardless, that's all it took.

We piled down the stairs and out into the woods, not even looking for the trail. We pushed right through the thickets, smashing into trees and tripping over logs and stepping in holes. We did not slow down until we saw the lights of 21st Street…even then we ran for the playground and into the school where there was light and life. Once inside, we burst into laughter, three Ghouls with leaves and twigs stuck to us, our faces scraped by sticks and our shoes black with mud. In the years to come, we would tell the story of that night and elaborate upon it until it was practically a full-blown ghost story.

We arrived just in time for some more drama: Rick had passed out. He had roasted like a chicken in his aluminum foil spacesuit and finally hit the floor. I remember watching adults peeling him open, pulling off strips of foil very carefully like they were unwrapping a mummy. His face was red and sweaty beneath and he was soaking wet. He was okay once he cooled off. But it was just another weird punch line to a weird day and one that I'll never forget.

What really happened at the house?

I don't know. George was a notorious practical joker so I'll leave it at that. Maybe there was someone up there with us. Older kids? Maybe one of the old bums that lived in the tarpaper shacks out there? I don't know, but I'll mark it down to an empty house and active imaginations on the scariest night of the year.

I live only a few blocks from the school now. In fact, it's no longer an elementary school but a preschool, I think. The woods are mostly gone and the haunted house has long been torn down. The neighborhoods expanded through the years and took over the thickets and fields and ponds where we played as kids. Some of the woods are still there, but just a fringe. They only exist because they're right in the approach path of a nearby airport, otherwise houses would have went in there, too.

It's all gone now, but Halloween 1972 has never left me and I never want it to.

The Dry Season

James A. Moore

The air was dry that year, dry enough that hair took on a static charge and the leaves fell from trees and commenced a hissing sigh when they were caught by the arid winds. Not that the kids seemed to care. If anything the dry atmosphere made costumes just a little easier to breathe in, and added to the snap of cheap plastic capes in the wind.

The air had the perfect bite of cold to it, and the wind carried hints of distant conversations and the far away sound of cars on the highway. The scent of autumn mingled with the bite of candle-roasted jack-o'-lantern. It was Halloween, and Linda loved that.

All around the town there were decorations aplenty, ranging from the cut-out paper pumpkins in front of the Mueller house to the elaborate displays of jack-o'-lantern artwork in front of Arielle Wilson's home. Arielle was a long-time fan of Halloween and spent most of her time running the most prestigious art gallery in town. Some of the pumpkins she carved herself and others were by special arrangement with her creative friends. Her house, as was traditional, would be saved for the very last, because all the kids wanted to go there the most.

On Harper Street the kids wandered mostly in groups, sometimes closely supervised by parents and sometimes barely watched over, but always with at least a token amount of adult supervision.

No one liked to talk about it, but everyone liked to make sure that the sins of the past never happened again.

There were rumors, of course. Always rumors. The man they caught, the man they arrested, the man they killed. Some people said he was innocent. Most people knew better. Some claimed he was a drifter. Some said he was a local who almost never came out of his house. In the end it didn't matter. He died for what he'd done to three children. That was enough.

Most days.

People felt differently on Halloween. The anniversaries of atrocities are often remembered better than the celebrations of happier things.

There were ten of them that moved closer to the house where the children were killed. It had been a long while back, since the adults in the group were children themselves, and the stories of what Martin Lundgren had done were little more than legends any more. That was for the best.

There were differences this year, however. For the first time in memory, the house where Lundgren lived and died was occupied. After decades of being locked in probate and becoming little more than a haunted myth, the legal issues had been resolved and someone had moved into the place.

Linda was delighted. The old house was a beautiful affair, with three stories worth of gingerbread shingles, three gables, and a wrought-iron and stone fence that added heavily to the creep factor, even after the entire place had been cleaned up. The large lawn was well-maintained these days and the seven old oak trees guarding the property were currently shedding the last of their leaves and were left reaching in all directions with long, skeletal limbs. She was staring right at the uppermost window—the one on the same level as the widow's walk—when Nancy started talking.

"There is something seriously wrong with that kid." Nancy laughed as she said it, but Linda couldn't quite tell if she was joking. Of course that was hardly unusual when it came to Nancy. The two of them had been friends since high school, well before they were married, settled down and had kids of their own, and Nancy was officially her BFF, but that didn't mean she could always tell what was on her best friend's mind.

Except, of course, that Nancy hated Halloween. She always had. Couldn't stand being scared. But she tolerated it for the sake of their kids. Nancy had her little girls, Katie—currently dressed as Cinderella—and Mary—currently dressed as a black cat, because she hated looking like her sister and they were twins naturally—and she had her newest, Tyler, who was only six and always half a second from getting himself into trouble. Currently his older sisters were reigning in his worst habits with threats of taking away his candy. Linda didn't really approve of using threats to manage her kids, but she wasn't about to criticize, especially if it was working. Tyler was dressed in a ratty old sheet that had been converted into a proper ghostly outfit—complete with chains and blood-stains, because if Nancy was going to put up with Halloween she would at least do it in style—and twirling himself in circles and then staggering around like a punch-drunk pugilist.

For Linda's part, Halloween was still fun. The kids loved it and she had a good time herself. On the weekend, she and her sister had got-ten their tykes together and make candy-corn balls and caramel apples and then watched a couple of kid-friendly Halloween flicks while the little ones were jazzed on sugar. Then they'd sat around and gossiped and caught up on life in general while the kids crashed and burned and slept off the end of the sugar rush.

Linda's kids were in the mix too, of course. Barry—Tyler's counter-part in the age department and currently dressed as Spider-Man—was firing imaginary webs at anything that moved. Jack was dressed as a witch. It was driving Linda's husband Mark just a little crazy that his son was dressed in a witch's dress, but Linda worked it out with him.

They had five other children they were watching over as well. The Hall's two little girls, both dressed as Powerpuff Girls, a very small Darth

Vader, one clown complete with rainbow hair and shoes so large they were comical when the kid wasn't tripping over himself, and a very large, glittery thing with antennae and wings that was either Toby Martin or the worlds tackiest giant butterfly. Apparently there was nothing more terrifying in the kid's eyes and he wanted to be scary.

Halloween is for kids, right?

The sun was setting. Nancy made sure to hand all the tykes their flashlights, complete with pumpkin shaped shades that lit up and made them noticeable from the street, even though there was still a good amount of light left. The sun set quickly in the neighborhood.

Linda found herself looking up at the window of the house again. There were no decorations up, and there weren't any lights, either, but someone had moved in.

"Honey, I know what you're thinking and not for all the chocolate in North America." Nancy's voice cut right through her contemplations.

"Seriously? How can you be like that? We haven't met them. We should meet the new neighbors."

"It doesn't look like there's anyone home, for one thing, and for another, we can meet them another time. Not tonight." Nancy's nasal voice had an edge to it, but as she joined Lisa in staring her voice softened a bit. "Wait a week. I'll even make them a big old pan of my lasagna."

"Forget that. Make me a big old pan of lasagna."

Nancy's voice was smaller when she spoke again. "Deal."

"You okay, Nan?" Linda looked toward her friend, frowning. Nancy had a very simple philosophy: if something scared her, intimidated her or made her in any way uncomfortable, she got louder, not quieter. That was her defense and always had been. That simple fact had caused no end of trouble for her when it came to relations in high school and college, back when every guy she liked automatically intimidated her. It took Robert to sneak past her defenses long enough to get to know her and marry her. Linda sort of loved Robert for that, platonically of course. Nancy would kill her if she ever got any ideas about messing around with Robert. And Mark would kick her to the curb besides.

She shook that notion away as she did at least once a month. It was silly, really, being her age and having a crush on her best friend's husband.

Nancy spoke up and broke her daydreams about being in Robert's arms. "Is there somebody up there watching us?" Nancy's hand raised toward the widow's walk of the old house and Lisa looked just in time to see what might have been a shadow and what could just as easily have been a person peering around the edge of the structure.

"Well, if I had that old place I'd be up there all the time. How neat is that thing?" It was an old discussion between the two of them. Nancy hated the house for what had happened there. Linda loved it because it was just plain the most unique structure on the block.

"You'd live with the Addams Family or the Munsters, too."

"Heck, yeah!" That did it. Nancy was properly distracted. That was the idea, of course. To lead her friend away from the bad nerves and back to the fun of having kids.

Speaking of which, Linda looked around and did a head count. They were all present and accounted for, though Tyler was terrorizing the tiny Lord of the Sith. "Tyler, leave Ollie alone."

"I wasn't doing anything," Tyler whined-explained.

"Don't sass your aunt Linda." Nancy's response was completely automatic. She was back to looking at the old house though they had moved on a few paces.

Linda looked back, too, frowning. "You thinking about sending the kids up there to get candy?"

"Not on your life. Don't even joke about that."

Nancy wrapped her arms around her narrow torso and shook. Linda couldn't help but smile a little. Scaring her friend on Halloween was almost too easy. Almost. She was about to make a response along those lines when the shadows shifted at the corner of the old house and a dark form slipped from the house to the closest old tree.

No damned way.

She looked at Nancy. Nancy had not noticed. For a moment she warred with herself over whether or not to point it out and then decided against it, because if Nancy freaked too hard, Halloween would officially be over and she didn't want to deal with a herd of unhappy, mostly candy-free kids.

Despite the logic of her inner argument and her satisfaction at winning the same, a chill ran through Linda and her arms pimpled into gooseflesh. She smiled at the notion of creeping herself out. When she looked at the tree there was nothing there, nothing moving.

And the kids were not suffering from that problem, so the whole lot of them moved forward.

The Addison place was up next and the Addisons knew how to do up a proper Halloween. There were three old mannequins dressed as a mummy, a witch, and a zombie in the front yard. Each of them had a lit lantern in wooden hand—LED lights because accidents happen when kids are involved—and scattered body parts lying around them. They all pointed toward the front of the house, where loud Halloween music was blaring and black lights added to the creep factor of several ghosts that had been drawn in glow-in-the-dark chalk on the walls leading to the front door. Adding to the fun was a long stretch of day-glow spider webs that turned the walkway into a sort of tunnel. The kids didn't know if they should be terrified or ecstatic.

Eventually greed for candy won over fear.

Linda and Nancy hung back. They were there for safety, not for getting in the way.

Nancy looked back behind them and frowned. The sun was almost gone now and the shadows were getting heavier. Dusk had taken the world and leeched away most of the colors, but the Halloween decorations, the slowly roasting jack-o'-lanterns, the flickering strobe lights, they all added their own illumination and their own deliciously creepy charm.

The kids knocked on the Addison door and hollered out a scattered "trick or treat!" as Mrs. Addison answered, dressed in a witch's hat and sporting a plastic cauldron filled with candy bars.

And somewhere behind them, a shadow moved and rustled the leaves that were bumbling along in the soft breeze.

"What's wrong?" Linda turned to Nancy, who was still looking the way they'd come.

"I thought I heard that old gate creaking open."

Linda's head snapped in that direction so fast she felt a muscle in her neck fire off a warning flare. She winced at the unexpected pain.

The gate to the Lundgren place stood open.

Another chill slid up Linda's spine. This one was not quite as pleasant. Before her imagination could do her in too heavily, however, Nancy came up with an answer. "I guess someone is braver than us," she laughed.

Linda was quick to recover. "You mean braver than you."

"Whatever, Linda." Nancy was good-natured about the ribbing.

"I wonder who finally moved into that place."

Before Nancy could come up with a response, the kids were ready to move on again, all of them bouncing with eagerness after the bounty from the Addison place. The street was full dark now, but the streetlights kicked in, offering pools of illumination amid the scattering of house lights and Halloween decorations.

They ushered the kids down to the Winston house. There was little by way of decoration, but they'd been warned that Stan planned on giving all the kids a proper scare—he was sitting on the porch, dressed in the ratty old clothes of a scarecrow, complete with a straw hat and a cheap rubber mask. And when they got close enough…Pow!

Both parents held back from getting too close and waited for the screams. There was a real chance that Toby was going to cry, but if he did, they'd be ready to handle it.

Nancy looked back at the Lundgren place again. "His mother."

"What?"

"His mother moved in," she spoke softly. "It was the family home before the dad passed away and the mother moved back to their old home somewhere in Europe. I think she's supposed to go back there after she sells the place or something."

"How could you know that?"

"Home Owners' Association Treasurer. Hello?"

"Well, I could never stay there." Linda frowned after she spoke. "I mean, if it had been my son. I still think the place is awesome."

"Well, I guess she has a few fond memories at least. You know, of before her son lost his freaking mind."

"Listen, don't." Linda couldn't apologize quickly enough. Sometimes it was easy to forget the connections. "I didn't mean to bring up all of that." Linda's tears, Linda's warnings had brought the wrath of the local police department down on the house so many years ago. She'd narrowly escaped getting done in by the bastard when he tried to grab her.

"It was a long time ago." Nancy's voice was soft. "I don't even really remember him." She shrugged and looked back over her shoulder again. "If I did, I would have moved away from this town a long time ago, you know?"

"Well, I'm glad you didn't." Linda put a hand on her friend's shoulder and squeezed with her fingers. The two of them shared a quick hug.

The kids broke the moment apart with a series of loud shrieks that had Nancy half jumping out of her skin before she remembered what was going on and started chuckling.

Sure enough, it took a few minutes to calm Toby down. The only kid in the world who was terrified of butterflies added scarecrows to his personal phobias that night.

After the chaos had calmed down and Toby stopped hyperventilating—candy bars have charms to soothe the savage breast—they continued on the way. By the time they reached the Wagner house even Toby was laughing again.

And Linda was convinced that they were being followed.

She felt positively paranoid as she looked over her shoulder time and again.

Nancy might have corrected her on it, but she apparently felt the same sensation of being watched.

"Seriously, Linda, what the hell?"

Normally Linda would have called her on the language, even if she was speaking softly, but she felt it too. "Should I call Mark?"

Nancy looked back the way they'd come for several seconds and finally shook her head. "What would you say?"

"That some creepy freak is stalking us?"

"On Halloween?"

Linda leaned in closely while the kids were talking with Mitzy Wagner. "He ever wants to sleep in the same bed with me again, he'll get his ass over here and never say a word about it."

"Yeah, that could happen."

They looked at each other for a long moment and then started chuckling. They were being silly. It was All Hallows' Eve and the night was surrounding them. Of course they had the creeps.

"Fine. I'll hold off, but when we get back to your place, I want Zin-fandel."

Another house, more candy, more creep out. By the time they were done at the Carpenter house, the feeling of being watched was far worse. Even the kids were starting to catch onto something, because now it wasn't just Toby who was making odd little noises and looking around.

It all came back to Lundgren. The very fact that the house was occupied was enough to be unsettling, but when you added in the weird stuff that seemed to go on around the place as the sun was setting and she was thinking about the murders, well, it was almost impossible not to get a freaky feeling in your guts, wasn't it?

"What do you suppose she's like? His mom, I mean?" Nancy's voice was strained.

Linda thought long and hard before she answered. "She's got to be at least in her eighties, right? I mean, he was in his forties and that was when we were in elementary school, so if that really is his mom in the place, she's got to be a little old withered crone."

"Yeah." Nancy snorted. "You know, that doesn't really help all that much on Halloween."

Linda wanted to laugh, but her skin was crawling again. "Let's just get to Arielle's place and then we're done."

Nancy shook her head, showing a bit of the backbone Linda knew she kept hidden for just such emergencies. "No way. If someone's follow-ing us, I'll call 'em on it. And if they have a problem, I have pepper spray and I'm not afraid to use it." Her hand patted the canister that Linda knew she kept in the back pocket of her jeans for any possible situation. When you considered that she'd narrowly escaped getting grabbed by the creepy bastard all those years ago, it was hardly surprising.

"There!" Nancy's voice was shrill and she pointed down the road, back toward the Addison house. "That tree, Linda! Someone's right there. I saw them this time." Her nerves were shot and Nancy couldn't control her natural tendencies any longer. She was afraid and she acted like she had since they'd met in middle school. She charged the source of her fear with her teeth bared and her back straight.

Linda wanted to go after her, wanted to stop her from either making a fool of herself or getting into a situation she couldn't get herself out of, but the kids were right there and Nancy was moving with a full head of steam.

And when she got where she was going, there was nothing to see.

Nancy circled the tree twice, a scowl making her pretty face ten years older the entire time. When she found nothing she came walking back with the same scowl locked in place.

And while she was looking at Linda and trying to figure out what to say about her rant and her acting out while the kids were watching, Linda saw the shadowy form that slithered up the tree and half crouched on a tree limb that creaked only slightly under the unexpected weight.

It must have shown on her face, because Nancy stopped and looked at her and then turned to where Linda was looking.

There was something solid up there. That much they could both see, but exactly what that something was became a bit more challenging. Whatever it was, it looked down at them in darkness and it laughed. The sound was exactly the sort of laugh that made witches so damned scary in movies.

And the thing slipped closer, crawling out on the long branch of the tree until it was almost directly over Nancy.

Nancy looked up and stared, her eyes half bugged out and her mouth hanging open.

Linda shook her head and stepped closer to her friend, but Nancy stayed where she was and trembled. The sound that came from that shape could not quite be called a voice, not really. It was more and it was less; it was the rustle of leaves, the hiss of the wind and the shifting of sand or fine debris but just the same it made words. "You told them tales, little Nancy. Told stories about my poor boy."

"I didn't." Nancy shook her head but her voice was so small that Linda could only barely hear her answer. "I never did."

It moved just a little and looked down on Nancy. Nancy, who looked up with wide eyes and did nothing but tremble.

"What are you doing?" Linda's voice rattled as she spoke.

Nancy did not look at her, but the shadow-thing did. And when it spoke the voice crept through her, slithered like sand into her ears. "Little Nancy hid the truth. She said such awful things about Martin." Linda blinked and in that brief instant the shadow shape disappeared. When it spoke again the voice was to her left and behind her. Linda turned fast and stared into darkened features in a field of gray, but oh there were eyes, weren't there, locked in a maze of wrinkles and withered, ancient flesh. There was hair, too, but like the rest of that shape it was wrapped in shadows, hidden in folds of night. "Little Nancy told a lie and my little boy died for her sins."

Nancy did not move. Her shoulders shook and her body moved as she wept, but she did not move, did not flee. Did not defend herself from the accusations.

That voice of grit and dust hissed in Linda's ear and breathed out a breath that was cinnamon and sand and ashes. "Do you know what it's like to lose your baby, little Linda?"

Linda shook her head and as she did that presence vanished again and was suddenly standing with Nancy. "So, a question, little Nancy. Answer now before I answer for you. Do I take you, my sweet girl? Or do I take your Tyler?"

Of course Linda looked. How could she not? She turned her head to Tyler in his ghostly costume and she looked hard for him because he was half buried in darkness, despite that tattered white sheet. He stood as still as his mother, his body frozen in place, the sack that carried his candy dangling from fingers that twitched as his ghostly features stretched in a painful, silent scream.

"I can take him. A life for a life. You can live on, little Nancy. Or I can have you. I can take you to Martin. He has been alone for so long, lost without anyone to hold."

Linda turned back to the voice and saw the shadow-woman open one long-fingered hand. Gray dust fell from her palm and the motes danced in the air, shifted and formed an image of a man she had never seen before, his arms crossed over his chest, his face locked in peaceful repose. He was dead, of course, and she could guess his identity. The image shimmered and blurred and changed, the dust swirling into a shroud of smoke and flames that consumed the corpse in moments.

"They burned my boy's body. I couldn't even give him a burial." Oh, the hatred in those words was a physical thing and Linda staggered back from it, unable to stay any closer to her friend.

Nancy shook her head and cried openly. Her eyes stared at Tyler for a long moment and then turned to the woman behind her. Woman, or ghost or demon or witch, whatever it might be that could come out on a Halloween night and demand payment for sins committed.

"Take. Take T—"

"Too late!" The dark thing slipped back and rose up, a fluttering cloud of shadows that opened arms wide and scattered more gray dust from both palms. The dust swept through the air, defied the mild breeze that should have sent it back toward the Lundgren place, and flowed over Nancy, coating her in a layer of gray that drained her of color. "Too late for you to decide, little Nancy. Too late by far!"

Nancy coughed and sucked in dust and coughed against her hands moving to wipe the dust from her eyes. She shook her head and staggered toward Linda before falling to her knees. And as Nancy took her steps and faltered, the shadow thing behind her fell away, little more than dust and sand scattered to the winds, gone in an instant.

Linda moved automatically, heading for her friend, horrified by the accusations, but also needing to know that Nancy was okay. Nancy had always been there for her, had always been her shoulder to lean on.

She was going to let that thing have Tyler.

That thought slithered unwanted into Linda's mind even as she reached for her friend.

Nancy coughed again and shivered. And as she coughed, a gust of gray spilled from her lips. She looked toward Linda for a moment and then toward her son, and she reached for Tyler, surely intent on going to the boy she'd almost betrayed.

Her fingers crumbled into powder and fell away, and that powder, heavy and gritty, slipped through the air and painted Linda's tongue. Linda closed her mouth instinctively and held her breath as she backed away, but the taste was already there.

Nancy looked toward her and tried to speak, but that was not meant to be. Her mouth split and collapsed on itself, her face following suit. In less than a minute, Nancy simply ceased to be. She fell into gray powder that spilled across the sidewalk and puffed into the breeze.

And Linda stepped back, horrified, the taste of ashes in her mouth. Ashes. She spit and spit but the flavor would not go away. Nor would the memories, or the screams of the children behind her.

T̄HE SPIRIT OF T̄HINGS

John Skipp

They were screaming downstairs, in Bob Wallach's apartment. He couldn't tell how many people Bob had down there with him. He couldn't even tell how much of it was human screaming. He really didn't want to know.

"Damn it all, I tried to warn him," Wertzel hissed. It didn't help. The floorboards thudded and death-twitched beneath his feet. Books and knickknacks threatened to tumble from their perches. Something snapped and shattered against a wall below: furniture, bone, he couldn't be sure. A window exploded into tinkling shards. The stereo died in mid-song, groaning.

The screaming got louder, crazier. Wertzel swallowed painfully and white-knuckled the handgrip of his .45. Something, decidedly not human, shrieked. The screaming got worse, if that was possible.

A single lightbulb burned in the center of the white ceiling. Jake Wertzel sat directly below it on a rickety wooden chair, his back pointed toward the only featureless wall in his third-story walkup studio apartment. To his right were the windows that faced Thirty-Seventh Street. To the left were the doorways to his closet, his bathroom, the hallway and stairs beyond. Before him lay the kitchenette, the unusable fireplace, his bed.

Every entrance to the room... the windows, the doors, the mouth of the fireplace... were completely boarded up and blockaded. He hoped that it would be enough.

The walls and the floorboards were ceasing to shudder. The screaming, which had continued to mount, now began to dissemble into its component parts. He could distinguish maybe a half-dozen voices, all veering off toward their separate grand finales: this one, a woman's, spiraling up toward the ultrasonic as if someone or something were slowly twisting a dial; this one, a man's, trumpeting dissonant jazz that closed with a jagged, moist burbling sound; this one, which could have been either sex, rattling off a string of syllables that ended, very clearly, with the word *no*. Wertzel knew for a fact that that was the word, because it hovered in the air for a good ten seconds before something made a sound like shredding paper and silenced it.

There was more. Much more. *Wallach must've been having some kind of a party*, Wertzel thought bitterly. *Maybe he thought there was safety in numbers*. A pair of voices warbled and whooped in screeching, agonized harmony. *Stupid goddam kid. I tried to warn him...*

The screaming stopped, abruptly.

And the feeding sounds began.

Wertzel cupped his hands over his ears, clammy shields against the horror. A blood-red ocean roared and surged inside his head. It was better, but it was not enough. He wanted to hum something, set up a monochromatic drone that would amplify itself against the confines of his skull, drown out the cracking and smacking and slurping from below. He didn't dare. The tiniest sound might be enough to attract them. Even his breathing was carefully modulated for silence.

It went on for five minutes that seemed very much like forever.

Jake Wertzel was a squat, stocky man in his late thirties: barrel chest, paunch beneath it, massive arms to either side. Twenty years on the loading docks will do that to you. His features were pinched and unlovely; his hairline had receded all the way to the back of his head, crowning him with a bald plateau that shimmered in the light from the bare bulb in the ceiling. He looked like a man who had known much hardship, very little happiness. He looked exactly like what he was.

He wished to God that he were not so horribly alone.

He remembered the dogs. Fleetingly, absurdly, he wished that they were still alive, wagging their tails or lapping at his cheeks or humping his knees with witless abandon. He had picked them up at the Humane Society three weeks before, anticipating the holiday rush: a pair of big, stupid, ungainly mutts that he named Haystacks and Calhoun. Wertzel had done his human best to remain detached from then, knowing what fate had in store. But three weeks is a long time: more than enough time to grow fond of them, their brainless devotion. More than enough time to make him miss them now.

At 10:45, the absolute latest that he could wait, Wertzel gave the last supper to Haystacks and Calhoun. The Purina Dog Chow was laced with enough sedatives to knock out an army: he wanted to make sure that they felt no pain. Fifteen minutes later, they were down for the count.

Wertzel had dragged them out into the hallway, gutted them, drawn a huge cross on the door with their blood, and left them on the matt: paws up, tongues lolling.

Then he had gone back into the apartment, locked and bolted and nailed the door shut, boarded it up with heavy planks he had taken from skids at the loading dock, and moved to the chair in the middle of the room.

To wait. And hope.

It was now twenty after twelve. The witching hour had struck.

And they had come.

"Oh, God," he moaned, and was startled by how loudly the words boomed in his ears. His hands jerked away from the sides of his head, and he realized that the downstairs had gone almost completely silent. There was a faint, airy sound that might have been the hissing of the pipes. Somehow, he didn't believe it.

Why me? he thought. *Why here? Why now?* Last year, the worst of it had gone down in Chelsea and the Village. The year before that... the first year... had laid waste to much of the Upper East Side. If there was a pattern there, Wertzel couldn't see it; but he'd hoped that the horror would focus itself uptown again, give him enough time to save up enough money to maybe get the hell out of New York before the fall.

As if there were anywhere safe to go.

Most of all, he wished that things would revert to the way they used to be. He wished for the sound of children's voices, giddy with laughter and hoarse with demands. He wished for cheesy plastic masks, eyeholes sliced in ratty sheets, prosthetic warts and theatrical blood.

He longed for the days when it was easy to pretend that the whole thing was just a joke.

Gone now, his mind whispered silently. *All gone. All gone...*

They were coming up the stairs.

Wertzel felt his bowels tighten like a hangman's knot. Ice water drained down his spine and gathered in the pit of his stomach. His scrotum constricted like a slug under a magnifying glass, and hot moisture like acid seeped into his eyes from the unlimited slope of his forehead.

They were coming up the stairs. He didn't know what they were, what they looked like, how they moved. He didn't want to know. They made sounds that his ears rejected as unreal, though his heart and soul knew better. They skittered and slithered and fluttered and muttered and howled like brain-damaged hyenas from Hell. One of them made a noise like a spoons-player in a jug band; it moved along the stairway wall with incredible speed, blasted down the hall toward him, clattered across the length of the door in a split-second, raced halfway up to the fourth floor and came all the way back before the others reached the third floor landing.

One of them made the walls shake as it approached.

I will not move, he urged himself with a silent, sickly whining voice. *I will not scream. I will not lose control.* He prayed that the sacrifice would work. Rumor had it that blood offerings had been known to, on occasion.

Wertzel found himself wishing, suddenly, that he'd sacrificed a child instead; supposedly, they worked the best. But killing the dogs had been bad enough.

At the time.

They were coming down the hall. They were coming to his door. The books and knickknacks that had threatened to tumble now made good on their promise, slamming and shattering against the floor, filling the room with gunshot echoes that ricocheted off the walls. The heavy chest of drawers rocked back and forth on its heels like a Bozo punching bag. The kitchen cupboard flew open; plates and saucers and glasses and cups exploded into the sink like a string of firecrackers.

Wertzel screamed and pissed himself. He couldn't help it. The crotch of his Lee jeans ballooned with moisture, and wet sticky tendrils crept down his thighs, while his mouth flew open and all the terror in his heart flew up, up, and out in a torrential spasm.

"NO PLEASE GOD NO PLEASE NO OH GOD PLEASE DON'T KILL ME! I...I..."

In the bathroom, behind the boarded-up door, the toilet flushed.

"...I...I..."

A light came on in the sealed closet. There was the sound of rending fabric.

"...I..."

Something scratched against the window, screeched, and flapped its leathery wings.

"I GAVE YOU A SACRIFICE!" he bellowed. *"I GAVE YOU A SAC-RIFICE, PLEASE DON'T KILL ME, OH GOD PLEASE I'LL DO ANY-THING YOU WANT..."*

Silence.

Jake Wertzel fell back in his seat, breath catching in his throat. The room had stopped shaking. Nothing moved. Nothing fell.

Silence from the bathroom.

Silence from the closet.

Silence from the windows.

Silence in the hall.

Wertzel held his breath for a good thirty seconds, not daring to believe.

Silence.

Slowly, then, he let out one long shuddering exhalation. The muscles in his face twitched; the corners of his mouth arced tentatively upward in a smile. He let the useless .45 dangle by one finger like an ornament on an artificial tree.

Then he started to cry.

And God, did it ever feel good to cry, to let out all the pent-up emotion, to bask and wallow in the fact that he was *alive!*, he was *alive!*, and no sound remained to haunt him but the manic intermingling of his own tears and laughter, punctuated by the steady...

(Drip. Drip. Drip.)

Of what? He laughed and cried some more. It could have been swollen teardrops, landing at his feet. It could have been the piss, still dribbling down his legs. Lord knew he had dropped enough fluids in the last few minutes to account for any amount of...

(Drip. Drip. Drip.)

It was coming from above him.

He opened his eyes.

The room was turning red.

(Drip. Drip. Drip.)

He looked up.

There was a quarter-inch of blood at the bottom of the lightbulb in the center of the ceiling, directly above his head. He looked up just in time to watch a tiny blue spark catch off the filament, just before the bulb blew up, showering him with blood and broken glass.

And total darkness.

Wertzel shrieked and hit the floor on his hands and knees. The glass bit through his clothes, his skin, sinking into the meat and lodging there like bee-stingers. He yowled and rolled over. His back erupted with pain.

The toilet flushed.

Light winked on under the closet door.

Something dragged its talons along the window-glass outside.

And the spitfire staccato of the wall-climbing thing burst out from the hole in the wall behind the oven, the hole he had forgotten to patch, the hole that now allowed it entrance. Like a methedrine freak with a pair of spoons, it clattered and streaked toward him so fast that he barely had time to aim the .45 in the direction of the sound and fire.

In the muzzle-flash, he could see the scuttling crabthing turn inside-out and spray all over the kitchenette. Then it was dark again, totally dark. Spots danced in front of his eyes. His ears were filling with the hiss of melting metal as the crabthing's guts ate holes in the oven, the Frigidaire…

No.

Not total darkness.

In the fireplace, something was moving. He could see it through the cracks between the boards, red and yellow and orange like flame. But brighter. More solid.

And moving.

A pair of tiny flaming hands pried their way between the boards. The wood crackled and blackened at their touch. A tiny head poked through the opening.

It stared at him.

And suddenly Wertzel knew why there would be no more plastic masks, no tattered sheets with holes for the eyes, no warts and scars and blood from the lab. Suddenly, he knew why they had come.

They had been watching, and waiting, for a long long time. They had watched the Church march arrogantly across the face of the earth, twisting the old pagan holidays to suit it, stripping and homogenizing away all meaning, then positing nonsense in its place.

And though centuries passed like seconds to them, it still dragged on too long. Where the Great Dark Ones had once strode the earth, there now stood Kolchak, The Night Stalker *and* Casper, The Friendly Ghost. *They had seen the shitty movies. They had read the shitty books. They had seen themselves turned into limp-wristed Bela Lugosis and carrot-headed James Arnesses, heard too many bad actors get the spells all wrong and conjure up demons that couldn't scare the fleas off a pink-nosed bunny.*

Worst of all, they had seen All Hallows' Eve transformed into a ritual for posturing, preening babies; had seen their glorious faces mocked and strung up in too many dime store windows. For far too long.

But that was over.

Wertzel understood it all, staring into those coal-black, ageless eyes.

He understood perfectly.

He started to scream.

Then the windows imploded, and the front door blew apart like a matchstick house in a hurricane's hands, and the Old Ones slithered and stalked and soared into Jake Wertzel's third-floor walkup apartment in beautiful Godless midtown Manhattan.

After a while, the screaming stopped.

And the feeding sounds began.

Halloween. It ain't just kid stuff.

Any more.

HAUNTING SEASON

Orrin Grey

I've always loved Halloween. It's the one time of the year when the rest of the world comes around to my way of thinking; when the evenings become the province of pumpkins and bats, ghosts and goblins, and all the things that go bump in the night. A liminal time, when the veil between the real and the numinous becomes thinnest, and the imaginary becomes just a little more real.

People have always assumed that I liked Halloween because I was born the night before, but the reverse is probably nearer the truth. I always saw the proximity of my birthday as more of an excuse to prolong Halloween for one more day than as a cause for celebration unto itself. Less a birthday, and more just Halloween-eve.

For all that, though, I was never much of a trick-or-treater. We lived out in the country when I was growing up, and while we could and sometimes did drive into town to go door-to-door in costume, that wasn't where the holiday lived for me. The heart of Halloween was beating beneath the floorboards of haunted houses. Not cobweb-strewn mansions tenanted by the restless dead—though I'm sure I would have loved those, too, had I been able to find any—but the haunted attractions put on every year in October, where animatronic beasts and very human ghouls in rubber masks contrived to jump out and scare passers-by.

Unlike horror movies and ghost stories, which could be brought out to enjoy at my leisure, the haunted houses came only once a year. Arriving on midnight trains, like Ray Bradbury's autumn people, they drifted down like changing leaves, and spun their webs in dark corners. That made them special, and every year I made sure to visit as many of them as I could: from the garages of local kids, where black trash bags made hallways full of groping hands, to haunts sponsored by movie special effects companies, their lobbies decorated with actual props and maquettes from *The Thing* and *Killer Klowns from Outer Space*. I've been to haunted houses in warehouses and parks, dark woods and strip malls, and even an abandoned doll factory.

One of my favorite haunted houses was actually a haunted island. It sat in the middle of the lake at Watson Park, more than an hour from where we lived, but I think I visited it more often than any other haunted attraction. The lines at haunted houses are always long, usually outdoors, and, since it's the middle of October, often in the rain. As an adult, when I go to haunted houses, I usually pay the few extra bucks to get tickets that let me skip the line. As a kid, standing in them was part of the ritual. The line at Watson Park wound around beneath one of the picnic shelters, and TVs had been hung from the rafters so those of us waiting to get in could watch scenes from *Tales from the Darkside* or *Halloween*.

The haunt itself is blended together in my memory, with different recollections from different years jostling side-by-side, broken out of their context, like sequences from a movie trailer. Crossing a floating bridge to the island, entering through the mouth slits of a two-story replica of Jason's famous hockey mask, walking on airbags sunken under the sandy ground, through stalks of corn in a scene that I would only learn years later was probably a nod to *I Walked with a Zombie*.

Near the end of the winding path that led around the island, there was a giant animatronic dragon—really just a silhouette of one cut from metal—that raised its head and roared as you passed, breathing a gout of real fire. The dragon was there all year round, even when the island wasn't in operation. When the trees were bare, you could just make it out from the road as you drove past the park.

I was never really very afraid of the haunts—except the parts with chainsaws, those scared me to death. Even as a kid, I could see the seams in them. I knew they weren't real, that the dragon was just some sheet metal and a torch. But that was always beside the point. I didn't go to them to be scared, I went to them to live inside them for the half-hour or so that it took to walk through. To wrap myself in their illusions, to let the night be transformed. Maybe that's why Watson Park was one of the best, because the island setting made the haunt feel boundless, made it easy to imagine that it would go on and on, that I would come to the shore and look out across the water at a different world, all dark forests and moss-grown churchyards.

My parents lacked my appreciation for all things creepy, and didn't usually accompany me to the haunts unless they had to. More often, they'd send me in the company of one of my grown-up brothers, or wait in the car while I stood in line for my chance to shuffle through dark hallways. My favorite haunted house memory is also one of my first haunted house memories, though, and in it, my mom is there with me.

Over the years, I've told the story a bunch of times, and as these things do, it's gotten fuzzier in my memory with each telling, until it's just a series of story beats that I hit while trying to fill in the blanks with whatever seems right at the time. So before I wrote this, I asked my mom to see what she remembered, and matched up the parts that we both had in common.

The haunt itself was set up in an orchard, and began with a hayrack ride from the parking lot. The wagon we rode in had slat sides, and we sat on bales of hay, while masked ghouls would jog up alongside and reach under the slats to grab at the ankles and feet of the passengers. I was sitting on the opposite side of the wagon from my mom, so that when a ghoul in a werewolf mask slipped up behind her, I saw what was coming before she felt it. When he reached up under the slats and closed the hairy fingers of his monster glove around my mom's ankle, she was startled, scared, but instead of screaming, she jumped, and instinctively kicked backward, trying to shake off whatever had touched her. She connected solidly with his face; the mask crumpled, and I imagine so did the nose beneath it.

The wolfman loosed a pretty human exclamation and pitched backward onto the ground. My mom tried to apologize, but the wagon was still moving on. Sometimes when I tell the story he waves us on, sometimes he doesn't acknowledge us at all. Neither my mom nor I can actually remember which happened, we both just remember the wolfman lying on the ground behind us, clutching at his mask.

I remember a little about the rest of the night, about the haunt itself, but it's all a dark blur compared to that moment. In some ways, I think I remember it because it's my mom to a T. She's a very practical woman. When a werewolf grabs her ankle, she's not going to scream, she's going to kick him in the head. I like to imagine that, no matter what else happens in my life or hers, that's how I'll always remember my mom: Sitting on a wagon in the October dark, accidentally kicking the wolfman in the face.

THE WITCH OF WALNUT

Elizabeth Massie

I grew up in a small town in a quiet residential area called the "Tree Streets." My house sat at the crest of a hill on Walnut Avenue. I lived there with my parents, two sisters, and brother. Halloween was a big holiday for us; there were factory-made costumes to be had at Roses and Newberry's department stores, but no, Mom created ours at her sewing machine. Best costumes ever.

This particular Halloween, my older sister Becky (aged 8) was a witch, in a flowing black gown and peaked black hat with a bright orange felt Jack-o-Lantern on the front. I (age 6) was a most lovely fairy princess (shut up) with a glitter-sparkly star wand, crown, and wings. My younger sister, Barb, (age 4) was a pink rabbit, complete with long ears and a white yarn tail that she continually tried to catch with her hand, causing her to spin in circles until the cycle was broken by an offer of candy or demand that it was time to go. My brother, Butch, was not quite 2 years old, so was costume-less that year.

Now, on the next block of Walnut Avenue, down the hill a bit, lived a witch. We knew she was a witch. My cousin Sue, who was my age and also lived on Walnut, had told me so. The witch lived in a house that was back from the street and obscured by tall, gangly trees and un-trimmed boxwoods. The ground was uneven, the sidewalk was buckled and cracked, and the house seemed to always be in shadows. Whenever we walked past the witch's house (this was in the day when kids could wander their neighborhoods *sans* parents or other worried adults), we heard her call out from her porch in a screechy, scratchy voice. We never saw her. We could never understand what she was saying and we didn't want to. It was clear was that she wanted our attention, wanted us to come up to her porch for some dreadful, unholy reason. When we passed her house, we always passed quickly.

So on that Halloween night we waited for the sun to set and then we ventured out to trick or treat. We went with my Dad (Mom stayed home to dole out the goods to other rabbits, witches, and sparkling fairies), fo-cusing on our block, collecting caramel apples, LifeSavers, Lemonheads, and Hershey kisses. Once those houses were covered, it was time for Barb in her bunny suit to go home with Dad. This left Becky and me and my cousin, Sue, who had joined up with us at some point, and Sue's older brother Frank. It was Frank who said we should go down to the witch's house. After all, it was Halloween.

The idea sent shards of ice up the spine of this fairy princess. I could see Becky was terrified, too, as was Sue. But Frank, being ten, was boss. We were scared of him as most kids who were short and less than ten years old were of a tall, loud-mouthed kid who was already ten years old. While the witch might scream at us from her porch, Frank could whack us right then and there. Frank, dressed as a pirate, herded us down past the other cheerfully and spookily decorated houses to the lot where the witch's house sat among the gangly trees.

We immediately heard the witch screaming from her porch, more of the unintelligible words that we knew comprised some kind of dreadful spell. Fairy arm-hair stood straight up. Becky dropped her Trick or Treat bag. Sue caught my arm.

"Okay, who's going to go up there?" asked Frank.

I would have suggested Frank but knew that would go over poorly. Becky was already digging in her heels, giving me the "I'm the older sister" look. Sue stared at me, I stared at Sue. I'm sure my eyes were as wide as hers.

"I mean it," said Frank. "Somebody better go up there. I'm not kidding." His balled up fists confirmed that he wasn't kidding.

A whack upside of the head or walking up to the witch's house. As an adult, now, I would go for the whack. As a six-year-old, I don't remember just what the hell I was thinking. Maybe I thought agreeing to go up to the witch's porch would delay the bad; maybe I thought I could run and hide before I had to actually look at her face to face, and then escape from Frank by running back home along the alley. I grabbed Sue's hand. We started up the witch's warped sidewalk, looking at our feet, our trick or treat bags swinging from our arms. I decided once this was over, I was going to tell on Frank. To my parents. But I knew I really wouldn't. Such are the dynamics of Southern cousin-hood.

I counted as I walked...a habit I still have when facing a frightful situation. One-two-three-four-five...up the walk, over the cracks in the concrete, until the toes of my shoes struck the lower step to the witch's porch. I saw Sue's toes strike the step at the same time.

And then the witch, her voice so much closer, screamed, "ORHA CALHA DOONA!" (Or something much like that...it's been a while.)

I dropped my Trick or Treat bag. I looked up, ready to turn and run. But at the top of the steps was a normal-looking old lady with puffy white hair and a very kind smile, holding out a bowl full of mini-chocolate bars. "Happy Halloween! You're our first trick-or-treaters!" She wasn't a witch, and she spoke real words. Understandable words. Sue and I looked at each other, mumbled "trick or treat," and reached out for some candy.

At that moment, from the dark end of the porch where the porch swing hung on heavy chains, came the witch's voice, "DAH ROOH HANA!" (Or something like that.)

We flinched, but the lady with the bowl said, "That's my sister. I hope she doesn't scare you. I live with her. She's needed help her whole life, but is quite sweet. And she certainly does love holidays."

I watched the porch swing; as my eyes adjusted in the yellowed porch light I could see a woman a bit smaller than the one with the bowl, sitting in the swing, hands on her knees, and grinning as if this was the best day of her life.

"Say hello, Mary," the lady with the bowl said.

"AHOOH," said the lady on the swing.

"These children are trick-or-treating. Isn't that nice?"

The lady on the swing said, "AHOOOH!"

I think Sue and I muttered a "Hello, Mary," or something close to that. Then we thanked the woman with the bowl and hastened back out to the road.

Frank laughed and told us not to eat the candy bars; he was sure they were poisoned. But later that night, I ate mine and they were fine. I'm still alive, after all.

That went down as the Halloween when I learned that old ladies that scream at you may not be witches after all. And that regular people—like big boy cousins—can be as mean and hateful as witches.

So there.

The Little Werewolf That Cried

Al Magliochetti

It's been said that the most wondrous Halloween of a child's life is when they're twelve years old, and for me that was definitely the case. You're still a kid then and it's your last hurrah before you're branded with the label of "teenager," and only a microscopic step away from the pressures and responsibilities of adult life. None of that exists when you're twelve and Halloween is still magic.

At that age I was totally addicted to classic monster movies. They played on TV every Saturday night and a world of merchandising sprang up out of nowhere. Models, t-shirt transfers, board games, posters…you name it; all of which I clamored to own. Nowadays they say we were "Monster Kids" but we didn't really have that distinction at the time, and in a small northeastern town like mine the words that were usually used to describe my fascination were Weirdo, Freak, Mental and, of course, Loser.

Don't misunderstand, it was a beautiful place, but puritanical New England was better suited to producing vapid blue-collar factory work- ers than anything of culture and substance. Coloring outside the lines on any creative level was perceived as arrogant and highbrow by the dullards in my class and it made you a target for every bully in the schoolyard, which is one thing my school cultivated very well. They delighted in terrorizing me every chance they had and eventually I spent all recesses either indoors or in close proximity to whatever adults were around.

Until I discovered The Wolfman.

For the longest time I'd only seen his picture in monster magazines. He looked really cool and the makeup was freakin' awesome, but until his exploits finally played on Creature Features I never knew his back story. This poor guy. He tried to be a hero and got cursed for his efforts; everybody hated him and he was downright miserable, which made he and I very similar. But when the full moon kissed the evening sky sud- denly he wasn't taking any shit from anybody anymore.

He changed—before my very eyes, I SAW him change through some unknown 1940's wizardry. My mom, noticing my rapture, loudly in- terrupted the absolute-coolest-scene-ever with the educational sidebar "They do that with mirrors, you know," which I immediately dismissed as her having some kind of stroke, since there were mirrors all over the house and none of them had ever reflected anything as mind-boggling as this. In that instant he became my hero…my Savior…my guardian. And I wanted to be him so very badly. I think somehow he knew that, and that's when I started sensing he was with me.

It started in little ways. Now when the bullies flashed The Look I didn't turn away like a coward, but gave my own dark, tortured look back instead. Then I'd tighten my lips and give a couple of twitches, baring my teeth just the littlest bit. Scared the shit out of them the first time. That felt good. But once they started getting used to my reaction they'd try to rile me for kicks, so by natural progression I really didn't have much choice but to throw one of them down the stairs. That felt really good.

It didn't go over very well with my parents, unfortunately. They'd al- ready been brainwashed by an unforgiving faculty that my love of monsters was an unhealthy obsession and had become halfway convinced that my only possible future involved sacrificing kidnapped infants over a torch, because clearly following the exploits of Dracula and the Frankenstein monster was a gateway into Satanism. I came home one afternoon to find that every monster poster had been ripped off my wall, my models were busted up in the trash and my entire collection of Famous Monsters was a pile of ashes in the fireplace. I cried for a very, very long time...and when I stopped the Wolfman wasn't with me anymore.

My parents were more than a little dismayed that their shock therapy hadn't produced the results of blind obedience they'd expected. I hardly talked anymore, my schoolwork tanked and no amount of lectures, punishments or beatings shook me out of it. With nowhere else to turn they vented their wrath on the educated professionals that gave them such sage advice in child rearing, who finally acquiesced that perhaps the treatment was a little too extreme. It was decided I could "play" with monsters again...a little.

But it wasn't the same. The Wolfman didn't come back. I figured he didn't trust me after my parents' betrayal and he wasn't going to risk having his feelings hurt anymore. And I missed him...so very much. Without him I was nothing.

Somehow I made it through the rest of the school year without being kept back but that minor victory was lost on me. I existed, but nothing mattered much anymore. I thought about the Wolfman all the time and cried myself to sleep during every full moon—wracking my brains trying to figure out a way to let him know I really loved him.

Salvation came in the oddest of ways; primarily because my old man was a paranoid cheapskate. A few months earlier he'd become convinced the Leyden twins, our paperboys, were hitting us up for more money than we owed so he abruptly cancelled our subscription; his excuse being that twins could easily show up twice and double charge him, which I'm still trying to figure out to this day. However, this lack of current events material cut way down on the available topics he could bitch about, so it was decided that my new chore would be to stop by Charlie Crook's drugstore on the way home from school every day and pick up the afternoon *Chronicle* to sate his after-dinner gripefest.

This activity sucked during summer vacation, since a daily drugstore trip was completely out of the way. On the plus side, the bully crowd wasn't usually around bumming smokes during the summer so that made the routine a little easier. It was all pretty uneventful until the day Paul Cachoply showed up.

As far as assholes go, Cachoply was easily the assholiest one around. He was three years older but being dumb as dirt he'd been kept back twice, so he was only one grade ahead of me. His age and size gave him status among the other reprobates, so he was naturally the leader of the troublemaking pack.

As luck would have it, one fine day, there were a couple of budding nymphets Cachoply was trying to impress with his skateboarding prowess, and since his tiny brain could only handle just so much multitasking, bullying at that point was not a priority. It was obvious to me from their giggles that he was not exactly scoring any points with these gals; rather, they were looking at him as though he were some bargain-basement Gong Show reject…it was almost cruel. My immediate plan was to speed up the usual convention, grab the paper and hightail it back home before the girls shined Cachoply on and he reverted back to ape mode. It didn't quite work out that way.

Greg Crook, Charlie's son, ("Greggy" to all us kids, which he hated—can't blame him) was at the register that day. I flew up the steps, whipped a *Chronicle* out of the rack and pitched the dime like a shot-put in his direction before wheeling around when he stopped me with "Hey, wait! I got something to show you!"

Me? The town weirdo? The momentary indecision as to whether I should ignore him and race home to avoid a neanderthal incident was jettisoned when I saw his smile. He was serious. Until that point I never really realized that Greggy was a cool guy, although back then being cool consisted of not treating me like I was much of a nuisance. Suddenly, out of nowhere, he was actually being friendly, which wasn't something I was used to.

"You like those monstah-books, right?" His New England accent gouged me since it reminded me of my old man snarling "Go play wit'cha monstahs!" whenever he was pissed off at me. He gave a glance to make sure his dad was occupied at the pharmacy counter, then reached under the register and produced a magazine I'd never seen before. The lurid cover made my jaw fall down into another dimension.

"They screwed up," he said, "we're not supposed to have this. My dad'll just throw it out since it's not on the order list so I saved it for ya." Or something like that. I was still entranced by the red, yellow and black cover and wouldn't have heard Greggy if he'd told me I was on fire. There was an ugly gray face in the lower corner and a three-step progression of photos showing a little boy who looked remarkably like me transitioning into a Pinocchio-nosed, green "WEIRD-OH," complete with helmet, goggles and exaggerated bloodshot eyes. The title burned itself into my retinas. "Do It Yourself Monster Makeup Handbook." Holy shit.

I shook like I'd grabbed an electric fence. I turned the magazine over and gazed at another eight horrifying faces. A hunchback, a couple of aliens, a skull and some guy that looked like he was made out of melting jelly. Greggy was still babbling but that was in a universe I was no longer part of. I rifled through the book and saw a dozen faces, mostly boys my age; each one wearing a fearsome painted visage. There were vampires, mummies…and suddenly I realized what had to be in there somewhere.

When I found it my heart sank. Werewolf Number One, it said, and it was probably the worst makeup in the book. It looked like some bratty little kid who'd scribbled black lines on his face with a Sharpie. This wasn't a werewolf…there wasn't even any fur on the kid; they'd just combed his hair down into a point. Useless. I started to hand it back to Greggy before I ripped that abomination to shreds.

"There's some bettah ones in the back," he said, freezing me in mid-motion. Of course. This was Werewolf number ONE; it was a basic makeup. So Werewolf number two had to be…

I flipped to the back and suddenly his eyes were staring right into mine; deep and foreboding. My Wolfman, in all his fuzzy glory. Razor teeth, killer gaze, fur on every square inch of his head. God, he looked outstanding. But more importantly he wasn't hurt anymore, I could feel it. He'd forgiven me.

Then the bottom fell out of my world when I saw the cover price. Sixty cents. It might as well have been a thousand dollars; I was lucky if my pockets carried two nickels in those days. The ache that signaled incoming tears scratched at the corner of my eyes so I slid the book back to Greggy while I could still see straight.

"You don't want it?" clearly puzzled, "I thought you'd go crazy for it. It's brand new—nobody else will have it for another few days. I told you, they screwed up."

"Greggy," I winced, seeing him wince, "I don't have the money! I got fifteen cents and a gumball penny. I don't even have anything to trade."

He shushed me down and checked the back counter once again. Dad was staying put. "Didn't you hear me? I'm not charging you for it. It's not on the list, so my dad will never know it was here. It's a present!"

Years later, I realized that when I'd finally met the woman of my dreams, it was the only other point in my life that came close to this moment and that still ran a distant second. Greggy grinned at me and slid the book back in my direction. "I like monstah stuff too," he beamed.

I thanked him profusely, at least I hope I did, as he tucked the magazine discreetly into the middle of the newspaper, but I was in such a fog when I left I blundered directly into the path of skateboarding studmuffin, Paul Cachoply.

Before I'd snapped out of my daydream his mitts were trying to yank the *Chronicle* out of my hands. Presumably his skateboard moves weren't quite helping him cozy up to the ladies so a brawny smacking down of a twelve year old would surely lob a hunk of pheromones in their direction.

With a war cry of "Hey, baby, lemme read that." he made his move. *You can read?* I thought, but kept it to myself; no sense in aggravating the situation even further, but I managed to squeak out an exasperated "Let GO!" in a voice that sounded way more immature than I'd intended. I snatched the paper away before he could get a good grip, but he skidded in front of me on that ludicrous board, made another lunge, almost lost his balance and managed to stay vertical by sheer dumb luck.

Unfortunately his antics caused the magazine to slide out and before I could hide it again he made his grab and snagged it. I clamped the paper tight before he could pull it completely away and now it was a moving tug of war; every motion I made was countered by Cachoply's idiotic rolling around. The makeup book, and the Wolfman, were about ready to rip in half.

My panic conjured up an adrenaline resolve I'd never known before I heard myself actually snarl "I-Said-Let-GO-of-me-You-FUCK!" and spun with all my weight into a circle. I don't know if it was his shock at the venom I spit in his face or the force I put into my swing but he slammed to the pavement on his tailbone, shooting the board into space like a cannonball, where it collided neatly with the crabby cop in the crosswalk.

I was already pedaling away when the cop stormed toward the dumbass daredevil, loudly spewing a veritable thundercloud of bile. In my handlebar mirror I saw Cachoply giving me the blood look as I gained distance. I couldn't care less. Me and my Wolfman were going home.

Even though I had permission to like monsters again, anything I brought into the house invited scrutiny so I snuck the makeup book in under my shirt. I bit my lip, playing it smooth, even though I was burning to run upstairs and dive into that greasepaint world. I lingered long enough downstairs to make some small talk with my mom and faked a half-hearted attempt to steal a cookie before dinner so no suspicions would be aroused.

Upon closing the bedroom door, which I was never allowed to lock, I began the camouflage ritual that I'd hit upon when all monster books became contraband. I pulled the bedspread down just enough to expose the pillows then sprinkled some comics (or "funny books" as my parents disdainfully referred to them) across the bulk of the mattress. This allowed me to read covertly as I could slide any subversive material directly under the pillows, undetected, replacing it with a nearby comic as a smokescreen if any adult happened to burst into the room in a boiling rage. I'd even learned to use comics I didn't particularly care for since they were known to be shredded in my face as a casualty of war. If there was one thing my dad hated, it was to see his son wasting his life by stickin' his fuckin' nose in a funny book.

The makeup book was Godly. It was written by an adult in a way that kids could easily interpret, and that alone filled me with warmth because it meant that somebody, somewhere understood and that there had to be other kids like me. I wasn't alone in the world after all.

I went straight to the Wolfman chapter in the advanced section and immediately got the wind knocked out of my sails as I couldn't even remotely understand the materials or techniques they were talking about. Spirit gum? Liquid latex? I knew latex was rubber but how it could come in a bottle like they showed in the pictures was totally beyond my comprehension. After a few frustrating minutes I forced myself to start at the very beginning and read every word. Slowly, very slowly, the glorious secrets of monsterdom unraveled themselves to me.

After the brief foreword, there was a glossary of all the makeup terms I'd need to know and even a list of suppliers where I could buy materials. My frustration faded as I realized I really could learn all this stuff and in the back of my mind I was already thinking ahead to October. It was still only mid-June and I had a few months to go before Halloween crept up and since it would be my last one before I became a teenager, I vowed then and there to bring my Wolfman to life.

The change that came over me that summer shocked everyone who knew me well. My quiet, withdrawn nature was eighty-sixed in favor of my first adventure into the world of capitalism. It turned out makeup materials weren't cheap and I had only a matter of weeks to amass the small fortune I needed to buy them so from that point on if anybody had a lawn that needed mowing, a yard that needed raking or even a fence that needed painting I was there underbidding all competitors. Normally this kind of drastic attitude adjustment would've raised an armada of red flags with my parents, but I lucked out when the bombshell dropped that my mother was pregnant.

Thinking back, it was kind of obvious that they hadn't been breathing down my neck nearly as much lately, but I didn't realize they'd been completely distracted by this turn of events. Mom was about forty years old, and as a second-rate mechanic my dad wasn't exactly bringing home Rockefeller wages. Consequently the revelation of an unplanned blessed event totally inverted their world and the least of their concerns was their idiot monster-loving offspring.

As the warm weeks lazed by it became apparent that the timetable was going to be tight. The "allow four weeks for delivery" disclaimer on the theatrical supply order blank got me thinking that I really needed to start prepping some of the necessary makeup appliances in advance, and while my income was steady it wasn't especially lucrative so budget cuts had to be made. The pricey bald cap I needed to make the wig was crossed off and a cheap swimming cap was substituted. Likewise, the dental acrylic necessary to make the fangs seemed to cost as much as a brand new car so I'd have to figure out a way to take standard candy-counter wax teeth and cobble them into the proper threatening choppers with matches and a craftily-wielded soldering iron.

Throughout all this I could feel the Wolfman at my side, like a hairy guardian angel, helping me figure out all the annoying little details that fell through the cracks. In spite of my complete lack of experience with all of these new techniques it seemed like I was born to them and gradually the individual pieces began to take shape.

I'd long since abandoned the idea of working in my bedroom since discovery was a real concern, especially taking the stench of the chemicals into account. Once again, my Wolfman—my muse—helped me find a solution. His murmurs reminded me of an old valise I could use to keep the materials in, as it sealed tight enough that no odors could escape. Then, since my bedroom window faced the woods, I rigged up a rope so I could lower the bag down and carry it deep into the trees to craft my paint and putty alchemy undisturbed. I felt like a pre-teen Victor Frankenstein, except my monster would be a lot scarier than his.

School started in September and I was finally able to relish the luxury of being a sixth grader. For the first time in my life there were no older kids to push me around since they'd moved on to the netherworld of Junior High, although I'd heard Cachoply had been shipped off to military school, which served him right. My new teacher, Mr. King, was a jovial butterball who smiled at the world in harsh contrast to the sourpuss harpy I was stuck with the previous year. My Wolfman was still with me but he wasn't as angry anymore and for the first time in my life I felt very different. I was almost happy.

The last couple of weeks greased by but I was on schedule for my Wolfman's Halloween unveiling. I was ecstatic to see the calendar noted a full moon for the thirty-first, thus making his terrifying debut even more perfect. All the pieces were completed and tucked into the valise, along with the appropriate adhesives and a carefully selected wardrobe, although I still hadn't quite figured out how I'd be able to apply everything without arousing suspicion. I mean, obviously on Halloween it wouldn't be out of character for me to stay in my room for a while to put on a costume, but this makeup would take hours. Then again, my mom had gotten gigantic lately and my dad was leaving me alone more and more to take care of her needs, so I might just sneak by with minimal parental interference.

The final hour of school on Halloween was excruciating with the clock ticking down slower than it ever had on the last day before summer vacation. The rain clouds rolling in were a little unsettling but in New England they were almost a daily hazard. When the bell finally rang, I tore out of class only to get mired in the Gordian Knot of canary yellow busses and remembered with impatience that mine had to make its usual twelve million stops before it finally got to my street.

I raced my Wolfman up the block so we could get a head start on the evening's activities. I was going to try to talk Mom into letting me scarf an early dinner since I couldn't eat once I started gluing crepe hair all over my face. But as I got closer to the house I saw my Dad's car in the driveway—way too early for him to be home from work. There's no way this could be good.

"Close the fuckin' door, are you tryin' to heat the whole goddamn world?" was my Dad's usual greeting when I came in during the fall and winter months, so hearing it this time wasn't any real shocker. What I wasn't expecting was "Keep your jacket on, you're goin' over to Gramma's right now!" Oh no. No way…

It couldn't be. Not tonight. Not after all my planning…all my months of work. My mom couldn't go into labor now. I had to figure a way out of this but I couldn't think straight. I started to protest that it was Halloween but that only got me the "tough shit" response I should've expected. I argued, Dad yelled, I argued more and he yelled louder. There was no way this wasn't going to get messy.

My mom showed up with her suitcase and the old man made a move to physically drag me into the car but I swatted his hand away in open defiance, ran up the stairs and locked the forbidden bedroom door behind me. I could hear him bellowing from the other side and saw the door shake violently with every punch he threw at it. I slammed open the window, flung the rope around the bed post, lowered the precious makeup bag to the ground and then scrambled down myself a few scant seconds before the remainder of the door became kindling.

I knew I'd catch the asskicking of all time later, but I was banking on my Mom's condition being more important to him than clobbering me, since the woods went on for miles and I literally could've been anywhere. For a few brief minutes his curses echoed as I escaped into the foliage, and I hoped to God he didn't decide to give chase. I ran until I didn't know where I was anymore and only then did I feel safe enough to stop.

I felt that ache peck at my eyes again and tears wanted to flow but I didn't have time for that nonsense now. I needed all the daylight left to get this makeup on while I could still see, and since we'd turned the clocks back I knew it would disappear fast. I caught my breath and pulled out my smeared little mirror, set it on a rock, and then stacked the grease-paints, sealers, adhesives and putties next to it. Before long the stresses and anxieties of the last hour melted into memory as I concentrated on transforming my reflection into my hirsute hero.

And it was working, as though my face was molding itself to fit the makeup. I didn't have the time or extra materials to do any practice tests, so seeing it all blend together for the first time was more magnificent than opening the one final present under the Christmas tree and seeing the toy you'd never thought you'd get in a billion years. I thought back to my Mom's naive concept that the Wolfman transformation was done with mirrors...maybe she was on to something after all, because I was certainly transforming in mine.

It was full dark before the last bits of spirit gum dried so I had to fudge the last few details, hoping I wasn't messing anything up. As the full moon began to rise through the encroaching cloud cover the colors of the world bled away, leaving me in a monochrome wonderland that looked just like the movies. From the mirror, my Wolfman gazed back at me; we were finally one. I wore his image proudly as I stealthily lumbered through the dim forest. We made a game of it, stalking our imaginary prey by the light of the autumn moon, pretending the dying honeysuckle was the scent of wolfbane until we saw the glow of familiar streetlights and made our way back down to civilization.

Chattering kids and their parents wandered the road by the dozens, mostly wearing store-bought cheesy costumes of popular cartoon char-acters. I felt a particular empathy for one sad little kid whose unimaginative parents had dressed up as a traffic light. He looked like he wasn't having any fun at all. I could fix that.

I crept down in the shadows to some brush under the streetlight; my heart racing as I prepared to pounce into the road and startle everybody. But something wasn't right; something was missing. I'd forgotten one critical thing.

I howled.

And everybody froze.

I slammed through the bushes and struck a fearsome pose, gnashing my ill-fitting wax fangs and trying to keep my drool from spilling out and spoiling the moment.

The entire crowd applauded.

They whooped, they hollered…parents patted me on the back. One, to my chagrin, ruffled my little wolfy head. Another twisted guy even shoved his young daughter right in my face just to make her scream while he laughed hysterically. Of every reaction I'd anticipated and even hoped for, being revered for my efforts totally blindsided me. These people liked what I did…appreciated my work…thought I was cool. I really was the Wolfman.

I bounded away before I wore out my welcome to commence the most awesome night in trick or treat history. Small problem, though; it suddenly occurred to me that I'd been so wrapped up in escaping from my house that I'd completely forgotten to bring anything to carry candy in. And while my priority for the night was to be a living, breathing Wolfman, it would've been nice to have at least some sugary profit.

I remembered that sometimes old Mr. Frenette had some burlap sacks laying out in back of his repair shop at the end of the block and I was sure he wouldn't mind if I borrowed one. I abandoned my loping gait in favor of an all-out run as the first drops of rain began to splash around me. Whenever I came to a group of trick or treaters I'd raise my claws up over my head and sprint howling through their midst. The cacophony of shrieks hit my pointed ears like the swells of a Mozart symphony.

The Frenettes' pitch-black yard probably would've unnerved me if I was my normal self, but Wolfmen aren't bothered by creepy, shadowy places. I padded through the crunching leaves over to the workbench near the gigantic willow tree and was elated to find a couple of sacks stashed underneath—which, of course, deserved a mighty howl.

But then another howl sang back. It was a weird howl. A stupid howl. Like some sound only an idiot would make. A drop of rain hit my snout as a dark figure rounded the tree. It was Cachoply...with a couple of beers...and a couple of goons. I saw something glint in the darkness and felt the ground crash into me as the empty beer bottle smashed against my knee. Then the three of them were on me and the clouds opened up.

Military school had apparently agreed with Cachoply since he was even more of an asshole than before and the buzz-cut made him look downright fiendish. He straddled my chest while holding both my arms and shoved his dopey howling face directly into mine while the other lackeys enjoyed the show.

"Hey, doggie," he belched, "where's your leash? You could get lost!"

Doggie? Seriously? Good grief.

Stevie-something, the short lackey, laughed way too hard at this pitiful attempt at humor, which I guess was his required activity in the group. Jeff-something, the fat lackey, piped up with "Maybe he's lookin' for a bone!" I could see the cracked light bulb fizzle to life over Cachoply's head, "Hey—maybe he's looking for MY bone!" and I really didn't like the sick grin on his face.

He tried to grab both of my wrists in one hand so he could unzip his fly but was uncoordinated enough that I got my right hand free and gave him a sock in the eye. It was more of a love-tap on my part, since I couldn't get any leverage, but he politely returned the favor by pasting me square in the mouth. The fangs crumbled into wax confetti and the coppery taste of blood trickled down my throat. In that one brief moment the illusion was shattered and my tears erupted to the surface in a torrent. I wasn't crying because of the pain, or the humiliation, or the senseless mistake that put me in this position. I was crying because at that moment I felt like I was the loser everybody said I was, like I was the useless little shitheel my dad always claimed I'd become. I deserved the beating I was getting. Cachoply could somehow sense that and it made him laugh...a lot.

His sophomoric cackle shot a bullet of rage through me and, spitting the wax shards aside, I sank my real teeth into the flesh of his hand. He yelped in shock and plowed his fist full into my face. My putty snout flattened and mixed into the blood and snot gushing out from under it. Between his weight on my chest and my broken nose I couldn't get a clear breath and with the rain now pelting down in buckets I felt like I was drowning. His fists kept pounding me but there was so much pain the blows didn't register anymore. And through the whole beating he just kept laughing and crowing out his insipid howl in my face.

My vision was starting to fade when I heard something howl back. Something that sounded like a demon straight out of hell. The beating stopped momentarily and when I cracked open a swollen, blackening eye I saw a look of naked fear on Cachoply's face frozen in a flash of lightning, right before a razor-clawed hand slashed in from out of nowhere and scooped out a chunk of his throat like it was made out of red velvet cake with gore frosting. His head, barely perched on what was left of his spine, spilled over backward and looked stupidly at the upside-down lackeys behind him before the rest of him collapsed into a pile of rapidly cooling meat.

The fat lackey never even got a chance to react before the claw slammed his head into the thick roots of the willow tree again and again. I hoped that first blow knocked him out because the second one definitely killed him. The third poetically left him looking very similar to the jack o'lanterns he'd smashed earlier that night.

The best part was the look on Stevie's face when the taloned hands pulled Cachoply's mangled corpse off of him. It was like there was a Vacant sign posted where his soul used to be, and his glazed eyes didn't react to the raindrops that ricocheted off them. Somewhere deep inside, that made me smile.

The last thing I saw before twilight embraced me was Cachoply's bulk being hurled into the path of an oncoming car. The rubbery skid shrieked through the night, along with a dull thud and soggy grinding that meant my enemy had been ripped sideways and was lubricating somebody's axles now. The Frenettes' front porch light blinked on and I went away.

I woke up in my own bed with sunlight streaming into my eyes and the seductive aroma of applewood bacon wafting up from downstairs. I thought I'd had the most vivid dream of all time until I saw the splintered bedroom door with my old man's fist prints still on display.

I was afraid to look in the mirror since I knew I'd see some Quasimodo-pummeled face looking back, but I was shocked to see that I looked perfectly normal with only a few greasepaint stains and stubborn spirit gum remnants as souvenirs of my previous night's escapade, along with a ton of ruddy, coagulated crud jammed under my fingernails.

In the kitchen I discovered my grandmother bustling away at a skillet full of the most glorious breakfast that had ever assailed my miraculously unbroken nose.

"Well, good morning, sleepynoggin'," she chirped, "I hope you're hungry."

I was ravenous. As I shoveled the mound of food into my face my gramma delightedly told me I now had a new little brother and admonished me for being a naughty boy and running away like I did. Apparently my dad was still a little ticked off at me, but the tragedy of the night before mellowed everyone's anger.

It seems some fat kid named Jeff was foolishly climbing a willow tree in the rain when he lost his footing and smashed his head wide open when he hit the ground. His best friend, Paul Cachoply, ran for help but instead managed to be mowed down and torn to bits by a motorist who didn't see him in the heavy rain. The worst part was a third party, a little goob named Stevie, who was so traumatized at witnessing these events that he would probably never talk again.

The sizzling bacon smelled really good…maybe I'd have a little more.

I never cried again.

The Boy in The White Sheet

Bev Vincent

There's a lot of blood, considering the victim is supposed to be a ghost.

It's Halloween night, which brings out the prankster in everyone. Sheriff Baker and his deputies have been busy responding to stupid calls all night long. If he were a crook, this would be the night he'd plan some big heist because the cops were sure to be busy. This is not an opinion he shares with anyone else.

The rain started half an hour ago, putting a premature end to the festivities for all but the hardiest trick-or-treaters. Baker is lecturing a couple of teenagers for starting a fire in a trash can when he gets the call about an automobile-pedestrian accident on Grove Avenue, only a few blocks from his location. He sends the kids home with a stern warning and gets into his squad car.

Lou and Ferg are tied up with a fender bender a few blocks away, so Baker is the first on the scene, except for a civilian vehicle pulled over to the curb with its four-ways flashing and its windshield wipers swishing. At first he assumes it's the automobile involved in the accident, but the driver soon disabuses him of that notion. The moment Baker exits his squad car, adjusting his poncho and the plastic covering on his Stetson, a large man leaps from the vehicle and approaches. Baker's hand drifts instinctively to his sidearm in case the man poses a threat, but the only thing the other driver is holding is an umbrella with a bank logo.

"Over here, officer," the man says, tipping his umbrella to indicate the direction.

"Sheriff," Baker responds. "What happened?"

"Damndest thing. Car ran right into this kid and kept right on going. No brake lights, nothing. I was behind him, so I saw the whole thing."

"Kid?" Baker says. He takes a deep breath. "Where? Show me."

"Over here. I called 911. They said an ambulance was on the way."

Sure enough, a siren wails in the distance. The other driver leads Baker to the grassy median. That's where he sees the ghost.

Based on the size of the body, he guesses it's a child of no more than nine or ten. He (or she—he can't tell yet) is lying on his back. The child's eyes stare through clumsily cut eye-holes in a white sheet that served as his costume. The *once-white* sheet, that is, for now it is soaked with blood that seems more orange than red in the uncertain light. The victim's eyes are unblinking, despite the large drops of rain striking them.

He waves the civilian away from what is now officially a crime scene, possibly a homicide. Sure, the witness said the boy was struck by a car, but Baker isn't taking anything for granted. People lie all the time, and for all he knows someone—maybe even this guy—deposited the body here. He crouches, trying to disturb as little as possible, and picks up an outstretched hand, feeling for a pulse. Nothing. He gets on his knees, ignoring the muddy water seeping into his pants, and does a more thorough check of the body. He considers CPR, but it has been a good eight to ten minutes since the call came in, so there doesn't seem much point.

More than the lack of a pulse, it's the eyes that tell him the full story. Those unblinking eyes that seem to be shedding tears.

He stands up and surveys his surroundings. The beam of his flashlight picks up a trail of strewn candy from the edge of the road all the way up to the body and beyond, which seems to confirm the citizen's story.

After Ferg and Lou arrive, Baker and his team try to gather evidence before the rain washes it all away, but there's little to be found. No skid marks on the road, nor any broken glass or other debris from the vehicle. They briefly consider erecting a canopy over the body to keep the rain off, but after the EMTs arrive and confirm what Baker already knows, there doesn't seem much point. Ferg uses his pocket gizmo to collect fingerprints while they wait for the justice of the peace to arrive and declare the victim dead so he can be transported. Lou peels the sheet back long enough to take a few photographs of the victim while Ferg documents the scene and bags up the strewn candy, but that's about all they can do.

Baker's last glimpse of the victim is that of a bloody ghost being tucked into a black body bag. He never gets a good look at the boy and later regrets that he didn't, as all he has to go on is a few blurry photos taken in poor lighting in the rain.

When the ambulance arrives at the morgue, the body bag is empty except for the blood-soaked sheet. The general consensus is that it was a prank, although no one can figure out how it was pulled off. Everyone at the crime scene, including the EMTs, was sure they were dealing with a corpse, so how it could have gotten out of the van is anyone's guess. No one reports a missing boy, and the fingerprints don't match anyone in the database. DNA from the blood on the sheet doesn't generate any hits, even when expanded for familial matches.

Baker thinks he's onto something when an elderly man named Victor calls the station the next day to say that he's pretty sure he hit someone the previous evening. When Baker goes to Victor's house, his wife takes Baker aside and explains that Victor has an OCD condition called "harming obsession" that makes him paranoid about having accidents. "It happens all the time," she says and, based on the tired look in her eyes, Baker believes her.

Minor damage to Victor's car and a jack-o'-lantern candy pail found jammed into the wheel well seem to support his claim, though, and the route he took to the store to buy more Halloween candy brought him past the location of the accident. However, any other possible supporting evidence, such as blood or hair, was washed away by the rain. The witness who reported the accident identifies Victor's car from a photo array but, given the lack of a body, the district attorney refuses to file charges.

Baker sees the bloody sheet again in his dreams the night after the incident, and then on and off again for several weeks after that. His wife asks him what his nightmares are about, but he isn't able to articulate them for her. It seems silly to tell her he's seeing ghosts.

Bloody ghosts are all the rage the next Halloween. It seems in poor taste to Baker, but that never stopped kids before, his wife tells him. After he yells at the first couple of kids who come to the door dressed like accident victims, his wife makes him go into the living room and watch TV, which he does to the accompaniment of a six-pack of beer.

The next year, he's alone on Halloween. An aneurism struck his wife down on New Year's Eve, fifteen minutes before the ball dropped in Times Square. One minute she was holding her glass awaiting the big moment with everyone else at the party. The next she was on the floor with a crowd gathering around her, and that was that.

He puts the outside light on out of habit, and he had enough foresight to buy a few packages of candy at Wal-Mart the previous weekend. The house is empty and quiet—too quiet—so he welcomes the distraction. For the first hour, it's mostly tiny tots, and he enjoys crouching down to their level as he hands out the candy and interacts with them. He's good with kids, his wife always said, and it was their biggest regret that they never had any.

When a bloody ghost shows up at a little after eight, Baker slams the door in the kid's face, turns off the porch light and retreats to the living room. This year, it's with a case of beer instead of a six-pack.

He waffles over running for sheriff during the next election campaign. By now, his hair is fully grey and deep lines have formed around the corners of his mouth, but his supporters say he looks dignified in his campaign photo and his victory is a landslide. His only opponent makes no mention of the child's body that went missing a couple of years earlier. There's been a lot of water under the bridge since then, and other cases have overshadowed that somewhat embarrassing incident.

The next Halloween, Baker doesn't turn on the porch light at all. He's had a dozen sessions with a grief counselor over the loss of his wife—something her sister encouraged him to try when she called to check up on him, which she still does from time to time—and he feels like he's in a better place emotionally. He's even starting to wonder if it would be appropriate to ask his former sister-in-law to dinner. He isn't, however, prepared to face another bloody ghost, so he decides it's safer to just watch TV.

Despite his precautions, the phantom visits Baker later that night. He awakens with a start and sees the white image in the bedroom doorway. There's enough light coming through his window, thanks to a neighbor's security light, for him to see the red splotches on the sheet. "What the hell?" he says as he starts to clamber out of bed. In his foggy condition, he wonders if he forgot to lock the door and a determined trick-or-treat-er wandered into the house in pursuit of candy. He glances at the bedside table. His alarm clock shows 3:13 a.m. Not a trick-or-treater, then. He can't blame it on booze—he stopped drinking around the time he started counselling.

He looks back at the doorway, expecting the sheeted figure to be gone, but it's still there. It makes no noise, but it wavers back and forth as if on unsteady feet. Baker sees something that stops him short. The eye holes are jagged, as if cut by a child's hand. All the ones he saw on the previous Halloweens were more regular, the work of older kids, parents or laborers in a factory in China. And the eyes within? Are they wet, either from tears or from rain drops? He takes another step toward the spectral figure. His foot hits something—his slippers, he discovers later. He looks down for only an instant, but when he looks up again, the doorway is empty and he's alone.

After several months of one-on-one therapy, Baker graduates into a grief support group. It takes him a while to open up to these other distraught people, but he has to admit that he feels better after an evening spent with like-minded individuals.

One week, the therapist introduces a new member to the group, a man named Victor who recently lost his wife of nearly thirty years to a heart attack. Baker thinks the man looks familiar, and once the new-comer starts talking he knows why. Therapy isn't new to Victor. Until recently, he's been in counselling for his obsessive-compulsive disorder, but his therapist recommended group sessions to deal with his grief. He doesn't mention the Halloween incident from a few years back, but Baker remembers how eager the man was to confess his role in the accident and his apparent disappointment that he wouldn't be punished.

After the meeting breaks up, Victor approaches Baker. "I know you," he says. "You're the sheriff."

Baker nods.

"I'm the guy who—"

Baker cuts him off. "I remember."

"Terrible thing, that," Victor says. "Terrible. I know people say it was a practical joke, but still. You want to get a cup of coffee? There's a place across the street."

Baker isn't ready to go back to his empty house, so he agrees and follows the older man out the door. Victor exhibits none of the traits of OCD that Baker sees on TV and in movies. He doesn't tap himself three times or turn the light switch off and on and off again or wait until exactly seventeen cars pass before crossing the street. He seems perfectly normal to Baker—as normal as anyone, he supposes.

"Halloween's coming up again," Victor says after they have their drinks and find a table in a quiet corner of the busy shop.

Baker nods. He isn't looking forward to it. He's taken that particular evening off every year since the hit-and-run incident, but he's thinking maybe this year he will work it.

"Sold my car," Victor says. "After Eleanor died. Just couldn't face driving any more."

"How do you get around?"

"Buses are fine. Taxis when I need them."

"And you don't have any issues when you're in a taxi?"

"So long as someone else is driving, I'm right as rain."

Victor has no way of knowing how the mere mention of that word in this context summons an image of the raindrops landing in the boy's staring eyes. Everyone has triggers, Baker has discovered, and he can't expect other people not to accidentally trip one of his from time to time.

Baker tests his coffee, but it's still too hot. "When did it start? Your problem? Were you in an accident?"

Victor shakes his head. "Nope. I've always had it. Ever since I started to drive. No one can tell me why. My therapist helped me manage it, but the only real solution was to stop driving."

Baker takes a sip of his coffee, giving Victor room to continue if he wants to.

"I see him, you know? At night?"

Baker almost chokes on his drink. "What? Who?"

"The boy. The one who vanished."

"What do you mean?"

"He comes to my bedroom door. Doesn't do or say anything. Just looks at me with those huge, unblinking eyes. In that bloody sheet."

"But…," Baker starts, then stops. "You never saw him. Or did you?" His cop radar starts to ping.

"Nope. Just the picture in the paper when they were trying to figure out who it was."

"Describe the sheet to me."

Victor sits up straight and frowns at Baker. "Eyeholes that look like they were cut by a kid. Raggedy, I mean. No mouth. Blood splattered here and here and here." He indicates parts of his body that match exactly what Baker saw. What he continues to see.

"Bad dreams," Baker says.

"Real bad," Victor says. "Real bad," he repeats, as if to himself.

While he's driving home that night, Baker is lost in thought. He keeps coming back to what Victor said. He doesn't believe in ghosts, nor in any sort of afterlife—something his grief counselor attempted to get him to embrace as part of his process—but it's hard to explain what they have both been experiencing.

He's only half paying attention to the road, so he doesn't see the pothole until the last second. He swerves, but one tire drops into it, jarring Baker's bones and rattling his teeth. He swears and, for a moment, his late wife is sitting next to him, chiding him for his language. He smiles, but then he has a thought. He glances in the rearview mirror. Was it a pothole, or had he hit something else? A person, maybe?

He applies his foot to the brake and pulls over to the curb. "Bah!" he says after a few seconds. Victor got under his skin with his obsessive compulsion. There's no way Baker is going to fall prey to that kind of rampant insecurity.

Still, he calls the dispatcher later that evening to see if any incidents were reported.

"Quiet night, Sheriff," Shirley says. "What are you up to?" She means well. After his wife died, she tried to fix him up with a couple of friends, and she still brings him a casserole or a tin of cookies from time to time. Her heart is in the right place. He tells her he's watching the game on TV with a few friends—a white lie meant to make her feel better.

Satisfied by Shirley's report, he hangs up and goes to bed, fully expecting a phantom visitation, but it is a quiet night.

The first snowfall occurs a week before Halloween, but the weather turns mild and pleasant during the final days of the month. The trees are in full autumn color and the streets and sidewalks are covered with leaves. Lou and Ferg try to convince Baker to take Halloween night off, but Baker declines. He doesn't want to sit alone in the house any more. Better to keep busy and forget about kids in bloody sheets. He'd rather spend the night rousting tricksters, sending drunks home or to the county jail to sober up, and responding to calls of suspicious activity on a night when almost everything is suspicious.

The streets are alive with kids in costume. Every now and then, he pulls over to make sure the children are being safe. That they have parental supervision where necessary. That they have their flashlights for when it gets dark. That they cross the streets only at crosswalks. He uses his best Officer Friendly voice and the kids always answer, "Yes, Sheriff."

He responds to a call at a convenience store where the cashier says someone walked out with a case of beer without paying. He records the complaint—the cashier provides a surprisingly detailed description—and makes a note to send Lou after the surveillance video footage.

Back in his cruiser, he feels tension in his shoulders and jaw. He has no reason to be nervous, but he can't shake the feeling that something is wrong. He checks his rearview mirrors and looks all about, but he sees nothing out of order.

The streetlights are starting to come on. As a kid, he remembers Halloween night lasting forever but now he can't wait for it to be over. He should have listened to Ferg and Lou and stayed at home.

Baker is jolted from his reverie by a dull thud. The steering wheel twists to the right and he fights to maintain control. His foot finds the brake pedal and he comes to a halt. He pulls over to the curb and activates his four-way flashers. He types the code into his computer that lets Shirley know he's leaving his vehicle to check on something and gets out of the car. It isn't full dark yet, but he takes his flashlight with him anyway so he can inspect for damage.

He circles the cruiser twice, but everything seems in order. Then he walks nearly a block back toward the convenience store, but he can't identify anything that might have caused the sound of an impact. He checks the median and the ditches, too. Nothing.

After a final pass around of his vehicle, he gets back in and heads toward the shopping center, where much of the evening's activity is taking place. The stores are holding special events and many parents have taken their younger kids there instead of allowing them to trick-or-treat.

A few minutes later, his computer gongs, indicating an incoming message. He glances at the screen. 10-57 on Newcomb Road. *Not again*, he thinks. His mouth suddenly dry, he acknowledges the call and marks himself as responding to the scene. After finding a place to turn, being extra careful to watch out for costumed kids, he heads toward the location of the hit-and-run accident. He puts on his flashers but doesn't activate his siren because traffic is light.

As he drives, he stares into the tunnel of light in front of him. It has gotten much darker in the past few minutes. In his peripheral vision, he sees kids around him everywhere. Some are running along the sidewalk, trying to keep pace with his squad car. He can't imagine where they came from all of a sudden. He doesn't let them distract him from the road, though.

A white sheet flutters off to one side, but he can't look. Won't look. How can they be keeping up with him? He glances at his speedometer—he's going nearly fifty, but still they swarm alongside him, so close that it seems like they're about to reach out and touch the car.

His breathing quickens. Sweat beads on his brow. One of the kids darts in front of the car, blindingly white in his headlights. He slams on the brakes and braces for impact, but there is none. Somehow the youngster flits away. He wants to roll down the window and yell at the kids, but when he looks out the window, he's alone on the street. There are no other vehicles around him and the sidewalks are empty.

He takes a deep breath, wipes his brow, and starts off again toward the accident scene. As he nears the location, he realizes where he's going. It's where he stopped after taking the report at the convenience store. The place where he thought he might have hit something.

He's almost gasping when he arrives, and the car interior feels like it's a hundred degrees. He has prepared himself to see another white-sheeted figure soaked in blood on the side of the road, but this time it's a little girl in a black witch outfit sprawled face down on the median, nearly invisible. If she crossed the street here, a driver probably wouldn't see her.

After checking in with Ferg, who got here ahead of him, Baker wanders back to his car. He gives it another good going over, checking for anything—a scratch, a dent, a piece of straw from a witch's broom—but he finds nothing. But he's sure, anyway. Sure that it was him who hit and ran.

When he thinks of the addition to his nightmares, the absolute certainty that the little boy in the white sheet won't come alone to visit him that night, he puts his head back and howls. His agonized wail blends in with the cry of the approaching ambulance.

CARRYING PRIMAL FIRE

Richard Gavin

As a child I carried Halloween with me year-round. My mind was a cobwebbed attic filled with every manner of ghost and ghoul. But I discovered early on that such interests were shared by my peers during the month of October but not much beyond that. I suppose that for many children, the morbid is a fun but ultimately requisite aspect of a cultural ritual one must endure if one wants a pillowcase full of candy. But for me, Halloween was the one season of the year when the rest of the world felt in harmony with my own obsessions.

Since roughly age five, the eerie and the macabre were a vital component of my life. I believed then (as I do now) in spirits, and horror stories and films were more than a passing interest with me. I was in their thrall, utterly and completely and deliriously. I built monster model kits and dragged my father through every "haunted" waxwork I could find. So whenever the yearly wheel brought Halloween back around, I would be overjoyed.

The first of October always brought about a marked change in my perception of the world. It was as if the very air had become tinted with orange and black. Walking in the streets or around the playground, I could practically smell the painted rubber of monster masks, could almost taste the earthy flavor of roasted pumpkin seeds. The fallen leaves would make hushing sounds whenever they were pushed along by a wind that I knew simply had to have come from a graveyard. Each successive day would thicken this atmosphere, would rarify my anticipation.

I am a child of the 1970s, and in those days Halloween was not the extravaganza that it is today. Department stores would devote perhaps an aisle to decorations and bulk candy. My costumes, however, came not from a retailer's rack but from my mother's sewing machine. *(Dear Mom—I still have the Dracula cape you made for me in 1979.)*

What few decorations my family did own were stored in our basement crawlspace. These consisted mainly of cardboard cut-outs (a skeleton with a mirthful rictus grin, a verdant-skinned witch hunched over a frothing cauldron, etc.) that could be taped to the walls; and a flickering plastic lamp that was molded in the shape of a black cat bracing a jack-o'-lantern upon its arched back.

Though these trinkets were undoubtedly the sort that could be obtained in any discount shop, to me they were masterpieces. The hanging cut-outs were as meticulous as any Gustav Doré illustration and that plastic lamp was a magic lantern. The fact that these talismans gestated out of sight in a darkened cellar for an entire year only increased their power.

Late October schooling would also be invigorated by seasonal activities, such as sing-alongs of the creepy traditional ballad "The Ghost of John" or scribbling in the details of haunted house coloring sheets.

The night of the 31st was of course a whirlwind of sugar, guttering pumpkin fire, and a citywide masquerade. After haunting our own neighborhood, my siblings and I would be driven to the houses of both sets of our grandparents for still more trick-or-treating.

What I recall most sharply from those visits was how strange the everyday sights and sounds of my grandparents' houses felt. I would step out of the cold October night that was bristling with the nearest thing I knew to pagan revelry, only to enter a well-lit living room with its television tuned to some unceremonious program. Watching sitcoms or the evening news on Halloween felt not so much *wrong* to me as…improper. So I would simply tune out the dayside intrusions as best I could in order to wring every last ounce of richness from the Eve of the Dead.

And so the night was observed for several years. But of course, as with all the rites of childhood, Halloween's carven grin began to fade incrementally with each passing year. Adolescence stained trick-or-treating, ghost stories, and Great Pumpkins with a varnish of embarrassment. While the dark fire in my heart was never extinguished, it *was* admittedly reduced to something of an ember as I trudged through those years where childhood is often shed in the manic (and often misguided) pursuit of seeming adulthood.

Sometime around the age of seventeen, I began to develop a much deeper and textured appreciation for how ancient, how vital these darker passions and pursuits were to the human condition. Just as I began to see that many of the macabre classics I still loved reading had deeper philosophical subtexts, Halloween also had its deep and dark history. But how to honor these roots? I was at something of a loss at the time.

By age twenty-one, I was living with my girlfriend (who would later become my wife). We both shared a deep Gothic inclination and because of this we resolved to celebrate our first Halloween together in a manner that was meaningful to us.

After a bit of brainstorming we hit upon the idea of hosting a Halloween soirée, a gathering that was deliberately modeled after the so-called haunted summer of 1816, when Lord Byron played host at the Villa Diodati for his friends Dr. John Polidori, and Percy and Mary Shelley. Through that unseasonably cold, damp summer the guests cloistered themselves in Byron's lakeside retreat, talking, wandering the grounds, and writing original ghost stories.

It was perfect. We selected a circle of our closest friends and mailed out handwritten invitations. They were cordially invited to our home on the 31st of October, but for a price: the cost of admission was a story.

Halloween night arrived, as did our guests in turn. We were all dressed in our "formal blacks." Food and drink were served. Our tiny apartment was aglow with candles and a freshly carved jack-o'-lantern. After convivial discussions, each of us read our story. Some were straightforward tales of horror, others personal accounts of eerie experiences. This was followed by much more food and drink and fellowship.

In the wee hours of the morning, our guests departed, each commenting on how this evening seemed to suggest something larger or more important than a one-off gathering.

We had inadvertently created a fresh tradition. And so it became…

For the next several Octobers, my wife and I played host and hostess to an annual soirée. Each year saw some new faces along with the stalwart ones. And the event became truly multidisciplinary; stories soon also included the unveiling of new paintings or drawings done by our creative friends, original compositions of haunting music were debuted, along with accounts of strange dreams. One particularly memorable year involved reaching back to my *file* (the ancient Irish word for Druid) roots. We extinguished all lights in our house shortly after our guests arrived. On a redbrick altar in our yard, a specially carved gourd sat burning. This represented the primal fire of the Underworld. Privately, we each ventured out to this fire armed with a candle. Each of us focused on a secret (a desire, a fear; whatever each person deemed appropriate) before igniting the candle from the gourd. Then, Prometheus-like, these flames of secrecy were carried back inside to illuminate our gathering.

But like the rites of childhood, few things in adulthood last indefinitely. Life eventually intervened as many of our friends went on to get married and have children of their own.

Halloween remains as important as ever for my wife and I, but we now have the joy of reliving those childhood pleasures as we help our children select their costumes. Every year we prepare a traditional Celtic supper of colcannon and soul cakes prior to trick-or-treating. Every October, my daughter helps me hang the decorations around the house.

Like its celebrants, Halloween seems to continually morph. It assumes ever-stranger forms. It tricks us with new disguises, treats us with fresh pleasures.

The Last Halloween

Ronald Kelly

In the little Tennessee town where I grew up, Halloween was for children. At the age of thirteen, you were pretty much expected to sit it out, hand out candy at the house with the old folks (your parents), or roll the principal's yard with two-ply Charmin. Nowadays, you can pretty much trick-or-treat until you're in your mid-twenties (freaky, but acceptable). Back in the late '60s and early '70s, you would be considered a "juvenile delinquent" if you showed up on someone's front porch with a greasepainted face and one of your mother's spare pillowcases. The neighbors would be ready to call Joe Friday to come and haul you off to juvie hall.

My last real Halloween was in 1972... at least the last one that held all the privileges and benefits of childhood. As it drew near, I knew the end of something special was approaching and it saddened me. For as long as I could remember, Halloween had always been my favorite holiday. The smell of wood smoke in the air, the crunch of autumn leaves beneath the soles of your Red Ball sneakers, and the sense of adolescent community that the sight of dozens of Batmans, ballerinas, and Frankenstein's Monsters roaming from house to house brought. That and the gradually-increasing heaviness of your candy sack taking on loot at each lighted porch or concrete stoop. Yes, it was downright magical… but those who held the Power… the *adults*… the mayor, the school superintendent, the local churches… said it all ended after the big One-Two. The pleasures of trick-or-treating were off limits for those acne-ridden, voice-changing, awkward creatures known as the common teenager.

I knew, for quite some time, that this had been coming. All good things—at least good *childhood* things—must come to an end. First Santa Claus, then the Easter Bunny, then your precious Mr. Potato Heads and G.I. Joes. I was a fighter, though. I wanted to cling to childhood with fingernails anchored to the quick and teeth bared… especially where All Hallows' Eve was concerned. So I decided I would do the last one up right. Pull out all the stops. Gather up enough candy to last me at least until I was twenty.

My brother Kevin and my cousin Donna also sensed my impending doom. Their beloved Ronald, the Lover of Monsters (and Dum-Dums and Bite-Sized Snickers) was making a transition, albeit a forced one. At the beginning of October we got together beneath the big magnolia tree in the back yard for a pow-wow. "Won't you ever get to go trick-or-treating again?" Kevin asked me with a pout. "No," I said grimly. "My time has come. Never again will I darken Old Lady Mangrum's door and hear her say 'Weren't you here an hour ago?' with her hair up in Coke can sized curlers and a Marlboro Light dangling from her lower lip." My confederates, ages eight and ten, still in their youthful prime, hung their heads in sorrow. Then we broke out the cherry Kool-Aid and Vanilla Wafers and partook of our final Halloween communion… and planned that season's festivities.

The following weekend we pooled our allowances and rode to town with our parents (for the entirety of our childhood, the city of Nashville was simply known as "Town," at least to us rural rubes). We endured hair appointments and shoe shopping (a torture unto itself) and finally found ourselves in the hallowed halls of Grants Department Store. While our mothers went to check the prices of cake pans and foundation bras ("unmentionables," to young ears), we loudly invaded the Halloween section of the store.

Grants was the best place to do one's Halloween shopping. The manager must surely have been a child at heart, because it was always decorated with plastic pumpkins, glow-in-the-dark skeletons, and cardboard cutouts of cackling witches and arch-backed black cats that looked as though they had stuck their claws in a light socket. The candy aisle with its three-pound bags of suckers, bubble gum, and candy bars was always fully stocked, enticing us with the sugary bootie to come. But the best thing about Grants' Halloween section was the costumes. For the little kids there were costumes in colorful cardboard boxes with clear windows with the masks of monsters, astronauts, and hollow-eyed princesses staring blankly through. Folded underneath those disembodied faces were silk-screened body stockings of shimmering polyester; the type that would make an Eskimo sweat and were, thank God, patently FLAME-RETARDANT!

We weren't interested in the baby stuff, though. We were interested in something else entirely. Grants had a long wooden bin that was perhaps six feet long by four feet wide… filled nearly two feet deep with rubber masks. Every sort of goblin or ghoul, werewolf or devil, could be found in that treasure trove of limp and garishly-painted latex. They were substandard in workmanship by today's standards, but back then they were wonderfully creepy works of art. With total abandon (and ignoring our mothers' forewarnings of "Don't you DARE try on those germy things!"), we picked through the heap of leering, grinning, fang-bearing rubber, trying on each and every one. Thinking back, I can still smell that powdery latex odor; feel the disorienting, but delicious, claustrophobia of staring through sagging eyeholes at the muted brilliance of Grants' overhead fluorescent lights, and the sensation of the mask cutting into the back of my head. For a moment, you were transformed. No longer human, but belonging to a time-honored fraternity of the grisly and ghoulish, hunted by torch-wielding mobs and cross-bearing Van Helsings in the mountainous wilds of Transylvania.

After the hunting was over, our choices were made. Mine was a pale-faced, widow-peaked vampire, fangs dripping with blood. My brother chose a leering, red-faced devil… then changed his mind and picked a werewolf when I convinced him that our conservative, Christian mom would never allow him to walk the length and breadth of Sunnyfield Drive bearing the unholy countenance of Satan. Cousin Donna opted for a different approach, shunning the latex and going with one of those bizarre transparent masks that showed a hint of your true face, while adding the benefit of bushy black eyebrows and mustache, or bee-stung lips the color of fire engine paint. She chose the Marilyn Monroe look and was certain that her mother would be more than happy to dye her hair platinum blond to complete the ensemble. Personally, I was doubtful that that would take place. My aunt Hazel was a bit more free-spirited than my mother, but I couldn't see her going down to the local Woolworths to buy a box of bleach-blonde Clairol to fulfill a ten-year-old's Halloween fantasy.

We left Grants satisfied, with masks and a couple of life-sized glow skeletons (if you can call five foot tall "life-sized") in hand. The first step of the planning and execution of my Last Halloween had been completed. But there was work still to come.

B efore I was a writer, I was known as an artist. Ever since I had scrawled my first Fred Flintstone and Touché Turtle on my stand-up blackboard at the age of four, family and friends honored me with distinction of being "the little boy who could draw."

It was no exception that October. I was on fire with artistic inspiration. Many a sheet of wide-ruled notebook paper fell victim to pencil-drawn renderings of the Wolfman, the Mummy, and my favorite, the Creature from the Black Lagoon, as well as assorted bats, rats, cats, and spiders. Perhaps I saw this as my last-ditch effort to purge myself of every Halloween image imaginable and share them with my friends. After all, that time the following year, I would see no jolly jack-o'-lanterns or grinning skeletons upon my classroom wall. Instead there would be boring charts of the food group pyramid, the American presidents (from Washington to Nixon), and the cryptic Table of Elements.

One drawing I was particularly fond of that year was a profile of a withered man with one bulging eye, a rat-gnawed ear, and a protruding chin sporting three ingrown hairs. The coup de grâce was a large ten-penny nail that had been driven through the bridge of his crooked nose. I was particularly proud of that addition. I could imagine that the Lunch Lady had put it there with a ball-peen hammer for the crime of not finishing his green bean casserole… or that he had done the piercing himself; a sideshow geek who had mutilated his Durante-sized schnoz for the enjoyment of the paying crowd.

That drawing was the most popular of my Halloween gallery and, before long, every boy and girl in my seventh grade class was requesting a copy to hang on their front door for Halloween night. Being the congenial and agreeable lad that I was, I readily agreed… but it was a daunting task. There were no office copiers in that day and age, only primitive mimeograph machines with royal blue ink so toxic it would give a paper bag full of airplane model glue a solid run for its money. So I set to work and hand-drew 32 of the one-eyed, nail-pierced geeks for my grinning classmates. Even the class bully wanted one. Inspired by his reign of terror, I added a word balloon hovering above the geek's snaggle-toothed mouth that pleaded "Here's my lunch money. Please don't hurt me!" The elementary school equivalent of Josef Mengle thought this was absolutely hilarious and so I was spared a purple nurple or an Indian rope burn (of my choice) for the following week.

After school, I would go home and continue the planning of my final trick-or-treating campaign. Since I was going as Count Dracula, I wanted my outfit to be as authentic as possible. I had no flowing black cape—there was none to be bought back then, to my knowledge—but my father did have a long, navy blue overcoat that hung loosely and dangled past my knees (giving me sort of a Dark Shadows/Barnabas Collins look). I convinced my mother to let me wear my white Sunday shirt and necktie, but there would be no slacks or patent-leather shoes to complete the illusion of undeadness. This was a definite setback. Who would ever believe the dreaded Nosferatu would terrorize the countryside wearing blue jeans from the boys' department at Sears and ratty basketball hightops?

Hours turned into days, days into weeks, and soon Halloween came to the picturesque town of Pegram (population 705). The weatherman had predicted rain, but our prayers apparently reached the Big Guy's celestial ears and the storm clouds held their bladders until well after nine o'clock. It was a chilly evening, blustery, sending dead leaves skittering across the streets like an exodus of withered, brown spiders. Kevin, Donna, and I donned our alter-egos and prepared for the "festival of groveling and begging," as my curmudgeonly Grandpa Kelly called it. We had our costumes satisfactorily in place (Donna with a fancy silk scarf wrapped around her head rather than the hair-sprayed helmet of platinum blonde tresses she had formerly envisioned).

Mama was in the kitchen, preparing her largest mixing bowl and filling it with black and orange peanut butter kisses (the standard candy giveaway at the Kelly household). She mugged a mock expression of terror as we paraded past in our garb. We had no plastic pumpkins or Halloween-themed bags to carry with us, so we went to the cabinet beneath the sink where Mama kept her spare grocery bags. We found three good-sized Kroger bags and, appropriating scissors, cut oval handles in the opposing sides. There were no "Pubic" grocery stores (as Aunt Wanda calls them) during that day and time; only Kroger, A&P, and good old reliable Piggly-Wiggly.

"Y'all be careful," Mama called to us as we started for the front door. Daddy sat in the living room, listening to George Jones on the big console stereo. He threw up his hand and grinned. We waved back and headed into the October night, the nasal tones of The Possum crooning "He Stopped Loving Her Today" drifting lazily behind us.

Now, you must understand; this was a different time. It was 1972. There was none of the fear of abductions and child molesters like there is today. Parents didn't follow their children around in cars and there was no such thing as trick-or-treating at the outlet mall or trunk-or-treat in the parking lot of the local church. Kids still had room to breathe and be kids, and one of the freedoms they enjoyed was venturing fearlessly into the night and trick-or-treating on their own.

I had secretly hoped for a full moon that evening—like any respectable vampire should—but if it was there, it was hidden behind a broad mat of dark clouds. We did our street first, going down one side, then back up the other. Although the temperature was hovering between the high 50s and low 60s, my rubber mask became sweltering. I began to sweat like a hog in a sauna and my frightening visage began to shift on me. I was leaving the McDowell house and heading across the yard, when the eyeholes of my vampire mask lost their alignment and, suddenly, I was as blind as a bat (no pun intended).

Suddenly, without warning, there was no ground beneath my feet. I took a spill and rolled into a drainage ditch. Fortunately, only my pride was hurt. I removed my mask and saw my brother and my cousin staring down at me. "What are you doing in that ditch?" Kevin asked me.

"Remind me to pound you one when I get out!" I snapped.

There was one casualty to my fall in the ditch; my Kroger sack had split down the middle and the majority of the candy inside had scattered, like shrapnel from a detonated grenade. "Get your bottoms down in here and help me pick this stuff up," I told them (we didn't say "ass" or even "butt" back then; my mother said it was a 'vulgarity' and if she ever heard it cross our lips, we'd be walking the woods, picking our own switch).

Soon, we had the candy gathered and accounted for, bundled in the remains of the mangled bag. I couldn't help but moan when I saw that the next stop was Old Lady Mangrum's house. I slipped my mask back over my head, made sure the eyeholes were properly in place, and then we headed up the porch steps.

Old Lady Mangrum had no curlers in her hair that night, but the cigarette was there, as well as a suspicious look in her eyes. She examined my brother's costume closely. "Didn't I give you candy a half hour ago?" she asked. "I know I saw a dog like you come up here." He was muffled, but I could hear the disdain in his voice. "I'm a werewolf."

When it was my turn, I held up my bag. "Do you have any Scotch tape?" I asked. She told me to wait and then returned with a J.C. Penney shopping bag. It was big and roomy and would have held a bulldozer battery. "Thanks!" I said as I transferred my candy. Maybe my luck was turning for the better. This was, without a doubt, the Cadillac of Halloween bags.

We ended up trick-or-treating across the entire town of Pegram, which is no mean feat, since it is scarcely a half mile from entrance to exit. We had no watch to tell the time, but we knew it was getting late. My last Halloween was slowly winding down.

Before we headed home, we decided to visit one more place. It was pretty ordinary; a ranch-style house with white brick and a big picture window in the front. There was a jack-o'-lantern on the porch and black and orange crepe paper draped from the banisters. Thinking it was a safe bet, we mounted the porch and knocked on the door.

A lady appeared; tall, skinny, with a beehive hairdo that had gone out of style with the Johnson Administration. She seemed excited to see us. "Come in, come in!" she urged. "I have something to show you!" Her enthusiasm was a little disturbing, but we went in anyway. I don't know why, but we did.

The living room was dimly lit and there were candles everywhere; on the end tables, the fireplace mantle, on the bar counter of the kitchenette nearby. "Come here!" the woman beckoned with a bony finger. "He wants to talk to you!"

Suddenly, a creepy feeling ran down my spine. *He? Who is he?*

Then we stepped further into the living room and we knew. It was a man—a pretty overweight man, perhaps 300 pounds or more—sitting in a reclining chair, dressed in a wife-beater undershirt, flannel pajama pants, and bedroom slippers. But that wasn't the odd thing about him. His pudgy face was painted up like a clown and he wore a huge multi-colored wig on top of his head. He smiled lopsidedly at us and waved his hand. "Come here, kids!" he said, laughing sinisterly. "Come here… I have something to give you!"

Cautiously, we crept forward. We were scarcely four feet from the chair when I smelled the odor of beer and perspiration in the air. I saw a Budweiser can on an end table beside him. Looking around, I saw that there were several more sitting on the carpet beside his Lazy-Boy recliner.

"Open your bags!" he urged, still laughing. "Open 'em up and I'll give it to you!"

My brother stared at me with frightened eyes. I'd never seen a lycanthrope look so scared before.

Then the drunken guy in the clown makeup and the rainbow afro dropped foil-wrapped popcorn balls in our treat bags and said "Happy Halloween!"

A few minutes later, we were outside and back on the street. We looked at each other and began to giggle… but there was more relief to our mirth than humor.

"That was so *weird!*" Donna said.

"You've got that right," I said. My heart was still pounding in my chest.

"What are we going to do with *these*?" Kevin asked, holding the crazy clown's popcorn ball in his hand.

We looked at one another, then tossed them in the nearest ditch and started home.

Halfway there, my brother turned to me. "So... you're not going trick-or-treating with us next year?"

"I can't dress up," I told him, "but I can walk with you."

He nodded quietly, then rummaged through his bag for a Bit-O-Honey.

Thinking back, I'm not sure if I ever did. The last Halloween I remember as a child, was the one we shared together in the fall of 1972.

These days I have three kids of my own. One has outgrown the joys and thrills of Halloween (having traded it in for a boyfriend, an iPod, and an Xbox), while two still indulge in the same autumnal rituals I enjoyed as a child.

Things have changed now. Small town Halloweens are similar to the ones I enjoyed, but they have an edge to them now; a constant awareness that things are not always right in our world. I'm always a few steps behind them, making sure they don't step off the edge of a sidewalk, or that they don't stray too close to a patch of darkness between trees or shrubs. I reckon a parent has a right to be overly-cautious in this day and time. There are dangers out there; dangers that were probably there when I was a kid, but not quite so apparent and identifiable.

But they have fun and, through the eyes of their masks and their infectious laughter, I relive the spirit of Halloweens past. Not as carefree and innocent as I once had it, but fun, nonetheless.

And if we end up with popcorn balls given away by demented clowns, we simply toss them in the nearest ditch and go our merry way.

Sexy Pirate Girl

Lisa Morton

The worst Halloween ever.

Annie was locked in her room on Halloween night, an act she thought must surely be one of the most unfair things in the long and miserable history of unfair things. "Christ, Annie," her father had said as he'd closed the door, his hand already on the knob, "you're fourteen. You're too old for trick or treat now anyway."

In the other room, she could hear her mother and father fighting. That wasn't unusual; they fought most nights. Since she'd abruptly sprouted prominent breasts, the fighting had worsened. Tonight she was glad, because it meant they'd be preoccupied with hurting each other and would ignore her.

She opened her window and gently pried the screen away. Their house was, like all the others in their neighborhood, only one story; but a thick, prickly holly bush grew just outside Annie's window. Her parents hadn't seen her with the hedge trimmers yesterday, when she'd cut away the back part of the shrub.

Annie stepped through the window, let her feet touch the ground, and edged around the holly until she reached the patchy lawn. She pushed the window mostly closed (just in case), and sprinted past the garage. On the sidewalks, costumed kids clutching plastic jack-o'-lanterns already half full of treats were parading by, ignoring Annie's unlit house. Of course her parents wouldn't be handing out candy. They were too busy drinking and blaming each other.

She found the side gate, pushed it open, and stepped through. Just beyond was the grate that opened onto the foundation of the house; she pushed it in, and felt for the plastic bag she'd stored there three days ago.

The one that held her Halloween costume.

Annie loved Halloween; dressing up had always made her feel somehow stronger, more confident. She'd been a comic book heroine, a secret agent, a female ninja, a cat burglar. But this year she wanted something different.

She wanted "Sexy Pirate Girl." Because this year, she had breasts.

A year ago, at a mere thirteen, she'd been a scrawny teen who hadn't yet had her first period. Then the blood had come, and not long after that her mother had taken away her training bra and given her an adult brassiere in a C-cup. It had taken some getting used to—suddenly having flesh in a place that had always been flat—but Annie had soon discovered that she could use this new development to her advantage. Boys, especially, stared at her in ways they never had before, and she *liked* it.

So this year, for Halloween, there would be no head-to-toe black leotard, no trench coat or concealing blouse.

Last week, she'd crept off alone, after school, to a seasonal Halloween store. She'd mowed lawns and washed cars and cleaned her parents' bathroom for weeks, she'd filched a few extra bills from her mom's purse and her dad's wallet, she'd saved it all for *this*. She'd seen the costume online, and knew it must be hers, with its low-cut red velvet corset top and flouncy black mini-skirt and naughty thigh-high boots.

She'd paid for it in dollar bills and coins, then taken it home and tried it on once in the bathroom, before her parents got home. She loved the way it barely contained her new curves, the ample expanse of flesh it offered, the wide belt that she hung a cheap plastic scabbard (an extra purchase) from.

She cast aside her t-shirt and jeans, dressing in the dark at the side of the house; she wished she had a mirror, but she'd have to trust that she looked the way she had three days ago. She struggled into the corset top, pulled on the boots, and—lastly—added the belt and scabbard. A few final tugs, a pillow case for pillage, and she was ready.

It didn't matter much to Annie that she would be trick-or-treating alone; even as a young child, her parents had often been too drunk to accompany her. They'd sometimes foisted her off on neighbors, but usually she'd wandered the dark Halloween nights alone, feeling invincible in her costume, experiencing the offerings of candy as rewards for her self-reliance.

She didn't care if she was fourteen, or if the other kids her age were off at parties or haunted houses or home doling out candy instead of receiving it. She wasn't going to give up that empowerment, that one special a night a year when she didn't feel like some barely-tolerated inhuman animal, trapped in the cage her parents dared call a home.

She reached the sidewalk, waited until a tiny vampire count accompanied by a princess and a smiling parent moved past, and turned right, heading for the first house. She barely knew the family who lived there—she thought their name might be Chavez—but they had candlelit pumpkins on the front steps and a grinning paper skeleton taped to the door, so she approached and knocked.

A smiling, black-haired woman in a cheap orange jack-o'-lantern t-shirt answered the door. "Trick or treat," Annie said, holding out her pillow case.

The fortyish woman squinted at her. "Is that Annie from next door?"

"That'd be *Captain* Annie," she answered, trying out what she thought was a swashbuckling accent.

Mrs. Chavez smiled and reached for a candy bowl just inside the door. "Are you out alone tonight, Captain Annie?"

"Aye," she growled.

The woman dropped two fun-sized chocolate bars in Annie's bag. "Well, you be careful…especially dressed like *that.*"

She closed the door.

Annie turned away, slightly disturbed. "*Dressed like that*"? That made no sense. Annie looked great. Was Mrs. Chavez just jealous? That had to be it.

Because she knew none of their other neighbors, Annie went unrecognized at the next four houses. In one, a twentysomething girl had grimaced and told her she was too old, but given her a peanut butter cup anyway. In another, a fat man in a running suit had gazed down at her and licked his lips. "Argggh," he murmured, obviously staring into her cleavage.

That response had given Annie a strange, fluttery sensation. She'd taken the offered candy and turned away with a combination of disgust and excitement.

She reached the end of her block and turned the corner; she was stepping into unknown territory now, sailing untested waters. The evening was growing late, and the number of trick or treaters was starting to thin; Annie saw a woman on the other side of the street blow out the candles in her pumpkins, marking an end to her participation in the night's rituals.

Annie was negotiating the stepping stones leading up to a front door lit by orange lights when she heard a voice say, "Their shit sucks."

She looked into the driveway beside the house, and made out a boy, lounging against the side of a parked car. She stopped halfway up the walk and watched as the boy approached her, stepping into the light. He was maybe a year older than her, a bulky blonde in a letterman jacket, and his eyes darted between her face and her chest. "I should know—I live here."

Annie thought the boy looked vaguely familiar; she might have seen him around school, but she couldn't be sure. Up until now, she'd paid little attention to the other kids in her classes; she had few friends, since she knew she could never bring one to her home.

The boy stopped before her, and leveled his gaze on her features long enough for recognition to hit him. "Hey, you go to my school. Annie, right?"

"Right," she admitted, her pirate voice forgotten.

The boy smiled. "I'm Josh. I think we have English together."

Annie shook her head. "We don't." She wasn't sure if he knew he was lying or was just stupid.

He giggled and shrugged. "You're right, we don't. I just said that because...well, I've noticed you, and I didn't want you to think that was weird."

"You've noticed *me?*"

"Sure," Josh said, as his eyes traveled the length of the deep divide between her breasts.

Annie liked the way he was reacting, and she arched her back, pushing herself out even farther. "What've you noticed, exactly?"

Josh's adam's apple bobbed and he forced himself to look away. "Are you actually out trick-or-treating?"

For the first time, Annie was embarrassed by that fact. "Well...yeah."

"Aren't you a little old for that? I mean, do you want to do something more fun?"

"Like what?"

Josh started down the driveway, heading for the sidewalk. "Come on," he said, waving at her to follow him.

She took a few steps before hesitating, uncertain. "Where are we going?"

Josh grinned, ran back, took her hand and tugged her down the sidewalk. "Just come *on!*"

The feel of his hand on hers was new and delicious, and Annie let him lead her down the street. Her pirate boots had slight heels, and it made her wobble as she ran, struggling to keep up with him. They dodged past the few younger children still out with parents until they came to the end of the street, where a brick wall intercepted the asphalt. Annie wondered what was on the other side as they jogged alongside for several hundred yards. The brick ended, replaced by a wrought iron gate, and she saw what they'd run past:

A cemetery.

The gates were closed with a length of chain and a padlock, but Josh approached and pushed, and the chain gave just enough to allow someone to enter. "You first," Josh said.

"You mean we're going in there?"

"Yeah. Why—you afraid?"

"No." Annie stepped through the opening.

A second later, Josh followed. "This way," he said, leading her a short distance down the main drive, then out over the grass and between the headstones and monuments.

After a few seconds they came to a crypt, squatting beside a table-sized tomb. The crypt was topped by a sobbing angel, the marble edges limned in yellow-gold from a dim sodium lamp high overhead. "Here," Josh said, as he sat on the edge of the tomb, motioning for Annie to join him.

"Why here?"

He shrugged. "Why not?" He reached out, plucked the pillow case from her hand, and tossed it aside.

Annie had to hop slightly to reach the lip of the tomb, and then she was seated beside Josh. Once she was in place, her right arm brushing his left, he turned to her, his eyes again seeking that shadow just above the rim of her corset. "So, Annie...why are you out alone tonight?"

She shrugged. "I like it. I mean, it's Halloween; we're all somebody else, right?"

"Yeah, I guess. Who are you tonight?"

"Sexy pirate girl. I mean, that's what the costume's called."

Josh reached into a pocket and pulled out a small silver flask. "It's a good name. I'm sorry this isn't rum, but maybe you'll like it anyway."

He held the flask out to her. Annie didn't reach for it. "What is it?"

Josh raised it to his own mouth, took a swallow, and grimaced. "Whiskey." He offered it to her again.

She took it, sniffed it. Her nose seemed to simultaneously open wide and shut down in response. If it was a warning, Annie ignored it; she tilted the flask up and took a huge gulp. It went down like lava and made her gasp, but Josh laughed appreciatively.

"Well, all right, pirate girl."

He waited, watching her, and the liquor hit Annie's stomach like a nuclear blast with a radius that went all the way to her brain; the sense of floating, of being intensified, hit her almost immediately.

"Your face just went all red," Josh said, smiling, as he leaned in.

He kissed her, and Annie froze in disbelief. She'd never been kissed by a boy like this; by a complete stranger. At first the sensation was so alien she was paralyzed, as if she were a machine, a computer, whose circuits had been overloaded and shut down.

Josh broke the contact and pulled back. "Don't you want me to kiss you?"

"Sure, yeah, but…I was just surprised, is all."

He smiled. "Just relax," he said, then held out the flask to her again. She took it, downed another gulp. Josh screwed the cap back on and set it on the cold stone of the tomb before leaning in to plant his lips on hers again.

This time she was prepared, and the feeling of his warmth, of his mouth on hers, was less unexpected. The alcohol made it easy to fall into the kiss, and it seemed to go on forever, charging every part of her with jolts of pleasure. His fingers were in her hair, his lips parted slightly, and Annie forgot everything else, everything that was outside of Josh and the kiss.

When they finally parted, both breathless, he said, "That was more like it."

The whiskey was working its full magic on Annie now, and Josh's face was hard to focus on; she wanted nothing but his kiss again, the lovely feeling of dissolving into him. He moved closer, this time his tongue ran along her lips—

And then his hand was on her shirt, clutching hungrily through the fabric of the corset top. Annie pulled back, confused, the alcohol making it hard to understand what had just happened.

Josh didn't remove his hand from her chest. "Don't you want to?"

"Well…I just…you know…"

Josh took her hand in his. "Baby, c'mon," he said, placing it against the bulging fabric of his jeans, "you're gettin' me all worked up here." He leapt down from the tomb and stood before her, removing any possibility of escape.

An alarm signal sounded somewhere in the back of Annie's mind, but it was muffled by whiskey. She wanted to say "no," to push him aside and walk away, but her tongue was too thick to create speech, and she knew she'd stagger if she tried to use her legs.

She didn't like the look on Josh's face now, the way his smile tilted up at the ends without compassion. She especially didn't like it when he undid his pants button and pulled the zipper down. "C'mon," he repeated, angling forward, his hands on her knees.

"No," she managed, a single breathy word.

"'No'?" Josh seemed to consider for an instant…then that feigned concern was gone. "Don't lie—I know you want to fuck me."

He pushed her legs apart.

Annie instinctively tried to close them, but he was strong and she knew where she'd seen him around the school: In the paper, as the football team's star linebacker. He'd taken on two-hundred-and-fifty-pound linemen with those hands.

"Just relax." His voice was throaty as he clawed at her underwear.

Annie was struggling to shove back away from him when a new voice interrupted: "What the hell's this?"

She looked past Josh's shoulder to see two figures approaching. At first she couldn't make them out, as they walked forward, silhouetted, through the cemetery's shadows; then they stepped into a pool of light cast by the sodium lamp, and Annie saw two boys about Josh's age and size. One wore a black hoodie, the other a half-assed costume consisting of butcher's apron and a placard reading "USDA INSPECTOR" on a string around his neck.

Josh saw them, and for a moment he was surprised…then he leered. "Yo, dudes—I thought you'd never get here."

The boy in the blood-stained apron thrust a chin at Annie. "So, what's with this bitch?"

"This bitch, Bobby boy, has had a shitload of whiskey and is ready to party."

Annie found her voice. "Fuck you."

Bobby and the other boy howled.

Josh smacked her. Not hard, but enough to shock her into silence. "That's the idea, dumbass." He wrapped his fingers in her panties, and with one pull had them halfway down her hips.

"Wait, hold on…" said the boy in the hoodie, as he brought out a phone and thumbed through the controls until he found the video camera. He pointed it at Josh and Annie. "We need to document this for posterity. Action!'

Bobby was already massaging his own crotch. "Just cut us in for our share of the treats, right?"

"Hey, bro, we're teammates," Josh said.

As he turned to look back at his friend's camera before continuing, Annie reached down to her side, fingers searching for the plastic scabbard attached to the belt. She found the handle of her makeshift dagger, and when Josh turned to her again, bending forward as he tried to rip her panties away and lower himself onto her, she thrust upward and buried eight inches of well-honed blade in his gut.

Josh's body arched and he uttered a small, strained cry. Behind him, his friends guffawed. "Oh man," said the cameraman, his eyes riveted to the image of his spasming friend on the tiny screen, "did you jizz already, you loser?"

While the others laughed, Annie grasped the knife—the one she'd taken from the kitchen cutting block at home this morning and placed in the cheap plastic scabbard—and twisted it, causing Josh to quiver and finally collapse on her, his strength ebbing with his life.

"Oh my fucking god," Bobby said, nearly doubled over, "you are such a retard."

Annie knew she'd have to move quickly, while they were still laughing. She yanked the knife free, feeling hot blood spray against her bare skin, and pushed Josh's dead body aside. Before the other boys had even stopped braying, she'd jumped from the tomb, moving steadily as adrenaline replaced alcohol. She stabbed the one in the hoodie, plunging the knife into his heart. He dropped, dead before he hit the ground.

Bobby took off running.

He was on the football team, too, and for a second Annie feared he might escape…but then he made the classic victim's mistake, risking a look back at his pursuer. In that interim, he tripped over a memorial plaque set into the grass, and fell, sprawling, screaming.

Annie was on him almost instantly. He had just enough time to turn, hold up his hands, and scream, "No, PLEASE—!" before the knife swung down, severing his jugular. Crimson streams fountained into the air and joined the fake blood on the apron, but Annie didn't pull back; she let it wash over her, confirmation of her victory.

The last blood to hit her was burbled up through Bobby's mouth, spattering her in a shotgun spread of droplets. Bobby died, then, and Annie straightened up, still holding the dripping knife, panting.

When she regained her breath, she went back to where the boy in the hoodie had fallen; she raised one pirate boot and ground his phone beneath it, continuing to stomp long after the picture had fizzled out, until it was nothing but electronic rubble. She went to Josh then, and used his letterman's jacket to wipe the flask clean. Just for good measure, she also ran the felt-covered arm along the granite top of the tomb. She knew she'd probably left some DNA, maybe even a print somewhere, but she wasn't in any databases yet, so it should be all right.

Of course her parents would know when they saw the news tomorrow. They'd figure out the window and put bars over it. They might even make good on their threat to send her away, to "some place where they know how to deal with people like you." She'd probably find herself stuck in a ward with guys who openly jerked off while they stared at her beautiful new breasts.

But, as she wiped the knife clean, returned it to the scabbard, and prepared to head home covered in blood that would barely be noticed on this one night, she didn't care. It had been completely worth it.

The best Halloween ever.

Monster Night

Brian James Freeman

Like every Halloween Jonathon could remember in his short life to date, his mother had spent the weeks leading up to the big day making his costume by hand.

When Jonathon asked his mother why everyone wore costumes to go trick-or-treating, she said the costumes helped little kids blend in with the real ghouls and goblins that walked around on October 31st.

"If the kids look like the ghouls and goblins," she explained, "the ghouls and goblins won't know the kids are really just kids!"

This made sense to Jonathon, but his friends had costumes their parents bought at the Party City store in the strip mall at the edge of town. Would the ghouls and goblins be able to tell he was human?

"No," his mother patiently replied, "A costume made by loving hands has extra special protective powers."

That also made sense, although Jonathon had once overheard a neighbor say his mother simply liked to keep busy this time of year because a drunk driver had killed Jonathon's daddy on Halloween night five years ago. Jonathon was too young to remember his father, but he understood his mother was lonely.

Jonathon wished she could be happy. Sometimes she was sadder than sad like when the bad person broke into their house a few weeks earlier. Jonathon and his mother had arrived home from a trip to Dairy Queen for vanilla ice cream cones to discover the kitchen window had been smashed. Their television and all of the change in the swear jar was gone.

His mother had cried a lot in the days that followed and nothing Jonathon did to cheer her up seemed to help.

Jonathon's mom had been a little happier the year before because she found a new friend named David, but that didn't last long and David didn't come around anymore.

Jonathon thought maybe they had a *fight*. He hoped it wasn't about him.

His mother hadn't liked how David came to the house so late at night sometimes. David would smell funny and talk too loud and Jonathon's mother would say, "Don't wake Jonathon," because she didn't realize Jonathon was already awake from the noise.

Jonathon also knew that his mother didn't like some of the things David told him.

David had been the one who told Jonathon about the Pumpkin Eater.

The Pumpkin Eater wasn't someone who ate pumpkins, as the name might suggest, but was instead a giant living pumpkin who ate *little boys*.

In their sleep.

In their beds in their darkened bedrooms.

This monster pumpkin pulled itself out of the field and dragged itself across the land and devoured those too small to defend themselves.

David said the Pumpkin Eater was awakened every October by people taking away its friends to carve them into jack-o'-lanterns. This angered the Pumpkin Eater, who then roamed the town every night seeking revenge, not returning to the field until Halloween was over. There it would sleep until the next October came around.

Jonathon believed the Pumpkin Eater had to be real. An adult had said it was, after all.

That was why thoughts of the Pumpkin Eater were gnawing through Jonathon's mind as the cold October wind howled against the side of the house.

He should have been asleep hours ago, but Halloween was tomorrow and the Pumpkin Eater was out there right now.

Lurking. Waiting. Hunting.

Jonathon's bedroom was on the second floor of the house, right next to his mother's, and that should have made him feel safe, but what if the Pumpkin Eater found a way inside?

The light of the big full moon passed through the skeleton branches of the lonely tree in their backyard, projecting bony shadow fingers through the window of Jonathon's bedroom.

These fingers crawled across his walls.

They waved, they shook, and they trembled.

"Go away, Pumpkin Eater," Jonathon whispered, his blankets pulled to his chin, his tiny fingers clenched tightly. "Leave us alone and don't come back."

Tomorrow was October 31st. After that the Pumpkin Eater would return to the fields to rest for another year.

Just one more night and Jonathon would be safe.

The children at school the next day couldn't contain their excitement. Most of the teachers couldn't, either. Halloween brought out the little kid in everyone.

The best part of the day was the school's annual Halloween parade.

It was a *big* deal.

The parade was also the first time Jonathon got to see his costume. In the weeks leading up to the 31st, his mother worked in her room in secret after he went to bed. She said the costume had to be a surprise or it would lose its protective powers.

Jonathon would lie in bed and listen to the hum of the sewing machine making stitch after stitch. The heavy sewing machine sat on a table at the foot of his mother's bed and Jonathon knew she lost a lot of sleep trying to get his costume just right.

When the time of the parade arrived, Jonathon and his classmates happily made their way to the cafeteria where their parents waited with their costumes.

When Jonathon passed through the double-doors of the cafeteria, he began searching for his mother.

At first he couldn't find her.

His heart sunk a little—had she forgotten?—but then he spotted her standing in the corner, holding a big black trash bag.

Jonathon rushed to his mother, waving and smiling. He hugged her.

She smiled and pulled his costume from the bag.

He felt the smile melt from his face. He knew his mother saw his disappointment, but he couldn't help himself.

She held a pumpkin costume as big as the biggest pumpkin they had ever seen in the farmer's field outside of town.

The costume was round and made of soft velvet. There were thick black stripes, a brown stem, and a traditional jack-o'-lantern face stitched on the front.

Narrow eyes holes had been made so he could see where he was walking.

The costume reminded Jonathon of the Pumpkin Eater so much that he found it to be *terrifying*.

Jonathon saw the look on his mother's face and he forced a smile, and his mother did her best to smile back, but he knew she was heartbroken.

That made him heartbroken, too.

Jonathon kept smiling as his mother draped the costume over his head.

He felt like he was being smothered. The costume was heavy and he had trouble walking, but he told his mother he loved it.

As Jonathon marched through the school with all his happy friends, he felt a deep sadness unlike any he had ever felt before, not even when their television was stolen or the many nights he had heard his mother crying through the bedroom wall.

Why did he have to be a giant waddling pumpkin that reminded him of his worst nightmare when all of his friends got to dress up like something fun?

That evening, as the lingering shadows reached across the neighborhood and a chilly breeze blew between the trees, the trick-or-treating hour drew closer and the butterflies of anticipation were a nervous wreck in Jonathon's stomach.

His mother helped him get ready and this time he was certain he had done a better job of convincing her he loved the costume.

He had decided it didn't really matter what his costume looked like as long as he got to go door to door with his friends collecting candy and having fun.

That was what the night was all about.

Once Jonathon was ready, his mother walked him to a neighbor's house where he met up with several of his friends. They were dressed as vampires and werewolves and zombies and Superman and Batman and Harry Potter.

Some of his friends had fancy decorated sacks for their loot, but Jonathon carried a generic plastic pumpkin with a black plastic handle. He hoped it was big enough for all of the candy he would be hauling home. His plan was to have enough to get him through Thanksgiving, which was when the Christmas cookies would be made.

Jonathon and his friends were off to the races, trying to make it to as many houses as they could before trick-or-treating officially came to an end at eight o'clock.

Although his mother and the other parents were trailing close behind, Jonathon barely noticed them as he rushed from door to door, knocking and waiting and then yelling, "Trick-or-treat!" as the door opened and some adult—sometimes an adult like a grandparent, sometimes an adult the same age as their parents, sometimes a bored teenager who wasn't technically an adult yet—distributed pieces of factory wrapped candy.

Most people gave you one piece, some people gave you two, and a few of the great houses let you select a piece of candy of your choice out of a plastic bowl.

All in all, though, the best house on the block was Doctor Brown's house. Mrs. Brown let you take your pick from a fancy crystal punch bowl filled with *full size candy bars.*

When given the choice, Jonathon always grabbed a Butterfinger because they were his favorite.

As he and his friends hurried from house to house, Jonathon couldn't help but wonder who among them were the real ghouls and goblins.

He knew his friends were okay, and their parents were okay, but this was the one night of the year when there were more strangers than friends on their street.

He didn't recognize many of the monsters carrying sacks of candy around his neighborhood. This worried him and made him nervous, but he knew his costume would protect him from the real monsters, just like his mother had said.

Like every previous year, his mother was right.

By eight o'clock, Jonathon arrived home safe and sound. Front porch lights were turning off across the neighborhood and the streets were almost empty again. Forgotten or discarded costume accessories dotted the lawns and sidewalks.

Jonathon's mother helped him out of his costume and she carefully hung it in his closet. She took ten minutes to inspect his candy before giving him his choice of one piece for a pre-bedtime snack. He selected a Butterfinger, of course.

Twenty minutes later, Jonathon was lying in bed, happy and content to think about all of the candy his mother had stashed on the high shelf in the kitchen to dole out to him over the next few weeks.

He hoped no one would break into the house and steal his candy, but he also knew that wasn't the worst thing that could happen.

It was still Halloween and there were still real monsters out there.

A few hours later, minutes before midnight, Jonathon couldn't tell if he was awake or asleep. He thought he might be awake. He certainly felt awake, but on the other hand, dreams could be tricky.

A few months earlier, he had been sure he was riding a horse with the knights of King Arthur's round table, but that had ended up being a dream, which disappointed him greatly upon waking.

Jonathon was about to pinch himself when something thumped on the side of the house.

He slowly turned his head in that direction and he couldn't believe what he saw.

Pumpkin vines slithered across the window glass, highlighted by the big full moon blazing brightly in the night sky.

A malevolent, brown stem rose into view from below the window.

The Pumpkin Eater continued his ascension of the house, rising as if lifted by balloons.

Just like David had warned, the Pumpkin Eater was a pumpkin from the nearby fields, maybe the biggest pumpkin.

Its skin was dark orange and wrinkled. Its eyes were slits that glowed from an angry fire burning within.

The Pumpkin Eater was grinning, too, a most awful grin.

"I've come for you, Jonathon," it growled from beyond the window. "I've come to split you open and eat your pulp and your seeds!"

"No," Jonathon whispered as he pulled his blankets above his head. "Please leave me alone. I told you not to come here again."

Jonathon heard the window smash.

The Pumpkin Eater was inside his room, slithering across the floor.

The vines found Jonathon's covers and pulled them back as the Pumpkin Eater towered over the little boy.

"No, please don't hurt me," Jonathon whispered.

"I told you I'd be back," the Pumpkin Eater said with a trace of sorrow.

One of the vines held a jack-o'-lantern carving tool. The Pumpkin Eater lowered the plastic tool to Jonathon's belly...

...and that was when Jonathon screamed himself awake.

He tumbled out of bed and landed hard on the cold floor. The window was not broken, but the full moon was out there, watching over him like in the dream.

Jonathon's heart was racing and he was disoriented. He heard a gruff voice say something on the other side of the wall where he had so often heard the sewing machine.

"Leave Jonathon alone," his mother answered quickly.

She had never sounded quite like that before, at least not that Jonathon could remember. She sounded terrified.

After a moment, Jonathon understood why: the Pumpkin Eater hadn't come for him. It had come for his *mother!*

Jonathon had to help her and fast. But how could he stop a real life monster? He was just a little boy.

He had no idea how to defeat the Pumpkin Eater, but he had to do *something.*

Just as despair grew inside of him, Jonathon's eyes widened and he realized the answer to his question had been with him all night: *his costume!*

He hurried to his closet where his mother had hung the costume with care. He grabbed the velvet orange pumpkin off the hanger and pulled it over his head, stumbling under the sudden weight.

He gently pushed open his bedroom door, tiptoed down the hallway as quietly as he could, and listened.

"Please, leave me alone," his mother said, her voice trembling.

Jonathon's heart raced a mile a minute and he could only barely see out of the eyes in the costume, but he had no time to waste.

He reached, slowly turned the doorknob to his mother's bedroom and pushed the door open a few inches.

The first thing Jonathon saw through the narrow eyeholes was that the window had been broken, just like in his dream.

But there was no Pumpkin Eater.

There was someone else.

A man stood by the bed, towering over his mother, who wore just her nightgown.

The man held a big hunting knife.

In some ways, this man looked like his mother's friend named David, but his hair was longer and dirtier, his clothes were grimy, and his belly was bigger.

He waved the knife around.

Jonathon's mother was crying.

The man was as scary as any monster Jonathon had ever seen, but he pushed the door open the rest of the way and ran into the room without the faintest idea what he would do next.

He ran on faith, trusting the costume would somehow save the day and protect him from the monster like it had during trick-or-treating.

As the giant pumpkin lurched toward him, the man turned and said, "What the hell?"

The man also sounded a lot like David.

"Jonathon, no!" his mother cried, rolling out of bed.

The man reached for Jonathon and Jonathon realized the man also smelled a lot like David had on some nights when he came to the house way too late. The smell was harsh and pungent as it seeped into the room with every breath the man exhaled.

The man pushed Jonathon off balance, sending the little boy in the giant pumpkin costume rolling across the room.

Jonathon cried out, reaching for anything that might stop his momentum. He smacked into the door, slamming it shut.

The man returned his attention to the bed just as the sewing machine crashed into his face. The sound of the impact was hollow and thunderous at the same time. The man roared in pain.

Through the eyeholes of his costume, Jonathon watched his mother drop the sewing machine, step forward, and push the man through the broken window.

The man screamed again on his way down to the ground, falling past the ladder he had placed there, but the scream ended suddenly with a loud thud.

Jonathon's mother hurried to her son and she rolled him over so he was sitting upright.

"Are you okay?" she asked as she helped him out of the costume again.

"I'm a little dizzy," Jonathon said, rubbing his head.

Jonathon's mother kissed him on the forehead. She was crying.

"That was very brave of you," she said.

"I thought the Pumpkin Eater had come for us. Was that a different monster?"

"Something like that," his mother replied, holding her little boy as tightly as she could.

"It's the worst part of Halloween," Jonathon said. "I can't wait for all of the monsters to go away for another year."

"Me, too," his mother said softly, kissing the top of his head. "Me, too."

SCREAMS IN THE ASYLUM

James Newman

I can recall countless wonderful childhood memories of this holiday we all love. But if forced to pick my favorite Halloween memory, it would be the October 31st of my twentieth year.

Back in the day, a friend and I were asked to help with a haunted house sponsored by our local chapter of the U.S. Junior Chamber, a civic organization for young people. While I admit I wasn't too familiar with the Jaycees' work at the time, it was obviously for a good cause and...we were being asked to work in a haunted house! We were aspiring horror writers who got a kick out of scaring people (the more things change, the more they stay the same; the friend in question happens to be Donn Gash, whose name *Cemetery Dance* fans will likely recognize). If you guessed that we RSVP'd with a "YES!" quicker than a vampire crumbles to dust beneath the first rays of the morning sun, you guessed correctly.

Both of our fathers had been in the military, so Donn and I acquired some old fatigues in order to create for ourselves two really cool "zombie soldier" costumes. Keep in mind that this was decades before every month saw the release of a dozen new DTV "zomedies"; before teenagers didn't spend all their free time machine-gunning undead Nazis in the latest violent video game; back when you could walk into bookstores without seeing titles like *Zen and the Art of Zombie-Killing* on the shelves. I can proudly say that our costumes were original. Plus, most of our fellow volunteers dressed like the anti-heroes of the slasher films that were all the rage back then. On any given night during the attraction's month-long run, you might see a half-dozen hockey-masked killers, or multiple versions of Michael Myers (short, tall, fat, skinny, all brandishing a butcher knife or—inexplicably, to those of us in the know—hefting a blood-spattered battle axe). Donn and I were determined to do something different. Our makeup was as far from professional quality as you can get, consisting mostly of green paint applied to our cheeks and forehead, but our hearts were in it all the way. The baggies of rice we hid in the front pockets of our fatigues were proof of that. When we stuck that stuff in our mouths and it oozed out from between our lips, it resembled masses of wriggling maggots. Disgusting? Sure. But that made it all the more fun.

The Jaycees' haunted house was held every year at an old V.A. hospital, a dilapidated building that the county eventually condemned. What a sublime location for such an attraction! With the exception of breaking windows (due to the possibility of injury to ourselves and others), volunteers were encouraged to do whatever was necessary to create the proper atmosphere: slamming doors and cabinets as if the site were a hotbed of paranormal activity, filling the place with the screams of the damned until our throats were raw and we could scream no more. To those waiting outside in the ticket line, the atmosphere was extremely effective.

There were some who refused, of course, to embrace the experience (begging the question: why were they there in the first place?). A handful in every group. Men who seemingly knew no fear…at least, that's what they wanted their friends to believe.

Sometimes we were able to expose a crack in that façade, if only for a second or two…

We were allowed to stake our claim on any part of the building that wasn't already occupied by volunteers. Donn and I took one look at the area called "The Slaughterhouse" and knew we had found our home base. We positioned ourselves near a small alcove located before a long hallway. Down the corridor, an actor dressed like Leatherface from *The Texas Chainsaw Massacre* awaited his "victims." All night long, the buzz of his Black-and-Decker echoed throughout that floor of the building. What made our vantage point so perfect was the fact that the guide who led visitors through the attraction would stop in the alcove, allowing stragglers to catch up before continuing on through the Slaughterhouse. Donn and I always waited a minute or two, giving everyone in the group just enough time to catch their breath...and then we would stagger forth from the dark doorways on either side of the alcove, moaning and hungry for brains.

More often than not, our patience paid off.

The most satisfying moments I can remember were those when we stood back, watching, patiently waiting, setting our sights on some macho guy who held his quivering girlfriend as he pretended to be unimpressed by everything he had witnessed.

When we got a jump out of that guy...oh, there was nothing better.

The kind of guy who tried to play it off. His kind always tried to play it off. The dude who would push out his chest like a bantam rooster, as if nothing could scare him, and there would be a new strut in his stride as the group went on their way...

...but we knew better. And all his friends did too.

We got that guy good. In fact, Donn and I were quite sure one or two of them pissed their pants a little bit.

How I loved that feeling.

I've been chasing it ever since.

UNDERFOLK

Tina Callaghan

"The dog still hates me."

"The dog doesn't hate you. She's adjusting to the situation."

"The situation. Very diplomatic."

"Which word would you like me to use?"

Which word? Disaster.

The dog did hate me though. She behaved well and didn't lose any of Gary's training but she lay in a corner of the room every night, as far from me as she could get. She always looked like she wanted to snap and she shied away from my attempts to pet her. She found one of Gary's shoes under the bed and kept it, lying with it between her paws, staring at me with her cold eyes. I stopped trying to pet her, but I walked her and fed her. Feeding her made me think of eating at least once a day, which I mightn't have otherwise.

Disaster. I hated him for what he did to me. I wanted to tear at him, scratch and rip and hurt. Of course, according to the priest, he was beyond all pain now. Good for him.

Funny how you could be living a lovely life and not know that you're seconds away from agony. Funny how your husband can kiss you good-bye and leave for work and you lock the door and head in the opposite direction, not knowing you'll see him only once more, for identification purposes. Funny how those lips are almost the only things you recognise. Long and a bit thin but quick to curl into a smile.

"You can make it through this, Maggie."

The cliché. How could anyone know what anything was like for another person? I knew and the dog knew, staring at each other in mutual, but separate misery, disconnected and aimless.

I took a leave of absence from the university, after a meeting where I was left with no other option. There were reports of me sitting in silence at my desk in front of big classes of students expecting Celtic studies. There were classes where I asked the wrong kind of question.

Where do the dead go?

"Where do the dead go?"

"Everyone decides for themselves what they believe about that, Maggie."

"What do you think?"

He looked at me with the same unfeeling eyes as the dog. I knew his answer. I had to figure it out for myself and it didn't matter what he thought. He didn't even care enough to offer me the comfort of belief, or a pretence of it. I should have gone to the priest, not a shrink.

The shops were full of black and orange, monster masks and candy bars. I walked through, almost fascinated by the jollity of strangers. Look at them, happy. It was a mystery, a marvel. They hadn't a clue what they were celebrating; knew nothing of the pagan origins and rituals of the holiday. To me, it was the end of the fertile season, the coming of the darkness. The ritual of fire and of welcoming the dead seemed appropriate. The car crash, the consuming flames that destroyed most of my husband, the feeling that the dead were near, all fit the season. Although

I wasn't sure if the dead were near me, or the other way around. I had shed life and my body just hadn't fallen over yet.

A week before the 31ˢᵗ of October, I threw some clothes in a bag, threw myself and the reluctant dog in the car and drove south. I drove until I came to a beach and the sea. I asked a woman in a shop if there was a hotel nearby but instead found myself in a holiday cottage that the shopkeeper let out to summer visitors. She swept me in, glad of off season money, gave me free milk and bread and sausages and left me to it.

The house smelled of the sea and when I opened the window, gauzy curtains blew in with fresh salt breeze followed by the cry of a seagull. Another cliché, but a better one. The dog sniffed everything in the house and then sat in the middle of the bright, timbered open plan room. She held her muzzle high as if afraid someone would hit her.

"Alright Tess. We'll go for a walk."

We were both used to city streets, urban parks. When she got her pads onto the sand, she seemed surprised and then surprised me by barking and taking off. I almost lost the lead, but managed to hang on, dragged into running. By the time I started to wheeze, she had slowed to a trot. We reached the end of the crescent beach, our feet now paddling in a little placid surf. She looked at me, her mouth hanging open, the cold noble face made friendly by a sideways hanging tongue. Her eyes seemed more golden but the sun had started to set. I risked a stroke of her head and for the first time, she allowed it.

The cottage was set slightly apart from the village, a part of it, but private. Its whitewash was peach colored by the sunset when we got back. I made sausages and shared them with the dog. She ate them and then, remembering that she didn't like me and everything was wrong, went to lie in the corner. I had forgotten to bring the shoe.

I walked every day with the expectation of something happening. I looked at the faces of the other October beach walkers, waiting for conversation or enlightenment or some craziness worse than my own. But everyone was within their own walls.

The sun shone once or twice but mostly it was misty, in that way that makes you think it's raining but it never quite commits. In the mornings, the dog and I came back damp and frizzy to the sea-smelling house and ate sausages and bread. In the afternoons, we walked again for want of anything else to do. On the afternoon of the 31ˢᵗ, Halloween itself, a man appeared on the beach with a little bundled-up boy. The boy cheered when the man threw a kite into the sky and the thin sound whipped away on the wind.

The kite was a monster. A green and red leering melting Halloween face. The dog watched it and her lip curled. We turned into the west wind and walked that way, getting salty.

On the way back, the man was down near the water untangling the knotted line and the boy was in our path, tossing stones. When he saw us coming, he chucked one at the dog and struck her on the nose. She yelped and stopped dead. The boy laughed, a light, bright sound, and weighed another stone in his hand. He looked no more than five or six. His eyes were a pale grey and he blinked seldom. His laughter had faded into a small smile, his soft lips tilting into dimpled cheeks.

The dog pressed against my leg, the first voluntary contact. The boy's hand blurred and the stone flew. It struck me on the head, the impact softened by the hood of my coat. The dog lunged to the end of the lead but I twisted sideways and pulled her enough to stop her reaching him. She started barking, a volley that the wind snatched and tore away.

"You ok?"

The man, suddenly closer, held his tangled kite between his body and us.

"What's wrong with your dog?"

He looked about seventeen, not a man at all.

"The boy hit her with a stone. He hit me too."

"What boy?"

Where do the dead go?

"Where do the dead go, Tess?"

She looked at me, serious face waiting for me to ask another question that she couldn't answer. We sat and looked at the grey sky through the picture window. The kid with the kite was probably still out there. A low pain settled somewhere between my stomach and my back, a miserable grumble that hadn't decided yet which way it would make me sick. The dog stared at me. Her eyes were warmer than usual, honey rather than gold.

A flock of dark birds blocked the grey light. A wheeling, crying mass, one hardly distinguishable from the other, carried on that west wind. I closed my eyes against the sight and instead saw other things in the darkness behind my eyelids. Lambs with their eyes torn out, injured foxes dragging useless hind limbs, babies left out in the garden for fresh air and forgotten, the carrion pickings from a car accident, burnt flesh black and red. And all with the mountain-bleak sound of dark birds squalling.

I opened my eyes and saw a flash of one bird close to the window. It was gone before I could do more than register it, but I imagined I could smell its dusty feathers and see the black shiny eyes considering me.

Zephyros. Greek god, bringer of light spring and early summer breezes. John Masefield wrote about the west wind, a warm wind. Maybe in Greece, but in Ireland, where the west meant desolate fields and nothing but three thousand miles of cold ocean, the westerly meant something different. Keats had it. *O wild West Wind, thou breath of Autumn's being, Thou, from whose unseen presence the leaves dead are driven, like ghosts from an enchanter fleeing, Yellow, and black, and pale, and hectic red, pestilence-stricken multitudes: O thou, who chariotest to their dark wintry bed the wingèd seeds, where they lie cold and low, each like a corpse within its grave.*

That's what this west wind felt like. Wild spirit, destroyer. I looked to the west windows of the house. One was open, carrying in a scent of something strange. I got up to close it. I had told my students often of the Sluagh, hunting the souls of the lost or dying, entering the house from the west on that winter-carrying wind. I pulled the window shut, my skin rising in goose flesh.

The wild hunt, the underfolk, the Sluagh, the name that shouldn't be said aloud. The stories that made up my scholarship. Years of young men and women seeking out sensational mythology alongside their study of culture and anthropology. The classes close to Halloween were popular. Halloween, the Celtic holiday, the holiday of the dead. I encouraged costumes in my lecture hall, allowed the spinning of suspense and delicious thrills, ending with a general laugh of relief. And yet, the west wind, the coming of winter. The underfolk. The host of the unforgiven and unrepentant. Where do the dead go?

The underfolk took the form of great dark birds, perhaps ravens. I looked back at the window. The sky was a blank grey except for one bright seagull riding the first wave of a coming storm.

The dog barked once and someone knocked on the door. For a stupid moment I wanted to hide and wait for them to go away. The dog barked again.

I opened the door. I opened it so that I wouldn't be afraid, forgetting that it's ok to be afraid of a stranger at your door when you're alone.

It was children. Five of them in masks and costumes. A smiling mother stood behind.

"Trick or treat!"

A cheerful chorus but the mother saw my face and her smile faded. I looked for pale eyes but saw brown and blue and green.

"I'm sorry, I don't have any sweets."

She faked a smile and bundled the children down the path and along to the next house, glancing over her shoulder.

"I'm sorry."

I shut the door and locked it.

I sat and watched the night draw in. I saw the birds again in the distance over the sea. Before full dark came, the sky had already darkened with the storm. Out there where the birds were, there were flashes of lightning. Not forks but sheet lightning, a sudden flashbulb going off, filling the sky.

We were in the terminator line. The line that runs across the world, pushing the light away and dragging the night behind it. The sunset was gone and everything was that grey twilight. I stood up. I heard them before I saw them. The rough cries of a great flock. They flew closer to the window this time and there were several thumps against the side of the house. One struck the window and left a greasy mark on the glass. The dog was growling low in her throat, shivers rippling through her. She pressed close to me.

A window smashed upstairs. I picked up a poker from the fire and stood at the bottom of the open timber stairs. There were rustling noises and then the distinct hop of bird claws across the floor. The dog started up the steps, claws scrabbling. When she reached the top, she stopped. All the hair on her back stood up. She started backing away and almost fell. She half skidded down the stairs and came to me.

When I looked up, the bird was standing on the top step. It was tall and thin, with an ugly bare beak. Its greasy plumage was black and ragged. The eyes were sharp and shiny. I reacted to its presence in the house, a dark smear against the bright timber. I threw the poker and it flew like an arrow and missed its target. The bird looked at it and hopped down a step towards me.

The window thumped and rattled behind me as something struck it. I looked around and the railing was full of birds, sitting, staring. As I watched, another flew forward and struck the glass. I think I made a sound then, some wretched caught-in-the-throat cry. It sounded like someone already lost. When I turned back, the bird was on the bottom step. Its head was cocked, watchful, speculative. I hated it. I suddenly wished I had made a fire, as the stories said I should. A fire to warm the beloved dead come to visit on this night. But there was no way back for the good. No way to call them from rest, even if you wanted to disturb that state. The unrestful were here instead.

I hated to take my eyes off it, but I needed a weapon of some sort. I backed away first, putting the chair between me and it. The dog came with me, stuck to my side. I didn't blame her for fear. My own hair was trying to stand up, my brain stem trying to tell me to run. But with the flock outside, flight didn't seem an option. Fight was all I had left. When I got close enough to the fireplace, I glanced sideways, thinking there was a fire shovel that would do.

The boy was there, his pale eyes happy and full of mischief. He clapped his hands and the flock outside rose briefly and settled again. I heard their wings and the impact of their mass coming back down on the railing. Behind the boy, a figure moved. A woman drifted into the room and wandered towards the bird. She had her eyes closed and moved as if she was swaying to music. As soon as I had the thought, I heard it. A strange lullaby. The boy followed her, grasping towards her skirt, but always missing. I grabbed the shovel and lunging without thinking, smashed at the bird. It caved beneath the impact. I saw a burst of blood and other material, but it puffed into dark powder that smelled of bird dander and fell into a stain on the floor. I leapt backwards and stood against the wall.

Something was there in the bird's place. I squinted my eyes and let them unfocus and that way, I saw it. Birdlike, tall, thin, ragged, something human about it, but corpselike, destroyed. It looked at me with dark shiny eyes and it was the Sluagh.

I thought of my father. He recovered from double pneumonia only to sit with his own father, dying far too young. He talked of it often. A room, silent but for the sound of a ticking clock. He sat and waited for death to come. Waited for that moment when the breath left and the body immediately looked like a wax figure. How the departure of the spirit was so obvious. I suppose he put the question in my mind, as it was in his.

Where do the dead go?

I looked at the unrepentant dead. It began to close the distance between us. The Sluagh is never satisfied with its number. It always wants more restless souls to join its ranks. I had called it to me in my misery but seeing it come for me, some scrap rose up inside. Some other Maggie, who just wouldn't quit. I hated her too. If she would let me quit, I could go to Gary. I called the Sluagh because I wasn't able to end my life but that other Maggie just wouldn't let go.

The dog moved from my side. She was staring at something else in the room. I was afraid to look away in case the Sluagh would be right beside me when I looked back, but I couldn't help it. The dog was making little sounds like whimpers and her tail thumped off my knee.

Gary was in the room. I could see him more clearly than the Sluagh but he was less solid, less present than the boy and the swaying woman had been. His thin lips curled in the smile I knew. He raised his hand in some gesture I didn't understand but the dog did. She turned with a snarl and leapt at the Sluagh. She should have passed through it, but contact with it made it more substantial somehow. She ripped and tore at its thin throat and I heard it scream, a thin sound that made me think of ambulance sirens, blood on the road, the cold of the morgue. It tossed her sideways, its throat open and spilling ichor. It lunged at me and I stuck my nails in its face. I didn't want to die. For a moment, the insistent scrap of Maggie within took charge and I didn't want to die. I felt the Sluagh's eyeballs puncture under my fingers and the dog grabbed the creature from behind and pulled it away from me. She shook her head and the thing came apart. The dog was left with a piece of spine in her jaws and she dropped it. It clattered when it hit the floor.

Outside, the sound of flight came again as the host rose into the sky. Normal thunder rolled and the flash of close lightening blinded me. When my sight cleared, the dog and I were alone in the room.

I could smell them still. The boy with the pale eyes. The swaying woman, the bird, the Sluagh. Gary. A tiny hint of him was still there. Not aftershave, or cologne. Just that smell that everyone has when you know them. The scent that a house takes on when it's lived in, every one different.

I went out onto the street. There were people about, some in costume, some not. They were looking at the sky.

"Did you see it?"

The kid with the kite was there, without his kite now.

"What? What did you see?"

He looked at me, his eyes clouded.

"It was…"

He looked around at an older man.

"Was it a tornado?"

The older man shook his head.

"A tremor."

"A lightning strike."

There was no answer. People drifted away rather than face the unanswerable. The street cleared of masks and costumes and the kite kid looked at me. His eyes were pale.

"Where do the dead go?"

Where do the dead go?

Not far. Restful or unrepentant. Not far.

Pumpkin Parade

Sèphera Girón

The smell of burning pumpkins always triggers me back to Halloween. There is a distinct charred, spoiled-vegetable aroma from candles flickering inside of jack-o'-lanterns that instantly reminds me of trick-or-treaters parading up and down the streets, stores crammed full with shrieking, flailing animatronics, Black Cat licorice gum, orange-and-black-wrapped molasses kisses, and disembodied sinister grins glowing in the darkness. Distinct memories of Halloween season include the carving of the pumpkins and the fearful yet compelling anticipation towards the big night itself.

When I was a kid, my brother and I were in charge of digging out the pumpkins with metal spoons, emptying them of their innards, scooping and slopping until the inside shell was smooth. The smell of the raw pumpkins guts and the stringy, spider-webby pulp that wrapped around my little fingers like seaweed grabbing my ankles in the ocean disgusted me, but this ritual was part of Halloween so I couldn't complain much.

My brother and I sat on spread-out newspapers, avoiding touching the cold, slimy mess as much as possible. Of course, little kids gingerly scooping pumpkins with metal spoons inevitably ended with someone getting guts or seeds on them. It was an accident of course, but the next thing I knew, we were flinging pumpkin guts, seeds, and all at each other. Squeamishness was abandoned as a battle of pumpkin entrails escalated between brother and sister.

There's something kind of gross about sitting in bathwater with pumpkin smeared across your face, orange wormy strings and the odd seed floating around you while your mom tsks at you with a soapy wash-cloth. I guess that should teach me not to torment my little brother with pumpkin guts…but it didn't.

One of the pumpkin rituals usually dictated that Dad carved the face and then Mom carefully placed the candle inside while my brother and I chattered excitedly about what we wanted to be for Halloween. Back in the sixties and seventies, most costumes were homemade or there were creepy plastic masks that cracked easily or had an elastic band with a metal bit that snapped off and stung me in the head or face or ear without warning. No one could breathe in those musky masks, and of course, hiking all around the neighborhood meant smelling my own sweat and sour breath while being barely able to see where to go. I could tell when I was nearly at the door by the smell of the burning jack-o'-lanterns.

Of course as the years rolled on, it was decided that perhaps masks should be created with large eyeholes so that one can see out of them, that costumes move towards becoming somewhat flame retardant with more creative fabrics, and that pumpkins could also be transformed into artistic creations beyond a couple of jagged eyes and a big toothy mouth.

But back then, I spent many a Halloween sweating through my painted plastic mask with the tiny eyeholes, holding the hand of a parent or brother, the other hand lugging my pumpkin basket, heavy with goodies. Some years, it was freezing cold and we had to fit our winter coats under our vinyl-plastic-body-tied-at-the-back-of-the-neck superhero or whatever suits. Lots of rips and crying ensued. One year when the skies decided to pour buckets of rain so that my real costume was impossible to wear, I made the bold move of donning my red fall jacket and carried a wooden-handled-apple-carton-basket, painted red circles on my cheeks and skipped around as Little Red Riding Hood.

The jack-o'-lanterns were the key markers for the night. If a porch had a lit jack-o'-lantern, it was supposed to indicate the family was home and ready to give out candy. If the pumpkin wasn't lit, we had to walk on by.

As the decades went on and people became more creative with the pumpkins, we determined that there was also a correlation between how cool was the carved pumpkin and the quality of candy being doled out. More than one fancy carved pumpkin in some kind of determined display might even signify a full-size candy bar. Sinister jack-o'-lanterns, especially ones that lined the sidewalks up to the house, were often signifiers that the homeowners got into Halloween and might even jump out at us or have creepy, hanging, blinking things in the front entrance or even the trees. Sound effects were a double bonus.

When I was a kid, I was a scaredy-cat. No question. For many years, a few days before Halloween, after I'd book-worm my way through the evening, I would be just dozing off when my door would slowly creak open. I'd sit up, pulling the blankets over my mouth as an "oooohing" noise filled the room. A scary jack-o'-lantern would enter, emitting scary noises, the candle flickering, the burnt pumpkin smell filling my room. I 'd scream and giggle and sometimes run to my brother's room and excitedly wait for the creepy pumpkin to taunt us there, too. In some ways, my dad tormenting us with the pumpkin was scarier than anything I saw trick-or-treating. You just never knew when the Great Pumpkin was gonna show up. In your bedroom.

The day after Halloween was always sad. There was usually at least one casualty, and sometimes many on our street. Smashed jack-o'-lanterns in the road or on lawns with their faces kicked in, candles crushed, their burned crushed cooked squashy smell mixed with leaves emitting from the damp earth as it almost always rained or snowed Halloween night. It was depressing to see the once enticing decorations destroyed so brutally.

The jack-o'-lanterns who survived Halloween hooliganism often sat on the porches or lawns, waiting for their next night of glory. Instead, their fate was comprised of shrinking and collapsing in on themselves, flies buzzing around them, rotting back into the earth from whence they came. Others were tossed into garbage cans or compost pick-up. As a kid, it struck me as almost callous that these pumpkins that had been pinnacles of the season were so quickly discarded, as a cheater discards a lover, yet that was the circle of life. And death. Just like the Christmas trees. Used for one spotlight moment and then forgotten. I used to feel sad for them, too.

As an adult, I created my own pumpkin rituals with the kids. I figured by having two sons that I would never have to touch pumpkin guts again. I was wrong. They wouldn't touch the pumpkin guts. Ever. So I had to disembowel the pumpkins myself while the boys booed with gleeful disgust. They each had their own mini-gourd to carve themselves with safety knives and then there was a big mama pumpkin as well.

Now the kids are grown and pumpkin rituals continue on with or without me.

This year since I had no place to put a pumpkin, I didn't carve one at all. I'll admit, it was because I didn't want to touch the pumpkin guts, or smell them. I have lots of decorative jack-o'-lanterns I've acquired over the years so they were displayed around the apartment.

For several weeks before Halloween, I noticed small signs around my neighborhood that piqued my curiosity. Several local stores and bars also displayed the sign in the front windows. They were on bus shelters and stapled to telephone poles. Some of the more extraordinary Halloween displays that I'd seen in the neighborhood had the sign in a wire holder smack dab in the middle of the lawn. Pumpkin Parade. Even lawns with no discernable Halloween decorations had the sign. I had a vague recollection I'd seen the signs another year but hadn't really paid attention. Halloween can be a very busy time when you're a horror author and a professional tarot card reader.

This year, since I had to work on Halloween night as a tarot reader for a corporate function, I thought I would check out what this November 1st Pumpkin Parade ritual might be. The sign was vague; it only listed the time and the park. There was no indication what happens at the parade. I wasn't too sure what to expect; after all, it was the Día de Muertos, Day of the Dead, so maybe this was some sort of celebration of that. Even more, I half-feared, half-hoped deep within my heart that it might be some kind of Wicker Man ritual. I doubted any of my imaginings would come to pass, though, since I was keenly aware of the cultural and religious heritage of the majority of the residents of my neighborhood from my gig as a census worker a few years prior.

The Pumpkin Parade was supposed to start at six. I donned my pumpkin earrings that had been given to me by one of my dear writer friends, my pumpkin turtleneck sweater, and stashed some candy into my winter coat pocket. My camera was loaded with fresh batteries and a memory card, so I felt confident I was ready for whatever a Pumpkin Parade included. The park was three blocks from my building, and I had no idea if it mattered what time I showed up.

As I left the glass doors of my building, it was clear: it was parade time. The sidewalks were filled with more than the usual nighttime walkers and joggers. Almost every clump of people held at least one jack-o'-lantern and they were all heading for the park.

At the edge of the park, the waft of burning pumpkin filled my nose, and I saw rows of flickering flames, although it wasn't dark yet.

There were already people bringing their jack-o'-lanterns to the bandstand, setting them down carefully beside each other, and lighting the candle within. As time went on, more pumpkins came, more were lit, and the weaving lines on display were growing. Most of the children wore their Halloween costumes, running around in glee with the thrill of wearing them a second night in a row. It was exciting to see all these jack-o'-lanterns able to glow one last time, with children playing tag around them and skipping over them. Perhaps the jack-o'-lanterns were no longer needed at their homes, but now they had purpose, pleasing children in the park and giving the neighborhood an opportunity to squeeze out one more night of Halloween. It was obvious that the parade was going to be contained in the park and in fact, that the "parade" consisted of lining up pumpkins that possessed no legs or feet, so it was a standing-in-one-spot parade. Since it wasn't dark yet, I decided to go for a walk.

I cut through the park and headed to the boardwalk by the lake. As the sky grew dark over the swelling waves of Lake Ontario, I thought about the people who were participating in this ritual. It was heartening to see dozens of strangers pulling together. The boardwalk curved around and I cut across another park and wandered through some townhouse yards. Finally I emerged along a sidewalk on the main street, many blocks away. As I walked back towards the park munching on a candy bar, I noticed that several families were moving away from the Pumpkin Parade, adults sternly hugging pumpkins, some pulling wagons stuffed with pumpkins, while other children cried and pleaded with their parents not to leave their pumpkins in the parade.

By now it was dark, and the spectacle of hundreds of pumpkins glowed from afar. The pumpkins lined the walkways into the park, towards the lake, across the bandstand, and in several rows winding around the park and along hedges and trees and even alongside the coffee shop, but mercifully away from playground equipment. The flickering of the jack-o'-lanterns, the shrieks of children, the laughter of adults, the crunching of leaves, the sizzling of candles, the distant screams and cries of perturbed seagulls…all combined to captivate me. I clicked my camera, but it didn't want to focus or take a picture no matter what tricks of the finger I used. There were pumpkins carved with names, of leering faces, scenes from movies, famous logos, pagan and folklore; so many amazingly creative pumpkins.

I wandered through the pumpkin lines, taking pictures when the camera deemed it was okay, admiring with other people some of the intricate artwork on these fabulous pumpkins. The aroma of burned pumpkin filled the air; the night sky flickered with seemingly hundreds of flames reflected in the emerging stars. A local charity handed out candy. The camera refused to focus, only taking pictures sporadically, as if it didn't want me to photograph things I wasn't meant to see.

Later on when I reviewed the pictures there were streaks like long black eels and blurry robed figures rising up from the tops of the pumpkins. In studying the pictures of the pumpkins, I could imagine that spirits were flying from their heads, or marching in a parallel parade above them. Years of paranormal investigation equipment study lead me to believe that the aberrations in the pictures were simply glares from flickering candles compounded by the dark, and by other people taking flash pictures. The patterns created by the emissions from the pumpkins created a pleasing Rorschach to muse over, nonetheless.

Some of the carved faces appeared poignant; the very last jack-o'-lantern that I photographed had a plaintive look on his face as if I were abandoning him. Which I did.

People pulled up with wagons full of pumpkins even after the designated Pumpkin Parade time had passed. Some piled out of the sliding side doors of vans that had pulled up to the sidewalk, grappling with their pumpkins. I stood at the edge of the park, hesitant to leave just yet. It was oddly magnificent to see all those pumpkins in their parade proudly displaying their beautiful faces flickering in the moonlight for one last time.

Finally, the compost truck rattled up, a huge, creaking, clattering monstrosity that disrupted the happy shrieks and chatter. The crowd parted as the vehicle pulled in. Children cried as parents hurried them away. The pumpkins stood in their lines, fiercely flickering, the thick smell of hundreds of them manifesting into a tangible smoke that rose above the parade. The pumpkins' spirits were escaping before their hosts were destroyed. I turned away, too, as I did not want to see those beautiful jack-o'-lanterns shoveled up and flung into the compost truck. In a way it was like some kind of pagan celebration. Day of the Dead. All Saints' Day. Wickerman. All those mutilated pumpkins lined up on display for us to stare at, to gawk at like they were freaks in a freakshow, and meanwhile the pumpkins' souls screamed in the night. Was it akin to cows being led to the slaughter? What about those screaming vegetable experiments that I heard about in public school science class back in the seventies? Were the pumpkins distraught to discover they had been lured to a parade only to end up as compost? I didn't hang around to find out.

The next morning, damp autumn lake mist hung heavy in the air as I walked down the street to the park and bandstand. I stood staring at the pavement, at the grass, at the playground equipment, at the stairs, at the steps. There was not one pumpkin seed, not one strand of pumpkin guts, or even a stray candle. No burning pumpkin smells. It was as if the Pumpkin Parade had never happened.

I closed my eyes, imagining their flicking faces in the darkness, a black ribbon of smoke rising from the holes in their heads. The veil between worlds? I swore I heard a distant scream but perhaps it was just a seagull. I opened my eyes again and looked around once more. A weary sense of loss nagged at me, piled upon generations of losses as I walked back to my apartment. I lit a candle and gave thanks that I was still here to see another Halloween, unlike so many of the Halloween-loving friends that I had so recently lost.

Halloween rituals change as our lives and needs change. In this era of environmental awareness that is so paradoxically paired with consumerism, it seems a Pumpkin Parade is a beneficial addition to the Halloween season. I intend to celebrate this ritual for years to come and to relish the smell of hundreds of burning pumpkins while watching the spectacle of the parade as their spirits escape into the night.

OCTOBER DREAMS

Michael Kelly

Her dreams were October dreams.

The girl was at that strange, carefree, happy age of dreaming and longing where one doesn't realize that they are unlikely to ever be that happy again. She dreamed of damp earth, crackling leaves, and wood smoke; warm spiced cider and cool winds; candied apples, and capering ghosts; grinning pumpkins and the boundless night.

The girl dreamed orange and black.

Then the girl grew older. She excelled in high school. And her dreams changed. They were filled with boyish grins, twining limbs, and soft smiles. She went to University. She found a job.

The world grew serious.

And still she dreamed, but she dreamed less, because now she wasn't a girl, but a woman, all grown up. And grown-ups, she knew, rarely dreamt. Grown-ups weren't expected to dream.

She fell in love and got married. And he wasn't the man of her dreams—who could be?—but he was good and kind and loved her. What dreams she still had she put on hold, and had a child, a girl, beautiful beyond words. She named her Autumn. And the woman who was once a girl was happy, yes, but it was a different happy. It wasn't the wild exuberance of infinite possibilities. It wasn't orange and black. It was contentment. And she was content to be content.

And life, as it does, passed.

The woman who was once a girl grew old. Her daughter Autumn dreamed too, but they were different dreams. Autumn found a good job, got married, moved away, and had children of her own. The woman's husband, who never knew of her dreams, grew infirm and passed away.

The woman who was once a girl wept quietly.

She grew older. She grew lonely.

She dreamed, again, of leering Jack-O-Lanterns, burning leaves, fresh-baked harvest pies, wet sidewalks, and pumpkin-scented winds. She dreamed of witches, demons, ghouls, and zombies.

She dreamed of darkest night.

She dreamed of the dead.

Time passed. The world quietened. The woman quietened. She waited...waited, and dreamed her October dreams. She could smell the season, the slow rot. Still she waited. And finally there came a knock on the door, and she could hear them outside, chuckling, shuffling, rustling like orange leaves in a damp wind, tiny feet stomping, nervous and excited chatter.

The old woman who was once a young girl with dreams smiled, eased herself painfully from her chair, and moved to the door. She pulled some candy from a bowl, opened the door, wishing—*hoping*—for a trick, a child-like prank. She stood there, grinning. And all the children turned, scampered and skittered away, shrieking, as if they'd seen a ghost.

Or something worse.

www.ingramcontent.com/pod-product-compliance
Lightning Source LLC
Chambersburg PA
CBHW030845030726
47495CB00005B/1381